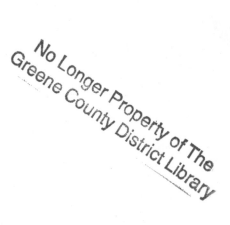

ALSO BY T.J. MACGREGOR

Blue Pearl

Storm Surge

Dark Fields

Kill Flash

Death Sweet

On Ice

Kin Dread

Death Flats

Spree

BY T.J. MACGREGOR AS ALISON DRAKE

Tango Key

Fevered

Black Moon

High Strangeness

Lagoon

MISTRESS OF THE BONES

MISTRESS OF THE BONES

T. J. MacGregor

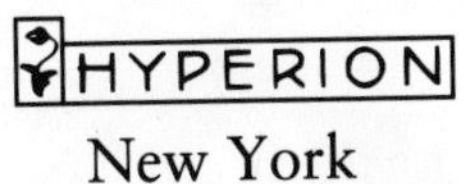

New York

 For information address Hyperion, 114 Fifth Avenue, New York, New York 10011.

Library of Congress Cataloging-in-Publication Data

MacGregor, T. J.
Mistress of the bones / by Trish MacGregor. — 1st ed.
p. cm.
ISBN 0-7868-6106-1
1. Saint James, Quin (Fictitious character)—Fiction. 2. McCleary, Mike (Fictitious character)—Fiction. 3. Private investigators—Florida—Fiction. 4. Women detectives—Florida—Fiction. 5. Florida—Fiction. I. Title.
PS3563.A31115M57 1995
813′.54—dc20 95-10123
CIP

Designed by George J. McKeon

First Edition

10 9 8 7 6 5 4 3 2 1

This one is for Linda Griffin, Phyllis Vega,
and Ed and Carol Gorman,
friends who have enriched my life
and whom I don't see often enough

Special thanks are due to Vicki Owings, who steered me through the complexities of the bail bonds business; to my editor, Pat Mulcahy, for her infallible sense of what works; to Mom and Dad for their relentless support; and to Rob and Megan for giving me all those weekends to work.

The notion that some events leave stronger imprints in the holographic record than others is supported by the tendency of hauntings to occur at locations where some terrible act of violence or other unusually powerful emotional occurrence has taken place.

—MICHAEL TALBOT, *The Holographic Universe*

Sing a song
for the mistress
of the bones

the player
on the black keys
the darker harmonies

—SAMHAIN

MISTRESS OF THE BONES

TANGO KEY, FLORIDA

Saturday, September 2

10:30 P.M.

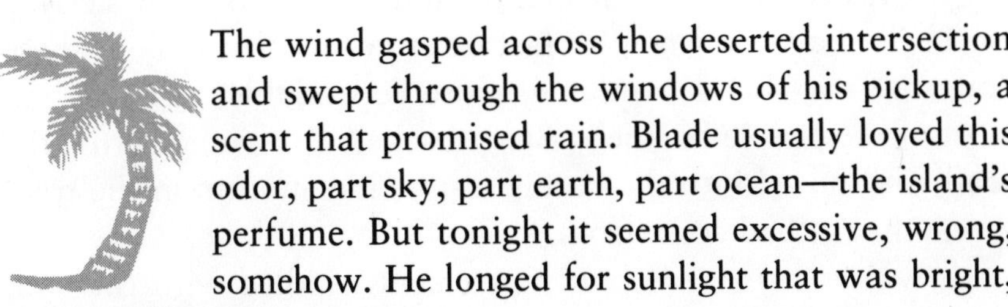

The wind gasped across the deserted intersection and swept through the windows of his pickup, a scent that promised rain. Blade usually loved this odor, part sky, part earth, part ocean—the island's perfume. But tonight it seemed excessive, wrong, somehow. He longed for sunlight that was bright, hot, and blinding.

Overhead, the traffic light swung like the hands of a grandfather clock, ticktock, ticktock, marking the passage of seconds that would never be reclaimed. Tomorrow he would be seventeen. At six A.M. exactly. Did his mother remember that? Did his old man? He doubted it.

But Lou would remember; Lou was his family now. Tomorrow morning they were going to take the houseboat to one of the smaller keys and spend the rest of the Labor Day weekend fishing. They hadn't gone fishing in months, not since the weirdness had started in the house.

But he didn't want to think too closely about any of that.

When the light turned, Blade sped through the intersection. A shimmering wall of green rose on either side of him now, pines and mango groves, the southeast side of Lou's property. Seconds before he reached his turnoff, a car exploded from the trees on his left, a blur without headlights, an airborne missile of glass and aluminum aimed straight at him.

Blade swerved violently to the right, onto the shoulder of the road, his pickup clattering, the tires kicking up gravel. He slammed on the brakes and the engine died with a pathetic shudder. Dust floated through the windows and covered his arms like a second skin. Shaken, his heart still hammering, Blade snapped around in his seat. The car was long gone.

Probably high school dipshits. They wandered back here sometimes to smoke reefer or drink and got spooked whenever they saw headlights. He knew how it was: He used to be one of them.

The truck started on the first try and Blade patted the steering wheel. Tasha wasn't new or fast or even much to look at these days, but she was dependable, more dependable, in fact, than most of the people he knew. Blade backed up, swung across the road, and nosed into the barely visible indentation in the trees where the car had come from.

It was an unpaved county easement, riddled with ruts and holes, which paralleled the fence that surrounded the grove. Blade followed it for better than a mile, Tasha rattling, her tires spitting out clumps of dirt.

The back gate stood open, as it usually did. A quick, warm wind rustled through the trees. Leaves fluttered from the branches, drifting across Tasha's hood. The mango season was almost over, but the fruit's rich, earthy odor lingered in the air.

The property was located on the western edge of the island, six hundred feet above the Gulf of Mexico. On a clear day, the view from the cliff was magnificent, blue as far as you could see, a band of violet where sky met water. The house should have been built here. Instead, it stood smack in the center of the grove, where there was no view at all, except of the pond, which didn't count.

The house had occupied this spot since pirate ships had sailed these waters. Only two rooms of the original house remained; the rest of the place had been expanded and rebuilt dozens of times. Every generation of Lou's family had added to it. Blade couldn't keep all the details straight, but Lou knew them by heart. The house was Lou's connection to his roots.

Blade had no such roots.

Thunder rumbled and lightning unzipped the sky. He could hear the birds—honks, quacks, shrieks, distress calls about the storm that was headed this way. Blade thought of the birds as his extended family. Wood storks, burrowing owls, Muscovy ducks, herons, egrets, crows, blackbirds, doves: He knew them all now. A year ago he couldn't tell a heron from an egret.

He parked next to Lou's battered Camaro, grabbed his pack from the passenger seat, and got out. The porch light wasn't on; the windows were dark. Lou rarely went to bed this early, especially on a weekend, but they were supposed to leave at sunrise tomorrow.

As usual, Lou hadn't locked the front door. Blade stepped into the yawning blackness, the total stillness, and stopped. Wrong, something was wrong, he felt it in the air. "Lou?" he whispered.

The hiss of the air conditioner answered him.

The car.

Blade slapped the wall for the light switch. When the floor lamp in the corner flared, he simply stared at the blood pooling on the tile, oozing along the grout. Lou, curled on his side next to the couch, knees drawn against his chest, twitched like a dying frog.

A low, terrible noise rushed from Blade's mouth. He flew across the room, dropped to his knees beside Lou, and lifted his head. Lou coughed, spraying blood.

"Jesus, Lou. Hold on, just hold on." So much blood. He grabbed a throw pillow off the couch, slipped it under Lou's head, and turned him gently onto his back. His hands fell away from his chest, from the knife that protruded from it.

His knife, a switchblade Lou had given him. The four-inch blade was jammed in to the hilt and he was afraid Lou would bleed to death if he pulled it out. "Don't move," Blade said hoarsely. "I'm going to call an ambulance."

But Lou's fingers dug into his arm and his eyes fluttered open. *Don't leave me,* whispered his eyes, bright and slick with pain. Then his lips moved again, a broken rasp, a word in Spanish that Blade didn't understand. "I'll be right back, Lou, I've got to call an ambulance, you'll be okay, just hang on."

But the wheezing stopped.

"Lou?"

His head went slack.

No.

Blade shook him, begging him to say something, to move, please please. He felt frantically for a pulse in Lou's neck, but there was nothing, nothing at all. A black hole tore open in the center of his chest, his head emptied. Sobs exploded from his mouth. Half a lifetime passed as he cradled Lou's head in his arms and cried.

Sound gradually penetrated his awareness: rain, the moan of the wind, a branch scraping across a window somewhere, and a noise here in the room, very close, a soft rustling like leaves blowing across asphalt. And now he could smell a faint scent of jasmine.

Blade's head snapped around. No one was there, but the rustling grew louder, the scent deepened, and the temperature in the room plunged. Blade scrambled to his feet, his terror suddenly as extreme as his grief.

Run, run while you can.

He scooped up his pack and stumbled away from the body, his breath erupting from his chest like gunfire. The rustling pursued him, surrounded him, and the scent rushed around him, thick as a liquid.

He didn't stop running until he reached his pickup.

1

Great pearl towers of clouds climbed the sky over Tango Key, absolute white against absolute blue. Sunlight pierced the center of the tallest one, rendering each swell, each sweet curve, with breathtaking clarity. It was the sort of sky, Quin thought, that could seduce you into believing in a god, an afterlife, in angels. It somehow fit the island, as though Tango were a place that existed not only in time and space but also straddled regions of the mind.

As soon as she and McCleary crossed the twelve-mile bridge between Key West and Tango, even the texture of the air changed. It seemed less dense, less exacting, less restrictive. She felt as though she were peering through a special lens that deepened the blues and greens, the reds and yellows, all the primary colors. It was like this every time she visited, part of the island's mystery and allure.

Tango Key rose from the Gulf side of Key West like the hump on a camel's back. The highest point was about a thousand feet above sea level and was marked to the west by a lighthouse and to the east by a fire ranger tower. Only the tower was visible from this distance, and it stuck up from the emerald green like a misshapen umbrella.

The toll was five bucks round-trip, thank you very much. It was a fairly recent development and a target of considerable controversy, because the island's property owners were issued cards that exempted them from the toll.

McCleary grumbled when he handed over the toll and asked for a receipt. It would be dutifully recorded as a business expense and filed neatly away in this year's IRS folder. Pity the tax man, she thought, who might one day audit the McCleary records. Her husband, a scribe at heart, didn't adhere to the three-year limit; he saved records in six-year clusters, every receipt, every deductible expense, everything and anything the IRS could possibly ask for.

"I bet this toll is part of employment contracts," McCleary remarked. "Like parking fees in Miami."

"The teachers' union got on the bandwagon a few years ago. They wanted the county to absorb the cost for the teachers who commuted."

As a former teacher of hormonal seventh-graders, she had sympathized. But mostly, she remembered, she had felt immensely grateful that she no longer numbered among their ranks. She hadn't taught school in fourteen years and still had nightmares about those days.

"What happened?" he asked.

"The county absorbed half the cost."

"What about the fishermen? The clerks? The dockworkers?"

"I don't know."

McCleary shook his head. "They should have found another way to pay for the bridge."

"And when you become governor, Mac, you can settle the issue."

He grinned and stabbed his thumb off to the left, where the ferry was pulling away from the Tango dock. "Hell, I'd tell everyone to take the ferry."

It was a car ferry similar to the one that operated between Cape Cod and Martha's Vineyard. The tourists loved this white elephant, a vestige from the pre-bridge days. Two bucks would get you to Key West if you had the thirty minutes to spare. The time factor wasn't due to distance; the ferry's aging engines were to blame.

Tango Key measured eleven miles at its longest point and seven at its widest. It was shaped like the head of a cat with major proportion problems—ears that were set too far apart, an excessively rounded jaw, a face that was much too long. There were two towns: Tango to the south, where most of the island's fishing industry was located, and Pirate's Cove to the north, which had more wealth per square inch than Palm Beach.

In between the two lay the rural heart of the island, rolling hills that were found nowhere else south of central Florida. The homes scattered through those hills belonged to snowbirds and old-timers who farmed the same plots of land their ancestors had tilled. The main crops were mango, guavas, pygmy lettuce, sweet green beans, and Tango citrus. Combined with the fishing industry and tourism, the economy on the island boomed even in the off-seasons when the snowbirds were elsewhere.

The road from the bridge branched at the mainland and McCleary turned the Explorer north, toward the hills. "You remember how to get there?" she asked, paging through her appointment calendar for the directions.

McCleary got a good chuckle over that one. "It's only been a year, Quin."

Only. Ha. Put her down alone in a place she hadn't glimpsed in a year and she would get hopelessly lost. But McCleary's sense of direction was as acute as a homing pigeon's. She wondered if there was any correlation between that and the focused clarity of his life.

She found the directions that Marion O'Connor had given her over the phone yesterday: *Follow Route 2 for three miles and at the produce stand hang a left onto Mango Road. Stay on that for a mile and a half, then look for the turnoff to Lou's place.*

"What time did Marion say she'd meet us there?" McCleary asked.

"Noon." Quin glanced at the clock on the dashboard. "We're late." Naturally.

The road wound up through the hills, deep green cushions shaded by Florida pines and banyan trees that resembled giant emerald mushrooms. The oppressive September heat drifted through the open windows, swollen with the odor of citrus and water, an almost jungle lushness. They passed several farms, a couple of people on horseback, a swimming hole that looked inviting.

As the rest of the peninsula vanished beneath asphalt and shopping malls, she thought, Tango remained relatively unchanged, as close to paradise as any Floridian was likely to see in this century. No wonder Lou had moved back here. The old saying that all Tango fritters eventually came home again was probably true.

The irony was that Lou had survived twenty years as a bail bondsman in Miami's Dade County without being shot at, mugged, or robbed only to be murdered three years after his return to Tango. Pundits argued that crime was rampant throughout the state, that your chances of being victimized were as great on Tango as they were in Miami. The crime rate on the island was nothing to brag about. Tango's seven thousand year-round residents took the same precautions that people did anywhere else in Florida. The court dockets in Tango County were jammed, the small police department was overworked, and the business of criminal law flourished. Just the same, it struck her as particularly significant that Lou had been killed here, in the home that had been in his family for forty years.

The turnoff from Mango Road was marked by a hand-printed sign that read: HERNANDO GROVES, 5 MANGOS $1. The dirt road was lined by mango trees that screamed for a trim. Their branches hung so low the unpicked fruit bumped against the Explorer's roof as they passed. Everything looked neglected: the hibiscus hedges along the inside of the wire-mesh fence, the clusters of gardenia bushes, the clumps of bougainvillea. In the absence of human intervention, nature rushed forward with impunity.

McCleary pulled up in front of the gate, which was shut and sealed with yellow crime tape. "Should we wait for Marion?"

"She's late. That entitles us to access."

"Yeah? That's written somewhere?"

The gumshoe broke laws when it suited him, but the ex-homicide cop wouldn't let him violate a crime scene, she mused. Go figure.

As she got out of the car, she was struck by the mix of scents—hot sun; ripe fruit; black, fertile soil; and the sharp tinge of salt from the Gulf. A blue heron swooped low through the light, its long wings whispering against the air. The mournful cry of a gull pierced the quiet.

She cut through the crime tape with a pocketknife, flipped up the latch on the gate, threw it open. It squealed like a pig in pain, the noise so shrill it startled a flock of blackbirds from the trees. They lifted en masse, a dark, shuddering cloud. McCleary drove through, she hopped in, and they continued for another three or four hundred yards.

The house appeared suddenly, without warning. It was two stories made of coquina rock and Florida pine, with a wraparound wooden porch that sagged at one end. The half-dozen windows were framed by faded blue Spanish tile that was chipped and cracked. Quin guessed the stuff had been there since the house had been built untold centuries ago.

There was no lawn, no sidewalk. Plants grew wild among the wood chips that were scattered across the ground from the edge of the grove to the bottom of the porch steps. About twenty yards off the right corner of the house stood an aluminum toolshed, a rusted eyesore with a padlock on it.

Just beyond the toolshed was a large pond surrounded by clusters of cats' tails and pampas grass. Some of the grass was so tall it drooped at the top, providing shade to a Muscovy duck and her line of little ducklings. An egret and an ibis stalked the muddy shores.

Lou's private little Walden.

When they were here a year ago, Quin's daughter had been fascinated by the wildlife. She was two and a half at the time and had waddled after the birds, her hands flying, her shrieks of delight loud enough to frighten even the placid, slow-moving turtles that inhabited the pond.

"I'm going to take a look inside," McCleary said.

"I'll be along in a second."

She was in no hurry to see the evidence in the house, a chalked silhouette marking the spot where Lou's body had been found. She had seen too many of them over the years and too many of them had belonged to people she knew. A friend of hers, a woman in Colorado, had once remarked that she was glad they lived on opposite sides of the country; too many of her and McCleary's friends ended up dead. It was said half-jokingly, but the truth in the comment had bothered her then and it bothered her now.

She walked over to the pond. None of the birds paid any attention to her, not even the ibis, which was usually easily spooked. She dug a pack of stale melba toast out of her purse, one of Michelle's post–day-care snacks that had escaped her last purse cleaning. She crumpled it, tore it open, and tossed a handful into the water.

The ripples broke up her reflection. A piece of her shoulder-length dark hair floated away. One of her ghost blue eyes drifted toward the bamboo. Her mouth split in two and the halves headed in opposite directions. The effect made her dizzy and she glanced up at the birds.

The egret and the ibis flew off, but the mother duck turned and swam toward Quin. Her ten little guys trailed behind her, a shining example of blind instinct. It was sort of how Quin had felt since Marion's call yesterday.

It somehow didn't matter that her last visit with Lou had been short, just three days. It didn't matter that she knew virtually nothing about his life since his move to Tango. One way or another, she and McCleary would find what they needed to nail whoever had killed him. It was the least she could do for a man who, at one point, had been the most important person in her life.

Years ago, when they had all lived in Miami, Lou had bailed McCleary out of a manslaughter charge, the only bondsman in Dade County who would touch the case. She had scraped together the $15,000 she owed him up front, ten percent of the bond, but it had left her perilously short on cash. Lou, for some reason she had yet to fathom, had proposed cutting his percentage in half if she would make up the difference by doing some investigative work for him.

She and McCleary had returned the favor over the years, but when Lou had needed them most, she thought, they hadn't been there.

Thoroughly depressed, she tossed the rest of the crumbled melba toast to the ducks and went up to the house. It appalled her that she had been here only once in three years. Lou had talked a lot about the place, his memories of it as a child, a teenager, as a young man home from college. During her first visit, she had felt she knew the place by heart just from his descriptions. Now she felt that the house, in some weird way, embodied Lou.

The door opened directly into the comfortable living room. Sunlight streamed through the picture window, details rendered in surreal relief leaped out at her. The wicker, the pine, the plants. The vast and horrible silence was as real to her, as palpable, as the chalked silhouette on the floor, the dark stains on the couch, the streaks of dry blood on the tile. This was no more and no less than what she had seen at hundreds of crime scenes. But this was different, and not just because she had known Lou. This difference was something she could taste, that she could lean against. It possessed weight and substance and she didn't like the way it made her feel. Creepy, she thought, and hurried into the hall.

The floor was Mexican tile, rust-hued and scuffed, and led straight toward the sunroom at the back of the house. The staircase to the second floor was just visible to the left of the sunroom. On the right side of the hall were Lou's den, a bathroom, a guest room.

"Mac?"

"In the sunroom," he called.

Her sandals clicked against the tile, a soft, reluctant sound that echoed eerily between the walls. Paintings hung wherever there was space. They were mostly simple watercolors in vibrant, tropical hues. Fish, animals, street scenes of some Caribbean village. They all bore Lou's signature.

Yet as far as she knew, Lou had never put a brush to canvas or expressed the slightest interest in any kind of art. Okay, so people changed and passions shifted, but these paintings, despite their simplicity, showed a sophistication and control that extended well beyond the dabbling stage. Even McCleary, a weekend artist for the last twenty years, couldn't achieve what these paintings had.

McCleary appeared in the doorway of the sunroom. For a moment, with the wall of sunlight behind him, just the sight of him stirred something so deep inside of her she felt like an adolescent with wild hormones. He stood six feet, had dark hair paling at the temples, and a neatly trimmed beard threaded with gray. He was wearing jeans and a T-shirt that announced he had successfully completed the 10K run for the Missing Children Network in Palm Beach County. He had actually come in second for his age group, not bad for a man who, in his forty-five years, had been shot and beaten, lost twenty years of memories to amnesia, and had died for twelve seconds during emergency surgery three years ago.

His appearance hadn't changed all that much in the more than ten years she had known him. But internally he was a vastly different man than the one she had married. She attributed much of this to his near-death experience.

"Looks like Lou had a passion we didn't know anything about," he said.

"You have any idea where this place is?" She motioned toward a painting of a street scene, the low, squat buildings, the suggestion of blinding sunlight, the breathtaking blue of the sky.

"Looks like my idea of Cuba."

Lou was Cuban, yes, but that was generations back and she doubted that he had traveled there. Even when travel restrictions had eased, Lou had sworn he would never contribute a dime to Fidel's coffers. She started to say as much, but McCleary had already turned back toward the sunroom. "You have to see this, Quin."

At first, when she entered the room, she thought McCleary was talking about the plants, dozens upon dozens of them. They burst from ceiling baskets, exploded from giant ceramic pots, flourished in the light that burned through the three walls of glass. But he was oblivious to the plants. He was standing in front of a portrait of a young black woman with the face of a goddess.

"*Lou* did that?" she exclaimed.

"His initials are on it." McCleary pointed at the bottom-right corner of the canvas, then poked through the cart of supplies that was parked next to the easel. Tubes of paints, an array of brushes, a nest of rags, various tools for scraping and texturing acrylics and oils. "Weird, huh."

"Weird isn't the adjective his ex-wife used when she walked in here," Marion said from the doorway behind them. "If I'm not mistaken, Felicity's exact words were, 'Fuckin spooky.' "

"And I bet she said it in Spanish," Quin remarked, turning around.

"You got it."

They laughed and Marion flung her arms out, hugging them

both hello. "Good to see you guys and thanks for coming so fast."

Despite her name, Marion O'Connor didn't look Irish. She looked as if she hailed from some Mediterranean country where the sun shone 350 days of the year and life was simple. Her ear-length black hair, which she wore in a wedge cut, was thick, shiny, and moved as she moved. Her skin, nut brown from the sun, was the kind that would never surrender to cancer.

She was, as McCleary had once said, a no-frills cop—no jewelry, no makeup, no polish on her nails—who looked like Athena on vacation. She was in her late thirties and was as laid back now as she had been when they'd first met years ago in Miami. Like Lou, she was a Tango fritter born and bred and her connections to the island went back nearly as far as Lou's.

"But where's Michelle?" she asked.

"With her grandparents for a couple of weeks," McCleary replied. "Time to meet the cousins and all that."

"She gets to find out how strange his side of the family is." Quin stabbed a thumb at McCleary. "Three weeks with the cows on a farm in upstate New York."

"Well, you could've brought her. I had a room at the lighthouse all fixed up for her. She could have had her choice of animals to share the room with—cats, a skunk, an owl, take your pick."

"*The* lighthouse?" Quin asked.

"Yup. I'm housesitting for another cop, Aline Scott. She and the guy she lives with are traveling in South America and I needed a place to stay after Carl and I split."

"When was the divorce final?"

"Six months ago. Carl's still living in Key West. I moved in with a friend for a while, but I got tired of commuting. This has worked out real well."

Quin had met Carl only a couple of times. He taught sociology at the community college, and although he seemed nice enough, she had never really understood the attraction. Marion obviously didn't want to discuss it and got down to business as soon as they were settled in the sunroom.

"We have a suspect, a seventeen-year-old kid named Ross Blade. He's an ex–car thief Lou took in about a year ago. His knife was embedded in Lou's chest when we found him. No one has any idea where he is. We've got an APB out on him. Personally, I think he's still on the island."

"Why?" McCleary asked.

"Just a hunch."

"What other evidence do you have on him?"

"He's the primary beneficiary in Lou's will. He's got a record. He lived here. I arrested him four times for car theft, okay? Then I got him into a rehab program for youthful offenders and he seemed to straighten out. That's where he met Lou. And you know Lou. Wounded animals, messed-up kids, forlorn women: He could never resist helping out. Blade moved in with him last fall, right after you all were here."

"Are you positive it was his knife?" Quin asked.

"His name's engraved on it."

"Were his prints on it?" McCleary asked.

"The only clear prints forensics got from the knife were Lou's. The coroner figures he was killed between ten and midnight on the second. He was stabbed once in the back, once in the chest. That one penetrated his heart. There was no sign of a break-in."

"When was the body found?"

"That's the odd part. About five on the morning of the third, 911 received an anonymous call that they tracked to a phone booth in Pirate's Cove. The caller was male. I've got a copy of the tape for you, as well as crime scene photos and Blade's file. He works at a garage in Tango and punched out at nine forty-two that night, so the timing fits. He hasn't been to work since."

"Does he have family on the island?" Quin asked.

"No. His old man lives in Miami and hasn't seen him for three years. He has a few close friends, though, and I've included their names in the file."

"What's Blade's motive supposed to be?" Quin asked.

"Well, according to the state attorney's office, he killed Lou for what he stands to inherit. This grove may not look like much, but according to the county, it's worth about half a million bucks. And that's just for tax purposes. It could bring two or three times that on the open market. Personally, I think Blade and Lou had an argument, Blade lost it, and killed him. I don't think the will has much to do with the motive."

"Who else benefits from his death?" Quin asked.

She drew her fingers back through her hair, a common gesture to which Marion lent an element of grace, of utter femininity. "I don't know. His attorney's a guy named Craig Peck—Peck the Prick is how he's referred to around the department. He was away for the weekend, so I got my information from his law clerk. She told me about Blade and, like I mentioned over the phone, that Lou had appointed you two executors of the will. Other than that, we'll have to wait for Peck. He's supposed to be back today."

"What'd the coroner say?" Quin asked.

"I'll have an official report for you by this evening. But basically he thinks Lou bled to death from a stab wound through the heart. He found dry sperm in the pubic area. He concluded that either Lou had intercourse some time before he was killed or, to put it bluntly, that he had jerked off. The other possibility, which the state attorney has brought up, is that maybe something was going on between Lou and Blade and that's why Blade killed him."

McCleary's incredulity matched Quin's. "C'mon, that's ridiculous. Lou wasn't gay and he definitely wasn't a pedophile."

Marion shrugged. "I'm with you, Mike. I'm just relaying information. There were rumors at one time."

"What about her?" Quin asked, gesturing toward the portrait. "Who is she?"

"I don't know."

"Look, I know you didn't ask us to investigate the murder, Marion, but since we're here, we'd like to poke around, if it's okay with you."

"It's fine with me, but the department can't pay you."

"We owe Lou this much," McCleary said.

"Any chance we'd have access to Lou's business records?" Quin asked.

"I've already talked to Gracie. You guys know her, don't you?"

Quin nodded. Gracie and Lou had been partners for as long as Quin had known him.

"She started to give me trouble, but I made it clear that if she didn't cooperate, I'd subpoena the records."

Bemused, McCleary said, "Subtlety was never your strong point, Marion."

Marion made a face. "Gracie doesn't understand subtlety. What do you think of her?"

"She's okay," Quin replied.

"She and I have never gotten along very well," Marion said. "I mean, if one of my snitches got busted, I could call Lou and ask him to hold off on bond for a day or two and he'd do it. Somewhere down the line I'd return the favor. That's how the system works. But Gracie has never been a player."

"Does she have an alibi?" Quin asked.

"More or less. She was in Key West, staying with friends. They verified that she was there, but hell, at night in the off-season, it's a twenty-minute drive from Duval Street to here. She could've left and come back without anyone knowing she was gone. I told her someone would be down at her office by four today to pick up the records. I hope you don't mind. I figured I'd pin her down while I had her there in front of me."

"Does Felicity have an alibi?"

"Yeah. It seems to check out. She and some people from the gym where she works spent the weekend on a boat up near Marathon." She glanced at the clock on the wall. "I've got to be at the station in a little while. Let me get the files and we'll go over to the lighthouse and get you guys settled in."

"We don't want to barge in on you," McCleary said. "Would anyone object if we stayed here?"

Marion seemed as surprised by the suggestion as Quin, who had no desire to stay in the rooms where Lou had died. "The lighthouse is huge, Mike. There's plenty of room."

"I think we'll stay here if it's okay with you and forensics."

Speak for yourself, Quin thought, but didn't say it.

"Forensics has finished up and the kid who's supposed to inherit the place is a fugitive," Marion said. "But if you have second thoughts, you're always welcome at the lighthouse. I'll get a cleaning service in here by tomorrow." She raised the rear door on the van and pulled out a small cardboard box of files. She set the box on the roof, then shut the door and leaned against it. "I guess you haven't heard the rumors about the house."

"Which rumors?" McCleary asked.

"Ridiculous rumors, actually. That the place is haunted."

Quin laughed. "C'mon."

Marion smiled.

"Who's the ghost supposed to be?" McCleary asked, clearly intrigued.

Marion shrugged. "Beats the shit out of me. I've never seen or heard anything weird in the house, but I guess other people have. And Lou did."

"Well, if we see or hear anything," Quin said, "we'll be knocking at your door."

"I know *you* will, Quin." Marion pointed her index finger at McCleary as though it were a gun. "But he won't."

"She's got your number, Mac."

He shrugged. "I'm tired of reading about weird shit that happens to other people. I'd love to witness a genuine haunting."

Or see a UFO, Quin thought. Or get abducted by the guys with the insect eyes. Yeah, swell. And pretty soon she, too, would be on Oprah, showing the scar on the back of her calf to five million people in TV land. "Be careful what you ask for, Mac."

He grinned, slid the box off the roof of the van, and walked toward the Explorer whistling the theme from *The Twilight Zone.*

2

McCleary was grateful that Marion left as quickly as she did. He and Quin had a particular way of doing things and it didn't work well if a third party was around, even someone they knew as well as Marion.

The routine was simple: first things first. They brought in their bags from the car and Quin promptly unpacked the numerous concoctions that she claimed mitigated her hot flashes. She lined the bottles up along the kitchen counter, eighteen different vitamins and nearly as many herbs, all with names that evoked the Orient and medieval England. There were also tea bags, lotions, and mysterious creams that supposedly reduced wrinkles and other ravages of aging. He thought she looked just fine the way she was, 120 pounds of sinew and muscle from daily jogs, her ghost blue eyes barely creased at the corners, and just a faint suggestion of white threads in her dark hair. But apparently when she looked in the mirror she saw middle age.

They picked the guest room with a queen-sized futon, an empty closet, and an empty pine dresser. There were two other bedrooms up here—Lou's and the kid's—as well as an attic, which he intended to explore. But not until he had unpacked.

Quin merely dumped the contents of her suitcase on the wicker chest at the foot of the bed. She pawed through everything until she found a pair of khaki shorts and a T-shirt, then changed into them and left her other clothes where they fell. "I'm going to see what I can rustle up for lunch from the bags of groceries we brought with us, then we can start making calls."

"What about this mess?"

"I'll do it later."

"Later when?"

Hand on her hip, a wry smile reshaping her mouth, those ghost blue eyes fixed on him: "Chill out, Mac. It'll get done."

Sure. Quin had been a clutter freak when he met her, was still a clutter freak, would always be a clutter freak. She could walk into an orderly room and within moments, with no effort at all, the order would break down. Entropy, he thought. Nothing he said would ever change that, but he couldn't resist a remark. "Your clothes would be less wrinkled if you hung them up."

"There's bound to be an iron around here somewhere," she said, and walked out of the room, the mess still on the chair.

She was burning up the phone line when he came downstairs, making appointments for tomorrow. They called his parents in Syracuse and spent twenty minutes on the phone, trying to decipher their daughter's stories about the cows, the chickens, the great rural outdoors. Over lunch they went through the files Marion had given them, a quick look. Later that night they would read through the material more slowly, make notes, and come up with the broad strokes of a game plan. Once the rhythm of the investigation was established, they would move into it like two parts of a single, pulsating brain.

Or, at any rate, that was how it was supposed to unfold. In practice it was rarely that simple.

Their exploration of the house, for instance, began haphazardly, with Quin in the basement and McCleary in the attic and the two of them working their way toward the second floor.

McCleary felt like a trespasser, an interloper, a voyeur. Even though he'd considered Lou a close friend, the closeness hadn't included an invasion of the man's privacy.

He didn't need to know, for instance, that Lou had rarely cleaned the shower or the toilet or his refrigerator. He didn't need to know about the green shit growing on the cheese. Or about the French tickler condoms in the nightstand drawer. Or about the junk in the attic, stuff that had probably been in his family for a hundred years. He didn't need to know about the grungy sheets in the master bedroom, the total chaos in the closets.

Yes, these details added up to something, the sum of one facet of the man, but in the end they raised more questions than they answered. Who had Lou been screwing? Was she the same woman who wore the negligee with the missing crotch that had been in Lou's dresser? And where did a seventeen-year-old kid fit into this picture?

The Lou he had known best was a compassionate, gregarious man with some eccentric ideas about how the world worked. He was the only child of Cuban entrepreneurs who had started at the bottom and worked their way into the American dream. At one point in their lives, they had been worth millions. But by the time they died, they had drunk away most of the family fortune. The ten acres of mango groves and this very odd house were Lou's primary legacy.

Lou's old man, if McCleary remembered correctly, had been a devout Catholic until Lou's mother had died. Then he'd become every priest's nightmare, a lapsed Catholic, a fallen soul, a bitter, irreverent alcoholic. His mother had been a practicing *santera,* a kind of Cuban witch who made offerings to the *santos*—the saints. She had lit candles for the dead, cast intricate spells, and had died twenty years ago.

Lou had been so deeply affected by his parents' alcoholism he had never touched anything addictive. No booze, no drugs, not even an aspirin. He had taken up running about the time McCleary had met him, a fact he remembered only because it was something they had in common. But to Lou, running hadn't been just aerobic exercise. It was a discipline you studied like tai chi or yoga, something that honed your body as well as your mind. As a result, he looked a decade younger than he was, lean and solid, with the salubrious good looks of a celebrity.

Given all this, the real puzzle was why Lou had become a bail bondsman. Of all the professions he might have chosen, he had picked one with a corrupt reputation, where sleaze was the norm. But maybe it wasn't all that much of a mystery, McCleary thought. After all, Lou had used it as a vehicle to help people like Ross Blade.

According to the records Marion had given them, Lou had bonded the kid five times out of seven arrests for either car theft or B and Es. Blade's career had begun when he was fourteen and working at the Tango docks with bogus ID. His old man, like Lou's, was a drunk. It was the only thing they had in common, but it was evidently enough. Maybe Lou saw a younger version of himself in Blade. Maybe he just felt sorry for him. Whatever his motive, he took the boy in, cleaned him up, helped him find a job, and then made the kid his major beneficiary.

Okay, so it was weird. But it didn't mean there had been a sexual relationship between them. If anything, Marion had hit it on the head: Lou couldn't resist taking in the wounded, the spiritually injured. Blade had needed someone and Lou had been there. And now he was supposed to believe this same kid had turned around and killed Lou for money? No way. That he had killed him in a fit of temper? Maybe, but it just didn't feel right to him. Even a man who killed in a fit of temper would have the presence of mind to take the murder weapon with him when he split.

"I think Marion's wrong about Blade," McCleary said.

"I suppose that comes from a higher authority."

"Such glibness."

They were in the sunroom now and Quin glanced up from where she was sitting. Her dark hair fell to her shoulders in unruly waves, her long legs rested on the corner of an old steamer trunk that served as a coffee table. She was munching chewable vitamin Cs as though they were candy.

"A prosecutor is going to find the evidence against him pretty compelling, Mac."

"If he stabbed Lou, why didn't he take the knife with him?"

"He wasn't thinking straight. He freaked. He lost it. You're jumping to conclusions, Mac." Her feet dropped to the floor and she went over to the portrait of the black woman. "She's really stunning. But she just doesn't seem like Lou's type."

"You can tell that from a painting?"

"You know what I mean."

Yeah, he did. The woman in the portrait didn't seem forlorn or lost enough to have attracted Lou. Or at least he hadn't captured it.

"Let's take a drive," he said. "I need to get a better sense of the grove's location. Then we can drive into town and meet with Gracie."

"Sounds good."

He dropped the file he'd been reading on top of the other files in the cardboard box and pushed the box over to the window. He briefly considered changing clothes, but decided that Quin had the right idea. Island casual was the way to go.

The island's shape made it easy to visualize the grove's location relative to everything else. The ten acres fell roughly below the cat's left ear, about four miles south of the old lighthouse where Marion was staying.

McCleary and Quin walked its western boundary, which extended for about half a mile along the edge of the cliff that overlooked the Gulf. The dramatic view was literally gothic in scope—the violent plunge to the rocks below, waves frothing over them, the startling blue that stretched all the way to the horizon. Heathcliff's country, he thought.

The wind whipped off the water, moaned through the mango trees behind them. He could taste the salt in the air, could feel it against his skin, a sticky residue.

Quin, clasping her hair behind her head, peeked over the lip of the cliff, then retreated to the edge of the trees. McCleary joined her a moment later. "Vertigo?"

"Don't be smug. It just made me dizzy to look down. How can this property be worth only half a million? The view alone is worth twice that."

"Tomorrow one of us needs to get the stats from the property appraiser's office." He took her hand. "Let's walk to the end."

They followed an overgrown footpath that hugged the trees. Rotting mangos littered the ground and here and there they spotted bright yellow mangos that clung tenaciously to the branches. Quin plucked one and held it up, turning it slowly in the light, an oval jewel the color of gold. "You have any idea how many vitamins are in one of these?"

"I'm sure you'll tell me."

She gave him a dirty look and dropped it in her bottomless bag. "Be nice or I won't share it with you."

The ground sloped gradually downward, then leveled out where the grove ended; they emerged in a noisy construction area stripped of trees, of brush, of any kind of greenery. A tractor rolled across the barrenness, flattening whatever was in its way. Half a dozen men beyond it were laying the foundation of a building. A six-foot wire-mesh fence stood between them and the construction area. A bright yellow sign hung from it that read: VICENTE CONSTRUCTION & REALTY, FUTURE SITE OF AMELIA RESORT.

"I bet Lou saw red over this," McCleary said.

"Maybe Vicente made an offer on Lou's land."

One of the workers saw them and walked over to the fence. "Help you folks with something?"

"We were out walking and noticed the construction," McCleary said. "What's the Amelia Resort going to be?"

The man raised his hard hat and wiped his handkerchief over his bald head. "You name it, this place will have it. Stables, horse trails, three swimming pools, indoor tennis courts, a gym, and forty chalets that'll rent by the season for more than I make in a year."

"Isn't most of the land around here zoned for agriculture?"

"Agriculture or residential, yeah. But this was rezoned about six months ago, when the county gave Vicente Construction permission to build the resort."

"You going to raze the grove, too?" Quin asked.

"Nope. Mr. Vicente doesn't own it. I heard they were willing to pay a pretty price for the land, but the guy who owns it didn't bite. Where you folks from?"

"Up north," McCleary replied. "We're visiting friends."

"Bad time to visit the island. Too damn hot. You oughta come back in January. Can't beat Tango in the winter."

"We will. Thanks for your time."

They walked back toward the path and once they were out of hearing range, Quin said, "Lou used to say there were two sources of information on the island—the media and the grapevine. Of the two, he trusted the grapevine."

"I'm with Lou," he replied, and decided that a visit to Vicente Construction was certainly in order.

Pirate's Cove was a rich man's haven, a little paradise at the north end of the island. Its tidy roads were packed with expensive boutiques, perfectly tended parks, and homes that were affordable only by multimillionaires.

Its history went back more than two hundred years, tales of pirate ships, lost treasures, beautiful slaves, mermaids. The history was evident in the Spanish style that pervaded the town—soft pink buildings, black iron trim, colorful inlaid tiles, cobbled streets. Logos of mermaids, anchors, and pirate ships festooned storefronts and restaurants.

Even the names of things were connected to the history—Doubloon Drive, Pieces of Eight Theater, Treasure Mall, Mermaid Beach Wear. The street signs themselves were gold with black lettering. The obvious hype would be tacky anywhere else, but Pirate's Cove took its history seriously and had gone to great lengths to preserve it.

All downtown buildings, for instance, were required to conform to a particular code in terms of color, height, parking, and landscaping. Shades of salmon pink, black iron trim in a variety of designs, inlaid tile, copious but tasteful shrubbery, and no building taller than three stories: Those were the basics. Here and there, an oddball building had been grandfathered into the eerie uniformity—a conch house or a brick structure, a cobblestone road or an exposed parking lot. McCleary welcomed these breaches, these blatant statements of individuality, and was pleased to discover that Hernando Bail Bonds was one of them.

The building, like Lou's house, was constructed mostly of coquina rock, a bleached white stone native to south Florida that was embedded with fossils. The iron gate at the entrance squeaked like a battalion of hungry mice and opened onto a courtyard that literally burst with plants. According to the hand-carved sign, Lou shared the building with Madame Janna Hilliard, a tarot card reader.

"I bet the town council nearly shit when the Madame moved in," Quin remarked.

"Hell, she probably got in here because she reads for the mayor or someone on the city council."

Lou's place had iron bars on the picture window and the glass was so darkly tinted it was impossible to see inside. McCleary started to knock, but Gracie suddenly opened the door, blinked against the cruel light, opened her mouth, closed it. Tears rushed into her blue eyes and she murmured: "Quin. Mike. You know about Lou?"

"That's why we're here, Gracie," said Quin.

As she drew her fingers back through her short blond hair,

her half-dozen rings glinted in the sun. Turquoise and silver, a topaz, a ruby, gold. Gracie Stevens didn't strive for uniformity any more than Lou had, McCleary thought. Her eccentricity simply took a different form. Even her clothes didn't match: a striped vest with a print skirt and flats the color of tarnished brass. And yet she was thin enough and attractive enough to pull it off.

"You're working for Marion on the investigation?" Her mouth puckered when she said the name. "Is that what you're saying?"

McCleary quickly set the record straight. "No one is paying us. Lou appointed us executors of his will."

"Executors? Christ. C'mon in." She shut the door behind them. "Marion should've told me you two would be going through the records. I don't have any problem with you all. I just didn't want some cop breathing down my neck. Bonds people aren't real popular on this island as it is."

They followed her into a room furnished in the basics but little else. Everything about it suggested that business was to be conducted quickly, efficiently.

"Marion didn't give me any idea which files to pull, so I gathered up the logbook and files on every bond Lou had written for the last year." She motioned toward a thin stack of file folders. "Which isn't all that much. The last six months or so, Lou hardly wrote anything. He wasn't here more than a day or two a week."

"Why not?" Quin asked as she and McCleary settled into the two chairs in front of the desk.

"I don't know." Gracie swept her fingertips across the desk's surface, as if to chase away motes of dust. "But even when he *was* here, part of him was absent." She twisted a ring, worked it off her finger and rubbed the joint, then plopped into the chair behind the desk. "Look, the business was in deep shit, okay? You're going to find out sooner or later anyway. Lou had written some bad bonds over the past year. He had to fork over more than two hundred thousand."

McCleary whistled softly. "Where'd he get the money?"

Gracie shrugged. "The grove and the house are paid for, so he took out a loan against the property and cashed in some stocks his folks had left him. For about three months he was totally obsessed, okay? He put in twelve-hour days, seven days a week. Then for some reason, he just . . . I don't know, seemed to lose interest."

Although McCleary was foggy on some of the specifics, he was familiar enough with the bond business to know it was high risk. It was run by insurance companies, a corporate mentality that grew fat by peddling fear. They issued the licenses, they limited the amount of the bond that could be written without special permission, they called the shots.

No one was guaranteed a bond. It wasn't in the Bill of Rights, denial wasn't any basis for a lawsuit. Whether you got a bond at all, in fact, was left completely to the discretion of the bondsman, two in the Cove, two in its freewheeling sister town to the south.

The risk statewide varied by county, but only because some counties had more murder or drug crimes, the two categories that demanded the highest bonds. On Tango, it was a combination of both and, for the most part, crime was seasonal. But in all counties, a bondsman was liable for the entire amount of the bond he wrote if the client skipped and the bond was forfeited. And to skip all you had to do was miss one court date. Most agencies couldn't sustain losses of more than two to three percent of the bonds they wrote. Not great odds.

On the other hand, thanks to the ten percent the bondsman required up front, the nonrefundable equivalent of his fee, there was a lot of money to be made in the business, particularly for an agency that wrote two to three million dollars worth of bonds a year. But it was not as lucrative as it had been twenty years ago.

In the old days, it was a sleazy business dominated by a few good ol' boys who ran things like feudal lords. Corruption was rampant, bribes were not uncommon. Now the industry was more tightly regulated and strove to be perceived as professional. Safeguards had been instituted to protect the insurance companies in case an agency went under.

"What were the bad bonds for?" McCleary asked.

"There were two," Gracie said. "Drug charges. A hundred grand each. Both guys skipped a court date and vanished. We hired a bounty hunter, we filed motions, but in the end, we got stuck."

"When was this?" Quin asked.

"The bonds were forfeited in late spring. Lou worked like a dog through early June, then nothing. Zip. It was like he woke up one morning and said, 'Fuck it. I don't care.' "

This didn't sound remotely like the man McCleary had known. "What was he doing when he wasn't at work?"

She slipped the ring back on her finger and brought her hands together, index fingers extended, touching the tip of her chin in an attitude of prayer. "Painting. He was in that goddamn house painting. Have you been over there?"

"Earlier," Quin replied.

McCleary noticed that she didn't mention they were staying at the house and followed her cue. "We didn't realize Lou had any interest in art."

"He didn't know ochre from magenta. But one day he was suddenly an artist. I think the paintings are actually pretty good. I figured if he wanted to paint rather than write bonds, fine, I could accept that. But then hire someone to take your place, Lou. Or buy me out. Something. He didn't want to hear about it. I'm not exaggerating when I tell you he spent weeks at a time locked up in that sunroom with his paints, his visions, his . . ." She stopped, her face bright pink, and made a dismissive gesture with her hand. "Well, whatever. I'd go over there every week or so. I'd plead with him to come back to work. I'd grovel. But it was like talking to a wall."

"What'd Blade say about it?" McCleary asked.

She snorted. "Please. Blade was the primo freeloader, what

the hell was he going to say to me? Don't worry, Gracie? He's having a lapse, Gracie? Uh-uh, I don't think so."

"You never discussed it?" Quin asked.

"Nope." Gracie shook her head. "I wasn't about to discuss my business with a kid."

"You think he killed him?"

"Christ, Quin. It was his knife. He lived there. He had every opportunity. I think they argued about something and Blade lost it, okay? He stabbed him, he split, and that's it."

"Was he paying Lou rent?" McCleary asked.

"Yeah, but it wasn't much. And I know for a fact that Lou turned around and put the money in a CD or a money market or something for Blade. That's how he was."

"Who's the black woman in that portrait?" Quin asked.

"I don't know." Gracie stuck a Marlboro in a corner of her mouth and lit it with a silver lighter studded with bits of turquoise. "Lou refused to talk about her."

"Was he dating her?"

"He never said, but that was my impression."

The French ticklers, McCleary thought. The negligee from Frederick's. "If he was painting around the clock, where'd he fit her in?"

Gracie cast Quin one of those female looks that made it clear she believed men thought with their cocks and that everything in their lives revolved around this fact. "He apparently managed," she said dryly.

The phone pealed and Gracie answered it with a crisp, professional voice. "Hernando Bail Bonds."

Quin got up to use the rest room and McCleary reached for the logbook that rested on top of the files. The headings were a bare bones history of each bond: the power or case number, the defendant's name, the date of the bond's execution, the amount of the bond and the amount of the premium that Lou or Gracie had been paid, the split on the twenty percent the insurance company took, the case disposition and date the case was terminated, the collateral receipt number, what was accepted as collateral, and the bondsman's initials.

Two facts were immediately apparent. In the last year, Gracie had written the majority of the bonds and for increasingly larger amounts. Only one of her clients had skipped, a B and E on a $5,000 bond, and he had apparently been found because the bond wasn't forfeited.

Despite Lou's absences from the office, he had managed to write half a dozen large bonds, between $70,000 and $150,000. The two skips among Lou's clients were charged with the sale and possession of cocaine. One bond was for seventy-five grand, the other was for a hundred and fifty grand. The bonds had been written several weeks apart in December and had been forfeited by tax day. Lou had filed a motion in both cases, which had given him time to look for the skips, but to no avail. He had paid the bonds in full and the canceled checks were included, both of them drawn on Tango First Union.

Given Gracie's description of Lou's indifference to work, it seemed unlikely that he had hunted the skips himself. But there was nothing in the log about whom he had hired as a bounty hunter.

Gracie hung up. "I've got to meet a client down at the jail in Tango."

"Just one more question, Gracie. Did you all hire a bounty hunter to search for Lou's skips on those two bonds?"

"Yeah, he did. I don't know who, I never met the guy." She dropped some papers in her briefcase, snapped it shut. "How about if we get together for lunch or dinner or something in the next couple days? That way if you have any questions about the files I can answer them for you."

"We're not sure what our schedule is going to be. But we'll give you a call."

"Where're you all staying?"

Quin, who had returned to the room, replied before McCleary had a chance to say anything. "At Lou's place."

Gracie wrinkled her pert little nose. "You don't have to do that. I'll ask a friend of mine to put you up at his guest house."

"Thanks for the offer, Gracie, but we don't mind staying there."

"The place gives me the creeps."

"We heard the house is haunted," Quin remarked.

"That's what they say." She started toward the door, McCleary and Quin falling in on either side of her. "Did you ever meet Lou's old man?"

McCleary shook his head.

"I met him a couple of times toward the end of his life, when he was living alone in the house. If he was six sheets to the wind, he would talk for hours about some of the weird stuff that happened when Lou was growing up in the house. Lights that came on by themselves, noises in the middle of the night, objects that floated . . . I mean, it sounded like shit straight out of Spielberg."

"What'd Lou say about it?" McCleary asked.

"Right after we opened our office here on the island, he used to joke about it. The spook did this, the spook did that. Then one day he just didn't talk about it anymore."

"Why not?" Quin asked.

Gracie shrugged. "I don't know. I never saw anything, but I definitely felt something every time I walked into Lou's den. That fireplace in there and in the kitchen are the oldest parts of the house. The stones are the originals. Just about everything else has been replaced or refurbished."

They walked outside, into the late afternoon heat. "What about the cellar?" McCleary asked. "Hasn't that always been there?"

"No. His grandfather had it dug when he added the sunroom and the two bedrooms downstairs. The original house was small—just the den, the kitchen, and the room across the hall from it."

"Gracie, hold on a second."

A woman with copper hair and a dusting of freckles on her

cheeks hurried across the courtyard, her turquoise skirt filling with air and floating around her, an exotic water lily. She looked like a New Age kook, McCleary thought. Her dangling quartz crystal earrings swung at the sides of her face. A large rose quartz crystal hung from a silver chain around her neck. A wide silver bracelet inlaid with different colored crystals graced her arm. Even her watch was studded with crystals. Hook her to a radio transmitter and you could probably contact Pluto.

"I don't mean to hold you up, hon," she said breathlessly. "I just wanted to tell you how sorry I am about Lou. I was away this weekend and just heard the news a little while ago. Didn't I tell him a hundred times that he was in the wrong line of work, Gracie? My God." She shook her head, her eyes darting from McCleary to Quin and back to Gracie. "I simply can't believe it. Do the police have any suspects yet?"

"I really don't know."

The chill in Gracie's voice was unmistakable, but if the woman heard it she didn't let on. She extended her hand to McCleary, her skin as soft as a peach. "I'm Janna. Janna Hilliard. I have the office on the other side of the courtyard."

Madame Hilliard, tarot card reader. "Nice to meet you," McCleary replied, and introduced Quin.

"You were friends of Lou's?" she went on in that same, breathless tone, one hand fixed to her narrow waist.

"Yes, they were," Gracie said briskly. "If you'll excuse us, Janna, I've got to run."

"Of course, hon, of course, I understand. Nice to meet you both."

Gracie was already halfway to the gate, as though she couldn't get away fast enough, but Quin didn't seem to be in any hurry to leave. McCleary heard her ask, "What do you charge for a reading, Mrs. Hilliard?"

"My usual fee is fifty, but for a friend of Lou's, it's thirty-five."

"I'd like to schedule something for tomorrow, if you have any openings."

"The day after, nine A.M."

"Great. I'll be here. Thanks again."

As Quin caught up to them, Gracie said, "Save your money. She's about as psychic as this sidewalk."

"What the hell. She knew Lou, that makes it a business expense." She winked at McCleary. "Right, Mac?"

"Until we're audited."

"Lou bailed Madame Weirdo out of a scrape not too long after we opened the office. One of her disgruntled clients charged her with fraud. She hired an attorney who got the client to agree to drop the charge if Janna refunded his money. So she refunded his thousand bucks, the case hit the paper, and suddenly she had more business than she knew what to do with. What's that tell you about the general gullibility of the American public?"

Meaning, of course, that Quin counted among their ranks. She caught the drift, rolled her eyes, and just laughed.

3

It was nearly dusk when Blade followed the Old Post Road toward the south end of the island. Traffic was light; it usually was on Old Post. Commuters preferred the four-lane highway that shot straight down the middle of Tango. The cops hung out on the four-laner, too, which was why Blade avoided it.

At one time, Old Post had been the only road on the island, twisting around its periphery from the ferry's dock to the fishing wharves on the Gulf side. In those days a mailman on horseback arrived once a month on a ferry from Key West and spent two days delivering mail to the several hundred residents. Blade sometimes wished he had lived back then, in a simpler time when the island was an exotic outpost of civilization.

Lou's stories about early Tango had always held a certain appeal for Blade, but that was especially true now, when his life was anything but simple.

He passed mansions and estates on the outskirts of the Cove. He passed an old cemetery, the lighthouse, and the construction site for the future Amelia Resort. When he saw the turnoff for

Mango Road, an ache a mile wide tore open in the center of his chest. In his head, he could still see Lou bleeding on the floor. He saw it in vivid color, in every goddamn stinking detail. It was burned so deeply into his memory that most of the time he didn't even have to close his eyes to see it.

He had spent the last three nights on the houseboat. It was anchored in a small marina on the Tango River, which meandered from the marshes on the north side of the island through the wilderness preserve in the cat's right ear, and into the channel between Tango and Key West. The marina was tucked back in a sheltered cove and during the off-season it was used mostly by old-timers who didn't ask questions.

Sooner or later, though, someone who knew about the houseboat might tell the cops. But until then, a dozen cops with dogs and choppers wouldn't find him. The three days had given him some time to begin growing a mustache, which would make him look older. His hair, which he'd worn in a ponytail, was now cut short. He had lightened it with lemon juice so that it was a soft brown streaked with blond. He wore a pair of reflective shades and a baseball cap to hide his face. There wasn't much else he could do to change the way he looked. As Lou once said, he'd been born looking like a brooding James Dean. Now he was James Dean after a three-week binge.

It was dark when he reached a cluttered neighborhood just east of the fishing docks. He felt at home here, probably because it wasn't so different from the area where he'd grown up in south Miami. The streets were lined with single-story concrete-block houses with fading paint jobs, carports, and jalousie windows. There were no rules here, no laws governing what you could or couldn't have on your property. Fences, satellite dishes, boats, trailers, trucks, vans, campers: everything was allowed.

If there were any rules at all, they were unspoken and they were all about how you treated your neighbor. You didn't snitch on him, didn't pry into his business, didn't ask too many questions. If he was growing pot in his greenhouse out back, well, so what as long as he didn't try to sell it to you. If he beat his wife and kids that was his business as long as it didn't cause any problems for you.

These unspoken rules had allowed Eduardo "Rico" Jimenez to prosper. No one cared that his yard was usually crowded with cars or that he played his music too loud. It didn't matter that he looked weird, that the rooms he lived in probably should be condemned, that this wasn't a place you would bring your mother.

Two cars were in the yard when Blade pulled into the driveway behind Rico's Jeep. The windows of the house were closed, the AC was on; he didn't hear music until the door opened. It pounded the air, the base throbbing so hard Blade felt it behind his eyes. Rico stood there in a black robe and a black pointed hat with bright white stars on them.

"Amigo," Rico boomed, his voice louder than the music, then threw out his arms as if to embrace the world. "I didn't recognize you with the hair on your face. Long time no see, come in, come in."

Blade stuck his fingers in his ears and shouted, "What's going on?"

"Groupies," Rico said, rolling his eyes, and waved him into the house.

He was a short, fat Puerto Rican with his fingers in a dozen pies, few of them legal. He had a double chin, curly hair that hung to his shoulders, and he wore enough jewelry to sink the *Titanic.* He waddled and wheezed when he moved, his rings clicking together, the diamond posts in his right ear grabbing most of the light in the hallway.

"Who're you supposed to be?" Blade asked.

"Merlin." Rico laughed and slung an arm around Blade's shoulders. "You know, seer of the ages, counselor to kings. Where you been, anyway? I heard about Lou on the news and then the next thing I hear is they're looking for you. What the fuck's going on, amigo?"

Still shouting: "I need a favor."

"You came to the right place."

Music blasted from the TV in the living room, where half a dozen people were watching MTV. Rico's groupies and his loud music were like Siamese twins joined at the hip of Rico's life. A decade ago in Miami, Blade's old man had called the cops to complain about the commie pinko across the street who played his music too loud. Rico was eventually evicted. He and Blade had hooked up again a few years ago at a New Year's bash on the Tango beach. It didn't matter that he was twice Blade's age, he loved Rico like a brother.

Rico shouted for someone to turn down the volume and motioned for Blade to follow him into a back room. It was like entering a snug, dark cave. The rug was black, heavy black curtains hung over the windows, and the black walls were graced with astrological symbols painted in a neon gold that glittered like sequins. The only light in the room came from a halogen floor lamp, which was also black.

Rico shut the door, whipped off his pointed hat, and tossed it on the black leather couch. He sank into the black leather chair behind the desk; it sighed noisily with his weight. "So let's bring up your chart and see what's been going on with you, m'man." He turned on his computer, a nifty notebook PC that weighed less than Blade's heart. "The moon and Neptune are about to conjunct in Scorpio, so there's plenty of weird shit going down."

"I'm not here for that," Blade said.

But Rico was already into it, tapping away on the keyboard, consulting his ephemeris, nodding to himself. "Yeah, yeah, okay. Both planets are transiting your eighth house, Blade. That means you're going to be dealing with the affairs of the dead, you know what I mean? Money from the dead, estates, inheritances, shit like that. It's going to shatter some of your illusions. It's all about Lou, man."

"Listen, Rico. I—"

"Lemme finish. Moving along here." Rico tapped his fingers against the edge of the desk in strange, rhythmic rolls as he studied the screen. "Pluto and Uranus are sailing through your twelfth house, amigo. That means sudden dealings with institutions—jails, hospitals, bureaucracies. It means the collapse of the old."

"The old?"

"Yeah. You know." His hand moved as if to snatch the right phrase out of the air. "The old way of doing things. The old belief systems and the people who run them. Politics, religion, health care, stuff like that."

Blade had no idea how "old belief systems" applied to his situation. But if Rico saw it, then in the grand order of things it was probably true.

"In other words, amigo, a crossroad, okay?" His fingers drummed the desk, his eyes were glued to the computer screen. "This is some past life thing you have to get through."

"I'm having enough trouble with this life, Rico."

"That's exactly what I'm saying. All these past life ties are coming up, okay? Karma, amigo, I'm talking about karma. Any questions?"

Yeah, a million. "Not about that."

Rico laced his plump fingers together on top of the desk. "You found him, right?"

All he could muster at first was a nod; his throat had closed up.

"Talk to me, Blade."

"My knife was sticking out of his chest."

"Sweet Christ."

"He was still alive."

Rico rubbed his hands over his face. "Was this a pocketknife or what?"

"A switchblade. It'd been missing a couple of weeks."

"Did Lou say anything to you?"

"Yeah, something in Spanish. It sounded like corridor."

Rico thought a moment, his frown pulling his dark eyes close together. "*Corredor?* Was that what it sounded like?"

"Yeah, that seems right. What's it mean?"

"Just like what it sounds. A corridor."

It didn't make sense. "Does it have another meaning?"

"A runner."

"Lou was a runner."

"Meaning that he stabbed himself? I don't think so. Maybe the person who stabbed him was a runner. Or maybe it was one of those bail terms, someone who splits, who takes off."

"They're called skips," Blade replied.

"I don't know what to tell you, amigo."

Thinking about it made Blade's head ache. "Listen, Rico, the sticker on my license plate has expired. I'm fucked if I get stopped. Can you help me out?"

Rico grinned, a flash of silver fillings, then crushed his cigarette and pushed himself to his feet. "How about a new license plate, sticker and all?"

"Great. That'd be perfect."

"No problem." He shuffled out of the room and returned a few minutes later with a new license plate, the green sticker attached.

"How much?"

"Forget it, amigo. Through you I cancel my karma. That's how it is with us."

As though karma were something that you could taste, touch, and feel. "Yeah?"

Rico laughed. "You think it's shit."

"Pretty much."

He laughed again and they walked outside. "Go see that movie *Dead Again*. We were brothers in the eighteenth century, see. We lived on the border between Spain and France. I was the prick, you were the good guy. Something like that. Choices, Blade. Karma is about choices, about making the right choices. Anyway, I owe you."

Rico, wheezing and sweating from the walk outside, watched

as Blade removed the old plate and screwed on the new one. Then he pressed his plump, dimpled hand to Blade's shoulders. "Where're you going to be?"

"On Lou's houseboat. It's at Colin's Marina in the preserve. I'll call you from there in the next couple of days. I need to move it pretty soon."

"Just call me and I'll pick up your car and drive it to you. I'm here for you, amigo. Remember that."

Blade's pickup climbed through the dark hills, her engine clacking like a tap dancer's heels. He kept glancing nervously at the temperature gauge, waiting for the instant when the needle would swing into the red zone and he would have to pull off the road.

Lou used to call Tasha a temperamental bitch, but Blade knew better. Tasha just didn't like the hills around the grove. The closer he got to Mango Road, in fact, the louder the clacking grew and the higher the temperature needle swung. He slowed, he shifted into third, then second, but the noise persisted. "C'mon, c'mon," he whispered. "Don't do this to me, Tash. It won't take long. I promise."

He rose over the final hill, hung a left on Mango. Before he reached the turnoff for the grove, he nosed into the trees and onto the firebreak that ran behind the grove. He killed his headlights, shifted into first. The clacking stopped, the needle on the temperature gauge swung into the normal range. Tasha had decided to cooperate.

Half a mile in, Blade parked alongside the fence, took the flashlight out of the glove compartment, and grabbed the flight bag off the floor in front of the passenger seat. He crouched in front of the fence and found the hole he'd dug months ago. It was filled with dead leaves.

He dug out the leaves with his hands, then reached into the flight bag for the thick gardening gloves. He slipped them on, took hold of the bottom of the wire-mesh fence, and twisted it toward him, then up. Perfect. He took off the gloves, dropped them inside the flight bag, and shoved it under the fence. Then he followed, snakelike, slippery and quick.

Leaves crunched under his shoes, dread clawed through his chest. The odors of the grove filled him, sharp smells that were neither sour nor sweet but some weird mix of the two. It didn't take him long to get through the grove. His feet remembered the way.

At the edge of the trees he dropped to a crouch. The moon hadn't risen yet and beneath the trees it was already very dark. An owl screeched in the silence, a noise he had heard every night for the last year, a noise as familiar to him as the sound of his own heartbeat. But it spooked him.

Goose bumps prickled his arms. His throat went dry. He didn't want to go inside that house, but he needed some of his things. No lights in the windows, the driveway was empty. He guessed the cops had whisked away Lou's Camaro and wondered if they had turned off the power in the house, too.

Behind the dusk noises of frogs and crickets lurked a terrible quiet, the same kind of quiet that had invaded his old man's house the day his mother had split ten years ago. That memory was like yesterday, as clear to him as the moment he had found Lou.

Blade crept toward the side of the house, certain that if he was caught he wouldn't be sent to juvenile court. Not this time. They would charge him with murder one or, at the very least, manslaughter, and he would end up at one of those joints for youthful offenders. Every second of his life would be ruled by someone else. They would tell him when he could work, eat, sleep, take a shit. And he would bug out, no doubt about it.

Who was going to believe he'd found Lou when he was still alive? That Lou had died in his arms? That he'd called 911 because he couldn't stand the thought of Lou just lying there in his own blood, drawing flies, maggots, worms.

He darted to the side door. It was locked, of course it was.

Locked and sealed with yellow crime tape. He ripped the tape away, climbed onto the air-conditioning unit to the left of the door, and felt along the top of the jamb for the spare key. It was there, dusty as hell and cold to the touch.

His hand was sweating as he fitted the key into the lock. The click sounded unnaturally loud, a sharp hiccup in the eerie silence. The door swung inward and the familiar odors of the house rushed at him.

But there was no scent of jasmine.

No rustling noises.

The air was cool but not chilly.

Blade stepped quickly into the utility room, shut the door.

He had never seen the ghost. But during the months he had lived in the house he had heard it—the rustling, the creak of the stairs when he was here alone at night. He had often smelled jasmine, too, and sometimes the lights came on by themselves, especially in Lou's den.

Lou had become obsessed with the ghost; Blade wasn't sure why. Deep down he hadn't wanted to know why. It had scared him, Lou locked up in his den for long hours at a time, Lou painting scenes of places he'd never been, Lou, for Christ's sake, who had never even touched a paintbrush until late last fall.

Flashlight on. Yeah, that was better. He hurried into the kitchen, the hall. Although his flight bag was empty except for the gardening gloves, it felt heavy on his shoulder. His old man had brought it back from the Bahamas four or five years ago. He had gone there with one of his girlfriends. Blade couldn't remember which one, there had been too many over the years to keep them all straight. But he remembered those three days, a long weekend by himself, hour after hour of freedom, of silence. Every now and then he had expected his old man to burst into the house, drunk and shouting, waving his goddamn belt and threatening him.

When he returned from the trip, his temper was worse than before he'd left. Anything could set him off. A couple of times a woman from Health and Rehabilitative Services had come out to the house and Blade had lied about the bruises on his arm, the cut on his lip. He had lied because foster care seemed worse than living with his old man's temper.

Shortly after Blade's fourteenth birthday, his old man had come home loaded to the gills and let him have it. The next day Blade had cut school and gone back to the house while his father was at work. He had packed up Tasha and driven away from the fucker's house, driven out of Miami and south to the keys.

Three months later he'd been busted for car theft by Detective O'Connor here on Tango. She had gotten him four times in the next year and had finally recommended that he be sent to the rehab program where Lou volunteered. And that, he thought, had changed his life.

So look at me now, Lou, sneaking through your goddamn house.

In the hall, his grief sprang free, crashing over him, crippling him. His knees buckled and he sank to the floor, his face pressed to his thighs. His sobs shoved upward through his throat and exploded against his jeans.

What the fuck am I s'posed to do now, Lou? What?

Only the silence answered him.

After a while, he pushed to his feet, ashamed and disgusted with himself. He ran upstairs, grabbed clothes from the drawers, the closet, and shoved everything inside the flight bag. Then he went back downstairs and into Lou's den. He stopped dead in the doorway, a ripple of shock coursing through him. Cold, he thought. It was cold in there. But he didn't sense her presence, didn't hear her.

Blade rubbed his hands over his arms and shone the flashlight around. The beam impaled a briefcase on the desk that he knew at a glance didn't belong to Lou. He moved into the room, opened the briefcase, searched it, and found files from Lou's office, a logbook that listed every bond Lou had written for the last year. He also found a file on himself.

He paged through it, wincing at his mug shot, the police reports on his various arrests, at Lou's hastily scribbled notes. He dropped the file back into the briefcase and pawed through the inner pockets.

An envelope with cash in it, insurance papers, photos, ID. It belonged to a dick from West Palm Beach named Mike McCleary. There were two women in his life—a wife and daughter, Blade guessed. He kept a list of important phone numbers—a cop in West Palm named Eastman, a Christine Redman of Lantana, a John Tark whose address wasn't given but whose phone had the same area code. Those were just the top three; there were at least a dozen.

This McCleary guy must be staying here. He had probably gone out to dinner or something and might be back any second. Seized with urgency, Blade quickly shut the briefcase and hurried over to the bookcase. He opened the cabinet beneath the shelves and pulled out the canvas carrying case that held his notebook computer.

Lou had bought it for him, a Toshiba 486DX. Lou hadn't known a damn thing about computers. The plan was that Blade would learn the ropes, then teach Lou. But Lou had turned out to be computer phobic.

From time to time, Blade had done stuff for him on the computer. He had gotten information off the electronic bulletin boards, had hacked his way into the computer at the local jail to check on guys Lou had bonded, and had accessed the court computer for hearing dates, dispositions, motions, the endless flow of judicial shit.

Blade unzipped the case and knew at a glance that no one had fucked with the computer. His program disks and the floppies were still in the side pockets. He put the strap over his shoulder, shut the cabinet door, then moved along the bookcase, scanning the titles for Lou's favorite book.

Anything ever happens to me, kid, you look for One Hundred

Years of Solitude *in my study.* Sure thing, Lou. That's crazy talk, Lou.

Not so crazy after all, Blade thought.

The book was on the fourth shelf, a thick sucker written by some guy named García Márquez. A Latino. Lou had a thing about Latino writers. Blade's taste in books was strictly gringo, the scarier the better, and Lou had known that. So why had he told him to look for this particular book?

Blade reached for it, but the book toppled forward onto its spine and part of the bookcase started to move, to squeak.

Jesus God, he wasn't kidding.

Blade stepped into a room that was about six feet square, with a ceiling so low he couldn't stand up straight inside of it. He guessed it was part of the original house, maybe the only part left standing except for the fireplaces. Everything was coquina stone—the walls, the floor, the ceiling—which kept the air cool, fifty-five or sixty degrees, he guessed.

The beam of his flashlight skipped across a rolltop desk and straight-back wooden chair; a cot with a pillow and blanket folded on it; a two-drawer metal filing cabinet. A large, battery-powered light rested on top of the cabinet. Next to it were a gallon of water, an unlit cigar, an ashtray, an empty bowl, an unopened bottle of Florida water, and a cheap religious statue.

And yet Lou had never smoked or gone to church.

Blade opened the lid on the rolltop desk. Several books were stacked to one side and in a small wooden bowl were various polished stones and differently colored crystals. He swept these things into his flight bag and picked up a fat little notebook that was tucked into a cubbyhole in the desk. The dated entry in Lou's handwriting began with: *Luz came to me last night. Her name means light.*

A journal, he thought. This was some sort of journal. He stuck it in the flight bag, too. The filing cabinet wasn't locked, the files weren't labeled. Blade chose one at random that held what appeared to be copies of blueprints, six of them. A date or dates had been jotted on each one and they spanned back nearly three hundred years, from 1984, when the last additions had been made to the house, back to the early 1700s.

The two earliest blueprints had come from the archives of Iglesia San Ignacio, a Catholic church outside of Tango. The other blueprints had come from the county or from the Tango Historical Society.

He didn't know what it meant, but he emptied the drawers and stuffed all the files in his flight bag. He checked the desk once more to make sure he hadn't missed anything and suddenly the air stank of jasmine. It was just that fast, one second nothing, the next second the odor seeping from the walls, the floor, the desk, the cot. It was so thick he could feel its stickiness against his fingers.

Blade backed out of the room, his heart pounding. He rushed over to the bookcase, shoved García Márquez's book back into place. The door started to close. *Run now!* shrieked a voice in his head. Not his own voice. This was no fucking voice he'd ever heard before.

His feet uprooted from the floor and he lurched toward the door, the jasmine stink drifting after him.

Blade threw open the front door and charged across the porch, into the warm, still darkness. He stumbled on the last step, lost his balance, went down hard on his knees. For seconds he just stayed like that, his breath exploding from his chest in quick, violent bursts, his heart hammering, the weight of the flight bag and the computer pulling at his shoulders. He still clutched the flashlight, his knuckles were bleeding.

A glare of lights impaled him, headlights, and he scrambled to his feet and tore toward the back fence where he had left Tasha. The car screeched to a stop and a man shouted, "Hey, you. Hey!"

Blade charged into the grove, weaving between the trees, the man so close behind him Blade heard the slap of his shoes against the ground, the crackle of dry leaves. His arms pumped at his sides, the computer and the flight bag banged against his ribs. He darted left, right, left again, trying to lose the bastard.

The fence was suddenly there, but he was too far from the hole to reach it before the man reached him. Instead he leaped onto the mesh, clinging to it like a spider, and scrambled six feet to the top. He dropped the flight bag to the ground on the other side, heaved himself over, and jumped.

He landed on both feet, scooped up the flight bag, and hauled ass toward Tasha. He hurled himself inside, turned the key, slammed her into reverse and raced backward down the firebreak. Dust flew, the engine roared, and for an instant the headlights pinned the man as he neared the top of the fence. Then darkness filled the space between them, Tasha's tires hit the road, and Blade pressed the accelerator to the floor.

4

I

McCleary stood in the dirt at the bottom of the fence, brushing off his jeans and staring down the road where the pickup had vanished. Fast little fucker. A man with mercurial feet who obviously knew his way through the grove well enough to navigate it in the dark.

Ross Blade? It was an intriguing possibility. He might have returned to collect the rest of his belongings and had flown the coop when he heard the car. But the more McCleary thought about it, the less likely it seemed that the car had surprised the intruder. Not the way he'd been moving. Given Blade's criminal history, he would leave by another door and he wouldn't be flying when he did it.

McCleary trotted down the firebreak, focusing on his impressions of the intruder. He weighed less than McCleary's 175 and stood about five ten, Quin's height. He was sinewy, fast, and obviously strong enough to scale the fence in half the time it had taken him. "Mac?"

Quin's voice drifted through the grove; the beam of a flashlight pierced the trees. "Back here." He went over to the gate, opened it, and she appeared moments later.

"Did you get a good look at him?" she asked.

"Not really."

"I did, just for a second when he looked into the headlights. Short hair, light brown, five ten or so, needed a shave, and young. Late teens. He didn't look much like Blade's mug shot, but I think that's who it was."

"Yeah, so do I. Let's see if anything's missing from the house."

Quin took the second floor and McCleary searched the first, beginning in the den. His briefcase was on Lou's desk where he'd left it and everything inside looked undisturbed. Address book here, checkbook there, each item in its place.

He pulled open the pocket where he kept some personal items. His photos of Quin and Michelle, a dozen family shots, nothing special, were stacked every which way. The slip of paper with important numbers on it was crinkled along one side. The little shit had definitely searched the briefcase. But none of the fifties tucked into his checkbook was gone. As far as he could tell, nothing at all was missing, not even his notebook computer, which was stowed under the desk.

McCleary turned slowly in place, looking around the room. The skin between his eyes—his hunch spot—burned fiercely, but he couldn't pinpoint why.

"Looks like he came back for some more clothes," Quin said from the doorway. "What about down here?"

"Nothing missing."

She rubbed her hands over her bare arms. "The AC works overtime in here."

He hadn't noticed that it was appreciably cooler in here than in the rest of the house until she mentioned it. He glanced around for the vents and located two in the ceiling, one at either end of the room. They were ridiculously small and very little air came out of them. And yet the temperature in here was at least ten degrees cooler than it was in the rest of the house.

"What?" Quin asked, coming over to him.

"Raise your hands toward the vent. Can you feel any air?"

"Not much."

"Then why is it so cold in here?"

Her arms dropped to her sides, she rubbed them again and glanced around. "Stone walls, stone floor, great insulation, a northern exposure, I don't know."

"I set the AC on seventy-eight when we left. The rest of the house feels like seventy-eight. This doesn't."

"Stop it. You're spooking me."

"Remember Gainesville, Quin?"

"I knew you were going to say that." She held out her arms, showing him the goose bumps. "My body remembers Gainesville just fine, thanks. If you really want to talk about this," she said more softly, "let's do it outside."

As they stepped into the hall, McCleary said, "This from the woman who doesn't believe in ghosts."

"I never said I don't believe." She sounded a bit defensive. "I'm just not obsessive about it."

"I'm obsessive?"

"You can be. In Gainesville you definitely were."

She was referring to his sister's murder three years ago. During the investigation, he and Quin had stayed at Catherine's farm outside of Gainesville. On several occasions he had caught the scent of his sister's perfume or walked into a room that was cold in the way the den was. An unnatural chill, a disturbing chill, the kind of chill he imagined you would find six feet under.

Ghost.

The word, as simple as it was, possessed a certain elemental power. It was the stuff of myth, folklore, superstition. It was Macbeth, Spielberg, Stephen King; it was kids huddled around a campfire in the pitch black of night, listening to stories that made your skin crawl. It intrigued him in the abstract, as a phenomenon, an anomaly, an inexplicable event. But in the real world, in the tangible world of solid objects and bills to pay, it spooked him just as deeply as it did Quin.

In the kitchen, Quin went immediately to her vitamins, her herbal remedies. She downed a handful with a glass of water, as though they were supposed to mitigate fear as well as aging. Then she opened the fridge and proceeded to bring out strawberries, cheese, crackers, stalks of broccoli, a dip, everything purchased on their way back from dinner in the Cove. It didn't matter that an hour ago she had finished a four-course vegetarian meal. Quin was a bottomless pit with an enviable metabolism, a woman who could pack away more food in an hour than McCleary could in a day and not gain a pound.

They settled at a nicked pine table next to the window. A million stars glinted in the panes of glass, ghost lights from places in the solar system too distant to imagine. In some ways, the spirit in this house was like those lights, there but not there.

"Okay, if we assume there's really a ghost in this house, what do we do?" she asked. "You're the expert. Do we light incense and candles? Hire a priest to do an exorcism? What?"

He shrugged and scooped a cracker through the dip. "I guess we figure out if she's trying to tell us something."

"She?"

He thought a moment. "I think so."

"Why?"

"I don't know. Did Lou ever mention a ghost to you?"

"Not that I remember. But from what Gracie said, the ghost was here when Lou's father was living alone in the house. So that goes back at least twenty years."

"How old is the house?"

"A hundred years? A hundred and fifty? I don't know. He never really said."

"It feels older than that to me. I'll check with the Tango Historical Society tomorrow."

"We could split up and cover twice as much ground," she suggested. "But it means one of us will have to rent a car."

"Maybe the department would release Lou's Camaro."

"I got the distinct impression that Marion doesn't mind our looking into the murder as long as we don't get in her way."

"We won't get in her way. And maybe for the time being we should just keep our findings to ourselves."

"Why?"

"Look, she's already decided that Blade is guilty. I'm not so sure. Until we have more information, I say we tell her the bare minimum."

"Then we're going to need an ally in the department, Mac."

"The chief of police is a guy named Gene Frederick. I knew him when I worked at Metro-Dade and he's a good friend of Tim Benson's." Benson was McCleary's ex-partner in Miami and was now head honcho for Dade's sheriff's department. "I'll give Tim a call and have him talk to Frederick. We'll work around Marion."

"And if she's right about Blade?"

"Fine. Then we go from there."

She smiled wryly and gave his hand a quick squeeze. "This from an ex-cop. There's hope for you yet, Mac."

II

Quin couldn't sleep. She had tried all the usual soporifics—warm milk before bed, Valerian, counting backward from a hundred, counting white sheep as they jumped an imaginary fence. Nothing worked. At two A.M., she was wide awake.

All those ghost stories, she thought, dropping her legs over the side of the bed. Her toes curled and uncurled against the soft throw rug. She rubbed her hands over her face, got up, and walked over to the rocker for her robe. She shrugged it on and gazed out into the moonlit grove.

Even Carl Jung had seen ghosts.

Shortly after he'd built his castle on Lake Zurich, he had been awakened one night by chanting. He had gone to the window and seen a procession of monks making their way across his front lawn, their lanterns swinging in the dark. He learned later that in the sixteenth century a monastery had stood where his castle did.

A story like that, coming from a man like Jung, didn't seem the least bit preposterous. But she was not Jung, she was not a mystic, she had no rational theories about ghosts.

When she thought about them, which wasn't often, they tended to fall into that catchall category with other general weirdness on the planet. UFOs, vampires, angels, poltergeists, things that went bump in the night. Ghosts belonged in the magic of childhood, not in the world she inhabited.

No monks traipsed through the groves out there.

She went downstairs, the skin on her bare feet recoiling at the chill of the floor. This house, she thought, was too big for two people. It needed animals, cats, a dog, something besides the multitudes of birds that flocked in the trees, that congregated in and around the pond. It needed a child, all that youthful energy that would shatter the quiet and undo the rooms. She missed her daughter. She missed her cats, her dog, her house, the routine of her life. She missed Lou.

There had never been any physical attraction between them, no chemistry like that. They had been friends, good friends, the kind of friends who could talk about gender differences without self-consciousness. In their sometimes lengthy discussions over the years they'd concluded that women were, indeed, from Venus and that men were from Mars. But Lou, the unrelenting optimist, had insisted that these basic differences weren't insurmountable. Quin hoped he was right but wasn't yet convinced.

She and McCleary had been married for nearly a decade and had known each other longer than that. They had shared bathrooms, toothbrushes, a child. They had lost friends to murder, to AIDS, to car accidents, to all the diseases of modern life. They had fought, separated, reconciled. And they had done it despite his affair with a woman he had known before Quin, despite her attraction to John Tark, a detective in their firm. Despite a million strikes against them, they had persevered as a couple and would still be together at ninety. It didn't matter that their relationship read like *Days of Our Lives*.

But she still wasn't sure who McCleary was. She could explain what he wasn't, what he liked and disliked, could enumerate the superficial things. Beyond that, she was lost. She didn't have a clue what he felt in his bones.

Tark was the opposite. Although he was reticent like McCleary, there were times when she knew she could penetrate to the core of who he was, when she could reach inside of him and pull out something she could identify, label, categorize. Tark, despite his complexities, could ultimately be discovered; she wasn't so sure about McCleary. This essential difference between the two men seemed vitally important and was best expressed, she thought, in the way each man would react to this house. Lou's house. This haunted place.

Tark would walk in here, take one whiff of the air, and walk out again, severing his connection. But McCleary would enter into it, would find the flow, the flux, the rhythm, and he would pursue it until he had his answers. The problem was that she didn't have the foggiest notion what questions he would ask or what, exactly, he would be searching for. The cosmic biggies? The macroscopic? The pieces to the huge, incomprehensible puzzles? What? Perhaps it was nothing more than an answer about his sister. Maybe it was as personal as that.

She paused in the doorway of the sunroom and hit the switch for the floor lamp next to the couch. It was a wonderful room, her favorite in the house. Against the backdrop of the bamboo blinds, which she had lowered earlier, the greenery created a certain snugness that appealed to her. Shoots of ivy spilled from the hanging baskets, birds of paradise poked up from nests of emerald leaves. In a flowerbox along the east window, a cluster of violet orchids languished like royalty.

The wicker couch and chairs with the tropical-hued cushions

invited you to sit down, to relax, to kick off your shoes. This was a room for quiet reflection, for reading, for painting. The portrait of the black woman still rested on the easel where they had found it. She gazed out with an imperial air that disturbed Quin. Her eyes moved when Quin moved, as if tracking her path from the doorway to the couch.

McCleary had taken a dozen black-and-white photos of the painting earlier that evening so they would have something to show people who had known Lou. If the woman and Lou had been lovers, then it was vital that they find her. But she didn't have to subject herself to the woman's scrutiny, she thought, and turned the canvas so it faced the wall.

She sat on the couch and scanned the files laid out on the coffee table. Marion's files, Gracie's files, a scattering of files that McCleary had pulled from Lou's desk in the den. The large corkboard they'd bought in town now had a number of index cards and other items attached to it. It resembled a family tree, except that none of the people mentioned was related by blood.

At the top were a mug shot of Ross Blade and an index card with a list of pertinent facts about him. Beneath these were two more index cards—one for Vicente Construction & Realty, another for Hernando Bail Bonds, with Gracie's name in parentheses. Beneath this card were three more with financial information that they'd lifted from Lou's bank statements. This included the loan for a quarter of a million, which he'd taken out in early April, as well as certain canceled checks that raised some intriguing questions.

There was, for instance, a check for five hundred bucks to Janna Hilliard. It seemed unlikely that Lou would get one tarot reading, much less ten readings at fifty bucks a shot, so exactly what service had she been paid for? Quin intended to bring it up when she had her reading with the woman.

Three other canceled checks had also struck her as odd and deserved closer scrutiny: $150 to the Tango Historical Society, $198.25 to a New Age bookstore, $60.50 to a Catholic church in

Tango. As far as she knew, Lou had never been a churchgoer, had dismissed most of the New Age as metaphysical babble, and didn't give a shit about history unless it pertained to his personal life in some way. All three places had gone on her "To Do" list.

She opened Lou's file on Vicente Construction & Realty and paged through brochures and PR material. She guessed that at some point Lou had considered selling the grove and the house to raise cash. But it wasn't clear to her whether he had intended to list the property with Vicente Realty or sell it to Vicente himself.

According to the construction worker they'd talked to at the site, Vicente had made an offer that Lou had refused. If that was true, why had he turned it down? The PR material in the folder made it clear that the man was certainly capable of shelling out half a million without blinking an eye. He and his wife owned property all over the island, had the largest construction company on Tango, and were civic-minded to boot.

They had built a shelter for battered women, a retreat for children with cancer, a theater in the Cove that they'd donated to the city. Not only did they have the money to buy the grove, but they also had the motive to pay whatever Lou might have asked. This ten acres, at the very least, would provide space for another swimming pool, stable, and chalet for the Amelia Resort.

Included in the file were articles about the Vicentes that Lou had clipped from the *Tango Tribune*. Society puff pieces, business news, and a front-page story about the Vicentes' purchase of the property for the resort. Lou had circled this story in red and underlined a quote by a woman named Doris Lynch. She was vehemently opposed to the resort and accused the owners of "selling out" to the highest bidder and blasted the county for rezoning the property.

"It's well known that the site of the future resort and the ten acres that comprise Hernando Groves are a wildlife refuge to such endangered species as the burrowing owl and the Florida wood stork. The county's flagrant disregard of this fact is symptomatic of the greed that will eventually transform Tango Key from paradise to nightmare." She was described as a philanthropist and patron of the arts whose grandfather had made his fortune in bootlegging during Prohibition.

Quin tacked the article to the corkboard and added Doris Lynch to her list of people to contact. She set the corkboard against the side of the wicker couch and walked into the kitchen to pour herself another glass of milk. An owl screeched somewhere outside; she leaned toward the window, hoping to glimpse it. But there was only the moon, a soft gold crescent that seemed to hover in the dark above the mango trees. Thunderheads drifted inland. They swallowed most of the stars and lightning flashed in their upper tips thirty thousand feet above the planet.

As she sipped the milk and watched the sky change, she thought she heard a dry, rustling sound, like a breath of wind across the surface of dead leaves. She turned, listening to it. The noise was definitely coming from somewhere in the house. She set the glass of milk on the counter, padded into the hall, listened again. Lou's den, she thought.

Quin turned on the hallway light, passed the front room, and stopped in the doorway of the den. The sound was louder, but she still couldn't pinpoint exactly where in the den it was coming from. It seemed to be everywhere, soft, innocuous, almost rhythmic. She patted the wall for the light switch, flicked it on, stepped into the room. She noticed it wasn't as cold as it had been earlier.

The noise continued. Swish, swish, pause, swish, swish, swish. The longer she listened to it, the more it reminded her of the sweep of a broom across a stone floor. She hurried over to Lou's desk, picked up the cassette recorder McCleary had been using earlier that evening, popped in a new tape, and turned the recorder on.

No more than twenty seconds later, the noise stopped.

The subsequent silence was thick, weighted, just the soft whirring of the tape running through the recorder. And then, without warning, a soft, terrible weeping suffused the air, a sound so personal, so private, so deeply sad, Quin felt her throat close up with emotion. She didn't move, couldn't move. She was frozen to the corner of Lou's desk, where she was half-sitting, hands clutching the tape recorder.

There was no precise moment when the weeping ceased. It seemed, instead, to hiss out of the air like gas from a balloon, growing softer, softer, until it was gone. For moments Quin remained as she was, motionless, her eyes dry and burning, her senses strained.

Then she heard footsteps in the hall and McCleary called, "Quin?"

"Here." Her voice cracked, she cleared her throat. "In the den."

McCleary, barefoot and wearing just his gym shorts, came over to the desk clutching his gun. "What the hell's going on? You have any idea what time it is?"

"I got it on tape." She hit *Rewind*, her excitement tempered somewhat by the gun. Funny, how a gun made you feel better, how just the weight of it in your hand conferred a certain self-confidence that would be lacking with a kitchen fork. Or a baseball bat. No problem, she understood the concept. But she didn't like it. A part of her desperately wanted a life where guns hadn't been invented yet.

"Got what?" he asked.

"Noises. From her. You won't believe this." She hit the *Play* button. Static, that was all. "Shit." She fast forwarded the tape, stopped it again, pushed *Play* once more. Nothing.

"What the hell," she murmured, and rewound the tape, then played it again. Blank. "I heard a noise like someone sweeping. And then crying."

"Crying? C'mon."

"That's what it was. A woman crying."

"And you turned on the recorder?"

"Definitely."

She kept fiddling with the dials. McCleary set the gun on the desk, combed his fingers through his hair, and seemed at a momentary loss for words. A rarity, for sure.

"I heard something," she insisted.

"Look, there're experts who study this kind of stuff, Quin. We're not here to investigate a haunted house."

"That's not the tune you were whistling earlier."

He shrugged, retrieved his briefcase from under the desk, put the tape recorder and blank tape inside of it. "I'm not discounting anything. But I'm not jumping to conclusions, either."

"We need a better tape recorder, Mac. And some infrared film and . . ."

He laughed. "Ghostbusters, huh?"

"It beats homicide investigations," she grumbled.

McCleary, perhaps sensing an argument in the offing, wisely avoided a smartass reply. He simply shut the briefcase and said, "I don't think there's much of a market for psychic investigations. We'd starve."

With that, he headed toward the door and Quin hurried after him. "I heard it, the recorder was running, it should have been on the tape."

"It's three o'clock in the morning and I'm bushed." He turned off the light and shut the door.

Quin snickered. "You're shutting it inside."

He opened the door. "There. Satisfied?"

"I heard it," she said again as they walked up the hall, turning off the lights behind them.

"Okay, we'll buy a better recorder."

"That's a good first step."

"It may cost you, though."

"Two seconds ago you were telling me how tired you were."

"Not that tired."

He pulled her closer and she leaned into the wall at the foot of the stairs, her arms locked at his waist, his body fitting against hers. His hands slipped inside her robe and he nibbled at her ear, whispering to her, arousing her with nothing more than words and the touch of his hands.

"Keep it up and we'll christen these steps," she murmured. "Let's go upstairs."

His mouth closed over hers, a familiar taste of sleep, wind, and something indescribably good that was unique to him. For the briefest moment, she thought of Tark, of herself and Tark in the darkness outside her house in West Palm months ago. The pressure of his mouth, the wild, dangerous taste of him, the quick, maddening heat of his hands. It was nothing more than a brief, stolen kiss, and yet certain details had remained bright and vivid in her mind.

McCleary, as if sensing her thoughts, her momentary distraction, reached under her T-shirt and rolled her panties down over her hips and slipped his hand between her legs. The exquisite pressure seemed to radiate from the core of her like spokes in a wheel. It shot down to her toes, into her fingers, and pierced the inside of her skull. She tugged on his gym shorts and they broke apart briefly to shed their clothes.

They stumbled up the stairs, groping at each other like hormonal adolescents, and fell back on the futon. McCleary's mouth dropped in a slow, languid glide down the center of her, pausing at a breast, a hip, her navel, his tongue inscribing the cryptic symbols of a passion that had been absent too long from the marriage.

His tongue slid over her, into her, quick and relentless and a little cruel. The line between pleasure and pain began to blur and she sank her fingers into his shoulders, urging him inside her. Instead, he merely paused, suspending her at the electric edge of some white-hot abyss and then he started again, playing her as smoothly as an instrument. She came suddenly, violently, twitching like a splayed frog. McCleary thrust himself inside of her and rode to his own completion.

She fell asleep with him still inside of her and woke abruptly sometime later, the vestige of a nightmare clinging to her briefly, then fading. Birds twittered outside; she guessed sunrise wasn't far off. As she reached to the floor for the sheet, she sensed a presence in the room. It was neither malevolent nor benign, it was simply there, waiting, watching, appraising.

"Mac," she whispered hoarsely.

And just that quickly, it was gone.

III

When Tom Roey wasn't working, he hung out at Lester's Bar. The place never closed, the beer was cheap, the food was good, he usually won a few bucks at pool, and the only tourists who came here were the ones who were lost. Good reasons to hang out anywhere.

Even at 4:30 in the morning the place was busy, regulars mostly—he recognized the faces. Roey threaded his way through the crowd. The twirling stools that lined the counter had been here since the bar was a neighborhood soda fountain way back in the fifties.

The walls were decorated with movie posters, most of them from old Hitchcock thrillers. Large glass containers filled with pickled eggs and beef jerky stood at either end of the bar. Nothing dated beyond 1960, not even the music that blared from the jukebox. Lester's existed in a permanent time warp and every time Roey walked in here he felt like a teenager again.

As he waited at the bar, he used the mirror on the wall to check out the scene. There weren't any women alone. At this hour, even the dogs were taken, paired up with guys who were seeing triple. It was just as well. As soon as the sun came up, he had things to do. But he was comforted by the fact that he was the best-looking guy in here, a Don Johnson lookalike with a body Johnson didn't have even in his dreams. White chinos, turquoise shirt, white sandals, a *Miami Vice* stud. That was what they called him on the island, Roey the Studman.

He ordered his usual tequila with a beer chaser, and walked into the pool room looking for a game. Amateurs were playing, they weren't worth a bet, so he wandered over to the booth where his bookie usually conducted business. Ferret, who resembled the rodent he was named after, was poring over racing forms and seemed oblivious to everything around him. His albino sidekick, a tall, skinny dude with bright red eyes, was talking on a cellular phone. These two looked almost ordinary compared to the others that were crowded into and around the booth.

Roey didn't know any of the others by name, but he had seen them around the keys at one time or another. They were street theater people, the nuts who performed at dusk on the Tango pier or the Key West boardwalk. The fire-eater. The escape artist. The tightrope walker. The sword juggler. The cookie lady. The spookiest one among them was the Grecian statue, the guy who spray-painted his body and costume white and stood motionless for hours on a white pedestal.

The rodent holding court, who needs it. Roey started to turn away when Ferret noticed him. He motioned him over to the booth and the crowd of weirdos parted to let him pass. As he slid in next to Ferret, the little man said, "You putting something down or what, Tommy?"

"What's looking good?"

"The afternoon races are shaping up nice. How much have you got to spend?"

"Three or four hundred."

Ferret glanced at Bino, who was off the phone now. "What've we got for that?"

"First race tomorrow afternoon, Tinkerbell to show. Sixth race tomorrow afternoon is Looking Good for a show."

"What're the odds?" Roey asked.

Ferret answered that one; he was the odds man. "Four to one for Tinker, six to one for Looking Good."

"Six to one," Roey replied, and passed Ferret an envelope under the table.

"Nice seeing you again, Tommy," said Ferret. "I'll be in touch."

His tequila and beer were gone by then and he was ready for another. Just two, that was all he ever allowed himself.

He walked out to the bar and someone tapped him on the shoulder. He glanced around. David Vicente stood there with a glass of beer in one hand, his mouth caught in a half-smile. "Morning, Tom. I've got a booth out back." He turned away before Roey could respond.

Since Vicente's wife had had a stroke eight or nine months ago, he kept weird hours. Roey had seen him in here a couple of times, Vicente dressed like he was now, in his tourist disguise—baseball cap, jeans, windbreaker, a T-shirt with "The Big Apple" on it. Vicente, hitting on the younger babes. Roey had made it his business to find out about Vicente and his other women just in case he ever needed to use the information. It never hurt to have a trick or two up your sleeve.

The back room was very dark, very noisy, and jammed with people. As soon as they were in the booth, Vicente didn't waste any time getting to the point. "Do you have any leads on the boy, Tom?"

"Yeah, I do."

Vicente didn't look up from the small plastic bottle of alcohol he had removed from his shirt pocket. He smiled and it threw his mouth out of whack. "Excellent."

Now he held a cottonball to the bottle of alcohol, tilted it forward, set it down, and ran the cottonball around the lip of his glass. It was all done with no more thought than the way another person might light a cigarette, but Vicente was the only person Roey knew who ever did such a thing. And he had known his share of fucked up weirdos, for sure.

"How long will it take?" Vicente asked.

"A couple of days, unless I run into trouble."

It impressed Roey that Vicente didn't ask what the lead was. He liked the fact that Vicente, eccentric as he was, assumed Roey was a professional, that he knew what he was doing.

The truth was that Roey sometimes knew what he was doing and sometimes he didn't have a clue. And then the consequences were big time. So twenty years ago, when he was fifteen years old—he remembered the exact date, the night, the circumstances—he had decided he needed every edge he could get.

He had stopped drinking, stopped doing drugs, he had given up smoking. He took up weight lifting, became a vegetarian, and lost sixty-two pounds. Although he drank occasionally—but no more than two of anything at a sitting—he had never relented on anything else. Maybe he wasn't as smart or as quick as the people he did business with, but his head was always clear. And that went a long way.

"I've got one other thing I'd like you to do, Tom." He was still running the cottonball around the edge of the glass and it squeaked, a noise like fingernails clawing a blackboard. "I'll pay you extra for it."

"What's that?"

Vicente pushed the cap farther back on his head and sipped from his sweating glass of beer. Roey guessed he'd been nursing it for some time and wondered how long Vicente had been here. "Some people are staying at Lou's house. I want them out. I don't care how you do it. Just make it clear that they aren't welcome and that if they stick around, it may shorten their lives considerably."

"Who are they?"

"Private eyes."

"Working for who?"

"Probably the police department."

"Which do you want me to do first?"

"Eeenie, meeney, miney, mo, Tom." Vicente raised his glass. "*Salud.*" Then he slugged down the beer, removed an envelope from a pocket in his windbreaker, and set it on the table. "That should cover it."

With that, he dropped the used cottonball in the ashtray, capped the bottle of alcohol, and walked off. Roey opened the envelope. A bunch of hundreds. He guessed it was another ten grand, pocket change to Vicente. That brought the grand total Vicente had paid him to twenty thousand. Yes siree, it sure was nice doing business with Mr. Vicente, a businessman, like Roey himself.

5

I

Sunlight pierced the mangroves, glinted against the surface of the river, and spilled through the porch doors of the houseboat. Gulls swooped through the brightness, a sloop drifted downriver. It was business as usual on the river this morning, Blade thought. But there was nothing usual about what he was doing.

He slipped the blueprints he'd taken from the house into a large manila envelope, sealed it, and put it in the flight bag. The next item was a copy of Lou's will, which had been in one of the files. Months ago, Lou had told Blade he was drawing up a new will and that Blade would inherit just about everything. But Blade didn't have any idea what that meant, exactly, until he had found these papers.

Lou had left him the grove, the house and nearly everything in it, the houseboat, some stocks, his social security pension, a life insurance policy, a retirement account, his car. The executors of the estate were Mike and Quin McCleary. The will was probably null and void now that he was the main suspect in the murder and on the run. Just the same, he sealed the will in another large manila envelope and put it into the flight bag, too.

He picked up the fat white envelope that had been in one of the files and removed the money. He had already counted it, twenty $100 bills. He put ten of them in his wallet, and stuck the other ten in a zippered compartment in the bag. He didn't know what the hell Lou had intended to do with the money, but it would help since he couldn't pick up his check from the garage.

He packed a few clothes in the bag, the backup program disks for the computer, a pair of shoes and socks. He sorted through the books that had been in the rolltop desk and decided to take the one that Lou had marked up. It was called *Ghosts, Poltergeists, Hauntings, & Other Weirdness.* He hadn't had a chance to read much of it; he'd been too absorbed in Lou's journal. He put it into a pocket in the computer's case.

He zipped up the bag, pushed it under the bed, turned off the AC. Then he picked up the computer and left the houseboat. The morning was already warm and humid, promising that today would be a scorcher. No one was out and about yet, but the smell of bacon and coffee lingered in the air. Only five of the two dozen slips were occupied and they were full-timers, like Lou had been. By Thanksgiving, when the snowbirds arrived, though, Colin would have a waiting list and the slips would cost three times what they did now.

The shack where Colin lived and worked was built of weathered Tango pine and listed slightly to the left. It reminded Blade of Mother Hubbard's house, except there weren't any kids, just eight plump and sassy cats who pretty much did as they pleased.

Three of them were on the porch, identical black-and-white cats, the Tuxedo Boys, Colin called them. They were preening in front of their empty bowls and only the longest of the three, Whiskers, trotted over to greet Blade. He stooped to scratch him behind the ears. "Hey, guy, how's it going? I thought you were going to keep me company on the boat last night."

Whiskers purred and rubbed up against his legs. When Blade opened the door, the cat darted in front of him and vanished in the aisles. The air smelled fishy, he could hear the drone of a TV from the back of the shop.

Colin was sitting behind the counter, his feet propped on the edge as he paged through a fishing magazine. His gold front tooth flashed as he grinned, the wrinkles around his small, blue eyes deepened. "Mornin', boy," he said in his cracker drawl. "Whatcha need?"

"Could I use the phone in your office, Colin? I need to hook up the modem on the computer. For some schoolwork. I don't know if Lou told you, but I've been taking GED courses at night."

"Don't know a modem from a golem, Blade, but be my guest." His feet dropped to the floor, he picked up a brass spittoon, and spat a wad of tobacco into it. "Lemme clear you a space at the desk."

They went into a back room jammed with clutter—unopened boxes of boating equipment and supplies and stacks of books and magazines on fishing and boating. There were small jalousie windows with dirty glass that looked out onto mangroves, the river, the flawless sky. Colin swept the desk clear of magazines and pulled the phone over in front of the chair.

"Go to it, boy."

"Thanks, Colin."

He kept standing there, pinching tobacco from a pouch and sticking it bit by bit into his mouth. "You doin okay out on that houseboat by yo'self?"

"It's okay. But it's not really the same without Lou."

"Yeah, yeah, can't blame you none for that."

Blade hooked up the phone to the computer and wondered if Colin knew he was the number one suspect in Lou's murder. Probably not. He would have said something. Even though he rarely read a newspaper and refused to watch TV news because he believed it was all propaganda, he would hear about it sooner or later from someone who was passing through. Or from the cops, when they found the houseboat. Blade wanted to believe that Colin wouldn't buy it. But he had learned to never second-guess another person's reaction to anything. His old man had taught him that.

"I still can't believe he gone and got hisself killed. I used to tell him to get out of that bizness, Blade. Dealin with convicts ain't a way to live. We even talked once about us bein partners. We'd build another dozen slips, advertise and shit like that. But in the end . . ." He shrugged his bony shoulders. "Hell, in the end he had the bond bizness in his blood." He paused. "Where was you the night he got killed, boy?"

"Working." He booted up the computer, activated the modem, and willed Colin to go away, to leave him alone.

"I reckon this ain't been too easy on you. You need anything you jus' holler, boy." Then Colin gave him a fatherly pat on the back and shut the door as he left.

Blade went into the file where he kept phone numbers and access codes and found the ones he needed for the Tango sheriff's department. Getting in was no problem. He'd done it for Lou a bunch of times. But now it was personal and that made him uneasy. He couldn't hang around too long.

He would get in, download what he needed, and get out.

Once he was in, he requested the file on Hernando, Lou.

Department?

Homicide.

ID, please.

He keyed in the same ID number that had gotten him into files in other departments. He figured it was some cop's ID number and since he hadn't used it that often, it wouldn't get flagged by the system's watchdog. Sure enough, it got him in but not far enough.

Enter case number.

"Shit." He took a stab in the dark, entered the date Lou's body had been found.

Insufficient data.

Okay, he was on the right track. Case numbers apparently had something to do with the dates the files were opened. He thought a moment, then assigned a Roman numeral to the end of it. A moment later, he was in.

Case 0902-I (Hernando, Louis). Press (D)ownload or (E)nter.

He pressed *D,* opened a file in his word processing program for the downloaded material, then hit *D* at the prompt. As soon as he had the information, he got out.

Blade disengaged the modem, unplugged the phone from the computer, and went into the file he had downloaded. He read through Detective O'Connor's description of the 911 call, the discovery of Lou's body, and the collection of physical evidence.

The autopsy report was included. Blade didn't understand a lot of the words and the coroner's dispassionate description pissed him off. But he struggled through it. Information was power: Lou had drummed that into him from day one.

When he got to the part about sperm, he stopped, rubbed his eyes, read it again. And again. Lou had been screwing someone? Who? He'd never said squat to Blade about any woman. Sometimes he talked about his ex or about Gracie, but he'd never said he was sleeping with either of them. Janna Hilliard had hit on Lou a couple of times when she was up at the house, but Lou hadn't seemed interested. So who?

He paged through the information, searching for some mention of Lou's will. He found it near the end, where Detective O'Connor had noted that Ross Blade was Lou's major beneficiary. The state attorney's office apparently believed this was sufficient for a motive, because a warrant had been issued for Blade's arrest on September 3.

O'Connor's notes implied that there may have been a sexual relationship between Lou and Blade, which in her opinion constituted a stronger motive for the murder than greed. Blade read that paragraph three times and something exploded inside of him. Sex? Him and Lou? What kind of fucked up people were these?

Blade saved to the disk, exited to the *C* prompt, and turned off the computer, shut it. All he wanted to do was get out of here and stash the flight bag someplace safe. He opened the door to the shop. A muscular man with sandy hair, wearing a tight T-shirt and jeans, was standing at the counter talking to Colin. His back was to Blade, but he could see the expression on Colin's face and knew the man wasn't a customer. A hunch told him the rest, that he was asking questions about Lou's houseboat.

Whiskers squeezed through the opening, then Blade shut the door to a sliver and strained to hear the conversation.

". . . my understanding was that Lou Hernando docked a houseboat here," the man was saying.

"We got a couple three houseboats, but none that belong to anyone named Hernando. You a reporter?"

"No. No, I'm not. Just a friend."

"Yeah? You got a name?"

"Jones, Tom Jones."

"Like the singer, huh? Well, like I said, Mr. Jones, we ain't got no houseboat here that . . ."

Blade shut the door quickly, soundlessly, and slipped across the room and out the rear exit. Whiskers charged along in front of him, leading him around the back of the shack and out onto the dock. As Blade untied the houseboat, the cat leaped on board. Blade was right behind him. He cranked up the engine and headed north into the canal, pushing the engine to the max.

He didn't look back.

II

McCleary ran alone that morning, down Mango Road. It hardly qualified as a major artery on the island and was utterly deserted at this hour. He shared his three miles of solitude with the heat, the goddamn mosquitos, a variety of birds, and a pair of Key deer that froze when they saw him.

They were no larger than a German shepherd and were poised at the edge of the pines, their liquid eyes huge and startled. Bambis, that was what Michelle would call them. The deer were more numerous on Big Pine Key, where more than fifty a year were killed by cars. All over Big Pine, for instance, signs were posted in their known grazing areas and speed limits were strictly enforced. McCleary suspected their life span on Tango was somewhat longer because most of them stayed in the wilderness preserve, where roads were few and far between.

A shiny black BMW turned onto Mango and sped toward him, the tires kicking up dirt and pebbles. It whizzed past, then braked, and rolled into reverse. McCleary stopped and the Beamer drew even with him. The window whispered down and a man with a soft moon face and carefully combed chestnut hair poked his head out.

"You Mike McCleary by any chance?"

He didn't walk over to the car. Six months ago, he had been shot while jogging outside the development where they lived and he no longer assumed that every car that stopped was driven by a lost tourist. "Who's asking?"

"Craig Peck. I'm Lou Hernando's attorney."

"Yeah, I'm McCleary."

Peck killed the engine, opened the door, stepped out. He looked like a well-dressed Pillsbury Dough Boy—expensive chinos, a cotton shirt with one of those fancy designer emblems on the pocket, and a psychedelic tie. He was maybe all of thirty and came toward McCleary with his hand extended and a shit-eating grin on his face.

"Nice to meet you, Mr. McCleary. Nice to meet you. Marion told me you and your wife were staying at the grove. I hope you don't mind my barging in like this without calling, but I was on my way into town and decided to take my chances. If this is a bad time, we can set up an appointment for later today. It's about Lou's will."

"Now is fine."

"Great, just great. Hop in and I'll give you a lift back to the house. You jog every morning?"

"Usually."

"I used to do it, that's how I met Lou. But Jesus, the heat got to me."

They were inside the car now, the air sweet with the scent of sun, new leather, and Peck's aftershave. McCleary noted the cellular phone, the portable fax. "You were on my list of people to see today," McCleary said. "You saved me a trip. I understand Ross Blade is Lou's primary beneficiary."

"He is, indeed. And you and your wife were named executors of the estate until Mr. Blade turns twenty-five. Did Marion tell you that?"

He nodded.

"Of course, at this point things are up in the air since Mr. Blade is wanted for first-degree murder. But that doesn't affect what you and your wife inherit."

"I thought we were executors."

"You are. But Lou also bequeathed you his shares of two computer stocks. Six months ago they weren't worth much more than what he'd paid for them. But today they're worth about seventy-five thousand."

"Goddamn."

"Yes, sir." Peck's grin was as odd as anything McCleary had ever seen, a kind of clenched-teeth grimace. "That's about the size of it." He turned through the gate and parked alongside the Explorer a few minutes later. He reached into the backseat for a spiffy black leather briefcase and they got out. Peck tugged at his tie and glanced around, nodding to himself. "A piece of paradise. I always loved this place. My folks used to vacation here in the winter and I can remember riding my bike along Mango Road and sneaking in here. It wasn't fenced in those days."

"When was that?"

"Musta been the early seventies. I was nine or ten at the time."

This guy was probably born the year Kennedy was assassinated, McCleary thought, and suddenly felt old. "Were Lou's parents living here then?"

"Yeah. It was before the booze had made them completely nuts. After they started losing it, the fence went up. The NO TRESPASSING signs were posted. And after she died, he would sit out on the porch at dusk sometimes, with a shotgun across his lap and a bottle of bourbon on the table beside him. Weird, very weird."

"So you didn't know Lou then?"

"Nope, he wasn't around. I think he was living in Miami."

As they stepped inside, McCleary said, "You ever hear any stories about this place being haunted?"

Peck laughed, whipped off his shades, and slipped them into his shirt pocket. "I was just about to launch into my haunted house story."

McCleary gestured toward the wooden kitchen table, inviting Peck to take a seat. "A personal story?"

"No way. Grapevine stuff. We used to hear that the ghost was a former slave who'd been brought here from Cuba by one of the pirate ships. She supposedly drove the Hernandos to drink and when the Mrs. died, she haunted the old man until he was nuttier than a fruitcake."

"How about some coffee, Mr. Peck?"

"Love some, thanks."

Quin was up, because there was a fresh pot of coffee on the counter. McCleary filled a mug for Peck and poured himself a large glass of ice water, which he gulped down. "Let me get my wife. Be right back."

She was on the phone in the sunroom, wearing the T-shirt she'd lost at the foot of the stairs last night. She pointed at the hall and mouthed, *Who is that?*

McCleary made an *L* with his thumb and forefinger and motioned for her to join them. She nodded and when she entered the kitchen five minutes later, she had changed into white shorts and a black T-shirt with bright orange letters across the front—

Tango Fritter, the island's response to Key West conchs. McCleary noticed that Peck's eyes lingered a shade too long on the words, which crossed Quin's breasts.

Now that Peck had both of them present, he didn't waste time with more stories. He removed some papers from his briefcase and went through them page by page: copies of the will for each of them, copies of the stock certificates.

"The original certificates are in a safe-deposit box at one of the banks on the island. Unfortunately, Lou neglected to tell me which bank and I don't have any idea where the key is. We'll get that straightened out."

Quin said, "We'd like to be present when you do that, Mr. Peck."

Although she was smiling when she said it and her voice was almost painfully pleasant and polite, McCleary detected a distrustful undercurrent. Quin didn't care for lawyers any more than he did, but he was pretty sure that what he heard was personal. It was Peck himself she disliked.

"No problem at all, Mrs. McCleary. Marion said you all would be staying here for a spell, so I'll just give you a buzz when things are straightened out. Now if you two would just sign these . . ." He pushed a pair of forms across the table. "I'll be on my way."

"One more question," McCleary said. "In the event that Ross Blade is caught and convicted, what happens to his inheritance?"

"Florida law prohibits inheritance through murder, so the courts would step in. I imagine his inheritance would be turned over to the county to make good on the lien against the house and grove. It wouldn't affect any of the other bequeathments."

"And what happens in the event of his death?"

"That's trickier."

Yeah, tell it to me, Mr. Attorney. "In what respect?"

"In the event of Mr. Blade's death, the property goes to the county for a wildlife refuge. The rest of the estate, except for what you have inherited, will be sold to meet the quarter-million-dollar lien against the property. The lien is actually going to be a problem regardless. Other than the land, Lou didn't have the assets to pay it off. So even if Mr. Blade inherits, part of the property will have to be sold."

"What about his business?" Quin asked. "Does that go to Gracie?"

"Yes, it does. Although Lou didn't own the building, he has a twenty-year lease and, considering the location, the rent is nominal. And of course she inherits everything pertaining to the business."

Quin, who was reading the will with considerably more care than McCleary had taken, looked up. "It says here that Blade inherits a houseboat. Where is it?"

"That's one of the details I have yet to find out."

McCleary glanced at the last page of the will; it was dated May 4, more than four months ago. According to Gracie, Lou had spent the last six months in an irresponsible fog and yet he had managed to draw up a will that covered every conceivable base. So what did that imply about Gracie's perspective on things? And what the hell had Lou actually been up to during all those months?

"So basically the people who have benefited from Lou's death are Blade, Gracie, and my wife and me."

"Well, if you read through the will, Mr. McCleary, you'll find several other people mentioned as well. But the bequeathments don't amount to much: a family heirloom that goes to his ex-wife, a portrait that goes to the church, a few—"

Quin leaned forward. "Which portrait?"

Peck paged through the will. "Let's see . . . Ah, here it is. A portrait of a black woman."

"And the other paintings?"

"They stay with the house."

"Which church?"

Peck consulted the will again. "San Ignacio. The contact person is a Father Rodriguez." He looked up at Quin and grinned in that clenched-teeth way that McCleary found intensely irritating. "What do you know that the rest of us don't, Mrs. McCleary?"

She rolled her eyes, touched the back of his hand, and in a soft, Southern drawl, said, "Why, Mr. Peck. Wherever did you get the idea I know anything at all?"

Peck's laugh was quick and nervous and made his double chin quiver. He knew Quin was making fun of him and wasn't quite sure how to react. Flustered, he dropped his gaze to the will again and slipped back into his lawyer routine. Quin glanced at McCleary, her eyes shouting, *Enough of this asshole.*

"I think that about covers it for now," Peck said. When he looked up again, he had regained his composure. "I'll be in touch about the safe-deposit box."

Five minutes later, he and Quin stood on the porch, waving at Peck as he left. "Hey, Mac, I've got a good joke for you."

"A lawyer joke."

"There's no other kind. If you ask a lawyer how many lawyers it takes to change a lightbulb, what does he say?"

"I give."

"How do you know it's really burned out?"

"Okay, he's an asshole."

"He's a crook," she said as they went back inside. "Lou was paying this turkey two or three hundred bucks an hour and he doesn't know where the houseboat is docked? Which bank the safe-deposit box is in? I don't buy it. I want a list of his other clients."

"We'll give that one to Marion."

Now that they had agreed on Peck, Quin turned her attention to her vitamins and herbs, which she doled out one by one. She swallowed them in clumps of seven; McCleary nearly gagged just watching her. Then she studied the contents of the fridge with the kind of concentration politicians reserved for Senate hearings. "How about pancakes?" she asked.

He didn't want to tell her that her pancakes were typically

too thick, burned on the outside, and raw and lumpy on the inside. Her pancakes, in fact, were characteristic of most of her cooking, which was why he had been the cook for most of the years they'd been married. Self-preservation. "I'll do it."

"Great. I'll go feed the critters."

He watched her through the window, doling out birdseed that she brought from the toolshed, Quin in her element. No wonder they had three cats and a dog at home, he thought. No wonder every Muscovy duck in Palm Beach County pecked through their yard, turning the sod to shit. The more the merrier, that was her motto. Given her druthers, she would turn her back on investigative work and buy a farm.

There were times when he indulged in the same fantasy, a vestige of his childhood on a farm in upstate New York. But the truth, as corny as it sounded, was that he was happy with the life he had. The last few months had been among the best in their marriage, and their firm had more business than they could effectively handle. More than this, though, was the fact that for the first time in years, he felt as though he had reached a place within himself where he felt comfortable, secure.

And then the phone rang and a rasping voice said, "Mike McCleary, please."

"Speaking."

"I could show up at the door any time now, Mr. McCleary, and your wife wouldn't know me from Adam. I'd make sure she was there alone and I'd show her a real good time before I killed her. I have a passion for long legs. Catch my drift? You have twenty-four hours to head back home."

The caller hung up and McCleary stood there with the dead phone in his hand, watching his wife move through the hot morning light.

"Who was on the phone?" she asked when she came back inside.

"Someone who wants us off the island."

She heard what he hadn't said and frowned, waiting for him

to go on. McCleary repeated what the caller had said. Her expression didn't change, but she rubbed her hands over her arms as if against a sudden chill. "I know what you're thinking," she said. "And you can just forget it. I'm staying here."

They had had this same conversation for this same reason before, and he knew enough not to try to convince her to do otherwise. "Just make sure you're always carrying."

"I know the routine, Mac." She went over to the stove, flipped the pancakes in the pan, then began setting the table, the caller's words like a third presence between them.

6

I

El Pueblito, the Little Town, was Tango's Cuban community, one of Quin's favorite spots on the island. On a map, it fell roughly to the right of the cat's mouth. It was smaller than its Miami sister of Little Havana and considerably older.

It dated back to the 1820s, when it was settled by Bahamian and Cuban seamen. They had fished the warm Atlantic and Gulf waters for turtles, stone crabs, crawfish, and whatever else the depths might yield. In 1831, when the cigar industry in Key West had burgeoned, so had El Pueblito. Fifty-some-odd years later, the industry was developed enough to attract cigar makers from Havana who were also seeking to escape the Nationalist uprising in Cuba against the Spanish. Some found employment in Key West factories, some turned to the sea, and the rest migrated to Tango.

In those days and long before, the church of San Ignacio had been the dominant force on the island. According to the brochures Quin had picked up at the Chamber of Commerce after she'd left the house, it was the oldest church on Tango. Construction on it began in 1697 by a band of Spanish pirates who had settled here after sweeping through the Caribbean, pillaging untold fortunes in gold and gems.

Their leader was a renegade from Barcelona named Juan Domingo—John Sunday—who supposedly had a vision that he was to build a church on "an emerald isle above the sea." His ship anchored somewhere offshore of what was today Pirate's Cove and he and his men fought their way inland.

During the three years it took John Sunday and his boys to build the church, more than half of his sixty men died of malaria or yellow fever. Of the thirty slaves he had brought from Cuba, only a handful survived. Domingo liberated them and paid them to finish building the church. Before its completion in 1700, Rome assigned half a dozen priests to the church, who, along with their predecessors, enabled the church to rule the island like a feudal lord for the next century.

But San Ignacio apparently wasn't on anyone's priority list these days. Panes of the stained-glass windows were missing, there was no bell in the steeple tower, weeds pushed up through the crumbling sidewalk out front. The priests' rectory to the side of the church was an eyesore. She couldn't imagine what Lou's connection was to this place or, more to the point, why he had bequeathed the church the portrait of a black woman who looked like a pagan goddess.

Unless she was one of the slaves brought from Cuba.

Now *that* was an interesting notion and if it was true, did that mean she was the spook in the house?

The young priest who answered the door had soft doe eyes, spidery fingers, and his breath smelled musty and stale. "*Buenos días*," she said in her awkward gringo Spanish. "*Puedo hablar con Padre Rodriguez?*"

"*Sí, señora. Entra, por favor. Esta en su oficina.*" He led her down a long, silent hall into a courtyard jammed with lush, tropical plants and invited her to wait on a bench in front of a pond. "Your name, *señora*?"

"Quin St. James."

He smiled at the "saint" part. "You are applying for the teacher position?"

"No, no, nothing like that." Never that again. "I'd like to speak to him about Lou Hernando."

"*Un momentito*," he replied, and hurried off.

She walked over to the pond. It resembled a small lagoon, plants tumbling over its edges, tendrils of crimson bougainvillea arching out over the water. A statue of the Virgin Mary stood at the end, her arms outstretched, her heart like a bright red badge against her blue robes. Coins littered the bottom of the pool at her feet, evidence of supplications, prayers, and offerings made to the virgin. Plump gold carp swam through the shaded waters, rising now and then to nab one of the numerous dead bugs that floated on the surface.

Quin's reflection gazed back at her, umber hair falling to her shoulders in frizzy waves, her blue eyes pinched with fatigue at the corners. Sunlight stroked the back of her head, making her pleasantly drowsy. She shut her eyes briefly and was immediately back in the bedroom early this morning, that presence like a weight in the very air that she breathed.

"Señora St. James?"

She turned, smiled. "Yes."

"I am Father Rodriguez," he said, and offered his hand.

He was very old, bald, hunched, and wrinkled. The skin on his palm felt like rice paper; if she squeezed too hard, it might split down the middle. "I understand you are here about Lou Hernando?"

"I was a friend of his and I'm also investigating his murder, Father."

Behind his thick glasses, his rheumy dark eyes seemed unnaturally small, diminished. "A terrible tragedy. Lou wasn't a member of our parish, but he was a good man and I was quite fond of him."

"How long did you know him?" she asked as they settled on the bench.

"I baptized him when he was six days old. His parents were members of the parish then. He attended our school through eighth grade, then transferred to the high school. After that, our lives crossed infrequently. When he moved back to the island after his father's death, we renewed our friendship. But I could never convince him to rejoin the church." The tone of his voice made it clear that he considered this a personal failure.

"Did you ever meet Ross Blade?"

"Only once. A nice young man with a troubled past."

"Do you think he killed Lou?"

"I leave such judgments to God."

How convenient. "You must have some opinion, Father."

He thought a moment. "Maybe he was a thief, but he's no killer, señora. They were like father and son, he and Lou."

"Do you think there was anything sexual going on between them?"

Behind his glasses, his watery eyes widened. "Certainly not."

Count one ally for Blade, she thought. "Can you tell me anything about this?" She brought the canceled check out of her purse. "Was it a donation or something?"

Rodriguez regarded it for a moment, but she couldn't tell if it was because he didn't remember what the check was for or didn't want to say. She wondered if one day she would be standing where the priest was now, trying to remember where she lived or how old her daughter was.

Rodriguez finally shook his head. "Lou spent a week searching the church's records and made copies of some of our documents. He insisted on paying for the time."

"What was he looking for?"

"References to his house—when it was built, who built it, who lived in it. In those days, the church had laid claim to much of the land at this end of the island. They collected rent and taxes from the people who lived on it. Our records go back to 1701."

"Was there any particular reason he was doing this?"

Rodriguez poked at his glasses, pushing them farther back on the bridge of his nose. "Lou had reasons for everything he did, señora, but he didn't always discuss them with me."

"What else did he look for in your records?"

"Census statistics for the early part of that century. Births, deaths, marriages. The Tango Historical Society helped us put most of the early records on microfilm because the parchment was so fragile. But Lou wanted to see the originals, so I arranged it for him."

"Did he find whatever he was looking for?"

"I don't know. Have you seen his house, señora?"

"My husband and I are staying there."

The change in his expression was slight but significant. "Of course, it is none of my business, but if I were you, señora, I would stay at a motel in town." Then, in a softer voice: "I believe there is something utterly evil in that house."

"The ghost, you mean."

Rodriguez rubbed his hands over his dark slacks. "Ghosts are folklore, señora. This is a . . . a presence, a succubus."

Quin struggled not to smile. "A female demon?"

Rodriguez made a surreptitious sign of the cross on his forehead. "A succubus is a female demon that has intercourse with a man while he sleeps. I believe this demon is what drove Lou's father to an early grave. Perhaps it is why Lou is dead."

"I don't believe in demons, Father Rodriguez."

"You will believe before you leave this island, señora."

The only demons Quin believed in were those that existed in the dark, shuttered rooms inside man. The very notion of a satanic being—incubus, succubus, any kind of uccubus—was nothing more than religious brainwashing, as simplistic and absurd as the concept of heaven and hell. It implied the existence of absolute evil, which she simply didn't buy.

And yet, open a newspaper on any given day and the evidence of absolute evil was there. Unimaginable atrocities shouted from the headlines and morning talk shows, sharing space at her breakfast table.

Several years before Michelle was born, she and McCleary had rented a cabin in the Adirondacks, on Blue Mountain Lake. There was no phone in the cabin, no television, and the nearest newspaper was thirty miles south. For a full week, the rhythm of her life had been vastly different. She had emerged from the cabin, from the woods, from the world of Blue Mountain Lake, with a heightened awareness of the interconnection among all things. She had emerged with trust.

Two days later, it had been shot to hell at a car wash in south Miami. A teenager in a souped-up Mustang had pulled alongside her car, leaped out, grabbed her purse off the seat, and fled. After that, she reverted to her old ways—locking all the doors when she was in the car, staying on well-lit streets at night, carrying a gun in the glove compartment. After that, she was vigilant again, she anticipated the worst, she prepared for it, she expected it.

And maybe that was the point, she thought. Her expectations. Her beliefs. Perhaps if she believed in demons, she would encounter them. Perhaps someone who didn't believe in spooks—her sister, for instance—would spend a night in Lou's house and never feel or hear or sense anything. It didn't mean the spook wasn't there or that it didn't exist. It simply meant it didn't fall within the skeptic's perception.

If she operated from this premise, then by opening herself more fully to the presence she should be able to perceive it more clearly. And maybe it would respond in the same way.

Sure, Quin, and you'll get a dialogue going.

As she approached the turnoff for Route 2, which would take her into town, she glanced in the rearview mirror to see if it was safe to change lanes. A chocolate brown Volvo was behind her. She was pretty sure she had seen it when she'd left the church, one of many details in her paranoid scan of the street. This didn't necessarily mean the driver was following her, but she was almost certain that he was.

Thinking of the call McCleary had taken earlier this morning, she reached for the gun in the glove compartment. It was a nine-millimeter Koch & Heckler with a thirteen-shot clip, a semiautomatic, powerful and precise. She snapped in a clip, set the gun in her lap. She didn't change lanes as she'd planned; instead, she hung a left at the intersection and drove through El Pueblito's bustling downtown.

The Volvo followed, two cars separating them.

"Okay, bud, we'll play it your way."

She cruised past Cuban restaurants and boutiques, past fast-food joints and outdoor parks. The Volvo darted in and out of cars, switched lanes, but didn't come any closer. At the next major intersection, she got her bearings and turned south on Route 2, just as she had planned to do earlier.

The Volvo caught the red light.

Quin laughed and sped ahead. Route 2 could hardly be called an interstate. Its two lanes meandered past patches of pines and small apartment complexes, gas stations and convenience stores, and grew more congested as you neared town. She turned at the first side road, cut through an apartment complex, and circled around to Route 2 again.

A mile later she spotted the Volvo putting along, a tidy brown box on wheels. She sped up until only one car separated them. She couldn't see the license plate, but she could see into the car well enough to determine that the only person inside was the driver.

The vehicle in front of her suddenly turned left and for a few seconds she had an unimpeded view of the Volvo. Tango County license plate, RUF-632. Thank you very much, she thought, and let up on the gas. Almost immediately, two cars whizzed past her on the left and darted between her and the Volvo. She followed him until he pulled into a gas station on the outskirts of town, then headed in the opposite direction and stopped at the first public phone to call Marion.

She ran the plate while Quin was on the phone. "The computer doesn't come up with anything, Quin. Are you sure you've got the numbers right?"

RUF. The noise a dog made. She was positive about the letters, but less certain about the numbers. "The three might have been an eight. Try that."

The tap of keys. A ringing phone in the background. The hot sun beating against her back. "Nope."

"A bogus plate."

"Or the numbers are wrong. Where're you headed now?"

"On my way to the gym to talk to Felicity."

"Call me if you see this guy again. And I'm working on getting you guys a list of Peck's other clients."

"How long do you think it'll take?"

"I've got to tread lightly on this one, Quin. Peck used to work as a public defender and has got some heavy political connections. Fortunately, his law clerk and I used to jog together."

"A punch of a computer key, Marion."

"I'm pushing, Quin, I'm pushing. By the way, Mac came by and picked up Lou's Camaro."

"I know. I dropped him off. Did he tell you about the call?"

"Yeah. I can put a tap on your line in case this guy pulls a repeat, but Mac said not yet. You okay with that?"

"For now." A half truth. "I heard sounds in the house last night."

"What kind of sounds?"

Quin told her; the subsequent pause was significant.

"You still there?" Quin asked.

"Uh, yeah, still here. These calls are recorded, Quin."

"We'll talk later," she said and hung up.

II

The headquarters for the Vicente conglomerate was located in a large warehouse in the wharf district. It seemed an odd spot for a businessman to set up shop, McCleary thought, unless you calculated the difference in rent between the docks and downtown Pirate's Cove.

This guy was definitely not worried about appearances.

McCleary squeezed Lou's Camaro into a tight space on the street. From his briefcase he removed a box of Marlboro Lights, flipped open the lid, and shook the cigarettes into his hand.

They were twenty in all, but only two of them were whole. The others were half the size and rested against a tiny cassette recorder that fit at the bottom of the box. He turned on the recorder and made sure the mike, concealed in one of the filters, was working. It was. He slipped it in the pocket of his shirt, locked the briefcase again, set it on the floor.

If man had never gone into space, he thought, gadgets like this might never have come into being. This particular item belonged to John Tark, who had lent it to him before he'd left on vacation a couple of weeks ago. Tark, he thought, who might or might not have slept with his wife. If it had happened—and he still wasn't sure, he had never asked and Quin had never volunteered the information—then it would have been last winter when he was in the hospital.

History, in other words.

Outside, the air was pungent with the odors of the Gulf—salt, smoke from the tugs, fish from the nearby docks where the fishing vessels were unloaded. The hot sun beat down against all of it, baking the smells into the very texture of the air.

The moment he stepped inside the warehouse the wharf odors vanished so completely it was as if the place were hermetically sealed against the exterior environment. The air here smelled of cleansers—bleach, a faint residue of ammonia, Windex. While the lobby was pleasant enough, it hardly classified as plush. He had seen better waiting rooms at walk-in clinics.

The artwork that hung on the walls, however, was something else altogether. These watercolors, acrylics, and oils, all by artists he'd never heard of, were rendered with such utter simplicity and beauty that just the sight of them made him ache inside for the road he himself hadn't followed. Pragmatism had pushed his artistic passions into a closet labeled "weekends."

The young woman at the desk directed him through an electronically controlled door just behind her. "Mr. Vicente is expecting you, sir, but you may have to wait a few minutes. He's on the phone right now."

Vicente, the busy man.

McCleary was ushered into a second, smaller waiting room. A long window overlooked the wharf, a bustling boardwalk of shops and businesses that stretched half a mile along the Gulf. There were no paintings here, but a map of Tango dominated one wall. Red pins marked Vicente's considerable real estate holdings on the island, each one meticulously labeled.

One of the two doors opened and a man in his late sixties strode out. He bore a striking resemblance to Sean Connery, except that he was more slender, sinewy, and moved with the mercurial quickness of a thief. His hair was pulled back into a nub of a ponytail, an odd touch for a Cuban businessman.

"Mr. McCleary, sorry to keep you waiting."

"Thanks for seeing me on such short notice." McCleary extended his hand, but Vicente acted as though he didn't see it. McCleary let his arm drop back to his side. "I appreciate it."

"Please, come in." He gestured toward the sitting area in his spacious office. McCleary noticed the odor of cleansers here as well, but it was masked by an air freshener. "Would you like coffee? Something to drink?"

Cuban hospitality. "Coffee would be great."

Vicente pressed a button on his phone. "*Margarita, dos cortos con azúcar, por favor.*"

Two short coffees with sugar. Vicente's melodic Spanish smacked of old Havana, when the warm Caribbean nights had throbbed with calypso music and lights burned from opulent hillsides. Batista's days, the same world Lou's parents had grown up in.

"I talked to Detective O'Connor at some length the day the body was found," Vicente said as he claimed the wicker couch across from McCleary. "Did she tell you?"

The businessman setting the stage: *This is where I am, where are you?* "Yes, she did. I just had a few other questions. I won't take much of your time."

"How can I help you?"

Vicente's bony hands lifted slightly, palms facing the ceiling, and in that moment, he seemed to merge with the figure in the mural behind him, Christ perched on a hill above Rio's Copacabana. McCleary was certain the pose was intentional—Vicente, the busy but benevolent businessman, granting an audience to one among the multitudes of peons way down below him. It pissed him off and he decided the hell with courtesy.

"Detective O'Connor neglected to mention how much you offered Lou for his grove. Or why he turned the offer down."

"Did you know Lou, Mr. McCleary?"

"For a number of years."

"Then I don't have to tell you that Lou was a walking contradiction. He needed the money and I offered him a fair price for the land—nearly a million dollars over a period of three years. But I don't think he really wanted to sell, Mr. McCleary. He was too attached to the property."

"Because it had been in his family for so many years? Attached that way?"

Vicente brought his folded hands to his chin, a contemplative gesture that was as sincere as the earlier gesture was false. "I'm sure that had something to do with it. But his rejection was also mixed up with the birds."

"Which birds?"

"The burrowing owls. The wood storks. The herons. The ducks and cranes and egrets. You name it, they frequent the grove. And Lou was the birdman of Tango, Mr. McCleary. He fed them, he cared for them, he took them to vets. They filled his life when his marriage went bad, when his business went bad. He was obsessed with those birds. And the house. He loved the house. He loved its history, its solidity, its realness. Do you know what I'm saying, Mr. McCleary? Toward the end of his life, Lou was as unbalanced as his father."

"You knew his father?"

Vicente sat forward. "Manuel Hernando and I went to school together in Havana. We immigrated here within a year of each other. He was a brilliant, eccentric man who made and lost a fortune in agriculture—citrus, mangos, you name it, he could grow it and grow it better than anyone else. But when he and his wife moved into that house, something happened to them. They withdrew from their business, they drank too much, they became reclusive. And finally, when Lou left for college, their lives literally fell apart.

"Lou's mother, Rosa, died of a stroke not long after he graduated from college. Lou spent almost two decades afterward watching his father sink deeper and deeper into some dark, fragmented world. The house, the land, that was all that remained of his family. So, yes, Mr. McCleary, you might say he was overly attached to the place."

McCleary didn't quite see the connection between the birds and Lou's family, but he let the point pass. "Would the ten acres have become part of the Amelia Resort?"

"Some of it would have, yes." No equivocation about that one. "But I agreed to maintain five acres as a wildlife refuge. And Lou could remain in the house as long as he lived."

"Then the house would revert to you when Lou died? Or to your heirs?"

"We never got that far in our negotiations. He wanted his heirs to retain the right to live in the house. I simply couldn't agree to it. He had no wife then, no children."

"But he felt responsible for Ross Blade."

"A juvenile delinquent."

"Whoever he is, whatever he did, Lou felt responsible for him."

"It was his worst mistake, Mr. McCleary. He and Felicity never had children and I think he hoped that Ross would become the son he never had."

Christ. An amateur Freud.

The receptionist arrived with two tiny cups of coffee and left without a word. Vicente opened his desk drawer, brought out a bottle of rubbing alcohol and a cottonball, wet the cotton, and casually ran it along the edge of the cup. This was obviously a routine with him, but McCleary found it no less shocking than if Vicente had suddenly started to pick his nose. There were things you did in private that you simply didn't do when other people were around because it wasn't fucking *normal.*

When Vicente was satisfied that the cup was germ free, he raised it, smiled, and said, *"Salud, Señor,"* and drank it down like a shot of whiskey.

Okay, so the guy had a germ phobia. The question was whether or not it was related to Lou's death in any way. "Did anyone else make an offer on Lou's property?"

"People were always making offers. That grove is a prime location on Tango, Mr. McCleary. Even if the zoning was never changed and it remained agricultural, it's still a fantastic piece of land."

"Did Doris Lynch make an offer?"

"More than once. She and Lou had birds in common, but I don't think he liked her personally. That might have had something to do with why he turned her down. Like I said, Lou was an odd man."

It takes one to know one.

"Have you seen Lou's paintings?" Vicente asked.

McCleary nodded.

"Before my wife's stroke, she used to collect art by unknown Cuban artists and unknown island artists. She thought Lou's paintings were among the best she'd seen in years, that they approached the brilliance of some of his father's works."

"I didn't realize Manuel painted."

"Magnificently. But like Lou he came to it rather late in life. He favored the same surreal landscapes of Cuba."

"Where are Manuel's paintings?"

"Lou burned them."

"*Burned* them? Why?"

"I don't know."

"He told you that?"

Vicente nodded. "And according to my wife, he burned them the day he buried his father. I think they reminded him of his father's madness."

"Have you seen the portrait of the black woman that Lou painted?" McCleary asked.

"Yes. It used to be in that wonderful room with all the windows and plants."

"It still is. Who is she?"

"Supposedly she's the ghost in the house. If you believe in ghosts, of course."

Vicente let out a belly laugh that was still resounding in McCleary's head when he drove away from the warehouse a while later.

7

I

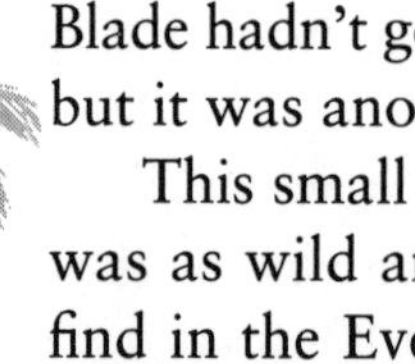

Blade hadn't gone far, four or five miles at the most, but it was another world.

This small mangrove in the wilderness preserve was as wild and primitive as anything you would find in the Everglades. Mosquitos swarmed in the hot, still air; alligators cruised silently through the tepid waters; birds flew through the shadows. The air vibrated with noises, clicks and shrieks, buzzing, an occasional splash. He hadn't seen another human being since he had steered the houseboat into the mangroves and vanished.

He sat on the deck, sharing a can of tuna fish with Whiskers, and wondered how far it was to the nearest phone. Too far to walk in the swamp, that was for sure. Best to wait until dusk, then take the Zodiac raft into the fancy marina in the Cove. He could call Rico from there and ask him to pick up his car. Then he would head to the bus station and stash everything in a locker.

Everything except the journal. It was his last link to Lou.

Blade put the can on the deck so Whiskers could finish it off and picked up the journal. It was warm from the sun and the warmth seeped into his palms. He was almost afraid to open it again. He had read random entries so far, opening the journal here, there, reading until his chest filled with sorrow and his eyes burned with tears. It was Lou's voice, all right, Lou speaking from that cold, shuttered room, that secret place.

He shut his eyes briefly and wished he knew how to pray. Wished he knew some magical incantation or ritual that would protect him from the power of Lou's words, from the darkness that surrounded them, the madness that shaped them. But since he didn't, he opened the journal to the very first entry and read it over again.

November 1

Luz came to me last night. Her name means light.

It was her light that woke me, a pale blue glow that seemed to rise from the floor and open like some exotic flower in the center of the room. I was terrified, awed, mesmerized, paralyzed.

The blue glow spread until it touched the ceiling, the walls on either side of me. It was neither cold nor hot, wet nor dry. It simply was. I somehow had the presence of mind to relight the cigar I had puffed on earlier. I sensed that the smoke would draw her out, pull her closer, encourage her to show herself.

I'm no longer sure if I saw her with my eyes, if she stood before me in her magnificent flesh, her lovely bones. Maybe I hallucinated her. Maybe I perceived her with some inner sense. I just don't know. It doesn't matter. I clearly remember the way the air rippled as she passed through it, the way tendrils of smoke curled around her legs, her arms, the way it draped at her throat, an etheric necklace.

When she touched me, when she placed her cold, dead hands at the sides of my face, a strange and powerful current coursed through me. The air smelled scorched. And then she touched her mouth to mine, her breath as sweet and warm as a piece of fruit, and my mind emptied.

I don't know what happened after that. I've tried to remember, but the memory just isn't there. The next thing I knew, I was sitting at the edge of the cot with a hard-on. I fled, fled with the stink of smoke in my lungs and the burn of her hands on my skin.

November 24

She inhabits my dreams. Every creak in the house, every moan, every whisper of wind, is her voice, calling to me.

So far I haven't stepped foot in the room again. I keep busy, find excuses not to go home too early, go running every morning at dawn and leave shortly after that. I am diligent about work. I am scrupulous in the lies I tell myself. But every night my resistance weakens. I stand in front of the bookcase, arguing with myself. If I go in, if I don't go in, like that. But the whole time the room tantalizes me. I think it's the only place where the barrier between us is as thin as rice paper. That sounds crazy, totally mad. And yet I know it's true. I know it.

December 1

Impulses. So many impulses. They come at me like bullets. Do this, Lou. Do that, Lou. What about this, Lou? Try it, Lou, just try it.

So I do.

I go to a botánica in town. I cruise up and down the crowded aisles, looking here, there, touching this or that. I do not feel real. Or the store does not feel real. I'm not sure which. But the impulses are real.

My hands choose for me. The bill is surprisingly low, considering the amount of shit I buy. Candles, incense, Florida water, a box of Cuban cigars, a couple of statues, a book of spells. I know what this is called. Santería. *My mother was a* santera, *trained by her black nanny in the days when Cuba floated in the Caribbean waters like a green pearl.*

She was powerful there. My dad told me that much. But here she was just a dabbler, some nutty weekend witch who had pretty much forgotten all the spells. By the time booze seized her, she was certifiable. Dad covered for her, but even he reached a point where he could no longer excuse her behavior.

My mother died when she was 42, I was 22. Dad lived the next seventeen years alone. Here.

With her.

With Luz.

I'm utterly certainly now that he knew her. That he knew about the secret place. That she painted through him, that he did to her what she is doing to me.

December 25

I hate Christmas. I hate the commercial bullshit, the family bullshit, the bullshit bullshit. I hate it even though Blade and I exchanged presents, even though Felicity dropped by and we had a mercy fuck. Her word, not mine.

I hate that I anticipate the dark, wait for it, that my real life is on hold until dark, when I near the bookcase, the door to Luz's world.

December 26

I went in at four this morning.

I came out at noon.

I have no idea what happened in between, except that we were together. The light and me. Luz and me.

There is no one I can talk to. No one. Not even Blade, who is into cars, animals, and girls. No one. Christ almighty, I'm afraid.

Blade slapped the journal shut. The cat was curled against his legs now, purring. The hot sun beat down. In his head, he could see Lou as he had been the last few months, painting hour after hour, day after day, night after night. He had rarely slept, rarely talked, rarely done anything but paint. Lou, obsessed with expressing something no one else could see.

By then, even Blade had felt the presence in the house. He had started hearing things, smelling the jasmine. The few times he and Lou had talked about her, they referred to her as the entity. Lou said she had lived in the house since it was first built, that her son had been born there, that she had died there when she was relatively young, a heart attack in her kitchen.

But what the hell does she want, Lou?

I don't know yet, kid. I just don't know.

Blade clearly remembered the day Lou had begun the portrait, the faint outline of the woman's features appearing first, then the startling detail on her eyes, her long neck, her hair, her forehead and nose. He had worked in a feverish frenzy, the sunroom awash in light, and had finished the portrait in a matter of hours.

For weeks afterward, though, he had touched it up, changing a minute detail here and there until he was satisfied. And from that day forward, Blade thought, the portrait of the woman had stood in the sunroom, a guard keeping watch, her spooky eyes fixed on whoever entered the room. Blade had grown to loathe the painting.

In the spring sometime, two of the bonds Lou had written were forfeited and for a while he snapped out of the weird space he'd inhabited. He considered selling the grove or, at the very least, several acres of it. But in the end, he had taken out a loan against the property and told Blade that he didn't want to sell the house, that Luz didn't want him to. And that was when Blade had lost it, shouting that Lou was a fucking fruitcake, crazier than his old man had ever been. He had moved out of the house and a week later Lou had come looking for him.

You're absolutely right, kid. But now I've gotten some help.

And that was when Madame Hilliard had entered their lives.

Blade dropped his head back and watched a great blue heron drifting on a current of wind too high up to touch him. He felt small and alone out here, dwarfed by all that he didn't understand. The ghost, the way she had possessed Lou, taken him over, the man named Jones who had come to the marina asking about him: How did any of that fit? And how had his own knife ended up in Lou's chest? How?

It had been missing for several weeks and the more he thought about it, the more certain he became that he'd left it here on the houseboat one weekend after a fishing trip. So either Lou had picked it up and brought it back to the house, where the killer had found it, or the killer had been on the houseboat. In either case, the killer apparently knew Lou well enough to visit the house or the houseboat.

If the killer had been on the houseboat, it narrowed the possibilities quite a bit. Felicity and Gracie knew about the houseboat, but who else did? Janna Hilliard, the weirded-out psychic? Doubtful. Doris Lynch? Maybe. Somewhere in the journal, Lou had mentioned that Doris knew about the house. But knew what? Did she know about the ghost?

Detective O'Connor might have been out to the houseboat because Lou had bonded some of her arrests. And David Vicente had been friends with Lou's old man, so Lou had kept in touch with him. Who else?

His head ached with questions that had no answers. He picked up the cat and went inside the houseboat to wait until dusk.

II

The Tango boardwalk stretched across the southern tip of the island, four miles of shops, cafes and restaurants, bars and discos, dive shops and windsurfing shops. It wasn't tacky yet, Quin thought. It wasn't a teeming carnival of T-shirt shops and sidewalk vendors like Duval Street in Key West. But it was beginning to strain at the edges.

Crumbling planks hadn't been replaced, metal had corroded from the constant assault of wind and salt, even some of the shop fronts seemed tired, worn down, almost impoverished. The gym where Lou's ex worked was the notable exception. It was the newest building on the boardwalk, a jewel in the island light.

Inside, it didn't look much different from the gym she and McCleary belonged to at home. The air was blessedly cool, rock music blared from invisible speakers to cover the noise of the clattering weights. The young woman at the desk looked as if she ate nails and steroids for breakfast and flashed a bright, Pepsodent smile as she chirped, "Hi, may I help you with something?"

"Is Felicity Hernando around?"

"You mean Felicity Paulson?"

Her maiden name. "Yes, that's right."

"I think she's doing a water aerobics class down on the beach."

"Thanks."

Sure enough, when Quin walked outside again, she spotted a dozen or more people doing jumping jacks just offshore. She trotted down the steps to the beach, kicked off her sandals, and carried them across the hot sand to the meager shade of a palm.

A boom box blasted from the sand near the water, close enough for the fat, older women in the class to hear. Despite the heat, they jumped and pumped and bumped right along with Felicity. The idea, naturally, was that if they did this faithfully, their bodies would one day look like hers. Damn unlikely, Quin thought.

Felicity's body was about as perfect as they came. She was tall, lean, solid, her skin a smooth, even brown from the sun. Her belly, glistening between the pale strips of cloth that passed as a bikini, was as flat as an empty envelope. Her bust, which Quin remembered as small, was now anything but and drew glances from the men on the beach. Quin wondered if the boob job had come before or after her divorce from Lou.

The class broke up a few minutes later, the fat ladies' bodies heaving from the exertion of making the transition from water to air. Felicity had no such problem. She emerged from the ocean with the lithe quickness of a creature at home in both worlds. She swept her towel off the sand, wrapped it around her waist so that it resembled a skirt with a long slit up one thigh, and headed toward the gym.

A woman with a lot on her mind, Quin thought. That was what her posture said. Quin caught up with her before she reached the steps and fell into step beside her. "You have time for coffee, Felicity?"

She stopped dead, her dark eyes wide with astonishment. "Goddamn," she breathed. "Quin."

"C'mon, it hasn't been *that* long."

"Almost five years." She gathered her long black hair to one side and squeezed the water out of it. "Coconut Grove. Lou and I met you and Mac at that crab place on Biscayne Bay."

"Joe's Stone Crab."

"Yeah, that was it. I had too many margaritas and upchucked dinner on the dock. Then I started to cry, right?"

Quin smiled. "Something like that."

"Hardly memorable." She rubbed her hands over her arms, looked down at the sand, and bit at her lower lip. When she raised her head again, her face was utterly naked with pain. "He was an infuriating man to live with, but Christ, I miss him."

Quin touched her shoulder. "So do I. C'mon, let's go someplace for coffee. Or a beer. Yeah, I could use an ice-cold draft."

They ended up at the Pink Moose, an open-deck bar a couple of blocks from the boardwalk. Even in the off-season the place was crowded with people: Europeans seduced by the low airfares, tourists from the mainland, old-timers who arrived when the place opened. The air smelled of hot sun, spilled beer, suntan lotion, and burgers that sizzled on the grill.

Quin claimed a table in a corner of the deck and Felicity, her bikini now covered with shorts and a T-shirt, threaded her way to the bar. She returned with a cold draft, a glass of cranberry juice, nectar of a workout queen, and a bowl of popcorn.

"I figured you'd be hungry," she said with a smile.

"Good memory."

She laughed. "The way you eat is hard to forget, Quin." She paused, the heat filled it. "How much do you know about Lou's life since he moved back to Tango, Quin?"

"Not enough." The icy beer slid down her throat. "I didn't know about Ross Blade, for instance."

"I hear the cops have an APB out on him."

The island grapevine. "What's he like?"

"I only met him a couple of times. I know he and Lou used to take fishing trips on that houseboat he bought when he moved back here."

"You have any idea where he kept the boat?"

"Some marina on the river, I don't remember which one. I'm jaded about Blade because I know what a sucker Lou was for wounded creatures." Her laugh was sharp, brittle. "Hell, I'm a prime example. I was a mess when Lou and I met, Quin. Teaching school to kids I couldn't stand, living with a guy who thought with his prick. I was twenty-seven years old and felt like I was fifty. Lou changed all that. He helped me see myself differently. That was a gift with him. He could see through the bullshit, he could see the best of what you could be."

"So what went wrong with you two?"

She shrugged and drew her fingernail around the edge of the glass. "I grew up, our interests changed. When we split, I moved here. Then when his dad died, he ended up here, too. Weird, how things turn out."

They exchanged stories about Lou for a while, something Felicity did with enormous relish. Lou the animal lover, Lou the bondsman, Lou as a Tango Key fritter, the only son of alcoholic entrepreneurs.

"The odd thing, Quin, is that we were together ten years and knew each other longer than that and I'm still not sure who the hell he was. The core of him is a complete mystery to me. That private part of him was unreachable. Do you know what I mean?"

"Sure."

She had felt that with McCleary, but not with Lou, perhaps because there had never been anything sexual between them. As soon as sex entered the picture, the landscape changed. The known became unknowable. Even McCleary sometimes seemed as if he belonged to a different species. Maybe it was a failure of perception on her part, maybe it was as simple as a gender gap. But the end result to her was the same, a sense of alienation, a fear that a tomorrow somewhere down the line would not include him.

"You involved with anyone?" Quin asked.

"Just dating, but there's no one special."

"Marion said you were up in Marathon the night of the murder."

The small, subtle changes in Felicity's expression made it clear she knew she was being asked about her alibi. And Felicity, who didn't beat around the bush when she was pissed, leaned across the table and hissed, "Jesus, Quin. Is that what you think? That I *killed* him?"

"Someone killed him, Felicity. That's a fact. Beyond that, it's all up for grabs."

Her eyes now narrowed and filled with a bright fierceness, sunlight glinting against aluminum. "Let me tell you something about your good buddy Lou. For the last six months to a year, he was fucked, okay?" She stabbed her index finger at her temple. "Nuts. Gone."

Quin didn't say anything. She watched Felicity gulp down the last of her juice, set her glass on the table, and not let go of it. "I saw him at Christmas. Big mistake. We ended up in bed, which is where Lou and I always ended up."

"That was the last time you slept together?" Quin was thinking of the coroner's report.

"That was the last time I saw him. And you know what he told me after we'd fucked our little brains out, Quin? That he was in love with a spook. I mean, please." Her thumbnails clawed erratic designs into the condensation on the glass. "A ghost, for Christ's sake. My Ex Loved a Ghost. It's a tabloid headline."

"Too tame for a tabloid," Quin replied dryly.

"My Ex Was Fucked by a Ghost."

"A Ghost Fucked My Ex."

They both laughed, but it was uneasy, restrained, the kind of laughter that signals the end of something. Felicity pushed her juice away. "Christ, I need a beer."

"This is my round." Quin made her way through the swelling crowd, murmuring, "Excuse me, excuse me." Then she waited ten minutes at the bar for someone to take her order.

She could see the parking lot from where she stood, a rectangle of asphalt shaded by acacia trees that had lost their summer blossoms but not their leaves. The cars were luxury models for the most part, their names a testimony to the good life. Mercedes, Lexus, BMW, Porsche, even a shiny black stretch that probably carried some celebrity traveling incognito. Sure, she could just imagine Alex Baldwin here at the Pink Moose, sucking down tequila while Kim Basinger stood at his side, munching on a bowl of popcorn. Uh-huh.

And back here on planet Earth, Lou had been in love with a spook. Yeah, great.

When she finally started back to the table with the beers, she saw that Felicity wasn't alone. A guy built like a truck had joined her. Muscles rippled beneath his tropical-print shirt. The cuffs of his white chinos brushed the tops of his white deck shoes. His sandy hair was slicked straight back from his face; he looked like a gringo actor trying to play a Puerto Rican in *West Side Story.*

He leaned into the frizzy nest of Felicity's hair until his face was hidden by it, swallowed by it. She drew back slightly, laughing at something he said, her hand at his arm. The intimate little moment had all the markings of a budding relationship and yet

Felicity had said there was no one special in her life. If she would lie about that, Quin thought, then she might lie about other things, too.

He was still at the table when Quin reached it. Up close, he bore a faint resemblance to Don Johnson, the same piercing gaze, the sun-bronzed skin, the sensuous mouth, the unbridled arrogance. But this guy, whoever he was, was better-looking than Johnson could ever hope to be.

Felicity introduced them and Tom Roey fixed his deep blue eyes on her and smiled as he stretched his hand across the table. "A pleasure, Quin."

"Quin's visiting from West Palm," Felicity said. "She and her husband were friends of Lou's."

"Real shame about Lou," said Roey, helping himself to popcorn from the bowl.

"You knew him?" Quin asked.

"We'd met a couple of times." He slipped his arm around Felicity's shoulders. "We had a mutual friend."

Felicity, visibly tense, shrugged off his arm. "What bullshit, Tom. You met him in the gym."

Roey laughed. "You misplaced your sense of humor, babe."

"You work at the gym, too?" Quin asked.

"No, I just work out there. This your first time on the island?"

Slick, she thought. He had immediately turned the conversation back to her. "Nope. So what do you do here on Tango, Tom?"

Felicity smirked. "Never evade a gumshoe's question, Tom."

"Yeah?" Roey's brows lifted, ruining the symmetry of his beautiful face. "That's what you do? You're a dick?"

"Not today."

He didn't seem put off by the sarcasm in her voice, but he answered her question. "I manage some apartment complexes here."

And in his spare time he turned on the charm and hit on

women, she thought. He probably scored fairly often, too. A face like that, a lonely woman, it was one of those single syndromes. But beneath the smile and the rest of it, Tom Roey was emotionally constipated. He was the guy who walks off the top floor of a fifty-foot building for no apparent reason; the loner who strolls into McDonald's with an assault rifle and opens fire; the husband and father who exits his life like a shadow and resumes his existence as someone else.

Tom Roey, she thought, was the kind of creep most women knew at least once in their lives, the tragedy that taught you circumspection.

Enough. She announced that she had to get going and slid off her stool. "Good seeing you again, Felicity. Nice meeting you, Tom."

"I'll call and we'll have lunch or something," Felicity said, even though they both knew it would never happen.

Roey mustered a halfhearted wave. Quin knew that as soon as her back was turned Tom would bury his face in Felicity's hair again.

On her way back to the boardwalk to get her car, she passed a New Age bookstore, Crystals, Books & Things. It was the name on one of Lou's canceled checks and had been on her list of places to go but not necessarily today. Now that she was here, she went in.

The store had the usual door chimes these places always seemed to have. The air smelled of incense or candles, something soft and sweet but not too sweet. Music played in the background, Stephen Halpern or one of those other New Age guys. There were signs inside about readers, psychics, palmists, classes, workshops, by people she'd never heard of who were renowned in the "consciousness field."

The shelves were arranged alphabetically by topics that ranged from auras to witchcraft. Bestsellers were displayed on the most visible tables: books on astrology, dreams, near-death experiences, healers, clairvoyants, topics that had brushed her life through the years.

She picked up *The Celestine Prophecy* and Castaneda's newest book for McCleary, then walked over to the shelves, to a section called Ghosts, Hauntings, & Poltergeists. Some of the books looked as if they'd been around since Lincoln had inhabited the White House. They were covered in dust, the print demanded bifocals, and the prose strained for credibility.

"Can I help you find something?" asked a young man who appeared at her side.

"I'm looking for something informative on ghosts. No hocus-pocus, just straightforward stuff."

He laughed and tugged at the gold loop earring he wore in his left ear. "Yeah, I know what you mean. Let's see." His finger trailed over the spines of the books. He picked out this one, that one, paged through several, and finally settled on a book by Hans Holzer. "This guy's good. In this book, he actually shows photographs of ghosts." The young man paged through it and stopped at a picture of a man and woman on a couch, etheric faces floating in the air above their heads. Famous faces. JFK, Marilyn Monroe, RFK, King.

"C'mon," Quin laughed. "This looks faked."

The man flashed a sheepish grin and shrugged.

"What the hell, I'll take it."

They went over to the counter and Quin asked if he took personal checks. With address, phone number, and a license, he replied. It seemed like a good point to ask about Lou Hernando and as soon as she mentioned his name, the young man looked flustered.

"You're the third person in the last week to ask about Lou."

"I am?"

"Uh-huh. A coincidence that isn't a coincidence. Is that the third or the fourth insight?"

"Excuse me?"

"*The Celestine Prophecy.*" He tapped her copy of the book. "It's one of the insights. I heard the author speak at a store in Key West. There must have been, I don't know, three hundred people there. I mean, these people think the lost manuscript is real."

"You don't think it is?"

"It's fiction."

"Are any of the insights about ghosts?"

"Ghosts?" He frowned, tugged at his earring again. "No, I don't remember any insights about ghosts."

Too bad. She could use some insights about ghosts right now. "So who were the people who've been asking about Lou?"

His frown deepened. "Why?"

"I'm investigating his murder, that's why." She dropped her PI license on the counter.

He didn't hedge after that. "A cop named Detective O'Connor was in here asking about Lou yesterday. Then right before Lou was killed, this old priest was in here. He said he knew Lou shopped in here from time to time and wondered if I could recommend something for a birthday present."

Fascinating, she thought. Lou's birthday was in May; it was now September. "Was the priest's name Rodriguez?"

"Yeah. Yeah, I think it was."

"I found a check Lou had written to the store for almost two hundred bucks. Do you remember what it was for?"

He leaned on the edge of the counter, his frown so deep now she was tempted to fit her index finger into it and smooth it out. "Books. I know he bought a bunch of books." He suddenly straightened and tapped some keys on the computer. "Uh-huh. Okay, here it is." He ticked off the book titles and added, "He also bought candles, incense, stuff like that."

One of the books Lou had purchased was the same one the young man had picked out for her. "I bet your business booms during the season."

"Definitely. It probably triples."

"So how come you remember Lou?"

"Look, a lot of people who come in here are looking for answers. They've been dabbling in past-life regression stuff and think they were Genghis Khan or Shakespeare. Or we get the ones whose parents or spouses have just died and they want to know if the deceased is going to be waiting on the other side when they bite the dust. But Lou was different, okay? He browsed, he hung out, he listened, he watched, and he read. He covered everything from Nostradamus to Ramtha to Seth. Lou needed answers."

"About what?"

"The house, I guess. About whether it's haunted."

"Do you think it is?" she asked.

"I was never inside the place, but it wouldn't surprise me, it being so old and all."

"How old is it exactly?"

"That was one of the things Lou was trying to find out. For a long time he thought it was built sometime in the eighteen hundreds. But he dug up blueprints from somewhere that dated back to the early seventeen hundreds."

"Dug them up where?"

The young man thought a moment. "The church, yeah, I'm pretty sure it was that church in El Pueblito."

Blueprints. Had Father Rodriguez known that and simply not told her? She wondered where a lie of omission fell in the church's list of sins.

"You ever been inside Lou's house?" the young man asked.

"I'm staying there now."

"Do you think it's haunted?"

"Something's there," she replied, and handed him her Visa card.

8

I

McCleary felt like a physician doing exploratory surgery, poking around through tissues and organs for some clue about the source of the patient's problem. He hadn't yet discovered the root of the illness, but he was certainly closer than he'd been two hours ago when he'd arrived.

He was seated at the back of the reference room at the Tango public library. Books and articles were stacked neatly around him, creating a barricade between him and the weirdo who had claimed the other side of the table about an hour ago. The guy bore a vague resemblance to a rodent and it wasn't just the angles of his face; he had the same small, compact body and a hungry look that got worse the longer he sat there.

Now and then, the weirdo glanced up from the racing forms he was studying and peered at McCleary over the rims of his Ben Franklin glasses, as if trying to place his face. His scrutiny was so blatant, McCleary finally gathered up his books and articles and moved to another table.

The weirdo stayed where he was, his amusement as obvious as his scrutiny. McCleary ignored him and went back to his books and articles. Thanks to the idiosyncrasies of the local bureaucracy, the historical society and the county offices occupied the basement of the library. This had greatly facilitated his research and allowed him to cull an enormous amount of information without leaving the building.

He had pulled everything he could find on David Vicente and his little empire and discovered, among other things, that he hadn't arrived here as a refugee with nothing but a few pesos in his pockets. He and Lou's old man had left Cuba a few months apart, several years before Castro had taken over, and had settled on Tango.

They had each bought modest homes on the island and had immediately gone into business for themselves. Lou's old man had grown and sold the produce for which the island was now famous—the pygmy lettuce, the guavas, the sweet green beans, and, of course, the mangos. Vicente had turned to real estate.

Both men had possessed that indomitable Cuban spirit that forged a burning path toward the American dream. Both had attained it. At one time Manuel Hernando was worth $5 or $6 million, not shabby even by today's standards. But only Vicente had held onto it and, like some Christ with the loaves and fishes, multiplied it.

In addition to the resort he was building and his real estate business, he owned a mansion and a complex of town houses up near the Tango reservoir, an apartment house in the village of Tango, two restaurants, a Cuban cafe, and he held the mortgage on a gym on the boardwalk. The same gym, McCleary noted, where Felicity worked.

He and his wife owned one of the largest collections of Cuban art outside of Havana and New York and, according to *People* magazine, enjoyed weekends on their hundred-foot yacht, *Amelia.* This article, however, was three years old, and according to more recent sources, Amelia Vicente had since had a stroke and was now confined to an exclusive rehab facility on the island.

The couple had two children, both grown and living in the

Northeast, and five grandchildren. They had been married in Havana in 1951, when he was twenty-one and she was eighteen, the only children of sugarcane barons. Their lives read like the Cuban equivalent of F. Scott and Zelda Fitzgerald. Except for the madness, he thought.

Amelia Vicente sounded about as sane as they come. European education. Sharp business sense. A charity fund-raiser. An equestrian. A sailor. An art collector. In other words, before her stroke, she had been a mover and shaker in her own right. A Cuban feminist. Considering the macho patriarchy she probably had to conquer, this was no small triumph.

Lou's mother, by contrast, had not been as outwardly successful. Although she had been involved in the family business, the important details had been left to Manuel. An arrangement more in keeping with Cuban traditions, he thought.

After his wife's death, Manuel Hernando spent seventeen years alone in the house, struggling to keep his life together. He failed, utterly and completely, and when he died there wasn't a whole lot for Lou to inherit. Just the grove and the house.

McCleary had pegged the house as between 100 and 125 years old. But he ran across one opposing opinion by a historian who believed that Juan Domingo, the pirate responsible for the construction of San Ignacio Church, had built the house for his mistress in the early 1700s. She was supposedly one of the black slaves he had taken from Cuba, and their bastard son had lived in the house with her.

This fit with what Vicente had said about the woman in the portrait, McCleary thought. But Vicente hadn't mentioned the other part of the story, which had to do with a fortune in gold and jewels that Domingo had allegedly plundered during his slow sweep through the Caribbean and still had with him when he landed on Tango. The fortune was supposedly spent to construct San Ignacio Church and the house.

McCleary was about to get up and search the computer for

more information on Domingo when the weirdo came over to his table. "McCleary, right?"

His lips pulled away from his teeth in an awkward, hungry grin. To his right and slightly behind him was a very tall, thin man with skin the color of pure cream. His eyes were bright rubies, small and sharp, eyes that missed nothing. An albino.

"Bino never forgets a face," Weirdo said, stabbing his thumb toward the albino. "It may take him a while to put it together, but eventually he remembers." The grin widened. "That's what I pay him for. What's his first name, Bino?"

"Michael," Bino replied. "Homicide, Metro-Dade." Those eyes bored into McCleary. "Investigated by internal affairs more than a decade ago for the shooting death of his partner, Robin Peters. Cleared of wrongdoing. Resigned shortly afterward." Bino paused. "Then there was a murder charge several years later. The bond was one-fifty. Lou Hernando posted it."

Weirdo's grin widened. "He has a mind like a steel trap, Bino does. Never forgets anything. That it, Bino?"

"He's married to Quin St. James. They have a daughter, Michelle, and live in Palm Beach County, where their PI firm is located."

"Thanks, Bino." His grin popped like a rubber band. "That's it in a nutshell, my friend."

McCleary's stunned silence was blatant but brief. "Okay, boys, I'm impressed. So you're a nightclub act? A carnival duo? You're with the psychic nine hundred line?"

Weirdo stuck out his hand. "Ferret's the name, Mr. McCleary. The pleasure's all mine."

Ferret. What the hell. At least the name fit. McCleary grasped his small, bony hand and had the sudden, overpowering impression that his luck was about to change.

"You play Calder, Mr. McCleary?"

"No."

"You should. At least once in your life you should play

Calder. Tonight's run would be a good one. Fourth race, Baby's Breath to win. The odds are going to be long, fifteen or higher to one. But if you bet at least five hundred bucks, the return on your money will speak for itself." He rapped his knotted knuckles on the table and grinned again. "With an extra seven or eight thousand under your belt, you may feel better about the two of us talking." He glanced at Bino, who dropped a business card on the table in front of McCleary:

ISLAND GARAGE
YOU BUST 'EM, WE FIX 'EM.
555-9871

"Ross Blade worked for me up until September second. So give me a call tomorrow morning, Mr. McCleary, and we'll have a chat about him and Lou Hernando."

McCleary pocketed the card. "Let's chat now."

Ferret grinned again, that weird, hideous grin that made him look hungry. "I don't think so. Play the horse, Mr. McCleary. The tip's free. And when the money's burning a hole in your pocket, then we'll talk." He turned around, signaling his taller, paler companion, and they strode out of the library without looking back.

McCleary watched them go, then walked over to the public phone. He called a Miami bookie he had known in the old days at Metro-Dade, a Puerto Rican he had once busted for possession. He placed a $500 bet on Baby's Breath to win in the fourth race.

"You crazy, man?" His voice sounded like air hissing from an AC vent. "Baby's Breath goin nowhere fast. You take-a Ramblin Rose, you got that, man? Rose she's somethin special. She gonna place or show. Play it safe."

"Five hundred, Baby's Breath to win, fourth race," McCleary said again.

The bookie sighed, a deep, exaggerated sigh. *"Muy mal, muy* fucking *mal."*

"Uh-huh. So let's make a side bet, two to one, your hundred against my fifty."

"You said it, not me."

"Nino, do you know a guy named Ferret?"

"Sure, man, everyone at the track they know Ferret. He the best caller around."

"What the hell's a caller?"

"My word, okay? A caller he has a feel for the horses. He knows how they run. He has, what's the word, insight, yeah, that's it. Ferret, he give you the word on Baby's Breath?"

"Yeah."

"Then play it like he says, man. Just play it. Make me eat them words."

"Fine, but who is he?"

"I dunno, man, he's Ferret, what can I say? On the island of Tango, he is, like, the man with information. A broker of information, okay? I think he owns a garage on the island, some houses that he rents, like that."

"And his albino sidekick? What's the deal on him?"

"He don't forget nothin. And you don't want to mess with him, don't want to piss him off. He and Ferret, they like Siamese twins or somethin. Real close."

"Thanks, Nino. Place that bet."

"You got it. Maybe Nino places a bet for himself, too, man. You want that I call you after the fourth race?"

"Definitely." He gave Nino the number at the house and hung up.

II

The late afternoon light spilled like fireworks across the Cove Marina. Sloops and ketches, catamarans and yachts, burned in vivid color against the sky. Blade drank in the sight of them.

Sometimes he dreamed of setting sail in a sloop, heading south to Panama and the locks. It took forty days to sail from there to the Marquesas in the Pacific. Forty days of swells and storms and skies so blue and vast you could almost taste them. That was how one sailor had described it to him. But right now, the South Pacific was no more real to him than the moon.

He was seated on a bench outside the supply shop at the marina, waiting for Rico. The Zodiac raft that had gotten him here from the mangroves was tied to the dock. It would still be here when he got back; people who docked at this marina were too rich to bother ripping off a raft.

They were rich, he thought, the way David Vicente was rich. And Doris Lynch. Doris's yacht had a special slip on the far side of the marina, where the river was deeper, and several people were getting off it. Blade barely resisted the urge to run for the Zodiac. Doris, after all, might recognize him. He had worked on her Mercedes at the garage, had driven it back to the house for her, had sipped lemonade on her back patio.

He sank lower in the bench, pulled his cap farther down over his eyes, and opened the book in his lap. One of Lou's books on ghosts. So where was Lou now? Was he a goddamn ghost? Were he and Luz together?

Blade raised his eyes and stole a glance at the people headed up the dock from Doris's yacht. There were two guys in uniform, part of the crew, and a woman in shorts and a halter top who had incredibly gorgeous legs. Definitely not Doris. In fact, as she got closer, he realized she was a girl about his age.

Doris's granddaughter? He had seen her picture once at Doris's house, a round pudgy face, a toothy smile, cute but not spectacular, not at all like the knockout who passed within a foot of him. She was good-looking the way all rich girls her age seemed to be, fairy-tale skin, not a zit or imperfection in sight. Her short hair was thick, shiny, the color of walnuts. Or hazelnuts. Some kind of nut. Her shorts were tight, she wore no bra under her cotton shirt.

She disappeared into the supply shop, her image permanently burned into his eyes.

He saw Tasha pulling into the parking lot, grabbed his flight bag, slung his pack over his shoulder, and hurried to the car. Rico heaved himself out, his big belly causing the buttons on his guayabera shirt to pucker. He gathered his long hair at the back of his head and fanned his neck with it.

"Hotter than goddamn Africa out here," he griped.

"Anyone see you?"

"Just some kid who thought I was stealing your pickup. He says he's your fishing buddy."

Blade nodded; there was a ten-year-old boy at the marina who he sometimes fished with. "He lives in one of the other houseboats. I really appreciate this, Rico."

"No problem, amigo." He tossed Blade the keys. "You drive. This car's a tank. Where're we going, anyway?"

"The bus station."

"I agree you should get off the island, Blade, but not when Mercury's retrograde."

Blade laughed, he didn't have any idea what Rico was talking about. They were in the car by then and it felt great to be inside Tasha again. "I'm not going anywhere."

"That's encouraging. So why're we going to the bus depot?"

"For a locker." Blade patted the canvas bag, which rested on the seat between them.

"A locker." Rico sighed and dabbed at his damp face with a handkerchief. "You want to tell me what's going on?"

"I'm playing it safe."

"Be specific, amigo."

Blade explained from start to finish because he knew if he didn't, Rico wouldn't stop bugging him. "Jones? Tom Jones?"

"That's what I heard him tell Colin. You know him?"

"Shit," Rico laughed. "They're seven thousand people on this island and no telling how many Joneses. Is everything you found in that room in the bag?"

"Just about." Blade unzipped it, pushed it toward him.

Rico went through the will first, the pages rustling. They were out of the hills when he spoke again. "I'm no lawyer, Blade, but it looks to me like you may be one rich dude."

"Not if I'm in jail."

"Good point. So first you beat the rap."

"Sure. With six arrests behind me, the prosecution will get up there and tell the jury my knife was jammed into Lou's chest and I'll probably get the fucking chair."

"In Texas, maybe, but not in Florida."

"That's not a real comforting thought, Rico."

"There's no chair in Texas."

Blade gave him a dirty look; Rico's plump, dimpled hands patted the air. "Okay, okay, so first we figure out who had reason to kill Lou."

"It's got to be someone he knew pretty well, since the person swiped my knife from the houseboat."

"Why's this Jones guy looking for you? Is he a cop? A dick? What's his business with you?"

"He's not a cop." Blade had enough experience with cops to know that. "I think he's working for someone who knew Lou well enough to want whatever he was killed for."

"The house and the land, in other words. Sure, with you dead it gets turned over to the county. And if the county boys see a way to make a profit without pissing off too many voters, they'll sell the land and fuck the wildlife sanctuary. Whoever's after you probably knows that and figures the county will be a cinch to deal with. Who're these McCleary people who're executors of the will?"

"Private eyes. They're staying at the house."

"They musta been friends of Lou's for him to name them as executors. Maybe you oughta talk to them."

"And say what? That I didn't kill him? Why the hell should they believe me? I'm not talking to anyone until I have something to say."

And until he had some answers. Then he would make his choices.

III

As Quin drove into the grove, the evening light clung to the trees with a kind of fierceness, as though the day wasn't quite ready to surrender to darkness. She knew the feeling, all right. The thought of spending another night in this house didn't thrill her in the least.

The Camaro wasn't out front, which meant McCleary wasn't back yet and she would be walking into an empty house. That didn't do much for her either. The place, in fact, looked long-abandoned, like some crumbling building in a dream that you knew was going to end badly.

She parked, gathered up her things, got out. She stood for a moment in the noisy twilight, watching the ducks settle in for the night on the banks of the pond. One of the owls was perched on the roof of the porch and its mate was just above it on the roof of the house. She wondered if these were the same two she had seen here a year ago. Did owls, like swans, mate for life?

Had she?

Six months ago she would have said no. But then, her marriage six months ago had not been as good as it was now. Granted, this might just be another phase, a mood of the moon, one of many in the last decade. Somehow, though, she didn't think so. Something fundamental between her and McCleary had changed, deepened. After all these years, they seemed to have reached a kind of acceptance of each other; it was as simple and as complex as that.

The individual quirks that had been a continual source of friction were now integrated into the complete package that they were as a couple. If, for instance, they were supposed to be someplace at seven, she told McCleary six so they would be on time. He, in turn, no longer griped about the electricity bill, the grocery bill, the amount of food she ate. They had learned to accommodate each other without complaint.

If anything, she thought, his chronic tardiness, his penchant for neatness, all the things that used to irritate her so deeply, had become objects of curiosity. They were intricate pieces of some vast and marvelous puzzle whose pieces she rearranged, seeking the key to the whole picture.

Did owls and swans look at their mates like that?

"Give me a few minutes, guys, and I'll be out with dinner," she murmured to the birds, and unlocked the door.

A cool, waiting silence.

Her stomach growled, she wanted to shower, to change clothes.

Fuck it, ghosts are a myth.

Righto. She stepped inside, shut the door, stood against it for a beat or two, then went into the kitchen. She dropped her purse and several bags of groceries on the counter. A frozen veggie pizza and a salad would do for dinner, she decided, and began unloading the bag.

As she sliced up radishes and cucumbers, she realized she heard a radio. Had a radio been playing when she had walked in? She set down the knife and wiped her hands on a dish towel as she walked out into the hall.

The sound was coming from the sunroom. Definitely from the sunroom.

"The high tomorrow is expected to hit ninety-five, with showers in the afternoon. The . . ."

She headed down the hall, but the phone suddenly pealed and the radio went off. What the hell, she thought, and hurried back into the kitchen to pick up the receiver. "Hello?"

Breathing on the other end, as if the caller had been running.

Or suffered from asthma or some other respiratory disorder. Then: "Is Quin in?"

She didn't recognize the man's voice. "No, she isn't. May I take a message?"

"Who's this?" he asked.

"The cleaning lady. Who's this?"

She didn't hear him breathing now. But she heard him waiting, heard it in her head, a language of patient silence that chilled her. He finally said: "You tell her something for me, okay? You tell her I can't wait to run my hand up her thighs, to stick my . . ."

Quin dropped the receiver over the hook. "Fuck you, too."

He knew my first name.

Was this the same guy who had called McCleary?

The phone rang, ten peals, fifteen, she counted each one as it exploded against the air. Then, silence, abrupt, thick, terrifying. He would call again, his type always did, he knew she was here alone.

As soon as the phone rang, she snatched up the receiver. "Okay, pal, I know you've heard of caller ID . . ."

"Yeah, we have it at home," McCleary said.

She started to laugh, laughed to shatter the lump of anxiety lodged in her throat.

"What's going on, Quin?"

Hello, Quin. Earth to Quin. Come in, please, come in. Over. A real McCleary question. "A perv call."

"What'd he say?"

She heard the edge in his voice, knew he was already planning the trip home. "Look, maybe it was the same guy, maybe it wasn't. I'm not going to lose any sleep over it."

"I am."

"This guy's hot air, Mac. That's all."

She knew he didn't believe it any more than she did. "I'll be there in a few minutes."

Quin hung up and stepped back until her spine was against

the cool stone wall. She suddenly felt like a character in one of Michelle's picture books, something darker than Barney, something along the lines of the Brothers Grimm. Power, she thought. These kinds of calls were about power. Gender power, physical power. Some things never changed, even Gloria Steinem couldn't argue with that.

The quiet in the house seeped around her, insidious, toxic. She thought she heard a noise in the sunroom and walked into the hall. No radio announcer, no music, no weather report. Just the ticktock of a clock and the soft breath of air from the ceiling vents.

Her shoes clicked against the tile floor and she stepped out of them, continued to the sunroom's doorway, the sleek, beautiful arch of stone, and stopped. Looked up. Where was the mistletoe? The Christmas tree? The presents? That was the kind of room this was, a space fit for traditions, rituals, magic.

The radio rested on top of an end table, a wooden antique shaped like Napoleon's hat. No automatic alarm on this sucker, she thought, and turned one of the knobs. Music issued forth, a mall tune, without soul. She jerked the plug out of the wall, then returned to the kitchen and punched out the number for a flight service office at Lantana airport, five minutes from her other life, her suspended life.

Christine Redman picked up on the first ring, almost as if she had been waiting for Quin's call. "Lantana Flight Service."

"Hey, Slick. Can you talk?"

"Goddamn girl, I really wish you wouldn't do that to me. You've been on my mind all day. You and Mike still in that dancin key?"

"Tango Key."

"Whatever. You sound kind of funny."

When Quin had met her last winter, Christine had been living under an assumed name, hiding out from the very woman Quin had been investigating. Now she worked at a flight service office south of West Palm and taught flying in her spare time.

"I was wondering if you had some free time to fly down for a day or two."

"Like a vacation, you mean?"

"Yeah, sort of."

"Shit, Bones. You can't lie worth a damn. What's goin on?"

"It sounds nuts."

"Comin from you that don't surprise me."

"I think this house where we're staying is haunted." It really sounded ridiculous when she said it out loud and she suddenly laughed. "See, I told you it was nuts."

"I ain't laughin, girl. You know I don't do this stuff anymore. Them wheels got too rusted. Besides, I never done nothin like that."

"What're you talking about? You were a clairvoyant for twenty-five years."

"That was different. Readings at malls, at psychic fairs, helpin the cops with a few cases. I never did no séance shit."

"No one's asking you to hold a séance, Slick. I just want to know what you pick up about this place."

"Listen, it ain't that easy, okay? I don't just walk into a place and absorb shit like some sponge."

"The ghost makes sounds. I heard her. The radio came on by itself."

"And that's s'posed to change my mind?" She laughed. "No way, Bones."

"I'll pay you for your time."

"I don't want your money."

"Okay, I'll grovel."

Silence.

"Slick?"

"Yeah, yeah. I'm lookin at my goddamn schedule. I could probably fly down the day after tomorrow. But I'm not promisin nothin, Bones."

"I know."

"Hold on, lemme look at a map." Papers rustled. Minutes

ticked past. "Okay, if I get out of here at five, I should be there by seven if I don't run into bad weather. Can you meet me at the airport?"

"I'll be there."

"I must have rocks in my head, gettin into this shit."

Or I do. "See you then unless I hear from you otherwise."

"Hang loose, Bones."

Sure. With a spook in chains rattling around the house.

9

I

The evening crowd at the Pink Moose spilled out across the deck like an ad for the good life, Roey thought. Young babes in stylish skirts and blouses who had just left work, slick businessmen on the make.

By nine, they would be soused and dropping like flies and the Lobes would arrive: the lonely, the bereaved, the perpetually horny. Most of them would be looking for company for the night and would be ready for lobotomies by midnight or one. The Hardcores would start to roll in around two. They were by far the most interesting group, bikers, insomniacs, lovers on the run, wheelers and dealers, the down and outs, the whole stinking melting pot of night people in the keys.

At one time or another during his five years on Tango, Roey had mingled with all of these groups. But he had never associated himself with any particular one. He was, even by his own assessment, the primo loner, and had been that way since he was a kid. When you were raised by grandparents too feeble to do much of anything, you learned early on to enjoy your own company.

In this way, he and Ross Blade were alike, loners who had left home when they were in their early teens and survived by their wits. Roey had wandered farther than the kid ever had and had drifted into much darker waters. But just the same, he had a sense about Blade and figured his best route to finding him was through his friends.

Roey spotted her as soon as he walked out onto the deck at the Pink Moose. All that copper hair, he thought. You couldn't miss it. She was standing off by herself, sipping from a tall, icy glass filled with something white, probably one of those sweet, fancy drinks that only women ordered. Her eyes roamed the crowd for someone to talk to.

Fat chance. At this hour, the average age of the cruising unattached male was about thirty-five, at least ten years younger than she was. But a woman's age had never bothered Roey when he wanted something. He came up behind her, slipped his arms around her narrow waist, and whispered into her hair. "Now don't you look pretty enough to nibble on."

Janna Hilliard laughed, a soft, girlish laugh, and turned around. "Tom Roey. It's been a while since I've seen you out and about." She poked him in the stomach, coy Janna. "You've still got that free reading, you know."

For fixing her car several months ago. "You have your cards with you?"

She laughed and patted the pocketbook hanging from her shoulder. "Always."

Shit, that's what this was, a crock of shit that people paid her money for. Incredible. But if he said no thanks, she would think he had something to hide. "Let's find a table."

What they found was a pair of stools along the counter at the far end of the balcony. He would get the reading out of the way and then move on to business. But Janna was wound up for small talk, how had he been, how was business, and the entire time she kept sucking at that sweet drink and her makeup slowly melted in the evening heat.

"Summers, Christ, they're slow for all of us," she was saying. "But I think things will pick up pretty soon. A big tour of French Canadians is due in the next couple of days and I'm on their list of tourist landmarks." She laughed at that and fiddled with one of her dangling earrings, a rose quartz shaped like a teardrop. "Gracie hates it, you know, all these tourists traipsing through the courtyard, but hey, business is business, right? At least my customers aren't cons." She paused long enough to sip at her drink. "You heard about Lou, I guess."

"Damn shame. He was a nice guy. I hear the kid who lived with him is the primary suspect."

"Ross Blade?" Her dark eyes widened. "C'mon. They were like brothers."

"A while back I heard they were closer than that."

Janna wrinkled her cute little nose. "Christ, just because Lou took him in people twist things around. Lou wasn't like that."

He noticed that she said it with a fierce loyalty, as though she knew this from personal experience.

"And he detested pedophiles. In fact, pedophiles and rapists were the two crimes he would never write a bond on."

"Well, if the kid's smart, he's left the island by now."

"He's smart, all right," she said. "But I doubt if he's left Tango. He's got friends here."

"If his friends have the kind of police record he does, it won't take long for the cops to find him."

"Ross doesn't hang around with those guys anymore. That was one of the conditions Lou handed down when he took him in. One of his closest friends is this astrologer I trade readings with sometimes. Damn fine astrologer."

"Yeah? She as expensive as you?"

He grinned when he said it. *No hard feelings, babe.*

"Fifty bucks isn't expensive, Tom. Rico charges the same for a chart."

He rubbed her arm, a friendly touch. "Just kidding."

Her slow, coy smile promised a night of surprises. She reached into her purse and brought out the cards. "This won't cost you a penny."

He watched her shuffle the cards, a slow, rhythmic shuffle. Then she fanned them facedown on the counter. "Pick four."

"Four. Okay." He quickly picked four, slid them up out of the fan, toward her.

Janna rested a finger against the card to the far left. "This is the foundation of the issue." She turned it over. "The king of coins." *Tap, tap,* went her finger. "He's the money man, at the peak of his profession." She flipped over the card next to it. Roey felt an instantaneous revulsion to the bound hands depicted in the illustration. "Nine of swords. This man makes you feel imprisoned, that your hands are tied."

Fuck. Vicente, she was talking about Vicente.

The third card looked better, a man, a woman, and a kid standing in an archway, in front of a pair of banners with coins on them that were crossed in a Roman numeral ten. Janna didn't say anything; she frowned and turned over the final card. Three swords piercing a heart, blood dripping from the blades. Yeah, real pleasant. What bullshit.

"You seem to perceive this guy, the king of coins, like he's the pot at the end of the rainbow. This ten's the Wall Street card, meaning he's got oodles of dough. But I got news for you, Tom." She met his eyes, then tapped the last card. "He's going to bring you nothing but big-time trouble and heartache."

"So let's have a name," he said with a laugh.

Janna didn't laugh. "Choose one more card."

He did and she turned it over. The six of swords.

"Looks pretty grim," he remarked.

"Whoever this king is, Tom, you're going to be moving away from him and the shit he's given you and toward something else. You could be moving to a colder climate."

It was hot where he wanted to go, San Miguel de Allende,

way south of the border. "I don't think so. But thanks, it was interesting."

She gathered up the cards. "Watch your back, Tom. That's the best advice I can give you."

"You ready for another drink?"

"No questions about the reading?" She sounded disappointed.

"Nope. You answered them all. What're you drinking?"

"Kahlua and milk."

Her glassy eyes said she had already had one too many; they followed him as he stood, followed him as he headed toward the bar. Such heat from her eyes. Too bad she was so weird. But with the lights off he wouldn't know the difference. Skin was skin, tits were tits, and it had been too long in between women. But more than that, he was intrigued by the possibility that she and Lou Hernando might have been lovers. He and good ol' Lou had a few women in common and he rather liked the irony in that.

II

The wilderness preserve was formidable terrain even when the sun was shining. But at night, McCleary thought, it might as well have been another planet.

The dirt road they were on angled through towering pines, ficus trees, banyans shaped like tremendous mushrooms and strung with shawls of Spanish moss. Everything, even the darkness, loomed with such magnificent grandeur that he felt Lilliputian in comparison, Jack in the world of the big, bad giant.

"There's got to be an easier way to this marina," he said.

"Yeah, by water, straight up the Tango River," Quin replied. "This is the only marina in the preserve, so it's got to be this one. There's a fork just ahead. We go left."

Quin was studying the map spread open in her lap. She held a flashlight in one hand and a half-eaten empanada in the other. They had stopped at a Cuban takeout restaurant on their way out of town, one of those south Florida jewels where the coffee was rich and cheap. Quin couldn't pass up the display of empanadas, corn tortillas filled with chunks of vegetables. Never mind that she had finished five slices of a veggie pizza no more than an hour ago.

Yes, he had counted.

Some people kept track of what their spouses ate because of health problems, obesity, high cholesterol. He kept track because her metabolism mystified him. She ate constantly and rarely gained weight. The heaviest he had ever seen her was when she was pregnant and even then she had barely tipped the scales at 140. Big for a woman of five two, hardly a bulge for a woman of five ten.

The odd thing was that food wasn't central to her life in the way it was for most people who enjoyed eating as much as she did. She didn't research restaurants before they traveled to a particular city or country. She detested cooking, didn't like to grocery shop, and given her druthers would just as soon eat yogurt and a grilled cheese sandwich for dinner.

He knew that in his wife's attitudes toward food and eating there was a message about their marriage. But he didn't have any idea what the hell it was.

"Tell me again what this guy's voice sounded like, Quin."

"I couldn't really tell. He was speaking too softly. But he breathed heavily, like maybe he'd been running. Did the guy you talked to sound like that?"

"No heavy breathing, just a rasp."

"Did he say anything about my legs?"

"That they were long."

"He said something about long legs to me, too. Maybe it was the same guy."

"Whoever he is, he obviously knows what you look like."

She nodded; he knew it bothered her.

"Let's switch on the cars tomorrow just to play it safe."

"You think men ever get perv calls from women?"

"Michael Douglas did in *Fatal Attraction.*"

"Real people."

"I did once."

"You never told me that."

"It was when I was selling insurance in Syracuse. Some woman called me every night for a week. At first it was annoying. Then it got weird, because she described the clothes I wore, the car I drove."

"Did you report it to the cops?"

"No. I moved to Florida about a month later."

"I can't believe you never told me this. What kind of stuff did she say?"

"The same shit a male perv says to a woman. I want to suck this, lick that."

"The words might be the same, but the threat isn't."

"Hey, this woman had obviously been watching me. Following me. For all I know she was some closet Lizzie Borden. It was creepy."

"Is that how you felt when you shot Robin Peters?"

He didn't expect the question. This was the second time in a day that someone had mentioned Robin and the fact that he had killed her. She had inadvertently brought him and Quin together, and yet it had all happened so long ago he could hardly remember the man he had been then. He knew he had been ridiculously in love with her, but was no longer sure why.

He clearly recalled, however, the moment when he had stood in front of her as she held a gun to Quin's temple and shouted at her to throw down her weapon. He clearly recalled the exact moment when he had squeezed the trigger on his gun.

"Mac?"

"I knew she would kill you if I didn't shoot her first," he said finally. "So yeah, you could say I felt threatened. What made you ask about Robin?"

"I guess it's this spook business. I started wondering where Robin was. And your sister. And Sylvia Callahan."

She placed no particular emphasis on Callahan's name, which had not been true a year ago. He had long since accepted the fact that Quin would never quite forgive him for his affair with Callahan. But maybe even the things you took for absolutes, he thought, were eventually transmuted.

The Explorer slammed into a pothole, bounced as it came out, and then the road angled steeply downward, toward the Tango River. The trees ended, the road ended, and starlight spilled across a sheltered cove on the Tango River. There were two docks and a couple dozen slips, most of them empty. A two-story shack stood alone in the shadows of the pines, a dilapidated structure that listed slightly to the left. Mother Hubbard's home. Its neon sign blinked off and on and several of the letters didn't light up, so it read: OIN'S RIN.

"It looks like whoever lives here has been in bed since the sun went down," Quin said.

"Let's check it out."

A breeze kicked in off the river, a warm, lush scent of water and earth, an odor as timeless as the river itself. Several black cats lazed on the porch and showed merely a passing interest in their presence. McCleary knocked and when no one answered, he turned the knob and opened the door. "Hello, anyone here?" he called.

"Yeah, yeah, jus' hold your horses." The man who shuffled out of a back room was zipping up the fly on his baggy shorts. He needed a shave, his gray hair needed combing, his hooded eyes were bloodshot, his cheek bulged with a wad of tobacco. He looked like a river rat coming off a six-week binge on belladonna. "Help you wit' somethin?"

"We're looking for Lou Hernando's houseboat," McCleary said.

"That a fact. And who're you?"

"A friend of Lou's."

"Uh-huh. Well, the boat ain't here." He glanced briefly at Quin, who had stooped to pat the black cat that had followed the man to the door. "Her name's Bessie. She don't take a likin to many people."

Bessie had obviously taken a liking to Quin, though. She rolled onto her back and offered her tummy for a scratch. "Didn't Lou dock his houseboat here?" Quin asked.

"Used to."

McCleary asked, "When was it here last?"

The man regarded McCleary with an animal wariness, his face like worn leather, those bloodshot eyes rooted in a rete of deep wrinkles. "You said you were a friend of Lou's?"

"That's right. Mike McCleary. This is my wife, Quin. Are you Mr. Colin?"

"Colin. Jus' Colin." He spat tobacco into a large brass spittoon that sat just inside the door. "How do you folks know Lou?"

"We knew him in Miami," Quin replied. "Where's his boat?"

"Ain't here."

"Lou was murdered on Saturday. Today's Thursday," McCleary said. "Was the houseboat moved before or after?"

"What's it to you?"

McCleary held up his PI license. "We're investigating his murder, Mr. Colin."

"Colin, no mister." He glanced at the license, then nodded. "You like that Rockford fella, huh? That was a good show."

Just what he didn't need, an aficionado of old gumshoe TV reruns. "I'd appreciate anything you could tell me about the houseboat."

He leaned into McCleary's face, his breath reeking of the shit he chewed. "And I don't mind tellin you I'm real tired of people waltzin in here with their cock 'n' bull stories about who they are. First it's some guy claimin he'd a buddy of Lou's, huh? Then it's a woman who says she worked with him. And before them it was some lady cop. So for all I know, mister, you could be the fuck who killed him. See what I mean?

"So I'm tellin you what I tol' the others. The houseboat ain't here. It ain't been here since Blade putted out into them blue waters and where he's gone nobody knows. And I reckon that's all I got to say about it."

"Ross Blade is wanted for Lou's murder," McCleary said.

This got a definite rise out of Colin. "You listen good, Mr. Detective. I seen them together. Like father and son, they was. That boy wouldn't do nothing to Lou and anyone who says otherwise got shit for brains."

"Who was the guy who said he was a buddy?" Quin asked.

"Jones, Tom Jones, like that singer. Didn't like him none either."

"When was he here?" McCleary asked.

"Since Lou was killed."

A cagey answer, but McCleary let it pass. "Can you describe him?"

"Big guy, lots of muscles."

"What color hair?" Quin asked.

"Hair?" Colin scratched his stubbly jaw. "Dunno."

"How tall was he?"

Colin glanced at McCleary, then back at Quin. " 'Bout like you, I reckon."

"And the woman?" McCleary asked. "What'd she look like?"

"Blond. Wore lots of jewelry, weird clothes."

Gracie, he thought. "Was she alone?"

"Came in alone, but there was a man waitin in a car outside."

"Did you see the man?"

"Nope. Jus' saw him sitting out there." Colin seemed to have forgotten that he didn't have anything more to say to them. "Slick, fancy car, don't know what kind. Bet it cost a bundle, though."

McCleary realized he didn't know what kind of car Gracie drove. "Where's Blade's car?"

"I done said enough, Mr. Detective. Now you and the lady scoot on outta here."

McCleary handed Colin a business card. "Give Blade this if you see him again. Ask him to give me a call. No cops, just him and me."

He stuck the card in the pocket of his shorts. "Ain't promisin nothin."

III

Doris Lynch lived on five acres of land high in the hills outside of Pirate's Cove. It wasn't an estate—no fence, no guardhouse, nothing like that. But it was one of the prettiest spots Blade had ever seen, a lush wilderness.

In his other life, the life before Lou's murder, he had worked at the garage and used to drive Doris's Mercedes back here sometimes; she was a good tipper. Sometimes she invited him in for lemonade and they talked about animals. Blade liked her, believed she liked him, and now he needed to know if he could trust her.

Tasha climbed the steep dirt driveway that angled through the banyans, the pines, the acacia trees. The darkness was noisy with insects, the cries and clicks of birds. As he neared the top of the hill, he heard the wind skipping in off the Gulf hundreds of feet below. Branches shivered as it passed.

The house came into view suddenly, a sprawling one-story place built of stone and brick. Lights burned in most of the windows, but there were only two cars out front, the Mercedes and a blue Miata. He wondered if it belonged to Doris's granddaughter. He hoped so, hoped even though she wasn't the reason he'd come.

Or, at least, not the main reason.

When the granddaughter answered the door, she looked like she had earlier at the Cove Marina. A knockout, the kind of girl who would never look twice at him. He was instantly tongue-tied. He couldn't look away from the steady cool blue of her eyes.

She was balanced on her right leg; her left foot was raised, the bare toes scratching at her right calf. She had a half-eaten apple in one hand and held on to the edge of the door with the other.

"So?" Her mouth twitched into a half-smile. "Cat got your tongue or what?"

"Is, uh, Mrs. Lynch home?"

"Doris? Sure. She's upstairs. C'mon in."

She turned away and he followed her into a wide hallway with a marble floor. The fact that she hadn't slammed the door in his face or run for the phone was encouraging. Either she hadn't seen his mug shot or didn't recognize him from it if she had.

She stopped at the bottom of the stairs, pressed a button on the intercom and said, "Doris, someone's here to see you."

Mrs. Lynch's voice crackled through the speaker a moment later. "Who is it, Charlie?"

"I don't know. He didn't give his name." She hit the switch before Doris could reply and laughed softly. "She hates it when I do that. You look like James Dean, anyone ever tell you that?"

"Yeah." He laughed nervously. "You look like Ali MacGraw in *The Getaway.*"

She grinned and combed her fingers back through her hair. "You have a name?"

"Ross."

"I'm Charlie." She tilted her head down the hall. "Let's get something cold to drink. You can wait for her in the kitchen."

"Is Charlie short for Charlotte?"

She thrust her hands into the pockets of her shorts. "God, don't even breathe that name. I hate it. I've been Charlie as long as I can remember. How do you know my grandmother?"

"I've worked on her car."

She tossed the remains of the apple into the trash can in the kitchen. "So you live on Tango."

"Right." He leaned against the long counter, watching her as she brought a pitcher of juice from the fridge. "What about you?"

"I'll probably be here till Christmas, maybe longer. I don't know. My parents got divorced right after I graduated, so things are kind of screwed up right now. I'll be working for Doris until I decide about college and stuff."

College. A cultural gulf an ocean wide suddenly tore open between them. Of course she would be going to college. Girls from money families always did. Blade had quit high school a year ago and had been studying to take his GED this fall. But that, like everything else in his life, had gone to hell when Lou was murdered.

"You into computers?" she asked, straddling a stool at the counter.

"Yeah. You?"

She nodded. "What do you have?"

"A Toshiba notebook, 486DX2."

Her huge blue eyes lit up. "I've got a Compaq. You on any of the nets?"

"Internet and GEnie."

"I'm on Prodigy and Internet. C.Lynch one."

"R.Blade."

A brief, awkward silence ticked past. She smiled at him, he smiled at her, and he sensed a sudden bond between them. Then Doris Lynch walked into the kitchen. She wasn't so bad-looking herself, an older version of her granddaughter—the same cool blue eyes, short salt and pepper hair that was very curly, a regal mouth. Her expression didn't change, but the moment she spoke, he knew that she knew the cops were looking for him.

"Ross. I didn't expect you."

"Sorry to just barge in like this, Mrs. Lynch. But I need to talk to you."

She leaned against the stove, her slender arms crossed at her waist, alarm flashing in her eyes as she glanced at Charlie. "Weren't you going to the store for something?"

Charlie didn't get it. "Huh?"

It was clear that Mrs. Lynch thought Blade was dangerous and that she wanted to get her granddaughter out of the house as fast as possible. Blade slid off his stool. "The only reason I came here was because Lou mentions you in his journal, Mrs. Lynch. He said you know about Luz, that you had a pretty good idea what she was guarding in the house. I need to know what it is."

"I'm afraid I don't know what you're talking about, Ross. I'd like you to leave now."

"Jesus, Doris, what's going on?" Charlie asked, sliding off her stool.

"I'm calling the police," Mrs. Lynch said, and marched over to the phone.

Blade crossed the room in a flash, tore the receiver out of her hand, slammed it down. "I didn't kill him," he said. "I didn't kill anyone. Someone's trying to frame me and it has something to do with that house."

She stepped back from him, her spine stiff, fear now shadowing her eyes. "Go out the back door, Charlotte."

Charlie stammered, "But . . ."

"Now!"

"Fuck it. I'm outta here." Blade swept past Mrs. Lynch, his shoes slapping the polished marble floors, her voice like the crack of a whip behind him.

This is Doris Lynch. We have an intruder here . . .

10

I

The lighthouse rose from the edge of a cliff on the western slope of the island, a great bleached white bone standing on end. It looked surreal against the moonlit sky, McCleary thought, a monolithic relic of the days when the sea was the source of everything—sustenance, transportation, riches.

"Goddamn, look at that thing," Quin breathed. "It's so New England. Whalers, foggy nights, like that. You ever been inside?"

"Just once, years ago. The county owned it then and the place had fallen into disrepair. They were trying to raise money for the renovations and were charging an exorbitant entrance fee. But the view was worth every dime."

McCleary pulled up to the gate and Quin hopped out to raise Marion on the intercom. The gate swung open as she climbed back into the Explorer and Marion was waiting in the doorway when McCleary parked behind her van. She had never looked less like a cop: baggy gym shorts, a tank top, the utter lack of pretense.

"What gives, guys?" she asked as they got out.

"We thought you needed company," Quin replied.

"Company?" Marion laughed and gestured through the doorway at a tabby cat with mismatched eyes. "Meet my buddies Unojo—that's Spanish for One Eye—and Wolfe, with an *e* at the end, thank you very much. Boys, meet Quin and Mike."

The tabby took off like a bullet as soon as they stepped inside. Wolfe, a skunk, backed up to the nearest wall, his tail flicking, twitching, threatening to spray them. "Don't worry, he's been deskunked," Marion said. "He just doesn't remember it. C'mon, let's go into the kitchen. I was online. You guys on the nets?"

"Mac is on three different nets," Quin said. "I just fiddle around on GEnie."

"You have access to the computer at the station?" McCleary asked.

"Sure, what do you need?"

"To run a name."

Marion's dark eyes skipped to Quin. "We ran the plate on the Volvo that followed you."

"It's not that. A guy named Tom Jones has been asking questions up at the marina where Lou kept his houseboat."

"Jones, huh? There're probably as many Joneses who've been busted in this state as there are Smiths. But we'll take a look. I could've saved you a trip up to the marina. That old codger's not about to tell anyone squat."

McCleary started to tell her what Colin had said about Blade, but decided to keep it quiet for now.

The kitchen was spacious and the only light came from the computer screen and the burning full moon that filled the picture window. Its light spilled a quarter of a million miles to the surface of the Gulf's black waters, a painted sea so placid it had captured the moon in its entirety. The view literally stole his breath.

As the three of them stood at the picture window, Quin said, "If I lived here, I don't think I'd ever leave."

Marion nodded. "It's really something, isn't it. I look out here at night and it snaps things right into perspective. Help yourselves to something to drink and I'll see what Big Brother has to say about Tom Jones."

Quin bustled around the kitchen and McCleary stood behind Marion's chair, peering over her shoulder as she initiated a global search on the computer. She came up with more than five hundred Tom Joneses.

"This could take days," McCleary said. "Is there any way to narrow it down?"

"Age, height, hair color, scars, crime—there're a hundred ways to break it down. But all you've got is this guy's name and it may not even be his real name."

On impulse, he said, "Try Roey, Tom Roey."

"I thought his last name was Jones," Marion said.

"Different Tom," Quin explained, strolling over to the computer with tall glasses of juice. "I met Roey when Felicity and I were at the Moose yesterday. They were awfully chummy."

Marion ran a global search for Roey, but nothing showed up. "He's never been busted in the state of Florida."

"Run his name through the MVD," McCleary suggested.

Marion glanced at him. "You never saw me doing this, right?"

"Got it."

According to the Motor Vehicle Department, Tom Roey drove a two-year-old Ford sedan and lived at 612 El Dorado, apartment four. He had no parking tickets, no speeding tickets, no infractions at all. Clean, absolutely clean. So clean it was as if he'd landed on the planet yesterday. Even model citizens, McCleary thought, occasionally got parking tickets.

"I'll check the FBI computer tomorrow at work. I can't access it through here."

With that, Marion turned off the computer, pushed to her feet, and played hostess. They settled in a spacious, comfortable room with several tall, narrow windows that overlooked the Gulf. Pine furniture, a colorful handmade throw rug, a fireplace, electronic equipment: McCleary felt instantly at home here. But Quin roamed about restlessly, touching this, that, until she reached the sound system.

"Nice piece of equipment," she remarked.

"It's customized and tops anything we've got at the department. We can filter out or enhance background sounds, speed it up, slow it down, you name it, this baby does it." Marion flipped through a box of tapes. "What's your preference?"

Quin pulled a tape out of her purse. The tape, McCleary thought, with nothing on it.

"Try this."

"What is it?" Marion asked.

"I recorded it at the house. Or tried to, at any rate," she added, and told Marion what had happened.

If there had been any question before about Marion's attitude toward the haunted house tales, McCleary thought, there wasn't now. Her mouth twitched into a smile, then she burst out laughing.

"I'm glad you find it so amusing," Quin said dryly.

"I'm sorry. It just sounds so bizarre. I mean, c'mon, Quin, it's an old house. When the wind gets under those eaves, there're all kinds of noises."

"I know what wind sounds like." Quin marched over to the recorder, popped in the tape. "And what I heard wasn't the goddamn wind." She pressed the *Start* button, fiddled with the knobs.

Nothing but silence issued from the home theater speakers. Outside, the wind prowled the lighthouse, an invisible beast that had sprung full blown from the sea. Suddenly, a faint noise drifted from the speakers. Quin turned a knob to distill the sound, enhance it, clarify it, and cranked the volume up as high as it would go.

The swishing noise drifted from the speakers as clearly and crisply as the drop of a pin in an empty, silent room. But the longer they listened, the more it sounded like a voice whispering,

Lou Lou Lou. It ceased abruptly and seconds later the weeping began, a wrenching tragic sound that rushed like water through the room.

The tape ended with McCleary calling for Quin.

She stopped the recorder, hit the *Rewind* button. "I told you I heard something," Quin said.

"It's something, all right," Marion said. "But I don't believe in spooks. This is probably an anomaly of some kind. A flaw in the tape. Maybe the tape already had something on it and you recorded over it."

"I don't think we should dismiss it quite that easily," McCleary said. "Let's assume for a moment that the ghost exists, okay?"

Bemused, Marion sat back against the couch and drew her legs up against her. "Big assumption, but go on."

"Historians seem to be divided on when the house was built. One faction says it dates back to the early seventeen hundreds, when a Spanish pirate named Juan Domingo built the place for his mistress, a black slave he'd brought from Cuba. I think Lou may have been trying to verify that through the archives at San Ignacio."

"Verify it for what purpose?"

She glanced at Quin when she asked it, as though this were a gender question. Quin shrugged. "We don't know yet."

McCleary went on. "According to Vicente, the portrait of the black woman Lou painted is supposedly the ghost. In other words, Domingo's mistress. If that's true, it gives us some idea about the strange places Lou was inhabiting in the months before he was killed."

Marion dropped her feet to the floor. "This is sounding more and more like an episode from *The Twilight Zone*, guys. If Lou was painting ghosts, then that tells me he was off the fucking wall."

"He saw her, we heard her," Quin said. "What's that make us?"

"You heard her, Quin. Mac and I didn't. That tape doesn't count."

Hardheaded, he thought. She just didn't get it. "The point isn't to prove or disprove what's on the tape, Marion. I think part of the key to all of this is the fortune in gold and gems Domingo may have been carrying when he got to Tango. Some accounts say he spent most of it in the construction of the church and the house. But suppose there was some left over? Suppose he buried it somewhere on the property? Or stashed it in the house somewhere? That would explain why Lou was scouring the church archives."

Marion still looked dubious. "Lots of ifs in this, Mike. I mean, you're implying that the reason the ghost has, uh, stuck around all these centuries is because of the treasure. She's guarding the treasure."

"What I'm implying is that the treasure may be somewhere on that property and it could be that Lou's killer suspected as much." It was more than he had intended to say to Marion, more than he wanted to say. But he was tired of her smug skepticism, the same smugness that he saw in her smile now, as though he were a mental case who had wandered in off the street with a story about aliens living in the White House.

"Sorry, but I just can't make the leap of faith, guys."

The phone rang and Marion excused herself and went into the kitchen to answer it. "Why bother?" Quin said softly, and proceeded to make a copy of the tape.

McCleary, wired and restless, paced over to the window. The Gulf was no longer placid. Fractured moonlight tipped the frothing white caps of waves and the wind lifted the salt spray and hurled it against the window. A buried treasure. A ghost. A pirate and his black mistress and their bastard son. A man haunted by visions. A gothic fantasy, he thought.

And yet, more than two decades ago when Mel Fischer had begun his search for the Atocha riches, people pegged him as just one more nutty treasure hunter chasing rainbows. But he held on to his convictions and, despite enormous personal losses, had proven all the skeptics wrong in the end.

Was that how it had been for Lou? Faced with a quarter of a million bucks in forfeited bonds, Lou's search for options had probably begun out of desperation. Should he sell the property to the highest bidder? Should he hold on to it and take out a loan? It seemed likely that he had already known something about Domingo and his alleged treasure and had decided to hold on to the property long enough to make a concerted search for it.

All of this certainly seemed feasible. Even the ghost seemed feasible. But not as a guardian of a long lost treasure, not as some sort of demon that had lusted for Lou's soul. There were limits, McCleary thought, to what even he considered possible, boundaries that sane, reasonable men didn't cross without risking madness.

II

Roey slipped out of Janna Hilliard's bed and dressed in the dark. He tucked his nine millimeter in the back of his jeans, under his shirt. He liked its cold hardness against his skin. Its certainty. Its reality.

He glanced at Janna, sprawled on her stomach, snoring softly. It would take a nuclear explosion to wake her now. She had been six sheets to the wind when they'd left the Moose and probably wouldn't remember much of anything in the morning. She definitely wouldn't remember that she had mentioned the astrologer by name.

Roey would be back by the time she woke, standing by the bed with a mug of hot coffee and a shit-eating grin on his face. *Rise and shine, babe. Remember me, babe?* Janna Hilliard, he thought, was going to be his alibi.

He drove south to a neighborhood that left a sour taste in his mouth. It had the same careless, shabby look of the south Miami neighborhood where he'd grown up. The lawns needed mowing, the houses shrieked for fresh paint, there were no garages, just old-fashioned carports. A redneck zone, and at this house, all the rednecks were asleep.

He found the house easily enough and was pleased to see just one car in the driveway, a Jeep. No lights shone in the windows. But there were houses on either side and houses across the street and for all he knew, an insomniac might live in one of them, some nosy neighbor sipping hot brandy at the window who would remember a strange car at the curb. No loose ends, not on this one, he thought, and drove past.

Roey pulled into a corner drugstore and used the public phone out front. On the fourth ring, a sleepy male voice said, "Hello? Hello?"

"Is this Rico?"

"Yeah. Who's this?"

"I've got information on Lou Hernando's murder that will get your buddy Blade out of deep shit. Be on the corner of Bristol and Eighth in fifteen minutes. I'll be the hitchhiker with his thumb out."

He hung up before Rico could reply, hurried back to the Volvo, and drove it into the lot behind the drugstore. Then he stood against the building and waited for Blade's buddy.

If he didn't show, Roey would switch to Plan B, he would make an appointment with Rico. He hoped it wouldn't come to that; Plan B posed considerable risk.

A Jeep cruised past the drugstore about twenty minutes after the call. Roey didn't signal, didn't do anything but watch the Jeep turn and come around the block again a few minutes later. This time he slowed and Roey walked over to the curb, and stuck out his thumb.

The Jeep stopped, the door opened. "You the guy who called?"

Rico was a fat man.

"I'm the guy." Roey climbed in, shut the door, and the fat man sped away.

"So what's the information?"

"Head north on the Old Post and turn into the wilderness preserve."

"What's the information?" Rico repeated.

Roey smelled rebellion in the air, but he wasn't going to do anything about it here. "David Vicente wants the kid dead," he said.

"Shit, *amigo*, that doesn't surprise me." Fat Man glanced at Roey, his double chin quivering. "Tell me something I don't know. Did Vicente kill Lou?"

"He wouldn't get his hands dirty."

"So he had him killed."

"Could be."

Fat Man was silent for a while, just driving, staring straight ahead like maybe he knew something wasn't quite right about the situation. Like maybe he was regretting he'd picked Roey up.

Roey felt for the gun, a sweetness he couldn't describe. Twenty years ago, he had killed a fat man in Miami. The fucker had cheated in a poker game, taken Roey's money. He was fifteen at the time, full of himself, and didn't have the dough to spare. He had stalked the prick, followed him, and shot him twice in the head in a parking garage.

Roey had never been caught and he hadn't been back to Miami since. He hadn't liked fat men then and he didn't like them now, and it was no sweat off his back if this guy vanished in a heartbeat.

"So what's your angle?" Rico asked finally.

"Just keep driving. The turnoff's a mile or so ahead."

"I don't think so, *amigo*. You're getting out here." Rico swerved onto the shoulder of the road.

"Think again, *amigo*." Roey pulled out the gun. "Keep driving."

In the wash of the headlights, Roey could see the gleam of

sweat on the fat man's face as he pulled back onto the road. He didn't say anything. Neither did Roey. Fat Man turned into the preserve, where the air was coffee black. "Where're we going?" he asked.

"I'll tell you when to stop." The Jeep bounced over the rutted road, trees seemed to lean inward toward the car like a line of ballroom dancers bowing to each other. Horseshit, Roey thought, and said, "Stop here."

Rico stopped.

"Give me the keys, keep the headlights on."

Fat Man followed directions real well.

"Get out of the car, nice and slow."

It had to be nice and slow, Rico was too big for it to be any other way. And Roey was so close behind him it was impossible for him to run without taking a bullet to the back. Fat Man even raised his arms as he stepped back.

"What do you want from me?"

Roey heard the terrible desperation in the fat man's voice. "I'm only going to ask you once. Where's the kid hiding out?"

"I don't know, man, I haven't heard from him since . . ."

Roey fired just to the right of the man's head. The shot echoed briefly through the trees, then the woods and the darkness swallowed the sound. "Wrong answer. But because I'm such a swell guy, Rico, I'm going to give you another chance. If you give the wrong answer again, I'll blow off a kneecap. Or your balls. If the bullet can find them in all that fat."

Rico was crying now and there was nothing more disgusting than a fat man who cried. Roey screwed the silencer on the end of the gun and Rico stammered, "I . . . I told you I haven't heard from him since . . . since he took off."

Christ, Roey thought, and fired.

The fat man squealed and toppled sideways, clutching his shattered kneecap, blood seeping between his fingers. A flock of birds lifted from the trees, squawking at the intrusion. Tough shit, Roey thought. Tough shit all the way around. His future was riding on this one.

When Rico's sobs subsided into a soft, pathetic weeping broken up by soft, pathetic pleas, Roey said, "Once more, *amigo*." He walked over to Rico, who was squirming on his side in the leaves, his eyes squeezed shut.

"I . . . I . . . Jesus, my knee, my knee."

Roey knelt beside him, jammed the gun to the side of his head. "Where's the kid hiding out, Rico?"

"In the marsh." The words hissed out through his teeth. "Somewhere in the marsh. North end of Tango."

"You've seen him? Talked to him?"

"Jesus, there's so much blood," he sobbed, wiping one hand and then the other against the ground. "Please . . ."

"Answer the question."

"I saw him. At the Cove Marina." He was curled up on his side, holding his injured knee against him. "He's staying on the houseboat, stashed it somewhere near there in the marsh."

"The marsh is a mighty big place, Rico. You'll have to be more specific."

"I . . . I haven't been there. I just met him once at the marina."

"Met him for what?"

"To give him a lift . . . into town."

Roey believed him; Rico was in too much pain to lie.

"Much better," Roey said, getting to his feet. "And it wasn't so hard, now was it?"

"Y-you can't just leave me here to—"

"You're right. You're absolutely right." And he fired two shots into the fat man's neck.

It was messy, but it did the job.

Roey unscrewed the silencer, put it into one pocket of his windbreaker and the gun in the other. He checked Fat Man's pockets for a wallet. There was about fifteen hundred in cash, which Roey slipped into his own pocket. He wiped Rico's wallet with a handkerchief, tossed it on the ground, and walked around the body, kicking leaves over it. His head raced but his thoughts were startlingly clear, precise, detailed. He knew exactly what he had to do.

He shrugged off his windbreaker, draped it over the top of the steering wheel, and used his handkerchief to turn the key in the ignition. He drove out of the preserve and, a mile south on Old Post, left the Jeep in the trees at the side of the road. With the handkerchief, he wiped off the steering wheel and everything else he had touched or might have touched.

He kicked the door shut, stuck his hands into his pockets, and started the hike back toward town, whistling to himself, certain there was nothing to connect him to the fat man's murder.

11

I

Blade woke in a blind white panic, sweat streaming down his face, his heart slamming hard against the walls of his chest. A nightmare. Something about Lou, about when he had found Lou's body, but already it was fading.

Close your eyes, he thought, and it's instant replay time. Christ.

He got up and lit a lantern in the kitchen. Whiskers, stretched out on top of the chipped wooden table, arched his back, yawned, leaped to the floor, and scampered over to his bowl. Blade filled it with some of the dry cat food he'd bought at the marina supply store on his way back from town. Then he dug Lou's journal out of his pack, sat down, and began to read.

December 30

There are places man is not meant to go, boundaries he is not meant to cross, worlds he is not meant to see. I know all of this but it doesn't seem to matter. I go, I cross, I see.

I have trouble remembering what happens in that room. My memories are fragmented, fractured. They glimmer like light through a prism and form tiny, sharp spears that pierce me to the core, that threaten to divide me, shatter me. But when I'm not in the room it's the only thing I think about. I am consumed with longing, literally sick with it.

It's lucky that Blade and I keep such different hours. I don't want him to know about this. Not yet. Maybe never. How would I even begin to explain it? Gracie has already noticed a difference in me. I sometimes catch her watching me, measuring my behavior against how I have acted in the past. I don't know what to say to her either, so I keep our conversations to a bare minimum. Morning, Gracie. How's it going, Gracie? You write the bond, Gracie.

I can't stand it any longer. I'm going back in on New Year's Eve. And this time I'll be prepared. I'll have this journal, a pen, the cigar, the Florida water, the little statues, the effigies. I'll have my wits about me.

December 31/January 1

I wait in the silence, my heart ticking like a clock. I am sitting at the rolltop desk I moved in here. I found it in the attic with Mom's things. When she was alive, it occupied a choice spot in front of the window in the sunroom. I also moved in a cot, a pillow and blanket, a battery-operated light, a few bottles of water, and all of my important files. Blade is out—working or celebrating, I don't know which—so this is the ideal time to do it.

The cigar is already lit, resting in the ashtray, smoke billowing from it. I have splashed Florida water around the room. It smells like a cheap cologne. But from what I've been reading, it supposedly purifies the air and facilitates the passage between worlds. This is her *thing,* her *belief,* her *religion.*

Several candles burn in ceramic holders on the upper edge of the desk, a red, a yellow, a white, each representing a different saint. A statue of Eleggúa *sits to the right of the red candle; he is the* orisha *who opens doors.*

Ritual, it's all ritual. This hybrid of Catholicism and paganism smacks of evil, of some unfathomable darkness, and yet I persevere.

I can already feel her presence, an unfocused cold that seeps like gas between these old stones. My teeth begin to chatter; I button my sweater. Then I feel that first caress, a breath so light it is barely more than a flutter of sensation against my cheek. Her arms encircle me. I feel the shape of them, the silken texture of her skin, and her scent drifts into me, an elemental scent of wind and earth and something wild.

Her voice whispers through my head, tall tales, intimate secrets, little white lies. Her nails glide up my arms, through my hair. Her mouth touches the back of my neck, the lips shockingly warm and passionate. A delicious sensation courses through me, a rushing tide that rises, rises until I can no longer write, no long—

January 15

My first dozen paintings were crude and simple, the way my old man's were. Landscapes, mostly. Beaches, fields, a bleached white village with cartoon buildings. And yet some of the scenes are familiar, recognizable from those that Dad painted.

I'm absolutely sure now that he, too, was a conduit for her. But I don't know what she wanted from him. Company, a diversion, or maybe the same thing she wants from me, whatever that is. He took up painting after Mom died, something he used to tinker with in Cuba. He had a natural talent for it, I don't. But I think that eventually she spoke to him that way, through the paintings that I burned in the yard that day after I buried him. I think he drank to obliterate her, to shut her out.

If he had been less proud, less stubborn, he could have sold the house and moved. But he had survived so many things in his life he refused to surrender to something he couldn't see. In the end, it killed him.

It will not kill me.

In a moment, I will go over to the canvas, sit in front of it, and open myself to her. She will come into me and use my nerves, my muscles, my hands and eyes.

In this way she will eventually communicate to me what she needs, what she seeks, what has kept her here all these centuries.

Emotion balled in his throat; he rubbed his eyes.

The noises of the river drifted through the open windows—frogs, crickets, insects, an occasional splash. More distant, he heard the mournful whistle of the ferry and wondered who rode it at two in the morning.

You never told me the whole story, Lou. Not about the spook, the women, not about any of it. But then again, it was personal and Lou was a forty-two-year-old man, not a seventeen-year-old kid. No matter how close Blade had thought they were, there was always a fatherly touch in Lou that he couldn't move beyond. But how many fathers told their sons about the women they screwed? About their dark fantasies? How many of them confessed that they were losing their minds, going slowly mad?

Blade's arms dropped to the table. The lantern hissed and flickered, the air smelled of kerosene. *Keep reading, just open the goddamn book anywhere and read.*

February 11

I ran into Roey tonight at the Moose and he asked me if I'd ever gotten a lead on the two skips. Which skips? I asked him. He sort of smiles, smiles in that way Roey has that makes my blood freeze. C'mon, man, he says, still smiling. It hasn't been that *long. What the hell, Lou, I spent three months looking for those fuckers and didn't make a dime.*

I didn't have a clue what he was talking about. Roey, though, filled me in and had a great time doing it. How two of my bonds, one for seventy-five and the other for a hundred and fifty, had missed their court dates. How Gracie had hired him to find them. How Gracie had refused to pay him a dime when he returned empty-handed.

It hit me then just how long I had been out of the office, completely removed from all of that. In my absence Gracie had fucked up big time. She had written large bonds and the clients had skipped and she had hired Roey to find them. And she never breathed a word of it to me.

I know I muttered something to Roey about the bounty rules, ten percent on delivery, you either brought in the skip or you weren't paid. Then I got out of there and drove over to the office. Sure enough, there it was in the files and in the logbook, for Christ's sake. Gracie had forged my name on bonds SHE had written.

I don't remember the ride to her place. But I remember the taste of my rage. I've never before wanted to kill someone, but I did then. And she knew it the second she opened the door to her apartment.

She stepped back, her hands snapped up like a shield, and she started to cry. What was I supposed to do, Lou? I didn't have any choice, Lou. You were holed up in that house talking to spooks, Lou, and we had bills to pay.

The bond for seventy-five grand will be forfeited next week.

The bond for a hundred and fifty will be forfeited tomorrow.

That gives me thirty days. Thirty fucking days.

March 31

I'm going to buy Gracie out. I'll sell David a couple acres of the grove. He needs it for his resort. Or Doris, sure, Doris has always wanted the land. Either one, I don't care which.

My only other choice is to bring charges against Gracie for forgery. But Tango being what it is, word would get around, people would find out I haven't been around much, I would get audited by the insurance companies, my license might be pulled. And assuming I got through all that, what the fuck would I do? Sell used cars? Hawk Girl Scout cookies?

I'll sell, yeah, that's the best bet. It'll give me enough to pay off the bonds, buy out Gracie, and save the business.

Blade hurled the journal across the room.

He sat there for a while, staring at his hands, at the nicks in the table. He struggled with his anger, his grief, and was unable to work completely through either of them. He didn't understand the world Lou had lived in and what he didn't understand might very well kill him.

Bottom line.

He finally got up from the table, walked across the room, and picked up the journal. He shoved it down inside his pack with a set of clean clothes, some money, his computer. He scooped up Whiskers and carried the cat out onto the back porch. The Zodiac was in the water, an oar inside. He untied it from the ladder and shoved off, out into the river. When he cranked up the outboard, the cat withdrew into a corner and meowed.

The only lights at Colin's were those that lit the number on each slip, a soft, dim glow, like a street lamp on a lazy neighborhood street. Blade cut the engine before he reached shore, but saw a light go on in the shack. Colin, who slept with one ear tuned to the river, had heard him coming.

He was out by his rusted pickup when Blade approached the shack, an old man who whispered hoarsely: "Git your ass in the back of the truck and pull that tarp over yourself, boy."

"But . . ."

"Just do it."

His voice communicated such urgency, Blade didn't argue, didn't ask questions. Whiskers jumped out of his arms before he reached the back of the pickup and leaped inside the truck when Colin opened the driver's door. Blade scrambled into the back with boat engines, cans of oil, a propeller from an airboat, and pulled a tarp over himself.

He felt every pothole, every rut, every ridge in the dirt road. He knew when the pickup hit asphalt. And he knew when it drove onto the ferry because he heard the whistle, shrill and close enough to blow out his eardrums.

Then, Colin's voice: "C'mon, don't got all night, boy. Out, fast, now."

Blade threw off the tarp and sat up. The ferry was moving. He climbed over the side and followed Colin across the empty deck. In the distance, the lights of Key West winked like stars.

They went up some stairs to the captain's roost, where a very old guy was hunched over the helm. White mustache. Strands of white hair poking out from under his cap. A tan, wrinkled face. He glanced at Blade, then looked back at Colin. "Him?"

"Yup." Colin walked right past him and threw open a door to his right. "Ain't much, but it'll do you for a spell. Sammy, he jus' goes back and forth to Key West and every twelve hours he and his mate trade off." Colin pushed Blade through the door, then squeezed his arm. "They're okay, I swear they are. Sammy's married to my kid sister, his mate's pokin my cousin. Stay low and stay quiet."

"What the hell's goin on, Colin?"

"Your buddy Rico? They done found his body in the preserve a while ago. They ain't sayin you done it, but jus' give 'em a while and they will." He shut the door. Blade just stood there in the dark, the words echoing in his skull.

Dead. Rico was dead.

Then he sank to his knees and pressed his hands to his face and the ferry churned toward Key West.

II

McCleary drifted in a half sleep, Quin's breath warming the back of his neck, the warmth of her body fitting against his own, a pair of old spoons in a drawer. Her mouth felt soft and light against his skin, a feather touch, echoes of the earlier days of their marriage, before Michelle.

He reached back and felt nothing at all.

McCleary bolted out of bed, groped for the lamp switch. Light fell across the empty mattress, the empty room. The bathroom door was shut, pipes clattered in the wall as the shower came on. "Shit," he whispered, rubbing hard at the back of his neck. Quin had been in the bathroom, not in bed.

And yet the temperature in the room hadn't changed, there were no anomalous noises. But a scent of jasmine threaded through the air, a scent so sweet he could almost see it.

He opened the bathroom door, the silhouette of his wife's body was visible against the frosted glass. "Hey, Quin. How long have you been in here?"

She slid open the shower door, her hair lathered into a nest of shampoo. "What?"

He repeated his question.

"I don't know, fifteen minutes or so, I guess. Why?"

I thought you were touching me. He couldn't bring himself to say it aloud. "Just curious. I'll start the coffee."

He pulled a T-shirt on over his gym shorts and went downstairs. The jasmine scent seemed stronger in the hallway but was completely absent in the kitchen. He started the coffee, walked into the hall again, backtracked to Lou's den and opened the door.

The odor was strongest here.

This was her lair, he thought, the place to which she returned like a vampire to a coffin, one of the oldest spots in the house.

A slice of violet sky was visible in the window at the other end of the room. He welcomed the sight of it and felt, just then, like some character in an old vampire movie, grateful that the sun was rising. He turned on the lamps, walked into the center of the room, and turned slowly, hoping for a nudge, the burn of a hunch.

Nothing.

He moved along the bookcase. It shot from the floor to the ceiling, ended at the fireplace, and resumed on the other side. Several shelves occupied the space above the fireplace mantel, but he would need a ladder to read the spines on the books. Lou's taste in books had run the gamut from dime-store westerns to literary works.

He felt he was close to something, but didn't have the foggiest notion what it might be. Then the phone on Lou's desk pealed, shattering his concentration. He was expecting it to be someone from their office in West Palm, and was surprised to hear his bookie's voice.

"This is Nino, man. Baby's Breath she paid off pretty fucking good. Your take is about seven grand. You want that I send you a money order?"

Goddamn. The rodent's tip had paid off. "Drop it off at the office, Nino."

"Since you passed on the tip, man, I took only five percent cut."

"Fair enough."

"You get any more tips from Ferret, you let Nino know, okay?"

"For sure."

McCleary called information for the number of the Island Garage. Ferret himself answered on the second ring. "Yo. Island Garage."

"Okay, I'm a believer, Ferret. How about breakfast at the Tango Cafe? Seven-thirty or eight?"

"Seven-thirty. On me. And bring your wife if you'd like."

"See you then."

The Tango Cafe was nothing fancy, just a mom-and-pop operation in downtown Tango. But the home-cooked food was good, the prices were cheap, and the coffee was strong enough to curl hairs.

He and Quin claimed a window booth, facing each other across the table. When the waitress arrived, a short, thin man was right behind her. He wore white levis, a white shirt, white sandals, and McCleary didn't recognize him until he whipped off his dark sunglasses.

"Mike," he said with that hungry grin, then extended his hand to Quin. "Ms. St. James. It's a pleasure."

"Quin," she said. "Nice to meet you. Slide in."

He did, then glanced up at the waitress. "You have any of that delicious Costa Rican coffee, Carolyn?"

"Sure do. Three mugs?" She glanced at Quin and McCleary, who nodded.

"And a basket of those fantastic biscuits."

"The granola's fresh this morning."

"Great. I'll take a bowl."

"Make it two," Quin said.

"Three," McCleary piped up.

"Nice woman, Carolyn," Ferret remarked as she walked off. "Kind of an interesting family. Her old man claims he was abducted by aliens. He's got scars that he says proves they did experiments on him. He wrote a book on his experience, made the round of talk shows, got laughed out of a couple of cities.

"But his book is on the bestseller lists because people are fascinated, because deep down we all want to believe there's something greater than us, wiser, more powerful. In some ways, I think ghosts fall into the same category."

Surprise, McCleary thought. This man spoke his language. "I

don't think most people see ghosts as being more powerful than aliens."

"It doesn't matter whether it's ghosts, aliens, or talking rocks. We're all hoping for easy answers about the biggies. Particularly the biggie about what it's like to be dead."

"You missed your calling, Mr. Ferret," said Quin. "You should have been a preacher."

He laughed, then spread his small, beautifully shaped hands as if to catch something, to hold something, to receive a gift. "Just think about it. Death is the single most powerful concept that we have. It's going to happen to all of us. And we don't have clue one about what it entails.

"Our religions try to explain but fail miserably, in my opinion. Even our various cultures don't explain it very well. Our music, our poetry, our arts . . ." He shrugged. "Attempts, that's all. The bottom line is that we just don't know if we're annihilated or if something of our consciousness survives or if we melt into the great void. I think we're getting closer to the answer with all this near-death research, but we're still looking for answers. We're hoping.

"Then along comes a ghost. And hey, this isn't just any ol' ghost. This one has got a very specific message to impart."

"Considering how long she's been in that house, she's taken her sweet time getting the point across," McCleary replied.

Ferret's lips drew away from his teeth in a disturbing parody of a grin. "Sure. She gets distracted from her goal. Understandable. We do it all the time. But she always comes back to it. Do you know who owned the house before the Hernandos did?" He glanced at both him and Quin.

"The Tripps," Quin said suddenly. "Lou used to talk about them."

"Do you remember any details?" Ferret asked.

"A tragedy of some sort."

"More than one tragedy. Husband, wife, two young kids. This was back in the forties. The parents are long dead and so is the daughter. The youngest, a man who is now well into his sixties, has been institutionalized since he was thirteen, when he put a butcher knife through his sister's chest."

"And you're blaming it on the ghost," McCleary said dryly.

"Nope. I'm just telling you that the weird shit that has happened in that house over the years beats the odds. And odds are something I know a little about."

"So who killed Lou?" Quin asked.

"Ask me something easy." Ferret sipped at the coffee the waitress had brought over. "Goddamn, but a whiff of this stuff makes me think I'm in some little fishing village on the Pacific side of Costa Rica. Ever been there?"

"Years ago," McCleary replied.

"The place hasn't changed much. It's like Lou in that respect. Costa Rica has just become more of what it always was."

"Are we talking about the same Lou? The Lou I heard about stopped going to work, Mr. Ferret. He closed himself up in that house and proceeded to lose it just like his father did. That's not the Lou I knew."

"Me neither. But that tendency always existed in Lou because he believed he would end up like his father."

"Did Ross Blade kill him?"

"My opinion is hardly infallible, but I'd be damned surprised."

"Have you seen him since the murder?"

"Nope."

McCleary laughed. He liked this guy, strange as he was. "You wouldn't tell me even if you had."

"That's absolutely correct."

"So if Blade didn't do it, who did?" Quin asked.

"Now that," Ferret said, pointing at her, "is a fascinating question."

The waitress returned with their breakfasts. When she'd left, McCleary said, "So what're your theories on who killed Lou?"

"His ex. His business partner. His psychic. Notice that they're all females."

"Who was his psychic?" Quin asked.

"Janna Hilliard."

"Why is she a contender?"

"At this point, Quin, I'd say that anyone who had more than a passing acquaintance with Lou is suspect."

"What about Vicente?" McCleary asked.

Ferret shrugged. "A good contender. Vicente certainly has a motive. But then again, so did the women in his life."

"What other women were there?"

"Doris Lynch."

"The conservationist."

"That's one of the hats she wears. She's also an animal rights activist, a philanthropist, a patron of the arts, a socialite, and a very strange woman."

"Who wanted Lou's land."

"You got it."

"To turn it into a wildlife sanctuary?"

"That's what she says. My own feeling is that she knows the history of the place and believes Juan Domingo's treasure is buried somewhere on the property."

"Why would Lynch give a damn about some pirate's treasure?" Quin asked. "She's worth a fortune."

The little man's shrug made it clear there was no accounting for the vagaries of human tastes and passions. "I know for a fact that she's been researching the history of the house for some time now."

"And just how do you know that?"

"We work on her car at the garage. You'd be appalled at some of the things people leave lying around on their seats, in their trunks and glove compartments. I make it my business to know what's going on around Tango. By the way, the cops are about to turn the heat up on Blade. A friend of his, guy named

Rico, was found in the preserve early this morning. He'd been shot through the neck."

"We hadn't heard," Quin said. "Why do they think Blade is responsible?"

"They don't yet, but they probably will. The kid's a convenient scapegoat, everybody's whipping boy. Blade stopped by Doris Lynch's last night. Christ knows why. Doris called the cops."

"We hadn't heard that either," McCleary said. "I'd like to talk to him."

"I'll tell you what, Mike. If I hear from Blade, I'll let you know. I'll try to set up a meeting."

His small, dark eyes darted from McCleary to something over his shoulder. A moment later, the albino slipped in next to McCleary and set a briefcase on the table. Ferret introduced him to Quin, then Bino removed a sheet of paper from the briefcase. His hands were paler than the paper, which he turned so both McCleary and Quin could see it. "This is a list of Craig Peck's clients. You'll notice that David Vicente and Doris Lynch are both on here."

"I think it's safe to assume they're both aware of the contents of Lou's will," Ferret said. "Peck isn't a particularly scrupulous attorney and Vicente and Doris Lynch have a long history with his firm."

"Peck's not old enough for a history," Quin remarked.

Ferret laughed. "Quite true. But he took over the firm when his father retired. And his father did business with Vicente and Doris for years. The point is that it's likely both of them know that if Blade is out of the way, they'll have easier access to the land."

"This may come in useful, too," Bino said, and set down a square box that was the size of a four-by-six card file. "A bug and a receiver. The bug is shaped like the plastic gizmo on the phone cord that pops into the wall. Just fit the bug over it and snap it into the wall. It's got to be a regular phone, not a remote.

The receiver's good for up to a mile. It'll give you any calls made to or from a regular phone in the house, the number dialed, and both sides of the conversation."

McCleary took the box but didn't comment on it. Ferret and Bino exchanged a glance and McCleary had the eerie impression that they were conversing. Then Ferret dropped a pair of twenties on the table, enough to cover eight breakfasts, and slid out of the booth. "We'll be in touch, Mike. Hope to see you again, Quin."

And just that fast, they were gone, rabbits that had disappeared into a magician's hat.

12

I

Lou's Camaro wasn't much to look at, Quin thought, particularly since the forensics department had ripped the interior apart and slapped it back together. But it drove like a charm, hugging Tango's hills with the tenacity of a spider and sliding with utter ease into a parking space at the curb in downtown Pirate's Cove.

Since she was early for her appointment with Janna Hilliard, she dropped by the office to see Gracie first. It took her a while to answer the door and when she finally did, she fell all over herself explaining that she had been in the back room and didn't hear the bell. She looked more disheveled than usual, her suit rumpled, her hair mussed, as if she had just pulled herself out of bed. She had lost her shoes on the way to the door, the toes of her stockings were stained.

"You just wouldn't believe how much shit Lou and I had stored in the back room. Empty boxes, broken furniture, old filing cabinets." She shook her head and invited Quin to sit in one of the chairs in front of her desk. She remained standing and seemed anxious, uptight. "How about coffee? Something cold to drink?"

"Don't go to any trouble, Gracie."

"Trouble? It's no trouble. I'll be right back."

She disappeared behind the divider that separated the rest of the office. Quin heard the creak of a door as it opened, shut. Curious, she got up and peeked around the end of the divider. There was another desk, several chairs, a copier, other office equipment.

Quin removed her sandals and stepped past a second divider, into a small, tidy kitchen where a full pot of coffee was already brewing. On the other side of the sink were two doors, both of them shut. The lone, barred window looked out into an alley, where Gracie and a man whose face Quin couldn't see were locked in what appeared to be the smooch of the decade. When they broke apart, Quin recognized Lou's attorney, Craig Peck.

No wonder Gracie had been acting so weird, so *guilty*.

Quin quickly returned to the front room and was paging through a magazine when Gracie appeared with two mugs of coffee. She had remembered to put her shoes back on. Her chair squeaked as she sat down behind the desk.

"So tell me. What has the investigation turned up?" Gracie asked.

"A couple of things. Like the items in Lou's will. Has his attorney talked to you yet?"

Blink, blink, went her eyes. "His attorney?"

"Craig Peck."

"Oh, Craig. Sure. Yeah, he came by yesterday. Lou left me the business. I hear you and Mike are executors of the will."

"Did he also tell you we inherited some stocks?"

Her unplucked brows lifted, forming odd loops over her guileless blue eyes. "No, he didn't tell me anything about the other bequeathments. That's privileged information."

"C'mon, Gracie. You're screwing the guy."

Every line in her face seemed to fall, pulled by a sudden surge of excessive gravity. Then anger leaped into her eyes, deepening all that blue. "Just who the hell do you think you are, anyway? My personal life is none of your business, it's . . ."

"Let me put it this way, Gracie. Lou's will may very well have something to do with why he was murdered. I figure you knew about the contents of the will before the goddamn ink was dry. And since Peck also represents David Vicente and Doris Lynch, just like his father did, I'm sure they knew about it, too. That brings up some rather intriguing possibilities about motives."

Gracie stood, her face livid with rage, her voice crackling with it when she spoke. "Get out of here. I don't have to listen to this bullshit."

"Neither do I." Quin slammed the door as she left and took enormous satisfaction that the glass in the window rattled.

It seemed that just about everyone Lou had known well would benefit from his death. So in the end the motive probably would boil down to greed, pure and simple.

She crossed the courtyard. The door to Janna Hilliard's office was open, and as soon as she stepped inside, Quin felt as though she were in a Victorian parlor. There were dainty lace curtains, lace doilies as frail and delicate as a butterfly's wings, red velvet cushions, lamps with stained-glass shades. Even the air smelled of some other century.

Janna stood behind a display case, where she was rearranging polished rocks, crystals, decks of tarot cards, and a selection of jewelry. Gone were the crystal earrings, the crystal pendant, the New Age kook routine. Today her jewelry was gold and she wore a pastel sundress that hugged her hips exactly right and which scooped just enough at the neckline.

"Excuse the mess. I meant to get in early this morning, but I overslept. Look around while I clear us a space to work."

"Is all the stuff in the case for sale?"

"You bet. I've got the best prices on the island."

Quin scanned the merchandise. "Which tarot cards do you recommend?"

"For you or someone else?" she asked, removing a pile of books and magazines from the end of a small rectangular coffee table.

"Me, I guess."

Janna strolled over, lifted the lid on the case, and removed a deck of cards. "I learned with the Morgan Greer deck. It's wonderfully illustrated." She slipped the deck from the box and handed it to Quin. "There's something about the artwork that makes the meanings of the cards easy to remember."

"Great. I'll take it."

"I'll throw in the book that comes with it. I'll use my Morgan Greer deck for the reading so you'll get a sense of it."

"Sure."

"Just sit right over here, Mrs. McCleary."

"Quin."

"Quin. What an unusual name. Is that with a double *n* like that Dr. Quinn on TV?"

"Just one *n.*"

"A family name?"

"Uh, no, my parents were playing Scrabble the night I was born. Their rules allowed proper names and that was the one my mother won with."

"Names, names, names." She brought out a deck of cards wrapped in silk. "My mother was a Superman fan, of the comic books, right? She identified most with Lana Lang, Lois's rival, and that's what she wanted to call me. Lana. But my father hated the name. He wanted to call me Janice. So they compromised on Janna." She shuffled the deck. "I'll just do a general reading. Is there any particular time frame you'd like to it?"

"The next couple of weeks."

"Now if that doesn't sound like a Gemini. Rush, rush. Lou was a double Gemini. Sun and rising, with a moon in Aries. Real tough combination."

"You read for him?"

"Once, must've been back in February. How long did you know him?"

"Years. What about you?"

"We moved into this building around the same time." She finished shuffling the deck, asked Quin to cut and shuffle. "Concentrate on the issues in your life. I'll do the horseshoe spread. It's the same one I did for Lou. It gives quite a bit of information in just seven cards."

She cut, shuffled, and handed the deck to Janna. She dealt seven cards right off the top, then laid them out facedown in the shape of an inverted horseshoe. She turned over the fourth card from the left. The six of swords. It depicted two passengers in a boat being rowed toward a distant shore by a man standing behind them. The floorboard of the boat was pierced by six swords. It didn't look like a particularly good card.

"This is the foundation of the issues in your life right now. Passage away from difficulties. The situation you're headed for may be better than the one you're leaving or may be worse. We'll have to see what the rest of the cards say." She turned over the first card on the left. The eight of cups. A forlorn figure was turning away from eight gold cups that were stacked behind him. The whole picture radiated disappointment, loss.

"You've recently released something, a situation from which you've withdrawn emotionally. A voluntary release."

Tark, she thought.

Janna turned over the card above it. The two of swords. A blindfolded woman stood alone with a pair of swords crossing her chest. "This represents the present. I always think of this card as the calm before the storm. It's like being in suspended animation. You're unable to take the necessary action to get things moving forward. You need to clarify what you want."

The third card, the five of wands, represented the immediate future. "This card usually indicates stress and confusion about a professional issue. It can also be about competition."

She tapped the card to the right of the six of swords. "This position is a person connected with the reading who may be of help." She turned it over. The knight of rods. "This guy is the bearer of good news, helpful news of some sort. Let's see if we can find out a little more about him." She dealt a card off the top of the deck and placed it next to the page. "The king of coins. Excellent. This man is over thirty-five, dark-haired, has strong convictions and he's financially secure. He's able to execute plans."

"And he's going to impart information?" Quin asked.

"Definitely."

Ferret? she wondered. "May I draw one more clarification card?" Quin asked.

"Sure."

The queen of cups.

"Interesting," Janna said. "You're apparently going to get help from a woman as well. She's over thirty-five and her gift is vision, clairvoyance." She glanced up, smiling. "Maybe that's me."

Quin doubted it. Christine Redman seemed the more likely contender.

"The next card represents the obstacle." Janna turned it over.

The Devil. Great. The goddamn devil.

Janna stared at the card. "The obstacle you're facing is your own fears. Lou drew this card in the final position. It sometimes indicates adversity, violence, destruction." Her voice softened. "Which is exactly what it represented for Lou."

She flipped over the final card. A man lay on the ground, ten swords sticking out of his back. "It doesn't represent violent death," she said quickly.

"He looks pretty damn dead."

"Metaphor, Quin. The tarot is about metaphor. This card is talking about treachery, betrayal, a stab in the back. It's the final outcome. But let's see if we can get more information." She pulled a card off the bottom of the deck, dropped it on the table.

The Tower. Fire leaped from its windows, lightning pierced its sides, the sky around it looked like the end of the world.

"Christ," Quin breathed. "What's that represent?"

"An abrupt change in one's life, transformation, knocking down the walls that imprison you. It's not necessarily a negative card. It just means that your life is about to go through a tremendous upheaval and then the six of swords will kick in. You'll find your passage away from hard times. Let's see if we can get a little more on this. Pull another card."

Death. A skull, a cloak, a scythe. Terrific.

"This isn't a death card either," Janna said. "But it's telling us that the transformation and upheavals are going to happen suddenly. It may very well have something to do with whoever or whatever the ten of swords represents." She scooped up the cards. "I'll do another spread and we'll get more information."

"Thanks, but that's enough. I get the general idea."

"If I were you, I'd get out of the line of work you're in, Quin. Do something safer."

"Is that what you advised Lou?"

"More than once."

"Why did he come to you for a reading?"

"I owed him a favor."

"Because he bailed you out when you were arrested?"

Her eyes narrowed. "I guess you've been talking to Gracie."

Quin reached into her purse and pulled out the canceled check that Lou had written to her for five hundred bucks. "What was this for? Ten readings? A loan? What?"

She was now a trifle defensive. "I don't have to answer that."

"Look, you either talk to me or you talk to the cops."

Janna returned the cards to the silk pouch, and pushed it aside. "That's thirty-five for the reading and twelve for the cards."

Quin handed her a fifty, made sure she had her deck in her purse and followed Janna to the register. As Janna gave her change, her eyes met Quin's. "I did an exorcism at Lou's house," she said softly.

Of all the things Janna might have said, this was the one thing Quin hadn't anticipated. "An exorcism?"

"That's what Lou called it." She rubbed her hands over her arms and shook her head. "I didn't really have any idea what the hell I was doing. I got some holy water from the church. You know, begone Satan, take a hike, like that. Except it's not a devil in that house. It's just some poor soul who's gotten stuck and doesn't know how to get unstuck. Maybe she doesn't even know she's dead. Or maybe she knows it but doesn't know how to escape where she is. Whatever, she's got unfinished business."

"About what?"

"I don't know. But I think Lou was pretty close to finding out. I think that's what obsessed him. You know those paintings of his? They were channeled. He channeled her when he painted, that's why they're as good as they are. She was trying to communicate what she needed before she can move on."

Channeled art. Hell, why not? Other people claimed to channel aliens and thirty-thousand-year-old entities with names no one could pronounce. "So what happened when you did your exorcism?"

"I walked through the house with the holy water, muttering incantations. I felt ridiculous. I mean, I'm not a psychic, okay? I don't walk into rooms and pick up impressions. I just read cards. Anyway, after I'd finished, Lou showed me his paintings. One thing led to another and we, uh, became lovers." She shrugged. "Right from the beginning it was more important to me than it was to Lou. He was too nice to just cut it off."

"When was the last time you saw him?"

"The week before he was killed. At the office. I walked in on him and Gracie arguing, and left. He stopped by here later."

"What were they arguing about?"

"A bond, that was all he said."

"So you weren't with him the night he was murdered."

She understood immediately what Quin was really asking, but unlike Felicity, she didn't take umbrage, didn't look incredulous. She merely seemed hurt by the implication and her eyes filled with tears. "I was in love with the man," she said softly. "I didn't kill him."

"Where were you the night of the murder?"

"At the Pink Moose."

"Alone?"

"Yes. The bartender will remember. I spent most of the evening talking to him."

"Was Lou sleeping with anyone else that you know of?"

"He never said and I never asked, but I'm sure he was. He was an attractive, single man who was too nice for his own good. He took to wounded people just as easily as he took to wounded animals. I know he saw his ex from time to time and I think he and Gracie were involved with each other off and on since his divorce. She denies it, but Gracie lies about everything."

"Anyone else?"

Her mouth puckered. "The ghost. She consumed most of his time."

"You can't have sex with a ghost."

"Tell that to Lou." Janna leaned forward. "Look, I know this is going to sound strange, but I think that's exactly what Lou was trying to do."

"Have sex with the ghost, you mean."

"Commune with the ghost."

Leave it alone for now, she thought. "I really appreciate everything you've told me, Janna."

"Wait. Take your money." She thrust the $35 into Quin's hand. "The reading's free. Just do me a favor. Finish what Lou started. That'll lead you to who killed him."

II

The houseboat was hidden in the mangroves on the Tango River, tucked away in the hot, noisy shade of the drooping trees. It had taken Roey nearly three hours to find it and now that he had, he knew at a glance that the kid wasn't around.

He throttled back on the outboard of the skiff he had rented, coasted alongside the houseboat to the rear, and killed the engine. He tied up at the ladder and climbed aboard. The door wasn't locked, the windows were wide open.

The stupid little shit figured he wouldn't be found. Wrong, Roey thought, and opened the door and walked in. A bedroom, a small, miserably hot bedroom that could belong to anyone. The bunk was unmade, clothes hung in the closet and cluttered the drawers. Lou's clothes, he guessed.

Roey jerked out the top drawer, dumped the stuff on the floor, and hurled the drawer across the room. It struck the window, shattering it. It made him feel so good, he did it with the next drawer, and the next. When he'd finished, when clothes and glass and splintered wood littered the floor, he unclipped the hunting knife from his belt and went after the room as though it were something living, the kid himself. He tore open the mattress from top to bottom, stabbed the pillows until feathers spilled out, scooped up one of the fallen drawers and swung it like a baseball bat at the mirror over the dresser.

It shattered with exquisite precision, glass showering over the dresser and floor. "Seven years of bad luck, kid," he muttered, and hurled the drawer through the back door.

Feathers drifted through the hot air and stuck to his sweaty skin. His shoes crunched over glass. He kicked the clothes out of his way and marched into the galley, rage rolling out of him in shimmering waves.

Little fucker, he thought. He'd show the little fucker.

He threw open the cabinet doors, scooped glasses off the shelves, flipped the plastic plates one by one across the room, spinning Frisbees that struck the wall and cracked like eggs. He yanked out drawers, dumped them on the floor, overturned the small fridge, stabbed bags of sugar and flour. He opened cans of beans and soup and corn and shook the contents onto the floor, the counters, the sink, the furniture. He stopped up the sinks, turned on the water full blast, and ripped apart the inside of the toilet so it would overflow.

The tide of his rage swept him along until he lost himself in the rhythm of destruction. This was how he had felt when he had stalked the bastard in Miami who had ripped him off, when he had cornered him finally in a parking garage and shot him twice. He felt renewed, invigorated, invincible.

Drenched in sweat, with nothing left to destroy, Roey shut the windows, blew out the pilot light on the stove's gas burner, and turned the knob as high as it would go. The sickening sweet odor quickly suffused the air.

He hurried outside and climbed into his skiff. It was at least ninety-five in the shade out here and it wouldn't take long, he thought, for the heat to ignite the gas. He would be long gone when it happened.

III

FROM: C. LYNCH 1
TO: R.BLADE

THIS MAY BE NONE OF MY BUSINESS, ROSS, BUT IF YOU NEED HELP JUST HOLLER. I KNOW HOW TOUGH THINGS CAN BE WHEN YOU DON'T HAVE ANYONE ON YOUR SIDE. I GOT PREGNANT WHEN I WAS 15. THE GUY WAS A JERK, I WAS A FOOL, BUT I WANTED TO KEEP THE BABY. MY PARENTS DECIDED I SHOULD HAVE AN ABORTION. I DON'T GIVE A DAMN WHAT DORIS SAYS ABOUT YOU. I HAVE A GOOD SENSE ABOUT PEOPLE AND I KNOW YOU DIDN'T KILL ANYONE. I HOPE YOU'RE STILL GOING ONLINE. CHARLIE.

FROM: R.BLADE
TO: C.LYNCH 1

CHARLIE, THANKS FOR THE OFFER (AND THE VOTE OF CONFIDENCE), BUT IT'S CALLED AIDING AND ABETTING A FUGITIVE.

I'M SORRY YOU DIDN'T GET TO KEEP YOUR BABY. MY MOTHER SPLIT WHEN I WAS A KID. I GUESS SHE COULDN'T STAND MY OLD MAN'S DRINKING, HIS ABUSE, HIS BULLSHIT.

I GET CHRISTMAS CARDS FROM HER SOMETIMES. SHE'S LIVING UP NORTH SOMEWHERE, GOT MARRIED AGAIN, AND HAS A TWO-YEAR-OLD DAUGHTER. SHE INVITED ME TO VISIT, I TOLD HER TO FORGET IT. BUT THAT WAS BEFORE LOU WAS KILLED AND NOW I'M BEGINNING TO THINK I'D LIKE TO SEE HER WHEN THIS IS ALL OVER. ROSS

FROM: C.LYNCH 1
TO: R. BLADE

WHEN I E-MAILED YOU LAST NIGHT, I WAS REALLY WORRIED THAT YOU WOULDN'T BE ONLINE. I'M GLAD YOU'RE SAFE. HOW OLD WERE YOU WHEN YOUR MOM SPLIT? MY PARENTS HAVE BEEN FIGHTING AS LONG AS I CAN REMEMBER. I'M ACTUALLY GLAD THEY'RE GETTING DIVORCED. THEY PROBABLY SHOULD HAVE DONE IT SOONER. THEY'LL BOTH BE HAPPIER, WHICH WILL MAKE ME HAPPIER.

YOUR PICTURE'S GOING TO BE ON THE FRONT PAGE OF THE TRIBUNE *TOMORROW. A REPORTER WAS OUT HERE INTERVIEWING DORIS. SHE'S ACTING REAL WEIRD ABOUT ALL THIS, WHICH MADE ME CURIOUS ABOUT WHAT'S GOING ON. SO I WENT THROUGH HER PAPERS AND FOUND SOMETHING THAT MAY BE OF INTEREST TO YOU. I SCANNED IT INTO MY COMPUTER AND UPLOADED IT. IT'S IN AN ATTACHED FILE TO THE NOTE.*

SOME GUY NAMED MCCLEARY IS GOING TO BE HERE PRETTY SOON TO TALK TO DORIS, SO I'D BETTER SIGN OFF. C.

ATTACHED FILE 09874

June 3
Dear Lou,

I've given your proposition a great deal of thought and I like it. I think the best way to proceed is for the two of us to get together and hammer out conditions that are mutually beneficial and agreeable. Then my attorney can put it all in legaleeze.

Just so we're both clear on what's what, here are the conditions as I understand them:

1. On or around 9/5, you will receive a certified check from me for $300,000. This will be enough for you to pay off the lien and interest and will pay for two acres of the grove that abut the site for the Amelia Resort to the east and the north.

2. A second payment for the same amount will be forthcoming on 10/5, which will buy me 1.5 acres (more or less) on the south side of the resort.

If this isn't correct, give me a call. Otherwise we'll get together in the next couple of weeks.

Doris

Blade disconnected the computer from the phone in the captain's quarters and walked over to the porthole. The ferry was churning toward Key West again, an endless journey, back and forth, back and forth. He was beginning to feel invisible, unreal, as though the ferry was actually the transporter of souls from the land of the living to the land of the dead.

He pinched himself hard on the arm. It hurt. Still alive, he thought, and walked back over to the table where he had set up his computer. He reread the letter Doris Lynch had written Lou. Not a word, Lou had never said a word about this. But it didn't take a financial wizard to figure out that Lou had been in deep shit. Blade just hadn't known how deep.

The interesting part was that he had somehow rigged a deal

where he would hold on to more than half of the grove, have enough to pay off the lien, with interest, that had covered his forfeited bonds, and still come out three hundred grand ahead of the game. Not bad. But he had been killed before he had received the first payment.

Did Doris have the legal documents? Would she try to use them if and when the will went through whatever channels it had to go through?

Blade went online again and did a search in the e-mail addresses for McCleary. There were eight, but only two in Florida, M.McCleary1 and Q.McCleary. Okay, they were online. But he didn't know them, didn't trust them, and until that changed, he would keep his discoveries to himself.

13

On a map of the island, Doris Lynch's homestead fell between the cat's two ears, a prime location by anyone's standards. But the house itself, McCleary thought, didn't reflect the fact that her personal fortune was estimated at about $40 million.

It was a single floor of brick and stone that occupied the top of a wooded hill. Like Lou's place, there was a certain wildness about the estate—unraked leaves, a lush, unpruned garden, branches that sagged with fruit. Nature, he thought, would have the final say here.

Just as he stopped behind a Mercedes parked in the driveway, a woman came around the side of the house. Her body was lean and compact, her jeans were dusty, her sleeveless shirt showed long, sinewy arms that glistened in the sun from sweat or suntan lotion, he couldn't tell which. Her floppy hat and sunglasses hid most of her face. "You must be Mike McCleary," she said, walking over to him, a smile fixed in place.

They shook hands. Her grip was surprisingly strong. "Thanks for seeing me, Mrs. Lynch."

"Not at all. Do you mind if we talk out back? I'm right in the middle of critter feedings."

"Sounds intriguing."

"It has its moments," she said with a laugh.

They followed a path along the side of the house to a tremendous backyard with a patio, a swimming pool, and a sweeping view of the Gulf on one side and the Atlantic on the other. In front of the gardenia bushes at the far side of the yard was a plastic kid's pool in which four baby ducks swam. Next to it were bags of wild-bird seed, containers of dry bread, and a cage of tiny white mice.

"Muscovys," he said.

She looked pleased that he knew his Muscovys from his mallards. "Yes, indeed, the ones most people detest." She whipped off her straw hat and tossed it on a nearby chaise longue. Her curly, salt-and-pepper hair shone in the sun. "Those four little guys have broken legs. I think one of the male ducks injured them. There's a pond about three hundred yards into the trees where a group of ten or twelve of them hang out. I found one dead baby duck the other day that looked like it had been pecked to death. So I took these four from the mother." She opened the container of dry bread and tossed a handful of crumbs into the little pool. The ducklings chased them, gobbling them up. "Their legs will heal as they get older."

"What're the mice for?"

"The owls." She picked up the cage and they squeezed between the bushes and walked through the thick shade of the banyans. "I let the mice loose near their nest. That way they still have to catch them, but since they're well fed, they won't go after the baby ducks."

"We've heard owls around Lou's place."

"That grove has more burrowing owls than anywhere else on the island. Is that where you're staying?"

"For the time being. I understand you made several offers on Lou's property."

Her smile was quick, bemused. "That's no secret, Mr. McCleary. David Vicente and I have made offers and counteroffers on that property ever since Manuel Hernando passed away three years ago. Lou's ambivalence about selling the property was a continual source of annoyance to both of us. I hoped to turn it into a wildlife sanctuary, David wanted it as part of the resort. He finally said the hell with it and broke ground. After that, I pretty much gave up. I figured Lou would never sell, so the property would stay like it was. And that's fine with me. I just didn't want it to be developed."

"By David Vicente, you mean?"

"By anyone."

"Why did Ross Blade come here last night?"

"How did you know he was here?" she asked.

"News gets around," McCleary replied, with a shrug.

"I never second-guess adolescents, Mr. McCleary. He works at the garage in town that I use. A couple of times he brought my car back to the house and we got friendly. I was shocked when I heard he was the prime suspect in Lou's murder. And then to come downstairs yesterday evening and see him just sitting in the kitchen with my granddaughter . . . well, you can imagine. I thought he might be armed and I'm afraid I didn't handle the situation very well."

The trees thinned, then gave way to a small field. Doris set the cage on the ground and pointed at a cluster of bushes. "The burrow is right over there. They're amazingly proficient diggers."

"Don't owls hunt at night?" he asked as she crouched and opened the door to the cage.

"You usually see them out and about at dusk. But I've found that they'll usually come out when I release the mice."

The mice, half a dozen of them, scampered around inside the cage, squealing, their noses twitching, working at the air.

They know, McCleary thought.

Doris tapped the cage. "Go on, guys."

They squeaked louder and huddled in a corner of the cage. She finally tilted it at their end and the mice tumbled through the opening and lit out in every direction, their shrill, pathetic squeaks a signal to every predator in the area. Sure enough, an owl about twice the size of his hand popped up from the burrow, swooped into the air, then dived and sank its talons into one of the mice. The mouse's shrieks echoed through the heat as the owl swept upward again. There was a deliberate cruelty to the whole thing that tainted his opinion of Doris Lynch.

"What did Blade say to you when he was here?"

She shrugged and snapped the cage door shut. "He seems to think I know something about the ghost in Lou's house. *Alleged* ghost," she corrected with a smile. "You've heard about it?"

More than that, Doris. "Yeah. It seems to be part of the island lore."

"I wouldn't go so far as to say that. But most of the people you're talking to probably know about it because they knew Lou. Anyway, Ross apparently thinks I know why the ghost has hung around all these years. Can you imagine?" She laughed and they retraced their path through the trees.

"Did he threaten you or your granddaughter in any way?"

"His presence here was a threat, Mr. McCleary."

That didn't answer his question. "Did he physically threaten you?"

"He grabbed the phone out of my hand when I was calling the police. Then he fled."

"Would it be possible for me to talk to your granddaughter?"

"Sure. She's probably upstairs on the computer. It seems she spends more time with her friends online than she does with real people."

"I had the same problem when I first went online."

"Personally, I don't understand the appeal. Excuse me, and I'll get her."

McCleary waited by the kiddie pool, alternately watching the baby ducks and a hawk that drifted through the vast blueness overhead. He was betting that the hawk, not the owls or the male ducks, had injured the ducklings and probably had eaten a few of them, too. It was something that Doris, given her interest in wildlife, should have considered. On the other hand, maybe she had and simply enjoyed interfering in nature's scheme of things, playing God up here on the top of her hill.

She returned shortly with a teenager who looked to be seventeen or eighteen. Even if McCleary hadn't known who she was, he would have pegged her as a relative. She had the same square jaw that her grandmother did, the same high, bold cheekbones. Doris had yet to remove her sunglasses, so McCleary didn't know what color her eyes were. He guessed, though, that they were the same blue as her granddaughter's. "Charlotte, this is Mike McCleary. He'd like to ask you some questions about what happened last night."

"Hi." Charlotte combed her fingers through her short, dark hair. "What do you want to know?"

"Just tell me what happened."

"Like I told the reporter, I don't really know a whole lot. This guy rang the bell, asked for Doris, so I told him to come in. We were waiting in the kitchen and suddenly Doris shows up and the shit hits the fan."

"There's no need to swear," Doris said irritably.

She shrugged, a teenage shrug that said, like it or lump it. "He asked."

"Could you leave us alone for a few minutes, Mrs. Lynch?" McCleary asked.

She didn't look very happy about it, but she walked over to the chaise longue where she had left her hat. "How long were you alone with him, Charlotte?"

"Charlie. My name's Charlie. We talked for, like, ten minutes. Fifteen. No more than that. Doris was busy upstairs."

"Did he threaten you?"

She folded her arms at her waist and let out a short, clipped laugh. There was something about her mouth just then and the way she tossed her head that reminded McCleary of a young Ali MacGraw. "No way. We talked about computers. About Internet and GEnie. I didn't have any idea who he was."

"And what did he say to your grandmother when she came into the room?"

"I don't really remember. Things happened pretty fast."

The giveaway was that she averted her eyes as she said this, looking down at the ground where her bare toes curled against leaves. She was lying. He thought Doris was probably lying about something as well, but she was far more accomplished at it than her granddaughter.

"What're you hiding, Charlie?" he asked gently.

Her blue eyes snapped to his face, narrowed against the bright light. When she didn't say anything, McCleary plunged ahead on nothing more than a hunch. "Look, I don't believe Ross Blade killed Lou. From what I know about him, he isn't capable of murder. I think he was framed. But I can't help him without talking to him about what he knows. So if you hear from him, please tell him to get in touch with me. It'll be between the two of us. He knows where I'm staying. If he'd feel more comfortable talking online, I'm on GEnie and the Net."

He jotted his Internet address on a business card and handed it to her. She pocketed it, glanced at Doris as she approached, then simply turned and walked off.

"A horrible, difficult age," Doris remarked, gazing after her granddaughter. "Do you have any children, Mr. McCleary?"

"A daughter. But she's a long ways from adolescence."

"I'm curious about something," Doris said. "It's my understanding that once Ross is found, he'll be booked on suspicion of murder. So exactly what is it you're investigating?"

"I think there's a good possibility that Blade was framed. If that proves true, then it changes the entire complexion of the case."

It didn't answer her question completely, but it was enough to shut her up for the time being. "May I use your phone?"

"Sure. Through the patio doors, you'll see it in the hall."

In other words, he'd been dismissed and the interview was over. Not quite, McCleary thought, and went inside.

He passed through a Florida room—tile floor, wicker and glass furniture, nothing ostentatious—and continued into the hall. The phone stood on a wicker table alongside the staircase. He paused, listening to the house. The only sound was music pounding from somewhere upstairs.

Opportunities didn't get any better than this.

He reached into his back pocket for the bug Bino had given him. Unsnap cord, fit bug around plastic gizmo, snap back into wall: lickety-split and he was outta here.

But as he stood, he glanced up and there was Charlie Lynch at the top of the stairs. Their eyes locked, then she touched her hands to her ears, to her mouth, and to her eyes, covering them. Hear no evil, speak no evil, see no evil. Her arms dropped to her sides, a half-smile teased her mouth, and she backed away.

Sudden allies, he thought. Ferret, Bino, and now this teenager.

He left the house through the patio doors and joined Doris out by the driveway, where she had turned a hose on a bed of bougainvillea vines. "I hope Charlotte's music didn't burst your eardrums."

"It's nothing compared to the noise level a couple of two-year-olds can generate. Thanks again for your time, Mrs. Lynch."

She said the expected things, call if he had more questions, good luck, and so on. He was certain she vanished as soon as he was out of sight. He removed the receiver from the glove compartment. It was one of those nifty high-tech gizmos that doubled as a tape recorder. He switched it on and pulled onto the shoulder of the road at the bottom of the hill. The receiver beeped a minute later, indicating someone had picked up the phone in the house.

A number appeared in the window: 555-9854. McCleary

didn't recognize it, but he knew the voice that answered with a crisp, "Hello?"

"Hi, David. It's me."

"How'd it go?"

"I'm pretty sure he suspects something."

"He's fishing," Vicente replied.

"No, I don't think so. He's going to be a problem."

"He's already a problem."

"What're we going to do about it?"

"I'm taking care of it, Doris."

"Pardon my skepticism, but I seem to remember you saying the same thing about finding Ross Blade."

"I'm working on that one, too. It would have been a lot easier if you hadn't overreacted last night."

"You weren't here."

"It's going to work out."

Their breathing filled the subsequent silence. "Which part?" Doris finally asked.

"Blade, McCleary, the property, us. All of it."

"I hope so," she said softly, and hung up.

Us? As in a couple? As in the merging of two massive fortunes? He wondered if Amelia Vicente suspected.

The receiver beeped again. He didn't recognize this number either, and when the ringing stopped, there were no voices, only static. It vanished completely when he was about a mile and a half from the house, out of the receiver's range. McCleary jotted down the number and realized that static was the same thing he heard every time he logged onto the computer boards.

And the subscriber in the Lynch household, he thought, had to be Charlie.

Gene Frederick was exactly where he'd told McCleary he would be, in a small park at the south end of the island, seated on a bench that faced the beach. He wore sunglasses, a red baseball cap, a fisherman's shirt with a dozen pockets in it, khaki shorts, and tennis shoes. He looked like a crusty old dog on vacation, not the chief of police.

"You're late," he said without prelude as McCleary joined him on the bench.

"I'm always late, Gene. That'll never change."

Frederick laughed and slapped him on the shoulder. "That's what I like about you, Mike. No bullshit. But this is my day off. C'mon, let's walk." They headed down toward the beach. "So how've you been? Any regrets about leaving Miami?"

"Occasionally. But I just couldn't see raising a kid in Dade County."

"Hell, Tango's the best place to raise kids. My offer still stands, you know. Anytime you want a job, say the word."

McCleary laughed. "That offer's eight years old."

"Shit, *tempus fugit,* huh? But I'm serious about the job."

"I've got a job, but thanks."

"Hell, you're an employer with headaches. How many people do you have working for your firm now?"

"Four full-timers, several part-timers."

"And overhead."

"Yeah, plenty of that."

"And bureaucracies to contend with."

"Right."

"And bills to pay."

"Get to the point, Gene."

"We're creating slots for special liaisons to various federal law enforcement agencies. They'll be independent contractors who report directly to me. The cases would run the gamut from computer crimes to drugs and customs violations to whatever other weirdness this island attracts. You work only on the cases that interest you. No benefits, but the pay is damn good. Have I tempted you yet?"

"Keep talking."

"We'd pay moving expenses. If your wife's interested in being a part of it, we'd be delighted to have her."

"What're the schools like here?"

"The best in the state."

Of course. To a Tango fritter, the island had the best of everything. "Day care?"

"Eight facilities so far on the island. All of them excellent. Your daughter will be reading before she hits kindergarten."

"When is this going to start up?"

"We'll be ready to roll by the first of the year. We're working out the details now with the feds."

"It sounds intriguing."

Frederick grinned. "That's the point. Look, think it over, discuss it with your wife, then we'll talk again."

They stopped at the edge of the ocean, where gulls swooped through the hot light and sandpipers scurried across the wet sand. "There's a certain magic about this island, Mike, and every time we have a murder here, some of that magic is eroded. That pisses me off. So the sooner you find Ross Blade, the happier I'll be."

"I'm not convinced Blade is guilty of anything except bad judgment for splitting. Listen to this." He slipped the receiver/recorder out of his shirt pocket, rewound it, turned it on. Frederick listened with rapt attention and didn't say anything until the tape ended.

"I won't ask how you got that."

"With a little help from some friends."

"It's not admissible evidence."

"I really don't think the kid did it, Gene."

Frederick jammed his hands into the pockets of his slacks and kicked at a clump of seaweed. "Frankly, I don't either. I went fishing a couple of times with Lou and Ross. He impressed me as a sharp kid who revered the ground Lou walked on. As for those ugly rumors about sexual abuse . . ." He shook his head. "I don't buy it. Lou was as heterosexual as a man gets. But Christ, the evidence is tough to argue with. It was Blade's knife, Mike."

"Suppose he was framed?"

"It has crossed my mind. With his police record, he'd make a convenient scapegoat. And David Vicente certainly had access to Lou's house. An old family friend and all that. But I just can't see Vicente killing Lou in the hopes that he would have a better chance of getting his hands on the grove."

"Maybe it's not the grove. What do you know about Juan Domingo?"

"That he was a marauding prick who pillaged a fortune in his travels through the Caribbean. The chamber of commerce hype makes him sound like he had some sort of epiphany that prompted him to build the church. I figure he just had a guilty conscience. Why?"

"There's some speculation that he may have built Lou's house for a black slave who was his concubine until he freed her, then she became his mistress."

"Yeah, I remember Lou mentioning something about it. But what's that got to do with anything?"

McCleary explained what he knew and what he suspected. To his surprise, Frederick didn't laugh when he got to the part about the ghost. About the noises in the house. About his experience this morning when he had felt someone touching him.

"Twenty years ago if you'd told me this story, Mike, I would've laughed. But I've seen things on this island that don't make sense to a reasonable man and I'm not as quick to laugh anymore."

"My theory, for what it's worth, is that Domingo buried part of his booty in that grove or maybe in the house and that's why Vicente wants the land."

"Greed." He nodded. "Yeah, I can buy greed as a motive, even when it's someone as rich as Vicente. You talked to his wife?"

"I don't know where to find her."

Frederick grinned. "The Tango Rehab Center three miles east of the Cove. Don't know how you'll get in to talk to her, but you'll figure out something. Just keep me informed directly."

"What about Marion?"

"It's still her investigation, but ultimately everything in the department is my responsibility. So if there's any doubt this kid isn't guilty, I want to know about it. I'll back you up as much as I can. If you get into deep shit, though, you're on your own."

Standard practice.

"Oh, by the way. A friend of Blade's was found dead up in the preserve."

"Yeah, I heard," McCleary replied.

Frederick looked amused. "You tapped into the grapevine damn fast, Mike."

"Lucky break. So are you going to charge Blade with the murder?"

"We're intensifying the search."

"And if you find him? What then?"

"I don't think we're going to get that lucky. This is a street kid, Mike, he knows the ropes, he's got friends. Besides, I'm banking on you finding him first."

"Why not just knock off the search?"

"C'mon," Frederick said with a laugh, pulling a cigar from his pocket. "You know how the game works. It's all politics, especially on Tango. If I suddenly called off the search, I'd have the goddamn mayor all over me. The news media would shit." He lit the cigar and blew three perfect smoke rings into the air. "You find him first, get him someplace safe, and we'll work out something. In the meantime, think seriously about my offer, Mike."

"I will."

"Now I'm going back to my fishing," he said, and strolled off without another word.

McCleary stopped at the first phone and called the Island Garage. Ferret answered the phone. "Yo, you break 'em, we fix 'em. What can I do you for?"

"Ferret, it's Mike. Can you meet me at the Tango Rehab Center? I may need someone to act as a diversion."

He chuckled. "Off to see Mrs. Vicente, huh? Sure, I'll meet you up there. There aren't any fences, so getting in isn't a problem. But you'll need to know which cottage she's in. When do you want to meet?"

"Half an hour. Wear a brown uniform. You'll be delivering a floral arrangement."

He laughed. "Got just the thing. See you there."

14

I

Quin took a shortcut through the hills to the Tango hospital, where Marion had said to meet her. Hospitals were not high on her list of desirable places to visit, she had seen too many of them in her years with McCleary. But this one was tucked back against a wooded area and had a certain charm about it, as though its designation as a hospital was only a masquerade, a cover.

The volunteer at the desk directed her to the morgue in the bowels of the building. She rode the freight elevator and stepped out into a dimly lit corridor, an eerie twilight of clanking pipes and cold concrete walls, where the air smelled of tight, dark spaces, earth, water, the inside of a coffin.

The door to the morgue was open and she could hear the drone of a man's voice somewhere inside. The stink of cleansers, Clorox and Pine Sol and other smells she couldn't identify, hung thickly in the air.

"Marion?"

"Back here, Quin."

She passed through a small office and entered a much larger

room where the walls were lined with silver drawers. *The dead's first stop en route to wherever,* she thought. Marion was standing several feet from an autopsy table, where a man in surgical greens stood over a body, speaking softly into a mike as he worked. When he wasn't talking, he whistled or hummed to himself, snatches from musicals, old Beatles tunes, nursery rhymes.

What the hell, she thought. Every coroner she'd ever met had some way of mitigating what he or she lived with day after day. If whistling while you worked did the trick, go for it. He raised his head and nodded as Quin walked over to Marion.

"Is that the guy who was found up in the preserve?" Quin whispered.

Marion seemed surprised. "How'd you know about that?"

"I heard it at the Tango Cafe." *Thank you, Ferret.*

"Christ, the grapevine on this island is better than goddamn television. His name's Eduardo Jimenez, his friends called him Rico. He was a buddy of Blade's. I think he was helping him out and Blade figured he couldn't have a loose end like that running around, so he wasted him."

"With a gun."

"You heard that on the grapevine, too?"

Quin nodded.

"It was a nine millimeter."

"A shot right through the carotid," the coroner said. "Point blank."

Marion introduced her to Bill Prentiss, the county coroner. "Quin was a friend of Lou's. She and her husband have been staying at his place."

"Lou was a friend of mine, too. Every coroner's nightmare is finding someone you know lying on this table." He turned on a hose and began washing blood and tissue down the drain. "At least this guy died fairly quickly. I wish I could say the same for Lou."

Quin tilted her head toward the body. "The shot to the neck killed him immediately?"

"Yeah, but the shot to the knee was first. It shattered his kneecap."

Tell me what I want to know or I'll blow off your kneecap. Mafioso stuff, she thought. She just couldn't imagine a seventeen-year-old kid like Ross Blade doing it.

"What about time of death, Bill?" asked Marion.

"You said he was found around five-thirty this morning, right?"

"Yeah."

"Then I'd have to place the time of death between two and five. There was blood and dirt under his nails and dirt in his hair. The perp shot him in the knee and he ended up on the ground, clutching his knee."

"In your autopsy report on Lou," Quin said, "you said he'd had sex shortly before he was killed."

"No, I said I found semen. Lou's semen. Since there were no other fluids except his own and forensics didn't find a used condom in the house, I'd have to conclude that he had masturbated sometime that evening and hadn't washed up."

"Or maybe the condom hasn't been found," Quin said.

Marion shook her head. "Damn unlikely. That house was turned inside out."

Prentiss pulled a sheet over Rico's body, removed his mask, peeled off his gloves, tossed both into a nearby receptacle, and began washing up. He was a nice-looking man and, considering what he did for a living, seemed remarkably ordinary, balanced. "It's a possibility, Marion. I mean, bottom line, only Lou knows for sure what happened and he isn't talking. As far as I can tell, there's nothing in this homicide to connect it to Lou's."

"Just because the MOs are different, doesn't mean the kid's innocent, Bill," said Marion.

"Hey, I'm just giving you my two cents' worth. How soon do you need the autopsy report?"

"This evening?"

"I think I can swing that. Nice meeting you, Quin," he said, then turned his back on them and finishing scrubbing.

Marion tilted her head toward the door. "I need some fresh air."

They left through an exit in the basement and emerged in the hospital parking lot. The hot air was a welcome reprieve from the odors in the morgue. "Bill's an excellent coroner," Marion said. "But I don't always agree with his conclusions."

"They sounded reasonable to me."

"You and Mike have already made up your minds about Blade, haven't you. That he didn't do it."

Hostility: that was what Quin heard in her voice. "Why're you so defensive about this, Marion?"

"Defensive?" Her brows shot up. "Is that what you think? My God, Quin, this kid's knife was sticking out of Lou's chest. How much clearer does it have to be?"

Leave it alone. But she couldn't. "Did you know Lou had an affair with Janna Hilliard? That tarot card reader?"

Marion burst out laughing. "C'mon. Tell me you're joking. Janna's a fucking fruitcake."

"Lou hired her to do an exorcism on the house."

Her smile vanished. "The more I hear, the nuttier Lou gets. What other little tidbits have you and Mike stumbled on?"

"Well, let's see. I don't know what all the implications on this might be, but Gracie is screwing Craig Peck."

It was obviously news to her. She shook her head. "You see what this island is like, Quin? Relationships are incestuous, they have to be, Tango's too small for it to be otherwise."

She had missed the point entirely. But then again, she was fixated on Blade as the perp, so why would it be otherwise? "I'd say that casts a somewhat darker suspicion on Gracie."

"It could. Except that I'm not looking for suspects. I already know who did it."

End of story, end of discussion. They had reached Lou's

Camaro and Marion ran her hand over the roof. "Piece of junk," she said.

Quin felt a trifle defensive about the car simply because it had been Lou's; it amounted to just one more irritating criticism of him. "It runs well," she said. "And it's fast."

Marion's eyes softened briefly. "Lou was lucky to have a friend like you, Quin."

"If I had been a better friend these last few years, maybe he wouldn't be dead."

"Things happen despite our best intentions."

It sounded as though she were talking about herself. "I've got to scoot," Quin said. "Talk to you later." She slid behind the wheel of Lou's car and took a kind of comfort in knowing that she was breathing air that he had once breathed.

When Quin got back to the house, she found a message on the machine from Christine Redman. "Slick, weather permitting I'll be there tomorrow morning at ten. If it's going to be later than that, I'll call. Hang in there, girl."

Quin doled out eighteen pills and capsules from the bottles lined up on the counter. Antioxidants, amino acids, herbs, a B complex, a mineral complex, calcium, enzymes. It seemed excessive even to her. But the fact was that before she had started this regimen five months ago, her hot flashes were so severe she couldn't sleep through the night and she had rarely gotten through a day without changing clothes at least once.

Worse than the hot flashes, though, were the extreme fluctuations in her moods, an emotional and spiritual PMS. Within two weeks of starting the program, she had noticed a marked improvement. Now she hadn't had a hot flash in four months and, although McCleary might disagree, her moods had evened out and she could look at herself in the mirror without wondering who the hell she was.

She gulped down the pills, then went upstairs. She tossed her purse and packages on the futon, stripped off her clothes. She could still smell the morgue on herself. Shower, a long hot shower, she thought.

The bathroom connected with the guest room, where they were staying. The absence of windows made it seem smaller than it was, claustrophobic. She left the door open to compensate for it and turned on the shower.

It was a glass stall, which exacerbated her claustrophobia. She wondered how the bathroom had escaped the numerous refurbishments to the house, why Lou or his father hadn't put in something more contemporary. The water, though, was hot and plentiful and she stood for a long time under the spray with her eyes closed, the needles drumming her shoulders and back. Her thoughts, untethered, drifted to that famous shower scene in *Psycho*. Her eyes snapped open.

What the hell.

The light had gone off, it was pitch black in here. At the very least there should be light coming through the door from the bedroom. She turned off the shower and for seconds just stood there, her heart hammering. Water dripped softly, steadily. That was all she heard.

So the bulb burned out and the door swung shut, big deal.

But in her heart she knew it wasn't that simple.

She pushed the stall door open, held it ajar with her hand, and fixed her eyes on the crack of light under the bathroom door. Then she lurched toward it, threw it open, and ran into the bedroom.

Light poured through the window, cool air hissed from the ceiling vents, her purse and package were still on the futon, her clothes were still on the floor. Nothing had changed. Nothing. She laughed nervously and glanced back at the doorway. The light was still off. Of course it was, the damn bulb had burned out. But that didn't explain how the door had shut.

Quin snatched up McCleary's towel from the back of the

rocker where he must have tossed it that morning, rubbed her hair with it, wrapped it around herself. She rummaged through the suitcase on the floor for clean clothes and kept glancing at the bathroom as she dressed. The light stayed off, the door remained open.

Go on, test it, get it over with.

She walked over to the door, nudged it with her toes. It was made of thick, heavy wood and barely moved. She reached inside the doorway, hit the switch on the wall, and the light winked on. Quin wrenched back, her heart thudding in her chest like some badly neglected engine.

"Do it again," she whispered. "Do it while I'm watching. C'mon."

The light stayed on.

"Coward." She didn't know if she meant the spook or herself.

She scooped her purse and package off the bed and flew downstairs. She deposited everything on the kitchen table and rummaged through the bag until she found the cassette recorder. She tore open a box of tapes, popped one in, and walked into the hall whispering, "Testing, testing." When she rewound it and played it back, her voice came through loud and clear.

Quin hadn't been into the den since she had recorded the weeping their first night here. The air was cool, but not appreciably cooler than anywhere else in the house. The blinds were lowered, not much light leaked through the slats. She stood just inside the door, her back to the wall, and listened to the thick, waiting silence.

"Okay, you got my attention." Her voice cracked. She cleared her throat and said it again, louder this time. She felt ridiculous, but what the hell, she was in here now, she would keep it up. "What is it you want?"

The cassette recorder whirred softly.

Language, sure, that was the problem. This was a Cuban spook. "*¿Que quiere?*"

Silence.

"How can I help you?" she asked in Spanish.

Nothing.

"Hey, you started this and now you've got an audience. So get on with it."

This didn't get any response either.

"Fine, have it your way. This was a stupid idea, anyway."

Quin was halfway down the hall when something crashed in the den. She ran back into the room, into a thick chill. Books were strewn across the floor in front of the bookcase, a dozen or more. On the shelf where they had stood, the books to the right had toppled inward to fill the space. But the books on the left were held upright by a thick, hefty hardback, and it was this which drew her across the room, drew her despite the eerie cold, the waiting stillness.

The book was García Márquez's *One Hundred Years of Solitude.*

She gripped it at the top to pull it off the shelf, but it dropped forward instead. Suddenly, a portion of the bookcase began to move, to yawn inward like a huge jaw. "Sweet Christ," she whispered.

Moments later, she walked into the oldest part of the house, a secret chapter in Lou's life.

II

On his way to the Tango Rehab Center, McCleary bought a bouquet of cut flowers at a shop in Pirate's Cove. Tiny pink carnations surrounded by baby's breath and a spray of ferns—just right for a woman recovering from a stroke.

The rehab center looked like a resort, three acres of rolling hills covered in Florida pines, wildflowers, two dozen or so A-frame cabins, and a main building that resembled a Swiss chalet. Just as Ferret had said, getting in wouldn't be a problem: no fence, no guardhouse, no one checking ID.

He parked in the visitors' lot, and while he waited for Ferret, he removed the blank greeting card from the envelope. On it he printed: For Amelia from Lou. He slipped it back into the envelope, printed her name on the front, and sealed the envelope.

When he glanced up, a white van was pulling into a space two cars down. Ferret trotted over and, sure enough, he was wearing a brown uniform with a tag across the shirt pocket that read, Tango Florist. He tugged his cap down lower over his forehead, stooped over so he was even with the window, and grinned. "How's this?"

"Looks authentic."

"It is."

McCleary guessed that Ferret and Bino had a room filled with costumes, disguises, electronic gizmos, vans, tanks, and probably weapons as well. He passed the flowers through the window and Ferret took them, then slipped on a pair of shades.

"Even your mother wouldn't recognize you," McCleary remarked.

"Good thing, since Mrs. Vicente has seen me a time or two." Ferret walked off toward the main building, whistling to himself.

Through the trees, McCleary saw a swimming pool, jogging trails, bike paths. People were out and about, some in wheelchairs, some walking with canes, some moving under their own steam. They were young and old and in between, victims of strokes, of nervous disorders, of accidents. It disturbed him to watch these people.

One of his greatest fears was that he would become like them when he was old, that he would be lame or addled or so infirm and out of it that he would not be able to care for himself. His daughter or Quin would be faced with the kind of choice that many people eventually had to deal with concerning their own parents. How old was too old? Seventy? Eighty? Ninety? A hundred?

Quality of life, the experts said, was the determining factor. That sounded like a line from an Ex-Lax commercial, but it happened to fit this point in his life. Given his druthers, he would rather grow old on Tango Key than in Palm Beach or Miami or any of the other places he had lived. This island possessed a peculiar magic that he had encountered nowhere else. Past, present, and future seemed to coexist here, as if Tango were some sort of portal that made such a disparity possible.

Right about now, he thought, he could use a little magic. What the hell was taking Ferret so long, anyway?

As soon as he thought it, he saw a man exit the main building with a bouquet and head up the jogging path. McCleary got out of the car and followed him at a discreet distance, then waited on a shaded bench near the pool while the orderly went inside one of the cabins. A few minutes later, he appeared again and walked back toward the main building.

McCleary remained where he was for a few minutes, watching the door of cabin 14 to see if anyone else came out. The air here was hot and strangely still. He could hear the whoop of a tennis ball as it was whacked back and forth on a court that wasn't visible from where he sat. He could hear birds, the cough of an engine. Then Ferret sank to the bench beside him, opened a magazine, and pulled a sandwich out of his jacket pocket. "Go on. She's alone in there. I'll make sure you aren't interrupted." He bit into the sandwich like a rodent would, a small, determined nibble, and paged through his magazine. When McCleary didn't get up immediately, he glanced at him over the rims of his shades. "What?"

"You mind if I ask you a personal question?"

"Depends on the question."

"Why're you doing this?"

His lips pulled back; a bud of grape jelly stained one of his front teeth. McCleary thought it vaguely resembled a drop of very dark blood. "You think I have some complicated reason for wanting to see Lou's killer strung up by the nuts?"

"Do you?"

"Nope." He poked his sunglasses back farther onto the

bridge of his nose and gazed out through the heat, the stillness. "It's really pretty simple. Inside of me there's a little old man who likes his tea in the morning, enjoys his afternoon naps, and finds a certain pleasure and comfort in the order of things. Murder shatters that order. And when the victim is someone I like and respect, I consider it a personal affront, Mike. Since I find bureaucracies tedious and beside the point, I do what I can to make things right." He patted McCleary's shoulder. "And that's where you come in."

"You're weird, Ferret."

He laughed. "Thank Christ."

McCleary got up and walked over to cabin 14 and knocked. The woman who answered the door was in a wheelchair, a tiny wisp of a thing with muscular arms and toothpick legs. The left side of her face sagged, her left leg was useless. But the shrewd intelligence in her eyes was unmistakable; she knew the flowers were from him.

She gestured toward the vase, which graced a low coffee table on the other side of the room. "Qui'tiful." Her speech was badly slurred, but it didn't seem to deter her in the least. "Yu'n'Lou?"

It took him a moment to translate it: You knew Lou?

"My name's Mike McCleary, Mrs. Vicente. I'm investigating Lou Hernando's murder."

The pain in her eyes was like some thick, heavy liquid. She motioned him inside, he shut the door, and she propelled her wheelchair toward a sitting area where a TV was turned on, the volume low. There was a work area in front of the window with an IBM computer that was on, an interactive game in progress. The computer, he noted, was a model that sold for about eight grand retail and did just about everything except fart.

She noticed his interest and said, "Kees'me . . ."

It sounded like "kiss me."

Her mouth twitched and she started over again, struggling to enunciate more clearly. "Kees. My. Bray. Shop."

Keeps my brain sharp.

"Would it be easier for you to type out the answers?"

She nodded and guided the wheelchair over to the computer. Considering how limited her mobility was, her hands moved with astonishing agility and speed as she exited the game program and went into WordPerfect. She opened a file and typed: *I was very fond of Lou. He was a good friend before my stroke and a good friend afterward. I can't say that about most people I know.*

"Did you know that two of his large bonds were forfeited?" McCleary asked.

She turned those dark eyes on him, nodded, started to say something, then resorted to the computer again. *Yes, I knew. He talked about it when he visited me. I offered to buy one acre of the grove for the amount he needed to pay off the bond. He refused. He was afraid my husband would use it to expand the resort. I was quite incapacitated then and Lou knew I wasn't in a position to stop David from doing anything.*

"So David wanted the land for the resort."

You'll have to ask him.

"I have. I'd like to hear it from you."

She looked at him again and he sensed the enormity of her struggle. Amelia Vicente, imprisoned in a body that no longer worked right, apparently forgotten by people she had considered friends and neglected by her husband, had reached a reluctant compromise with life. Lou's friendship had mitigated her loneliness, but her loyalty to him didn't extend to betrayal of her husband. She wasn't about to tell McCleary everything she knew or suspected about her husband's business affairs.

He prodded her. "I need your help to piece things together, Mrs. Vicente."

She rubbed her eyes and gazed for a moment at the TV, where Ross Blade's mug shot and Lou's photo stood side by side in the lower-right-hand corner of the screen. She pointed, then typed furiously.

What's there to investigate about the murder? The police already know who did it.

"I'm not convinced they're right."

Was Lou a friend of yours?

"Yes. Eight years ago he bailed me out of a murder charge, the only bondsman in Dade County who would touch the case. I was framed, just as I think Ross Blade was."

By my husband? Is that what you're saying?

"I'm not accusing anyone, Mrs. Vicente. But I think your husband wants that grove for something other than the resort and that you know exactly what I'm talking about. I'd appreciate anything you can tell me."

The line sounded like something you learned in a PI correspondence course and he immediately regretted saying it.

"Ti'fo'y't'lea." Time for you to leave.

She spun the wheelchair away from the computer and headed for the door. McCleary hit the *Escape* button on the keyboard without saving to the disk; he didn't want a record of her responses.

"G'bye, Ms'ter McCler," she said, holding the door open.

McCleary shut the door and she backed up her wheelchair, gazing at him with an eerie acceptance. If he suddenly pulled a gun on her, he knew her expression would remain unchanged. This was a woman who had learned to roll with the punches.

"If you're protecting your husband, Mrs. Vicente, you'd better think twice about it. He isn't sitting around waiting for you to improve."

"Wha'spo't'mea?" What's that supposed to mean?

A wall went up, her expression turned to stone. McCleary slipped the receiver/recorder out of his shirt pocket, rewound it, turned it on. It was a deliberately cruel thing to do, certainly worse than any of the games Doris Lynch played with her wildlife up on her hill, but he needed what Amelia Vicente knew.

The voices of Doris Lynch and David Vicente curled like smoke through the stillness. Amelia's expression didn't change until Vicente said: *It's going to work out.*

Which part?

Blade, McCleary, the property, us. All of it.

That word, *us,* brought a rush of blood to her face and turned her eyes as dark as wet streets. "*Ge'ou!*" she snapped.

"If you change your mind about talking to me, Mrs. Vicente, here's my card." He dropped it in her lap and left.

She slammed the door, threw something at it that shattered. The glass tinkled like wind chimes as it rained to the floor.

He glanced at the bench where he and Ferret had sat; the rodent was gone.

"Quin?" His voice echoed in the hallway.

When she didn't answer, he figured she was upstairs napping. He went into the kitchen for something cold to drink and saw the packages on the table, the empty box that had held a cassette recorder, and a pack of tapes with one missing.

And she called *him* obsessive?

He did an about-face, hurried down the hall, and felt the chill before he reached the doorway of the den. It drifted from the room like an invisible fog and smelled faintly of earth, a freshly dug hole.

Goose bumps broke out on his arms, the skin between his eyes tightened and burned and itched like crazy.

"Quin?"

Part of the bookcase on the wall in front of him stood ajar, revealing a small room made of stone. Quin was sitting at a roll-top desk inside, hunched over something, her hair falling like a veil at the sides of her face.

When he said her name again, her head turned slowly, as though the neck muscles were stiff. Her expression was completely blank, empty, as though she had just awakened and didn't realize yet that she was awake.

He stammered, "How . . ."

"Mac." She looked puzzled, as though she couldn't figure out what he was doing here. Then she dropped the pencil she was holding, rubbed her hands over her arms, looked at the pad of paper in front of her.

McCleary was inside the room then. The cold seeped through his clothing, his skin, and sank into his bones. He touched Quin's shoulders, felt the chill of her skin through the fabric, and pulled her to her feet. "C'mon, you're ice cold."

Her teeth were chattering now.

She began to tremble.

He picked up the pad and got her out of the stone room and into a rocker on the porch. Then he hurried back into the house, whipped the afghan off the couch in the sunroom, and sprinted back to the porch. Her eyes were squeezed shut, and she was clutching the pad he had dropped into her lap. McCleary draped the afghan around her shoulders.

"Tell me what happened," he said.

And she did, in a slow, halting voice. The light in the bathroom, the tape recorder, the books falling from the bookcase, *One Hundred Years of Solitude.* When she was finished, she showed him the pad; three pages were filled with a slanted, ornate script that was nothing at all like her handwriting. Some words were large, two to a page; others were very small, squeezed together, difficult to make out.

"Did you write this?" he asked.

"I don't know. I remember . . ." She squinted as if against the sun and gazed out toward the lake. "No. No, I don't think I did."

"It's not in English or Spanish."

"Then what the hell is it?"

"I think it's Latin."

"Latin?" She emitted a soft, choked laugh. Her face was very pale, beads of perspiration had sprung across her forehead, her upper lip. She threw off the afghan. "I don't know Latin. I never even took a course in Latin. I definitely didn't write that, Mac."

"What's the last thing you remember?"

"Sitting down at the desk to search the cubbyholes. The next thing I knew, you were here. I'm almost afraid to ask what time it is."

"Five-thirty or so."

Her eyes widened. "My God, I was in there for two hours, Mac."

He pulled a chair over in front of her and sat down. "Do you want to move to a motel?"

"Definitely not."

"You weren't crazy about staying here to begin with."

"I'm not crazy about the idea now. But if we move, we might as well hang up this investigation and go home. Luz's legacy is the key to all of this, Mac."

He agreed, but there were limits to what even he would risk for answers.

"Look," she went on, "this case is no riskier than any of the others we've investigated. The difference is that we don't have much experience with"—she gestured toward the house—"with whatever's in this place. I'd like to see what Christine picks up."

"Well, we've got Gene Frederick on our side now."

She touched his beard, ran her hand over it. "I hear a story."

"Over dinner. I'm cooking. We'll eat out here."

"Such service."

The squeak of the rocker followed him into the house. He popped leftover pizza in the microwave, then went into the den. The cold was gone now and the stone room yawned, a black hole. He gathered up the books from the floor and stacked them on the shelf next to *One Hundred Years of Solitude.*

It was tilted forward, resting on the spine, and when he tried to pull it off the shelf, it wouldn't budge. A lever was stuck between the inside of the spine and the binding of the book. A push upward made the movable part of the bookcase creak inward; a pull forward opened it wide once more. A nifty little gadget. He wondered which generation of Hernandos had devised it.

McCleary turned on all the lights in the den and walked into the room. Desk, filing cabinet, a cot, and some other items that he recognized as staples in the practice of *santería*. He knew Lou's mother had been a practicing *santera,* but he was fairly sure Lou had never dabbled. Did that mean Luz had?

Luz: as though she were a real person. He had started thinking of her like that, as a name, a personality. Let a shrink in on this, he thought, and he and Quin would be found wanting in the mental clarity department.

He picked up the recorder from the desk, hit *Play*, and listened to Quin's voice as he opened the drawers in the cabinet. Empty. But they hadn't always been empty; he found several plastic label holders. The desk didn't yield much of interest, some unpaid bills and several small drawing pads that contained rudimentary sketches of some of the scenes in the paintings. He was sure someone had been in here since Lou's death and Blade seemed the most likely possibility.

The tide, he thought, was definitely beginning to turn. But in whose favor was anyone's guess.

15

I

Roey stood on the wharf, listening to the wind as it whipped in off the Gulf. Up and down the docks, fishermen were preparing their boats for the morning, pulling in their nets, packing up for the night. In another twenty minutes, even the fast-food joints that catered to the fishermen would be sealed up until five tomorrow morning.

He waited by the Shrimp Shack, watching one of the fishermen wolf down an order of fried shrimp. Deep-fried shrimp with more fat per square millimeter than a slice of pecan pie. Grease glistened on his lips; Roey felt like puking.

He ordered a cup of espresso and walked down the dock a ways. The manila envelope zipped into his windbreaker felt like an extra appendage against his ribs. The last time he'd been here he'd also been carrying a package, a box with an engagement ring in it, a sapphire surrounded by diamond chips. He had offered it to the only woman he'd ever given a shit about and she had told him thanks, but no thanks, it's over, finito, finished.

He had stood at the edge of the dock that night with a gun at his temple, his finger squeezing the trigger again and again and again. Russian roulette, four tries total, that was what he had allotted himself. And when he'd popped out the clip, the bullet had been the next shot. The fifth shot. Then he had taken the ring from his pocket and hurled it out into the dark.

Now he hated her, hated her because she had reduced him to such desperation. She was the only woman who had ever gotten to him. She had wiggled under his skin like a succulent worm until he was unable to tell where her flesh ended and his own began.

He claimed a bench at the end of the dock and pretty soon he heard Vicente's footsteps—quick, light, urgent. Vicente didn't sit on the bench, he stood in front of it in his jeans, his windbreaker, his baseball cap, his tourist disguise. "You lost him, Tom." His voice was as flat as three-day-old Coke.

"He had help."

"I don't give a shit if God helped him." Vicente slipped a handkerchief from his back pocket and smoothed it out over the bench. Then he sat down on it. Roey expected him to whip out his little bottle of alcohol and sterilize the bench on either side of him. "I want the kid gone. I can't make it any clearer than that."

"I've got a few other cards to play."

"I do hope they're better cards than what you've had so far."

"He's just a kid, Mr. Vicente. And he's running scared."

"He's also very bright, very shrewd, and he evidently has some friends on the island who're willing to hide him."

Roey didn't say anything. For several long, uncomfortable moments, he and Vicente sat in silence, the noises of the wharf drifting around them.

"McCleary dropped in to see my wife today."

There it was, Roey thought. The bottom line. And the way Vicente said it implied that the Mrs. had been enlightened about her husband's affair with Doris Lynch. Personally, Roey didn't give a damn one way or another who slept with whom. But a long time ago he had made a point of uncovering dirt on each of his employers just in case he needed it for leverage.

"His visit has created certain problems for me," Vicente continued. "His presence on the island, in fact, has become something of a nuisance. I think it's time the welcome mat was jerked out from under him."

"I already have something in mind," Roey said.

"It'd better be good, Tom, because if they don't take the hint, I'll have to take more drastic measures."

"Seems to me it'd be easier to just get rid of them and the kid at the same time."

"It may come to that." Pause. The clicks and hums of the darkness punctuated the quiet. "We would renegotiate, of course."

Roey followed the cue and also hesitated before he spoke. "It would have to be quite a bit more than what you've paid me so far."

Bemused, Vicente said: "It's premature to talk about more money, Tom. I have yet to see results for the twenty thousand I've paid you to this point."

"The twenty would be deductible."

"We'll talk about it if and when it comes to that."

"I'd like to settle on a fee now."

"We'll discuss it when I've seen results." Vicente's voice held an unpleasant edge that irritated Roey.

"Look, Mr. Vicente. I've worked for you off and on for five years now. When you wanted dirt on the zoning commissioner, I got it for you. When you . . ."

"I know what jobs I've hired you for." The edge in his voice was sharper now. "And I'm well aware that you've been discreet and efficient. But the fact remains that I haven't seen any results yet for what I've already paid you."

The ball had now fallen in Roey's court. Once he reached inside his windbreaker, he knew he better be prepared to get up and walk away from the whole goddamn thing, if it came to that. He thought about it for a moment, San Miguel de Allende as an event in some other man's life, his future merely more of the same. He had nothing to lose. Nothing.

He unzipped his windbreaker and brought out the envelope. He unclipped a penlight from his shirt pocket and handed both items to Vicente. "Those are just copies."

There was something almost tragic about Vicente's silence as he went through the photographs inside. They were color glossies of Vicente with Doris Lynch on her yacht and his. They were sunbathing in the nude, swimming in the nude, embracing on private, hidden beaches in the Bahamas. The deckhand who had taken them had since moved on to another job, but Roey had paid him a small fortune for the pictures.

They weren't as incriminating, however, as the two photos of Vicente with a woman who was maybe eighteen, a sweet young thing he had picked up at Lester's one night.

Roey had snapped the picture about seven months ago, when the two of them were coming out of a motel in Key West, their arms around each other, their heads thrown back as they laughed at something, their faces perfectly visible. Mrs. Vicente might tolerate Doris Lynch, but no way in hell would she put up with eighteen-year-olds. Vicente couldn't afford a divorce or a scandal that might put a glitch in the construction of the resort.

"So," Vicente said, as he slipped the photos back into the envelope and set it on the bench between them. "Just how much money are we talking about, Tom?"

Roey pretended to consider it. "I'm not a greedy man, Mr. Vicente. Two-fifty would do it. Half up front, half on delivery of positive proof that Blade and McCleary are out of your hair. You get the negatives and I buy a one-way ticket out of the country."

He could almost hear the wheels turning in Vicente's head as he weighed his options. What this would cost him, what that would cost him. "I'm afraid one-fifty is as high as I can go, Tom."

"I guess I'll have to get the difference from your wife."

"For a quarter of a million dollars I can hire a professional from Atlantic City who would take out the McClearys, the kid, *and* you."

"Then do it," Roey said, and got up from the bench and started back up the dock.

The distance between them filled with warm, black air, the silence on the dock. Roey imagined that he could hear a door creaking shut behind him, a door closing on a future he might have had.

"Two hundred," Vicente said, coming up behind him on feet of silk. "Twenty-five tonight, another twenty-five by noon tomorrow and I get the negatives of myself and the young woman. Two more payments of seventy-five when the boy and McCleary are taken care of and I get the rest of the negatives."

Roey considered it, but not for long. "I can live with that, except that the first negatives you get are of you and Doris Lynch."

Vicente didn't like that part, but there wasn't much he could do about it. "Then let's go back to the office and get that first payment squared away."

Just that fast, Roey's future burned like some bright new sun.

II

They had agreed to meet at nine in a conference room in cyberspace. Blade was early, he was fed up with waiting, going stir crazy in the captain's quarters. When he wasn't watching the clock, he was staring at the low ceiling or listening to the engines of the ferry as it churned from east to west to east again and again.

On the island, the search for him had heated up. He had made it to the evening news and had heard the lies, seen the interview with Doris Lynch, listened to the broadcaster talk about Rico as though he were just one more miserable statistic. And here he was, hiding out as if he were actually guilty of something. Hiding out because he was afraid.

Lou deserved better than this. So did Rico. *So do I.*

<R.BLADE HAS ARRIVED.>

<R.BLADE> CHARLIE, YOU AROUND?

<C.LYNCH1> DOWN HERE IN THE RIGHT-HAND CORNER. :)

<R.BLADE> I THOUGHT I WAS EARLY.

<C.LYNCH1> WE BOTH ARE. DID YOU CATCH THE NEWS?

<R.BLADE> YEAH.

<C.LYNCH1> DORIS GOT HER FIFTEEN SECONDS OF FAME. WHAT DO YOU THINK OF THE ATTACHED FILE?

<R.BLADE> A SHOCK. LOU NEVER SAID ANYTHING.

<C.LYNCH1> MIKE MCCLEARY WAS AT THE HOUSE TODAY. I THINK HE'S OKAY, HE SAID HE DOESN'T BELIEVE YOU KILLED LOU. I SAW HIM BUG OUR PHONE.

<R.BLADE> MAYBE HE DID IT TO FIND OUT IF YOU'RE IN TOUCH WITH ME.

<C.LYNCH1> THAT WAS THE FIRST THING THAT CROSSED MY MIND. BUT I JUST DON'T GET THOSE KIND OF VIBES FROM HIM. YOU NEED TO TRUST SOMEONE, ROSS.

<R.BLADE> I TRUST YOU.

<C.LYNCH1> WHY?

<R.BLADE> I'VE MET YOU. I'VE NEVER MET HIM.

<C.LYNCH1> BUT I HAVE AND I TRUST HIM FOR THE SAME REASON YOU TRUST ME.

<R.BLADE> OKAY, YOU WIN. :) FOR THE TIME BEING LET'S SAY HE'S TRUSTWORTHY.

<C.LYNCH1> SO TALK TO HIM. IF YOU DON'T WANT TO DO IT FACE-TO-FACE, DO IT ONLINE.

<R.Blade> I'll think about it.
<C.Lynch1> Silence.
<R.Blade> LOL. C'mon, talk to me, Charlie.
<C.Lynch1> Thinking.
<R.Blade> Think out loud.
<C.Lynch1> You first, Ross.
<R.Blade> Do you sail?
<C.Lynch1> Sometimes. You?
<R.Blade> A couple times. I'd like to buy a boat and name her Someday and sail her to the Marquesas.
<C.Lynch1> Through the Panama locks?
<R.Blade> Definitely.
<C.Lynch1> Sign me up.
<R.Blade> Company would be great.
<C.Lynch1> Now or then?
<R.Blade> Either. Both.
<C.Lynch1> (Blushing) I could meet you somewhere.
<R.Blade> When this is over.
<C.Lynch1> It's not going to be over until you make a move, Ross.
<R.Blade> I'll move when I'm ready.
<C.Lynch1> In the meantime, do you need anything?
<R.Blade> Whatever else you can find in Doris's papers that pertain to Lou. Also, could you call the Island Garage and tell Ferret I'm okay?
<C.Lynch1> Ferret? That's his name? Ferret? What kind of name is that?
<R.Blade> The only one he's got. If he's not in, give the message to Bino.
<C.Lynch1> Ferret and Bino. Right. Tell me those are code names or something.
<R.Blade> LOL. No code names.
<C.Lynch1> OK. I'll pass on the message. Anything else?
<R.Blade> Yeah, someone killed my buddy Rico. Eduardo Jimenez. You hear about that?

<C.Lynch1> On the news. I didn't know he was your friend. I'm real sorry, Ross.

<R.Blade> I seem to have become a liability to my closest friends.

<C.Lynch1> No one knows we're friends.

<Q.McCleary has arrived.>

<Q.McCleary> Hello? Anyone here? This is Quin McCleary. Ross, if you're here, Charlie left us a note in e-mail to meet in here. We'd like to talk to you. We can do it here, if you feel comfortable with that. It's private. If someone drops in, we'll know it and we'll just stay quiet until they leave.

<C.Lynch1> I'm here. How do I know absolutely for sure who I'm talking to? Handles don't mean anything.

<Q.McCleary> What kind of proof do you need?

<C.Lynch1> Something no one else knows.

<Q.McCleary> I'm only posting that with Ross's permission.

<Q.McCleary> If you're here, Ross, now is the time to speak up.

<R.Blade> I'm here. Post your proof, Mrs. McCleary.

<M.McCleary> This is Mike, Ross. We found the room. You know which room I mean. *One Hundred Years of Solitude.* Is that good enough?

<R.Blade> That'll do. I didn't know it existed until that night you chased me, Mr. McCleary.

<M.McCleary> And you cleaned it out?

<R.Blade> Yeah. Some blueprints for the house, a journal, files, some money.

<M.McCleary> What's in the journal?

<R.Blade> A lot of it is about the spook. The rest is about him. About him and different women, him and his thoughts, shit like that.

<M.McCleary> Did you make the 911 call to the cops?

<R.Blade.> I found him. He was alive when I found him.

He said one thing to me, "Corredor." Runner. I don't know what the hell it means. My pocketknife was in his chest, I was afraid that if I pulled it out he'd die. Maybe he wouldn't have died, maybe I could've saved him, I don't know.
<C.Lynch1> Doris wasn't home that night. That might be significant.
<Q.McCleary> Charlie, do you have any idea where Doris was that night?
<C.Lynch1> She said she was going out with friends. I'm pretty sure she was with Mr. Vicente. He'd called earlier that night. He never identifies himself, he always disguises his voice. But I recognize his voice.
<Q.McCleary> Aren't they antagonists? She's conservation, he's development and they bid against each other for Lou's land.
<C.Lynch1> I don't know a whole lot about it. The few times I've mentioned him to Doris, she kind of brushes him off as an annoyance.
<R.Blade> Right before I turned into the firebreak that night, a car flew out of the trees. It was too dark to tell anything about it.
<Q.McCleary> Can we meet, Ross? I'd like to see the journal, the blueprints, whatever else you've got.
<R.Blade> Gotta split.
<C.Lynch1> Hold on, Ross.
<R.Blade has left>
<Q.McCleary> Charlie, don't go yet.
<Q.McCleary> Charlie? Look, we'll work through you if he prefers.
<C.Lynch1> I'll let you know.
<C.Lynch1 has left>
<Q.McCleary> Shit shit shit.

III

"Hurry up, boy," hissed Sammy. "We just got word that someone from the sheriff's department is coming on board when we pull in. That's about sixty seconds from now. Lemme take your things."

"No." His pack and his computer were parts of himself, the only baggage he carried. "I'll hold onto them."

He was already on his feet, the pack slung over one shoulder, the computer over the other. There wasn't time to glance around the room for clues the trained eye might pick up. Sammy was already opening the door and moving past his mate, who stood at the wheel. He popped out a panel in the floor and motioned Blade inside.

"Git. Fast. It's going to be noisy and hot, but it's the best I can do."

Blade squeezed inside a space no larger than the cabinet under a bathroom sink. Sammy fitted the panel back into place. A horrible claustrophobia crashed over him, he could hardly breathe. The engine shrieked as the power was throttled back. He shut his eyes, clenched his teeth against the noise, and pushed back into the hole as far as he could go.

The cops are going to search the ferry.

Not a breath of air seeped through the narrow crevices between the planks of wood. Sweat rolled down the sides of his face and dripped over his brows, into his eyes. The ferry slowed to an idle, he felt several hard bumps as it hugged the dock. Now: footsteps, voices, sweet Christ, he was going to be found.

Chill out, kid.

That was what Lou always said to him when he was struggling to reel in a fish. *Take a couple deep breaths.*

Blade sucked at the air, pulled it deeply into his lungs, let it out slowly. It helped, it put a little distance between him and his fear. It was as if he were standing outside of his fear, watching it. He moved his head a fraction of an inch. He could see the first mate's feet, a curve of the steering wheel. Lights flared, illuminating the dirty floor.

More footsteps.

Voices again.

". . . apologize for the intrusion, Captain . . ."

Detective O'Connor's voice. Christ, anyone but her. Anyone. Even the chief of police was better than O'Connor. She hated him. She'd shoot him on sight.

There. He could see her now, a slice of chin, of mouth, of nose and forehead, a connect-the-dots cop. ". . . just checking with . . ."

Her voice faded in and out of his awareness, an echo of the past.

". . . young man . . ."

Don't move, don't sneeze, don't do anything.

"I don't see everyone who comes on board, ma'am," replied Sammy. "But I don't recollect seeing this boy."

"What's in there?" Detective O'Connor asked.

Blade could see her finger, pointing toward the captain's quarters.

"My room," Sammy said. "Feel free to take a look, Detective. And excuse the mess."

Moments ticked by.

The heat grew more oppressive.

Then, O'Connor's voice again: "How many more trips does the ferry make tonight, Captain?"

"Just two more. Then we don't start up again until six A.M."

"And you dock on the island for the night?"

"Yes, ma'am."

"Beginning tomorrow morning, I'd like to have an officer on board who would spot-check all passengers."

"No problem, ma'am. You just send him on over around half past five and we'll get him squared away."

"Thanks very much, Captain. And sorry for the intrusion."

"Not at all, ma'am."

The footsteps receded and after what seemed a long time but probably wasn't, the engine clattered and clanked and the ferry pulled away from the dock, headed for Key West again.

16

I

Roey slipped through the grove with the ease of a snake. Thanks to the clouds that had covered most of the sky, the darkness was like India ink. The crackle of dry leaves underfoot was absorbed by the night noises and the soft, aching moan of the wind through branches. He hoped the rain held off long enough.

He had left his car in the trees on Mango Road half a mile from the grove. It was close enough for him to make it back on foot in a matter of minutes, but far enough away so that the car wouldn't be heard when he took off.

The trees thinned out about a hundred yards from the side of the house. Roey paused, even with the lopsided metal shed that stood between him and the building so that he was hidden from view. He dropped his large canvas bags on the ground, a pair of them, and crept to the edge of the trees. A single light glowed from a second-story window, a bathroom. It provided enough illumination to see the hose fastened to a faucet on the wall.

Roey darted forward, made three quick slashes in the hose

with his pocketknife, and moved along the side of the house until he reached the cable boxes, three of them, each one labeled. He popped open the Tango Bell box, cut the cables with a pair of wire clippers, and trotted back to the bags. He unzipped one and brought out a pair of latex gloves, which he snapped on. He removed a spool that contained a long fuse and soaked it in kerosene.

Roey tied one end of the fuse to the base of the nearest tree and threaded it through the crook of a low-hanging branch. He splashed kerosene on the tree, soaked the leaves on the ground around it, and began to unwind the fuse as he slipped around the shed and the corner of the porch.

The fuse reached only as far as the porch steps, so he poured kerosene over the plants and dry leaves on either side of the steps. He paid special attention to the wooden parts of the house, that sweet Florida pine that would burn like money if the fire was hot enough.

When the can was empty, he sprinted into the trees, peeled off the gloves and shoved them and the empty container into the first bag. He removed another can from the second bag, slung it and the other bag over either shoulder, and lit the fuse with a long lighter. It was a Home Depot special for lighting barbecues and cozy fires in the family hearth. A tongue of flame raced along the fuse and sparks leaped from it to the kerosene-soaked leaves.

Roey splashed kerosene to either side of him as he quickly made his way back to the fence. He pulled up on the bottom of the wire mesh, widening the opening he'd made earlier, pushed his bags through, then slithered under. He swept dry leaves and twigs into the hole and soaked them with the last of the kerosene.

He zipped the bags shut, flicked the Home Depot special again. The leaves burst into flame and the fire sped across the ground, crackling and hissing and splitting off to follow the fuse and other trails of kerosene. Birds lifted suddenly from the trees, dozens of them, their shrieks piercing the darkness. Then it was ducks and cranes and owls. And frogs, Christ, he'd never seen so many frogs in one place, all of them croaking, frantic to escape. He saw snakes, opossums, squirrels, raccoons, a regular zoo of terrified creatures scrambling to outrun the flames.

Mesmerized, Roey stood there as flames sped up trunks. The wind fanned them, fed them, swept them higher and higher and higher until they reached branches and leaves and ate into the bark itself. He could feel the quivering waves of heat, smell the burning wood. The sight of it awed him. The fire was alive and it rushed through the grove with malignant, conscious intent, a beast of unimagined power.

He wrenched back, so filled with elation he felt lightheaded, almost giddy. Then he spun around, grabbed his bags, and charged through the dark toward his car.

II

Quin bolted upright, blinking hard and fast against the darkness, blood pounding in her ears. The room was cold, that deep, disturbing cold that seemed to work its way under the skin like hundreds of tiny, sharp needles. The scent of jasmine suffused the air, a smell so thick she could nearly feel it between her fingers. And then she caught a whiff of smoke.

She shot out of bed, ran to the window, jerked up the blinds. Flames raced through the grove, long furious tongues that wrapped around branches at luminal speeds, incinerated bushes, and sped from the edge of the grove to the brush in front of the house.

"The grove's on fire!" she shouted and lurched for the phone.

It was dead, the line was dead. Quin dropped the receiver and charged out of the bedroom after McCleary. They flew down the stairs, into smoke that was seeping in under the front door, and ran into the kitchen. They filled pots and pans and bowls with water and hurried to the front door. The wood wasn't hot, the flames hadn't reached the porch yet. But when McCleary threw open the door, clouds of smoke poured in, burning Quin's eyes, filling her lungs.

"The hose at the front of the house is closest!" McCleary shouted, and they stumbled down the steps, hurling water to either side of them so that they had a clear path to the spigot. McCleary got the hose connected, spun the knob, and turned the spray on her, on himself, soaking them both to the bone.

He stumbled forward, the spray aimed at the flames that were closest to the house, then at the Explorer, which was parked less than a hundred yards from the wall of fire in the grove. She darted around to the side of the house, where there was another hose. The smoke rolled toward her in thick, undulating clouds, forcing her to hunker over as she ran.

She spun the faucet and water spurted from the hose like blood from a severed artery. It had been cut, the damn thing was useless. She sprinted back to where McCleary was. He had gotten the cellular phone out of the car, tossed it to her, then aimed the spray at the flames again. Quin punched out 911. "Fire," she wheezed to the man who answered, and spat out Lou's address.

"It's already been reported, ma'am, a truck's on the way." Sparks now darted like fireflies through the air and smoldered in areas where the flames hadn't reached. McCleary had stretched the hose as far as it would go, but it was obvious he wasn't going to be able to hold off the fire much longer. It was like trying to kill a dragon with a straight pin.

Sprinklers, she thought. There were yard sprinklers here, but where the hell was the switch? At home it was in a metal box behind the house, near the pump for the sprinklers. But she didn't remember seeing a pump anywhere outside this place. Utility room, of course, where the circuit breaker panel was.

Quin dashed for the porch but before she reached the door, it slammed shut and the knob wouldn't give. It was locked. She tried to open the closest window, but it wouldn't budge. She spun around to grab a chair, a table, something she could use to break the glass, and saw McCleary stumbling back toward the house.

Beyond him, great arcs of water shot upward from the invisible sprinklers and whipped across the grove. The water shimmered in the firelight like thousands of bright silvery fish that had risen from the sea at the same moment. The shriek of sirens shredded the air.

Lights from the emergency vehicles flashed blue and red against the layers of smoke that clung to the grove. She expected to see the headless horseman gallop out of the singed trees, through the scorched air.

But all the people around her had heads and although they weren't on horses, they moved with considerably more energy than she had. Firemen, cops, paramedics. She was sitting in the open doorway of the ambulance, breathing from an oxygen mask a medic held over her mouth and nose. She pushed his arm away. "I'm fine now."

"I'd like to take your blood pressure, ma'am."

"You just took it five minutes ago."

"Yes, ma'am, that's right, but . . ."

"I'm fine."

She swayed as she stood, held on to the door to steady herself, and walked over to the back of the fire truck. McCleary was seated in a folding chair, holding an oxygen mask to his face as a medic took his blood pressure. He looked as if he had been in a car accident, his face and arms streaked with soot the color of dried blood, his gym shorts and T-shirt ripped and filthy. He rolled his eyes when he saw her and she smiled and squeezed his hand. He pulled the mask away from his face and handed it to the paramedic.

"You okay?" McCleary asked her.

"I've had better days."

"Your pressure's fine, Mr. McCleary," said the medic, removing the cuff from his arm. "You'll live to be a hundred. Breathing okay now?"

"Fine. Thanks."

"You were both real lucky. If those sprinklers hadn't been working, the fire would've spread pretty fast to the trees near the gate and we would've had a hell of a time getting in here."

McCleary pushed to his feet. "Thanks for the air."

"Take it easy."

"I didn't turn on the sprinklers, Mac," she said as they walked away. "I couldn't get into the house. The door was locked. There must be an automatic timer on the sprinklers and it clicked on."

"There's no timer on the sprinklers."

"Then how the hell did they come on?"

He shrugged, refusing to say what they were both thinking.

"Show me the switch for the sprinklers," she said.

They went inside the house, where the power was off, the air smelled of smoke, and the floors were covered in two inches of water from the firemen's hoses. McCleary dug a flashlight out of a kitchen drawer and Quin followed him into the utility room. There were two electrical panels, one for circuit breakers and one for the sprinklers. McCleary opened the latter. "See?"

And he was right, sure he was, details were McCleary's specialty. Up for on, Down for off. Simple. Except that it wasn't simple at all. "A ghost can't turn on sprinklers, Mac."

"Or knock books off a shelf or cause air to turn chilly. But those things happened, right? We agree on that?"

"Spooks aren't my specialty."

"What gives?" Marion asked, coming up behind them, the beam of her flashlight skipping across the walls.

"I think we're having a metaphysical discussion," McCleary replied.

Marion's smile was small, hesitant, as though she thought she might be the brunt of a joke. "I must've missed something."

"Neither of us turned on the sprinklers and there's no automatic timer," McCleary said. "How's that going to appear in your report?"

She hesitated, as though she didn't quite believe them, then shook her head. "It's not." She shut the door and lowered her voice. "But I'll tell you one thing. It looks like this fire was deliberate and it wasn't set by any goddamn ghost. The hose at the side of the house had been sliced to shit and we found pieces of a fuse. I don't have to be an arson specialist to know that someone wants you two off this case in the worst way. At the very least, you should move out of here and stay at the lighthouse until we get this place cleaned up."

"Sounds good to me," Quin said.

"You go if you want," said McCleary, looking at her. "But I'm staying here."

First she wanted to leave and he didn't. Then it was vice versa, now it had come full circle again. "The power doesn't work, the floors are covered in water, the phone is dead . . . It's ridiculous to stay here."

He pulled a mop and a bucket from the supply closet and left without another word.

"Stubborn, isn't he," Marion remarked.

"Pigheaded."

"Well, the offer's open either way."

"Thanks, Marion. Let me think about it." She squeezed her arm. "C'mon, help me take inventory of the damage around here."

"Sure thing."

They sloshed through the water in the hallway and Quin opened the door to the den. There was little damage in here, just a thin film of water that had seeped in under the door. The stink of smoke wasn't quite as pervasive either. Quin opened the rear windows, then pulled García Márquez's book toward her and the door to the stone room began to swing inward.

"What the hell," Marion said softly.

"I found this by accident last night." They stepped into the room; the floor was completely dry. "Weird, huh."

"Jesus, this is like something out of a gothic novel. A desk, a cot . . . was Lou living in here or what?"

"I think he spent a lot of time in here. At that desk." Quin told her about the pages in Latin that she'd found, but didn't mention anything about her odd fugue. "I'm going to talk to the priest again and ask him to translate it for me."

Marion ran her hand over the surface of the desk, sat down on the cot, looked around, and shook her head. "I don't get it. I don't understand anything more about Lou now than I did when he was alive. I mean, what the fuck did he do in here, Quin?"

"Talked to the spook, that's my guess."

The beam of Marion's flashlight struck her in the face. "Be serious."

Quin stepped to the side, out of the light. "I'm being perfectly serious."

"Right." Marion got to her feet, she didn't want to hear about it.

"Look, whether you accept it or not, there's something in this house, okay? And I think it's connected somehow to Lou's murder."

With a sudden, inexplicable fury, Marion snapped, "Blade killed Lou, Quin. The sooner you and Mac accept *that* the better off we'll all be."

So much for telling her about their online chat with Blade last night, Quin thought. "Chill out, Marion. Go home and get some sleep."

She rubbed a hand over her face, her shoulders slumped, she looked suddenly old, used up, shriveled. "Christ," she whispered, rubbing her hands over her face. "I'm sorry. I didn't mean to snap at you."

Quin wasn't feeling particularly forgiving at the moment, but managed to say, "Don't worry about it."

Marion's hands fell away from her face and Quin realized she was crying. "I've made such a mess of things," she said softly, and sank onto the edge of the cot again.

"What things?"

"Everything."

This had all the markings of a confession about Marion's divorce. Quin was hardly in the mood to give advice, but she could certainly listen. She sat down on the edge of the cot. "Between you and Carl, you mean?"

"Not exactly." She paused, rubbed her hands over her face once more. "Lou and I ran into each other at the Pink Moose one evening last spring. I was off duty, I'd had too much to drink, he drove me home, stuff happened."

"Stuff?"

She nodded.

"You slept with him?"

Another nod.

Sweet Christ. The list of Lou's women was growing longer by the day. Felicity, Madame Hilliard, Gracie (maybe), and now Marion. Were there others she didn't know about? And just what did this tell her about Lou? He had been divorced for two years before he returned to Tango and became Lou the stud. Had this been some sort of delayed reaction to being single again?

It just didn't fit, she thought. The Lou she had known had used work, not women, as an emotional pacifier. He hadn't been an opportunist or a deliberately cruel man. But maybe these women had been his attempt to break free of whatever spell this house had held over him. Perhaps his sexual forays had been the final acts of a desperate man who believed that he had been going slowly and inevitably mad. Bizarre as it was, it made a certain sense.

"Say something, Quin."

"You threw me a loop with that one."

"It didn't last long. We were lonely, we had things in common. But we were both afraid it would compromise our jobs. Then that little fucker kills him, Quin, and I feel like I'm dying inside." Her misery was as tangible as the cold floor against Quin's feet.

"When did you split up?"

"Early summer. I couldn't risk this coming out. There's no hard-and-fast rule about cops and bondsmen getting involved, but it's definitely not something that would go unnoticed. The powers that be figure one or the other could be compromised. I knew the shit would hit the fan if the captain found out."

"Does anyone else know?"

She shook her head. "We were never in public together. I thought I had a pretty clear sense of who he was, you know what I mean? But then he's killed and . . ." She raised her arms as if to embrace the room. "And I start finding out shit like this, a secret room. Women. A man who talked to ghosts. I never knew him at all, Quin."

Her lament was familiar. Years ago, a man Quin had been living with in Miami had been murdered and Quin had said those very words: *I never really knew him.* She wanted very much to offer something comforting, but anything she might say would sound like a platitude. "C'mon, let's get out of here."

Quin pushed the García Márquez tome upright, the door swung shut, and they walked out onto the porch. A milky light seeped through the smoky air and oozed over the scorched trees, the blackened trunks, the broken branches, and blackened fruit that littered the ground.

The ruin depressed her and echoed The Tower card in her reading with Janna Hilliard. Catastrophe. Sudden change. Yeah, the fire certainly qualified. But the real thread of this case, its theme, its texture, was the six of swords, flight from something by nearly everyone involved.

Lou had been fleeing his financial problems and whatever had been happening to him in that house. Janna Hilliard had been fleeing loneliness, Felicity had been fleeing her ten-year marriage to Lou, Marion had been fleeing the pain of her divorce. And Blade was now fleeing for his life. And Gracie? What had she been fleeing? And what about the spook? What was she running from or toward?

There were too many loose ends, too many possible branches. It was like some interactive computer game where a click of the mouse would determine which branch she would follow and how the story would end. A little like life, she thought.

The branches were called Janna Hilliard, Doris Lynch, David Vicente, Felicity, Gracie, Marion, Luz the spook, and Ross Blade. Quin didn't think Janna Hilliard had killed Lou; her only crime seemed to be faulty judgment. Doris Lynch was obviously up to her eyeballs in something, but whether that extended beyond her being in cahoots with Vicente was open to debate. Vicente himself had the best motive so far, but Quin somehow couldn't imagine the man McCleary had described as being the type to stab someone to death. A bullet would be more his style, quick and sweet and indifferent. But even then, she couldn't see him doing it himself. He would hire someone.

Her impression, culled from the forensics and police reports, was that Lou had been stabbed in the heat of passion, a brief instant when the mind breaks down and all that is primal and dark surges. Her instincts said the killer was female.

III

At this hour of the morning, Cove Park was crowded with bizzo joggers, the movers and shakers who ran with their beepers and their cellular phones. They pounded out their two or three miles with a kind of joyless focus, as though they were doing time.

McCleary watched them as he started his warmup on the

grass and spotted Gene Frederick among them. He was rounding a curve, his short, muscular legs stretching, reaching, his shoes pounding the packed dirt path.

"Late again," Frederick said as McCleary joined him. "But I guess you've got a good excuse this morning. How much damage was done to the house?"

"Water damage, lots of smoke, and a third of the grove was decimated."

"So someone wants you off this case in the worst way."

"Sure looks that way."

"You hear anything from the kid?"

"Online."

"What?"

McCleary explained. "I think I can convince him to meet with me if I promise him a safehouse somewhere."

"Uh-huh."

"Love your enthusiasm."

"Shit, Mike. You're asking me to give a fugitive immunity."

"I'm not asking you for anything except backup if I need it."

Frederick mulled it over. "A safehouse where?"

"I don't know yet."

"But you'll arrange it."

"Yeah, I think I can."

"One condition."

"I know, I know. If I fuck up, you didn't know anything about it and I take the heat."

"You got it." Frederick grinned. "You remind me of my buddy Kincaid, the guy who lives in the lighthouse with one of my cops. He and I have worked deals like this over the years. And I've found that if he takes the risk, it usually means he has a real clear picture of what's going on. He has to. And he's a lot more careful than he might be otherwise because his ass is on the line."

"You're a swell guy, Gene."

He chuckled. "Don't I know it. You willing to play by those rules?"

"Only if you agree not to bring Blade in for at least seventy-two hours after I've talked to him."

"Make it forty-eight and you've got a deal."

"Forty-eight."

"Done," Frederick said.

17

I

"Church? Is that what you said?" Christine Redman laughed and shook her head. "No way, Bones. Stop the car. Take me back to the airport. I don't do church. I walk into a church, the whole thing collapses, you hear what I'm saying?"

"We're going to the rectory, where the priests live, not to the church. I need a priest to translate something for me. It won't take long."

"Translate what?"

Quin motioned to the briefcase on the floor at Christine's feet. "In there."

Christine reached for the briefcase, opened it, glanced at the pages. "I got enough trouble speakin English. Where'd you find this shit? No, never mind. Just tell me from the beginning."

Quin talked as she drove away from the airport and through the Tango hills, cushions of green against the September sky. Six months ago, Christine's name was Loretta Henderson and she was forty pounds heavier. The weight had been shed with the name and the lie she had been living. It had brought out the dramatic boldness of Christine's features, a sharp topography of the distance she had traveled from her dirt-poor childhood in the Carolinas to this particular moment in time. A true metamorphosis, caterpillar to butterfly.

"Jesus God," Christine muttered when Quin had finished. "I think I shoulda stayed home."

"Too late for that."

Christine still had the suitcase balanced on her lap and held up the pack of tarot cards that Quin had bought from Janna Hilliard.

"You readin cards now?"

"Yeah, sure, Slick. I'm a whiz at tarot."

"What're you carrying them for?"

She shrugged, not entirely sure why she'd bought them or why she hadn't removed them from her briefcase. "I don't know. I guess I thought I'd learn how to do them."

"Way back when I used this deck at psychic fairs and shit." Quin expected her to pull out the deck and spread the cards. But she merely nodded and set the deck back into the briefcase. At some point, Quin knew, they would get into the cards, but not today, maybe not tonight, maybe not tomorrow. Christine moved at her own pace, in her own time, and when it came to her spiritual life, she talked about it only when she felt compelled to do so.

Quin nosed into a parking space behind the church and Christine said, "Now let's go see how the church's stories differ from the historical versions."

"They say there isn't any difference."

"Ha."

At the church rectory, the same young priest answered the door, Father Esteban with the soft doe eyes, the spidery fingers, the quiet voice. "*Señora McCleary, un placer.* Please, come in. Come in."

"Nice to see you again, Padre. This is Christine Redman, a friend of mine."

Those doe eyes smiled. "Welcome, Señora Redman."

Quin noticed that he automatically assumed Christine was married, that she was a señora, and wondered if this was a result of Catholic church brainwashing or just the priest's assumption that all women over thirty-five were married.

Father Esteban took them to the same courtyard where she had waited before. Rodriguez appeared shortly afterward and he looked to be mostly skin and bone. Although he greeted her politely, she sensed his courtesy was strained, that her visit was an imposition. He shook Christine's hand when Quin introduced her and asked what he could do for them.

"I was wondering if you could translate something for me, Father Rodriguez. I think it's in Latin."

"My Latin is not so good these days, but I will certainly try. Let's go inside where it is cooler."

They settled at a table in the rectory library, a wonderful room with a skylight, floor-to-ceiling pine shelves crowded with books, pine furniture scuffed and nicked with age. An almost sacred stillness infused the air. Quin handed the priest the sheets of paper and he slipped on a pair of Ben Franklin bifocals.

"All right. Let's see here." He glanced at them, then looked up, his eyes like huge dark grapes behind his bifocals. "Do you mind my asking where these papers came from, señora?"

He recognizes them. "They were among Lou's things."

A pulse throbbed at the priest's temple and for moments he didn't say a word, he simply stared at the pages, struggling with his conscience. "An abomination," he said finally, his voice barely a whisper.

"What is?" Christine asked.

His eyes slipped to her, then back to Quin. "You think I don't know the source of this material? When I told you there was something evil in that house, señora, I was not speaking from hearsay. Lou talked to me about it. He asked me to bless the house, so I did. He asked me to hear his confession and I did that, too. But in the end, it didn't matter, no? He still consorted with the demon, he still painted for her, listened to her, he . . ."

"Hold on a minute, Father," Christine said. "Just hold on. I'm a little slow about all this, you know what I'm saying? What makes you believe the spirit in that house is evil?"

He hissed, "She is a succubus. She consorts with mortal men. She wanted Lou's soul."

Quin leaped in before the conversation could go any further. "What do the pages say, Father Rodriguez?"

He slapped the first sheet down against the table. " 'Help me, please help me.' "

"That's all?"

"On this page, yes." He slapped the second sheet against the first. "This says 'Release my son from the grave of the pauper. Bless him, set him free, set us both free.' "

The chill licked its way across the back of Quin's neck. "And the last page?"

His fingers twitched against the sheet, then crumpled it. His knuckles turned white. His face turned white. And his dark eyes burned with the light of a fanatic. "She professed her love for him. Over and over again, *te amo te amo te amo*. A blasphemy."

"Maybe she was talking about her son," Quin said. "What was his name again?"

"Tomás Jacinto. He took her name. And I do not think her declarations of love were for her son, señora."

Christine bristled at that. "Now just how can you know that?"

"Let me tell you about the spirit in that house." He was leaning forward, his voice hushed yet sharp and urgent. His face seemed to age by the second, each wrinkle deepening with every word he spat out. "She was originally from Nigeria and was taken to Cuba as a slave, as a concubine. The Spaniard who built this church"—he flung out his arms—"was in love with her and San Ignacio was his penance."

"Uh, excuse me," Quin said, "but the man who built this church was a pirate. He pillaged and killed. He took whatever he wanted and he wanted her, Luz."

"Señora, please. I know about Domingo. He was a man who was at sea for many months at a time and when he got to land, he satisfied his urges. It is human to be weak."

Make me gag. "Weakness doesn't excuse murder."

"There is no documented evidence that he killed. He liberated his slaves when he reached the island. He paid them to build this church. He himself worked side by side with the slaves he set free. As for the woman, she seduced him with her magic, she . . ."

"C'mon," Christine laughed. "It was okay for him to do the dirty deed, but when she did it she was seducing him with her magic? That's a crock of shit, Father."

His mouth pursed with disapproval. "There is no need for profanity, señora."

"I knew I shouldn't have come to no church," Christine snapped and sat back, her long dark arms folded against her. "You're talking like all them cardinals in Rome who're tellin good Catholics to mess around all they want without birth control so we can have more and more babies in the world that no one wants. Just who the hell are you protecting?"

"Take it easy, Slick," Quin said softly.

The priest stammered, "I . . . I . . ."

"You what?" Christine sat forward, her face inches from the priest's.

Hang it up, Quin thought, and wished the floor would open up and swallow her.

The priest sat in a stunned silence, his eyes blinking, blinking, blinking, as if to dispel or at least break up the contempt that rolled from Christine in waves. And then he simply pushed away from the table. "I have nothing more to say about this."

As he shuffled toward the door, Quin shot to her feet and went after him. "Just a minute, Father."

"I have nothing more to say," he repeated.

"I do. You're afraid of something and it isn't a spirit or a succubus or anything like that. So what is it? Did someone threaten you? Has someone promised you money for the church or the school if you refuse to talk about this?" The light, the shadows, the silence, his astonishment: It all coalesced in his tragic eyes and she knew she was right. He started to turn away but she caught his arm. "I'm sure David Vicente is at church every Sunday, isn't he, Father? He certainly has the means to refurbish the church or build a new wing for the school or the rectory. So in return for a few pieces of silver you betrayed Lou."

"I betrayed no one." His voice was choked. "I did what is best for my church."

She released his arm. "And what did that entail, Father?"

He looked down at the floor like a kid who had been shamed into feeling remorse. "I showed Mr. Vicente the material that Lou studied in our archives and agreed not to discuss it with anyone."

"In return for what?"

He still wouldn't meet her eyes, his voice was soft when he spoke. "A sizable donation that will pay for an expansion of our archives."

And it probably had been agreed upon without either man spelling out the terms, she thought. A gentleman's agreement. "I'd like to see the material."

He didn't look happy about it, but he wasn't about to put up a fight at this point. "I'll take you to the archives."

Quin glanced back at Christine and motioned that she would meet her outside. Christine mouthed, "Told you so," then she winked and left.

The archive was at the back of the church, a cramped room where the air smelled ancient and light struggled through a stained-glass window in dire need of some soap and water. The keeper of the books was Father Esteban, who smiled hello. At Father Rodriguez's request, he brought a leather-bound ledger over to the table where she and the priest were sitting.

"Mr. Hernando was most interested in this document," he said in Spanish. "It is the church's official record of vital statistics on the island between 1704 and 1888. Births, deaths, baptisms, marriages, burials, who bought and sold property, even epidemics are recorded here. The pages have been laminated to preserve them, so some of the entries may be difficult to read."

When he opened the ledger, the smell of the distant past seemed to emanate from the pages—the heat and wind of those lost decades, the exotic history. He turned to an entry marked with a strip of paper. It was dated 1704 and was written in black ink in an ornate script that slanted to the right.

"This is where Mr. Hernando began his search. His marker is still here. I believe the other pages are also still marked." The young priest drew his finger down the list to the name Tomás Xavier Jacinto, born on April 3, 1704, to Luz Rosa Jacinto. The father's name was not given.

"Has anyone else used the ledger since Mr. Hernando was here?" she asked, slipping a notepad from her purse.

The priests exchanged a glance; Rodriguez shrugged. "You can tell her."

"Mr. Vicente."

"Thank you for your help," Rodriguez said to the younger priest, an abrupt dismissal.

Father Esteban nodded and walked off. Quin turned to the next marked page, 1706. On January 4 of that year, Juan Domingo purchased ten acres of land from the church for the sum of one hundred gold coins. The boundaries were described in terms of landmarks that had existed then and extended from the northwestern edge of the island to a point well inland. In other words, this was the land that had eventually become the Hernando groves.

In June of 1708, several acres of the land and the house that

Domingo built on it were deeded to Luz Rosa Jacinto and her son, Tomás. By 1710, Luz was using part of the property as a school for the children of freed slaves. That same year, Domingo married a seventeen-year-old Spanish girl from Madrid.

Quin paged back to the year that Luz's son was born and went through each entry, searching for baptisms. "There's no mention of a baptism for Tomás Jacinto," she remarked, looking up at Rodriguez.

"My understanding of church law, as it existed then on the island, was that bastard children could not be baptized. The children born to blacks were particularly discriminated against."

Quin thought of the enigmatic reference to the grave of paupers in the Latin material. "Where were people buried in those days?"

"Dignitaries were buried in the church cemetery. It is still out back, but there are no more than a dozen marked graves left. Most everyone else was buried in what is the island cemetery today, up near the cat's right ear, on Nuevo Mundo Road. There was also a seamen's graveyard near the lighthouse, but I believe that wasn't in existence until the eighteen hundreds."

"Where is Domingo buried?"

"Behind the church."

Of course. The pirate as a church dignitary. "And Luz Jacinto?"

"She and her son are both buried in the island cemetery."

Quin didn't think he would lie to her at this point, but she wasn't about to leave anything more to chance. She checked the remaining pages that Lou had marked and found that Luz's son had died of malaria on July 20, 1734, when he was thirty years old. She had lived another year and died of unknown causes at the ripe old age of fifty. She and her son were buried "on the pauper's hill."

"Pauper's hill? What's that?" Quin asked.

"It was where non-Catholics, slaves, and unbaptized people were buried."

No outright lies, she thought, just small sins of omission. "In the island cemetery."

"Yes."

"Why didn't you just say so?"

"I won't have anything to do with the succubus, señora."

Right. He wouldn't offer information, but he would answer her questions if she asked the right ones.

The last two entries that Lou had marked were labeled "Casa de Juan Domingo." Both were sketches of the house that Domingo had built for Luz, one of the exterior and the other of the floor plan. It was considerably smaller than the house as it existed now, just the kitchen, the den, and an adjoining room with a window. She guessed it was the secret room, but it apparently hadn't been secret then. Both sketches were dated the same year that Domingo had bought the property.

"Is there anything else Lou looked at while he was here?"

"You will have to ask Esteban." He signaled the young priest, who came right over. "What other documents did Mr. Hernando study?"

Esteban thought a moment, then replied in English. "Some maps and other items that were among Domingo's things when he died. Should I get them?"

"Yes, please."

As he vanished into the stacks, another priest poked his head in the door and told Rodriguez he had a phone call. He excused himself and was still gone when Esteban returned, carrying a long aluminum container. It was labeled with Domingo's name and an inventory number. Esteban popped off the lid. "Please don't open the transparent bag. It's sealed so the objects inside don't oxidize. You can handle the maps and papers; they've been laminated."

"Did Mr. Vicente see these things?" she asked.

Esteban's eyes glinted mischievously. "No."

"Why not?"

"He did not ask the right questions, señora."

Quin laughed. "Too bad for him."

He grinned. "My own feeling is that we don't need to expand the archives."

A priest like this might convert her to Catholicism. "Do you remember if Mr. Hernando was interested in something in particular?"

"The pages. Those are all that remained of Juan Domingo's journal."

The ornate script was very small and the ink had faded over the centuries, so it was difficult to read. The first page she stumbled through was about one of Domingo's seafaring voyages. The second was a letter and her Spanish wasn't quite good enough to grasp the nuances in the language.

"Would you mind translating this for me?"

"It would be my pleasure, señora." He sat down beside her. "I have always wondered about this. The flow is almost like a verse, poetic in its way."

"You've read it before?"

He seemed surprised that she was surprised. "Of course. I'm responsible for these archives. These documents, these books . . . I am filled with the past." He gave a self-conscious laugh, then cleared his throat and began to read. " 'My love, moonlight spills through the window in your room, a pale buttery light so sweet and thick I can taste it against your skin. I know this taste. I have known it for a thousand years. I have even dreamed of it at sea, when it mingles with the sharpness of wind and salt against my tongue.

" 'And yet, when a cloud passes in front of the moon, swallowing the light, you melt from sight, you are lost to me, and I am no longer whole. I am uprooted, nomadic, no more substantial than the shadows that drift across this floor, these walls. I seek your body in this terrible darkness, the cool, familiar smoothness, the curves, the infinite surprises, and discover a cold, unforgiving sharpness.

" 'I sometimes see us as we are in that picture you sketched, a pair of suns around which the other people in our lives swirl like planets. Tomás is one such planet; my wife and our daughter are two other planets; and then there is the church, which sits in judgment of who we are and who we might become.

" 'I have never loved a woman as I love you. All that I have is yours. Hide it, bury it, keep it for our son, for the future I hope we will one day possess. Juan.' " Esteban set the page down. "That's it. Front and back."

"What do you think he's referring to when he talks about burying *it?* Hiding *it?*" she asked. "What is *it?*"

"The treasure, of course."

"I thought his riches were spent building the church."

Esteban shrugged and ran his finger around the inside of his clerical collar. "I am never sure where legend ends and fact begins, señora. Domingo was one of those people who, historically, seems larger than life. But he was only a man and not a very nice man most of the time."

"Father Rodriguez would differ with you on that point."

"Please. Don't misunderstand me. I fully respect Father Rodriguez's opinion. My opinion simply differs, that's all. I think that Juan Domingo was much richer than anyone thought and that his gold was stained with the blood of men he had killed. During his final voyage from Cuba, I think his own nature troubled him so deeply that God visited him in a vision. In that sense, I believe Father Rodriguez is quite correct. This church was Domingo's penance.

"But he never lived up to his bargain with God because he loved a woman he could not possess, could not buy, could not cajole. They had a son whom Domingo refused to acknowledge as his own, thus robbing Tomás of his rightful identity. He continued to see Luz even after he was married, so he was also an adulterer. She was, too, of course, but my feeling is that she continued to see him in the hopes that she could somehow ensure her son's future."

"And yet the church has Domingo on a pedestal."

The young priest's shrug was one of embarrassed resignation; he had long ago accepted the church's hypocrisy.

"If we were to meet these people today, señora, I would rather know her than him. She ran a free school for the children of liberated slaves like herself, nursed the sick with her secret potions and herbs, and was always true to her own vision."

"It sounds to me as if you've already met these people, Father Esteban."

"I guess it does," he said with a soft laugh. "But in many ways, they are more real to me than the people I see every day. To me, Domingo was a guilt-ridden despot, Tomás was the forgotten son, and Luz was the one who was trying to hold it all together. The mistress of the bones, that is how I think of her.

"I believe Domingo's guilt finally got the best of him and he gave her what remained of his considerable fortune. She then hid it somewhere in that house or on the land. So your friend wasn't killed because his property is valuable or because of the business he was in. He was killed because a woman who has been dead for nearly three hundred years hid a pirate's secret somewhere on the land or in the rooms where she lived."

Quin put her arms around Father Esteban's neck and hugged him. "You're a gem."

Clearly embarrassed, the young priest laughed nervously and stepped away from her. "Now you, señora, must do what Señor Hernando did not live long enough to do. You must find the truth."

II

FROM: C.LYNCH 1
TO: R.BLADE

IT WAS GREAT TO HEAR YOUR VOICE ON THE PHONE, ROSS. AND THERE WASN'T ANY RISK, DORIS WASN'T HERE. NO ONE WAS. I TALKED TO FERRET AND EVERYTHING'S SET. THE '68 RAMBLER WILL BE IN THE REAR LOT AT THE BUS STATION. DIRECTIONS ARE IN THE GLOVE COMPARTMENT. ANYTHING ELSE? C.

FROM: R.BLADE
TO: C.LYNCH 1

YOU'VE DONE ENOUGH, CHARLIE. I'M STARTING TO FEEL GUILTY OR SOMETHING. NOW YOU'LL HAVE TO GO SAILING WITH ME, IT'S THE ONLY WAY I CAN REPAY YOU. I HAVE JUST ONE STOP I REALLY NEED TO MAKE EN ROUTE TO THE MARQUESAS. THE BALBOA YACHT CLUB. IT'S IN THE AMERICAN ZONE IN PANAMA, IN THE TOWN OF BALBOA. LOU HAD BEEN THERE, I'M NOT SURE WHEN, BEFORE I MET HIM, ANYWAY. IT'S WHERE THE AMERICAN SAILORS HANG OUT WHO'RE HEADED THRU THE LOCKS TO THE SOUTH PACIFIC. NOSTALGIA, OKAY?

THANKS FOR ALL YOUR HELP, CHARLIE.

LOVE, ROSS

FROM: C.LYNCH 1
TO: R.BLADE

GUILTY??!! PLEASE. THE DRINKS AT THE BALBOA ARE ON ME, OKAY?

I'LL MEET YOU WHERE AND WHEN WE AGREED—ON TANGO, I MEAN, NOT IN PANAMA, AT LEAST NOT YET. :)

LOVE, C.

From: R.Blade
To: C.Lynch 1
I can walk to the bus station, Charlie. You don't have to do this. R.

From: C.Lynch 1
To: R.Blade
Forget walking. It's more than six miles to the bus station in broad daylight. Bad idea. I'll be there. Love, C.

18

I

The Island Garage stood at the end of a dead-end street in downtown Tango. The building wasn't much to look at, McCleary thought, just weathered concrete block shaped like an *L*, with four stalls along the longest part of the *L*. But business was booming. Cars were lined five deep in front of the stalls and more cars were parked at the side of the building. The noise of machinery surrounded the place like a wall.

McCleary went inside to look for Ferret or Bino. The man behind the counter was painfully thin, with hollowed cheeks and haunted eyes. He wore his black hair in a brush cut, sported a diamond post in his right ear, and might have been thirty or fifty, it was hard to tell. He also looked vaguely familiar.

"Morning, sir, how can I help you?" he asked, his voice quick and cheerful.

"Is Ferret around?"

"No, sir."

"How about Bino?"

"Nope. Can anyone else help you?"

"Not really. What time do you expect Ferret?"

"Let me check." He reached for the phone. "Your name, sir?"

"McCleary. Mike McCleary."

"Oh." He replaced the receiver and grinned. "Mr. McCleary. Go through that freezer door." He stabbed a thumb over his shoulder. "Ferret's back there unloading cartons."

As though his own name were a password. "Have we met? You look familiar."

"I got an act down on the boardwalk. The escape artist."

Of course. Lou had taken them down to the boardwalk last fall and they had watched this guy squirm his way out of a strait-jacket and chains. "I saw you perform last year. You're incredibly good."

He took a mock bow. "Thank you, thank you. Music to my ears. Better catch Ferret before he disappears."

"Thanks."

The freezer door opened into a dimly lit hallway lined with metal shelves that were jammed with automotive supplies. Ferret was at the far end, unpacking cartons. "You're a tough man to track down," McCleary said.

"At least my phone works." He sat on one of the cartons. "Pull up a box, Mike. I've been calling Lou's house since six this morning. I heard about the fire."

McCleary pulled over another box, sat down. "The phone's been out of commission since the house was hit by lightning the other night. Who told you about the fire?"

"Heard it on the police scanner."

"I talked to Blade." McCleary told him about the online conversation they'd had. "Has he contacted you?"

"Not personally." His small, hungry eyes impaled McCleary, scrutinizing him, measuring him against some standard in his own mind. "Charlie Lynch called to tell me Ross Blade says he's okay. I think we'll have something worked out by tonight."

"What kind of something?"

"Moving him someplace more secure than where he's at now.

The cops must've figured he might get in touch with me. They've got the garage under surveillance. So how about if we meet on the boardwalk around dusk? It'll be easy to lose a tail there."

"Meet to go where?"

Ferret's lips pulled away from his teeth. "The less you know right now, the safer Ross will be."

"Fair enough. See you at seven."

As McCleary got up, Ferret said, "Wear dark clothes and make sure you're armed."

In the light of day, the grove was a nightmare turned inside out. The blackened trees, the scorched and barren branches, the blistered ground strewn with ashes: It was the manifestation of all that had gone awry at the end of Lou's life.

But some of the wildlife had returned already. Half a dozen Muscovys were foraging in the weeds at the edge of the pond and one of the burrowing owls was perched at the apex of the roof, watching him. McCleary trotted up to the porch and filled one of the aluminum pans with birdseed from the twenty-five-pound bag Quin kept out here.

He carried the pan out to where the Muscovys were hovering around, fifteen or twenty yards from the house. McCleary remembered Quin telling him about her little experiment with the birds and tested it for himself. When he set the container eight yards from the porch steps, the ducks refused to come any closer. He finally moved the container beyond the ten-yard mark and sure enough, they descended in droves. It wasn't just the ducks either, but blackbirds and doves and mockingbirds that seemed to appear out of nowhere.

They felt it, too.

McCleary returned to the house and stood for a moment in the front room, listening for noises that didn't belong. There were none. He and Quin had cleaned up the water downstairs, but the air still smelled of it, of old cellars, wet earth.

He had turned the power on before he'd left the house earlier, but the phone was still dead. Even though Tango Bell had promised someone would be out today, he wasn't holding his breath.

He walked down the hall to the sunroom, glanced at the portrait of the black woman, of Luz. Her eyes moved as he moved. She watched him as he removed her portrait from the easel and set a blank canvas in its place. She watched him as he opened Lou's paints, prepared an easel, opened a bottle of water and poured some into a plastic cup.

"So now you'll have to talk to me," he said softly.

The paints were acrylics, which he liked working with. Even though they weren't as rich as oil and you couldn't do the same kind of texturing with them, they were easier to use. They were water soluble. You could make mistakes that weren't irreparable.

Quin and Christine weren't back yet, he was alone here, so why not? Why not indulge himself? Why not test the waters where Lou had drifted? At least he, unlike Lou, had been painting for twenty years. They could dispense with the basics and get to the real stuff. Assuming, of course, that she had something to say. That she wasn't just jerking them all around.

He had read about spooks like that, the gleeful imp that banged pots and slammed doors in the middle of the night, the nasty little shit that knocked priceless vases off coffee tables. Luz seemed to have a distinct preference for more intimate connections, but it still might be just a way to pass the time. Maybe Lou had been merely a curiosity for her, a man willing to step off into the void and meet her halfway.

He looked at her portrait again, at those compelling eyes that Lou, despite the fact that he was an amateur, had captured with such realism. Eyes that seemed to stare through him, to scoop him raw inside.

"So get on with it," he said, then opened another box and plucked out a brush.

A blank canvas was like a blank computer screen, something

that begged for expression. He focused on all that white until the shapes and colors in his peripheral vision dropped away and his vision blurred. Images fluttered through his head as they often did right before he dropped off to sleep, with the rapidity of light. Slow it down, he thought. Focus. Concentrate. Find the right one.

Since the moment he had realized that the paintings in the house were Lou's, he had avoided doing this. He had avoided it because at some deeply personal level he knew he would be asking for trouble. He had avoided it because it frightened him. The whole business of automatic anything, whether it was writing or painting or speaking for Indian chiefs who hadn't walked the Earth since the pilgrims had landed, offended him. And yet. Here he was.

Open, waiting.

And then he began to paint.

Now and then he was aware of birds outside, of the heat of the sunlight pouring through the windows. But mostly, his sense of hearing had shut down. So had his sense of taste.

Sight, smell, and touch, however, were exquisitely attuned to what he was doing. The colors. You could lose yourself in these colors. Vivid, bright, tropical, hallucinogenic. And there was the scent of the paint itself, the way it smelled when it touched the canvas, as it mingled with other colors, as it dried. Even the sensation of the brush in his hand seemed heightened, possessed of some preternatural clarity, strung as tightly as a cord that stretched from someplace inside of him then out into the world.

He was barely aware of how the painting took shape. The brush became an extension of his hand, moving as if of its own volition. He paused once, like a seafaring mammal surfacing for air, and replaced the canvas he'd been working on for another. He referred to it as he tackled the new blank canvas, noting the suggestions of shapes and textures and deepening them this time, enriching them.

His shoulders began to ache. His bladder filled. He was hungry and thirsty, his eyes burned. He set the brush down and pushed up from the stool without looking at the painting. And that was when he became aware of the distinct, pervasive coolness in the room. This wasn't the sharp, biting chill he had experienced in the den; this was friendlier. And with it came the faint, sweet fragrance of jasmine.

He used the bathroom, polished off an apple, worked the kinks out of his shoulders, and was shocked to see that only an hour had passed. He returned to the sunroom, where nothing had changed.

The air was still cooler here than it was in the hallway and the early afternoon sunlight spilled across the hanging plants. But an eerie silence now suffused the room, as if it had been hermetically sealed. And as he sat down on the stool, something brushed the back of his neck, something light and almost feathery, neither cool nor warm. It raised goose bumps on his arms, sucked the moisture from his mouth.

He looked at the canvas, frowned, picked up the first canvas and compared them. Neither was complete. But there was enough in both to recognize they were different versions of the stone room. The first, the room as it existed now, didn't have a window. The second version did, a tall arched window that started low to the floor and extended almost to the ceiling. It looked out into trees, a suggestion of light and shadows.

He felt sort of foolish now, but what the hell, he had started this, he might as well finish it. If he operated from the premise that there was a message in all this, then the window was key. He picked up both canvases and carried them into the den.

The room was cold, dim, very still. He set the canvases against the wall, turned on the lights, and raised the blinds. There, much better. He carried one of the lamps over to the bookcase, plugged it into a nearby socket, and turned the shade so the light would shine into the secret room when he opened it. Then he pulled *One Hundred Years of Solitude* toward him and the bookcase began to creak, to swing inward. He picked up the canvases, entered the stone room, and set the paintings side by side on top of the rolltop desk.

If the painting was correct, then there had once been a window in here. But in which wall? Just pick one, he thought, and chose the wall directly across from the door, the south wall, where the cot was.

McCleary moved the cot into the center of the room, pushed the filing cabinet away from the wall, and stretched out on his back to measure its length. He was six feet tall and with his feet flat against one wall, his head nearly touched the other. Call it six feet. Then he stood to measure the height. The ceiling at this end sloped and he couldn't stand up straight without his head touching it. Call it five feet ten.

He glanced at the painting with the window in it, then knelt and proceeded to rap his knuckles against the row of stones closest to the floor. He was looking for one that sounded different from the others, but as far as he could tell there was no difference. He went on to the second row of stones and began, as before, at the far left and worked his way across to the far right.

Nothing.

But two feet in on the third row, he struck a stone with a hollow ring to it. He marked it with a pencil, then rapped the stone directly above it. Nothing. Okay, forget simple stuff like straight lines. He tapped the stones in the immediate vicinity and located another at roughly two o'clock. He marked it as well and began knocking on the stones that surrounded it.

The light from the lamp didn't reach far enough, so he stopped and went into the den for an extension cord. He connected it to the lamp, carried the lamp into the room, and set it down next to the wall where he was working. Thanks to the additional light, he noticed a significant detail that had escaped him before.

The baseboards along each wall, which had been hidden earlier by the furniture, had obviously been added since the house had been built. But the baseboard on this wall looked newer than the others. Just above one section of it, the coquina stone looked as if it had been mixed with cement.

McCleary tried to pull the baseboard away from the wall with his fingers, but it wouldn't give. A hammer and screwdriver would do the trick, he decided, and headed into the kitchen and down into the cellar where Lou had kept his tools.

The doorbell rang as he was on his way back upstairs, a sharp, impatient peal. He expected someone from the phone company, but it was Felicity, standing there in her workout attire, luminous blue tights and a matching halter top with an unbuttoned shirt thrown over it. A large leather bag hung from her shoulder.

This was the first time he'd seen her in five years. She didn't seem to have aged; if anything, she had gotten better-looking. She smiled and gestured at the hammer and screwdriver. "You were expecting Jack the Ripper?"

"Home improvements. Good to see you again, Felicity."

"You, too." She hugged him quickly, as if Lou stood between them, and stepped back. "I'm relieved you're okay. I heard about the fire. Christ, I felt sick driving in here. Lou loved these trees. Was there much damage to the house?"

"Some water and smoke damage, but not much else. C'mon in."

"Is Quin around?"

"No. I'm not sure when she'll be back. She had to pick up a friend of ours at the airport and was going to run some errands."

"I kept getting a busy signal when I called."

"The phone's out of order."

They walked into the sunroom, where Felicity hesitated briefly and rubbed her hands over her arms. "Jesus, it's chilly in here." Her eyes fixed instantly on the portrait of Luz. "That painting has always spooked me."

"I know what you mean." But he didn't want to get onto that subject with Felicity. "So what brings you out to the house?"

"Well, other than the fire, I wanted to make sure you and Quin know about the paintings Lou's father did."

"I heard Lou had burned them."

"He burned the big ones, but kept some of the miniatures. When I was here during the Christmas holidays, he showed them to me."

"We haven't run across them. Any idea where they might be?"

"I'm pretty sure Lou brought them out of the den."

"We've been through that den with . . ." And then it struck him and was suddenly so obvious he laughed.

Felicity frowned. "I said something amusing?"

"You have a few minutes? I want to show you something."

She glanced at her watch. "I've got an aerobics class pretty soon, but what the hell. The old biddies can wait."

He took her into the den, where the bookcase was still open to the stone room. Her shock was genuine. She looked at him, then back at the room, then at him again. "I don't understand," she said finally, softly. "Lou never told me about this room."

"He didn't tell anyone." Except Blade.

She stepped to the doorway, gestured at the two paintings he'd done. "Are those Lou's?"

"No. Mine."

She gave him an odd look, glanced back at the paintings. "You think there was a window in here at one time?"

"Yeah, I'm sure of it." McCleary walked over to the desk, removed a large flashlight from the bottom drawer, and handed it to Felicity. "And I've got a hunch that those miniature paintings are where the window used to be."

She turned on the flashlight and followed him into the secret room.

II

The island cemetery, Quin thought, was about adjectives. Emerald greens, cool shade, brilliant flowers, a pastoral rendition of the afterlife in technicolor. It covered more than twenty acres of prime real estate on a hill just south of the wilderness preserve and offered one of the finest views on the island. She could see the rooftops of Key West, the bridge that spanned the two islands, the ferry churning through the channel waters.

"Waste of space, if you ask me," Christine said. "But I guess if you're goin for burial instead of cremation, this is the spot to be."

"Personally, I'd rather skip this step."

Christine laughed. "I hear you, girl. There's another one of them signs just ahead."

The signs she was referring to were courtesy of the Tango Historical Society, bits of macabre information about the bygone days, battles won and lost, blood that was shed, historical figures and celebrities who were buried here. But thanks to the signs, they found their way to paupers' hill.

It was in the oldest part of the cemetery, the forgotten part, where the trees weren't trimmed and the grass had died. For the most part, the gravestones had toppled and the inscriptions had been worn away by time. The historical society had only one sign among these graves:

> In the early 1700s, this part of the cemetery was known as Paupers' Hill. Here are buried the destitute, the despised, the forgotten. But for the grace of God, here lie you and me.

"A real cheery thought for the day," Christine muttered.

"Don't pay attention to that stupid sign." The man who had spoken raised up from behind the only bench in sight. He had a pair of hedge clippers in one hand and with the end of it he nudged his baseball cap farther back on his head. He looked about seventy but moved around the side of the bench with the wiry spryness of a man twenty years younger. "I've been thinking about knocking that sign down ever since they put it up. All it does is spook people." He grinned. "Now you're going to say you're from the Historical Society, right?"

Christine snickered. "Nope."

"We're looking for the graves of Luz and Tomás Jacinto. They were buried here in . . ."

"Different years." The man pointed with the clippers. "She's down yonder." He pivoted slowly, pointing at a spot ninety degrees away. "The son's over there. Least he was till six, seven weeks ago."

"The grave was moved?" Quin asked.

"Moved?" He laughed, exposing stained, broken teeth that begged for the services of a dentist. "Dug up is more like it." His sudden frown threw his face into a dizzying network of creases; suspicion burned in his voice. "You cops?"

"We're amateur historians," Quin said quickly.

His small, dark eyes glanced from Quin to Christine, assessing, judging. "With the historical society?"

"Hon, we're just a couple of tourists from Jacksonville," Christine said.

"You can't be too careful these days." He whipped off his cap and fanned himself with it. "People nose around, ask questions, feed you a line, they could be anyone."

Christine nodded. "I hear what you're sayin."

"Which grave is it?" Quin asked.

"Right over here."

They accompanied him to a cool, thickly shaded spot beneath an acacia tree that had lost nearly all of its crimson flowers. The dead buds littered the ground like bloody footprints. The headstone had long since fallen over, but the name was still faintly visible. Tomás Xavier Jacinto. No date of birth, no date of death, just the name, short and sweet.

"Gravestone's still there, the ground doesn't look like it's been bothered in a million years. But one morning back in late July, I guess it was, I came to work and I knew that grave had been messed with. Oh, you couldn't tell it just by looking at it. Whoever'd done it was real careful about putting the sod back just right. But I been here a good long while. I know every shrub, every grave, I know when things don't look like they're supposed to look."

"Did you notify the police?" Quin asked.

"Sure thing. And some cop comes out here a couple days later, asks me some questions, leaves. End of story. Nothing came of it. Why should anyone care, right? Tomás was a nobody.

"Now, if it had been one of the fancy mausoleums on the west hill, that'd be different. Those graves are new, the bodies get buried with wedding rings, china, crystal, you wouldn't believe some of the stuff they put in the coffins. Some of them have been broken into. We got our share of grave robbers here on the island. But Tomás?" He shook his head. "No way is a cop going to bother with this."

"Maybe an animal was diggin around here," Christine said.

"Uh-uh. I dug the grave up myself just because I needed to know. And I'm telling you there's nothing in there but an empty coffin."

Release my son from the grave of the pauper. Bless him, set him free, set us both free. The words from the Latin translation drifted through Quin's head; she rubbed her arms against a sudden, penetrating chill.

III

Felicity was kneeling next to him, holding the flashlight on the spot where he worked at the baseboard with the screwdriver and hammer. She didn't say anything, but now and then the light trembled.

When he finally tore the baseboard away from the wall, there was one section about two feet long that was mostly cement mixed with bits and pieces of coquina stone. It looked as if the stones had shattered when they'd been removed and someone had tried to plaster them back together.

He tapped the cement lightly with the hammer.

"Hollow," said Felicity. "It sounds hollow."

He slammed the hammer against the plaster just above where the baseboard had been. After a dozen hard blows, it caved in. McCleary scooped the bits and pieces out with his hands, marveling that in many ways this house was the perfect expression of Lou's life, filled with dark compartments, private spaces, secrets.

When the opening was relatively clean, they could see the inner surface of the exterior wall of the house. "Is it entirely hollow behind this wall?" she asked, hunkering down for a better look.

"I don't know. Hold the light steady." He reached down inside with his right hand, his fingers digging through crumbled plaster and stone until they hit something hard. "There's something here." He shifted and thrust his other hand into the opening. He found either side of what felt like a small wooden chest and worked it slowly out of the opening.

It looked like a vastly scaled down version of an old steamer trunk, something that women forty or fifty years ago had used to pack away silks and other fineries from their trousseaux. He guessed it had made the journey from Havana with Lou's parents. It was badly scuffed, with rusted metal corners, but the padlock was bright and shiny.

"That's it?" Felicity sounded disappointed. "There's nothing else in there?"

"Maybe the paintings are inside of it."

McCleary took the hammer to the padlock and the lid gave with a soft pop. He raised it.

The paintings, half a dozen exquisite miniatures, rested in a nest of Styrofoam, the popcorn stuff that was used to pack items for shipping. They removed them, Felicity nodding as she lined them up against the side of the trunk. "Yeah, these are the ones I saw. Scenes of Havana."

"Why would he save these and not any of the others?"

She shrugged. "Damned if I know."

McCleary scooped out the rest of the popcorn Styrofoam and uncovered a thin blanket of beach sand at the bottom of the chest. An object wrapped in black plastic rested against it. He unwrapped the plastic and a tide of bile surged in his throat. Felicity made a harsh, choking sound and wrenched back.

It was a human skull.

McCleary slammed the lid.

19

I

At ten past noon, Roey broke his vigil of the Island Garage, certain that he was on the right track. Something was brewing. Something major.

He had seen the boardwalk weirdos arriving at the garage, the sword juggler, the fire-eater, the Grecian statue, the guy who thought he was the next Houdini. And he had seen McCleary pull in, go inside, and come back out again a while later.

But even if he had missed all that, he would still feel the tightening in the air, a certain tension that his body absorbed like vitamins from food. The cops sensed it, too. They had been cruising past the garage all morning, as subtle as ticks on a dog's back.

Roey walked into Lester's Bar twenty minutes late for his rendezvous with David Vicente, something he never would have done in the past. But the past was dead; this was the beginning of his future.

A few regulars were at the bar, some bikers were playing pool in the back room, but otherwise the place was pretty quiet. He ordered a pickled egg and a glass of cranberry juice and when he turned to find a booth, Vicente had already claimed one at the back, where the light was dim.

He was dressed like a farm worker—dusty dungarees, a blue work shirt, the usual baseball cap. Roey strolled over with his briefcase in one hand and his pickled egg and juice in the other. He slid into the opposite side of the booth and felt a secret, exhilarating thrill.

Vicente didn't say hello. The first words out of his mouth were "I'd like to see the negatives first, Tom."

"Let's just exchange briefcases, David."

David: The impropriety hung in the air between them, a breech of some long-standing unspoken rule. Roey liked it; it meant they were equals now. He set his briefcase on the floor in front of his feet and Vicente did the same. They never took their eyes off each other. Moments later, Vicente's briefcase was on the booth beside Roey. He opened it and paged through the neat stacks of bills inside. Twenty-five grand. This brought the total to fifty.

Vicente turned on the little lamp at the booth, looked at the negatives, put them back into the briefcase.

"Satisfied?" Roey asked.

"For the moment. I'd like to see your plane ticket."

Roey pulled it out of his windbreaker, a one-way ticket from Tango to Miami to Mexico City.

"This is for tomorrow night."

"Right."

"You expect things to be wrapped up by then?"

"Yes." With a little luck.

"And you'll have the other negatives."

"If you have the money, I'll have the negatives, David. A deal's a deal."

"A rose is a rose."

"What?"

"Gertrude Stein."

"Never heard of her."

Vicente seemed amused by this. "Not surprising. She was a poet. I'll wait to hear from you." He slipped out of the booth and left.

Roey finished his pickled egg and his juice, irritated about the reference to Stein. Vicente and his intellectual bullshit, he thought. The old man was just making it clear that even though Roey was soaking him for two hundred grand, he remained his intellectual superior. Fuck him, fuck his intellectual crap. After tomorrow, he'd never have to see the asshole again.

Roey knew it was a risk. But he didn't care. He had something to offer her now, something she could see, taste, touch, feel, something more than pipe dreams.

He was waiting for her in the parking garage, watching for her as she stepped off the elevator, her shoulders slouched, hunched, as if beneath an unbearable weight. It hurt him to look at her.

He popped out from behind a concrete post like a jack-in-the-box. "Hi, babe."

She stopped dead. The expression on her face turned him inside out like a dirty sock. He noticed how she tightened her grasp on her bag like some nervous twit who thought he was going to jerk it off her shoulder. "Tom."

"Hey, you remember my name."

"Very funny. Excuse me, but I'm in a hurry."

"I'll walk with you to your car."

"I'd rather you didn't."

"Fine. Then let's talk here."

"We don't have anything to talk about."

"Certain people would think differently about that."

"Frankly, I don't think anyone would give a shit."

"The McClearys would."

That got her attention. She paused and glared at him.

"I think the McClearys would be real interested. And David

Vicente. And the chief of police. And Ross Blade. Yeah, the kid would be interested in hearing what I have to say. I'll be sure and tell him when I see him."

She recognized his threats for what they were—so much hot air. "You're going to find him when no one else can?" She laughed, a sharp, biting laugh. "Get off it, Tom. You couldn't even find the guys who skipped bond. You're just not that good."

"Vicente thinks I am."

"Right." She started walking again and Roey fell into step beside her. Their footsteps echoed in the garage, shadows pooled at their feet. "And the next thing you're going to tell me is that he's paying you a fortune to find the kid."

"You hit it on the head, babe."

"And just why the hell would he do that, Tom?"

"I figure it has something to do with Lou's will. With who inherits the land and the house."

"C'mon, the land's worth a million and a half tops. That's peanuts to Vicente."

"Unless the land is rezoned, which it probably would be if Blade wasn't around to inherit. Or maybe Vicente bought into those tales about the treasure."

She glanced at him as they walked but didn't say anything. He wanted to touch her face, to feel her skin against his knuckles. There was a time when he would have done that, would have touched her. But that time had long since passed. He had caught her on the rebound, the worst time to catch a woman you might love.

And of course it had ended badly, as most rebounds did. Even though she had dumped him, had told him to hit the road, Jack, here he was. In his mind she existed in a perpetual suspended animation, unchanged since the first moment he had seen her in the Pink Moose during a happy hour two years ago. Hell, in his mind she walked on water.

"You ever think about us?" he asked suddenly.

"Sometimes."

That surprised him, that she admitted it, that she actually thought about it. "And what do you think?"

They had reached her car. She unlocked the door, then turned to him. "What do you want from me, Tom?"

He felt light-headed, dizzy. An eternity passed before he responded. "You ever seen Mexico?" he asked.

She laughed again and fixed a hand to her hip, a gesture he remembered well. "No, Tom, I've never been to Mexico."

"You want to go? I mean, would you go with me?"

He expected a hostile remark that dripped with sarcasm. To his complete shock, her eyes glistened. "C'mon," she said softly. "Don't bullshit me. We talked about all that before. People don't just quit their lives and run off to fucking Mexico or Tahiti or wherever."

"They do if they have enough money."

Something new crept into her expression then, something he didn't know how to read. "How much is enough, Tom? Fifty thousand? A hundred thousand?" She opened her car door. "A million?"

"Two hundred thousand."

She shut the door slowly, deliberately, and looked at him as she used to, with a mixture of puzzlement and surprise. "You're not serious. Vicente offered you that much to find Blade?"

It entailed a little more than that, but she didn't need to know that now. He nodded.

"So what the hell do you want from me?"

"Just a few answers. Does Mexico interest you? I've heard it's got some pretty places where you can hide away. I don't really give a shit where we go, as long as we go together."

She regarded him for what must have been a full minute or more. Then she said, "Get in the car, Tommy."

Tommy: That was what she used to call him in the old days, the days when she claimed that Lou was no longer in the picture.

Lou, Christ, it all came back to that sonuvabitch, didn't it. That was the problem with life on this island. It was incestuous.

In a normal world you meet a woman in a bar and, unless she turns out to have some terrible communicable disease, you don't think about whom she might know, whom she might have slept with or been married to; you never think about how it might impact your life in the future. But life here was not normal. It was not ordinary. It was not business as usual. Everyone knew everyone else. The grapevine buzzed with lies and truths and everything in between and sometimes you couldn't figure out which was which.

And knowing all this he still got into the car with her, slid into the passenger seat, and they sat there for a long time, sometimes talking, sometimes not. For a while, it seemed to Roey that the car was actually moving, that he could smell the green of the hills where they used to picnic, to make love.

"Did you kill him, Tom? Did you kill Lou? Is that what Vicente hired you to do?"

"No."

"No to which one?"

"No to all of them." A beat passed. "Did you waste him?" he asked.

"No."

He didn't know what to say after that. It didn't make any difference to him who had killed Lou Hernando. He was just glad the fucker was dead.

"I almost called you a couple of times," she said finally.

Roey touched her hair, that was all, just a light stroke, his fingers combing through it. "Same here."

"How come you didn't?"

"You ended it. I figured if you wanted to see me you'd call."

She rubbed the heel of her hand against her temple. "I've been so . . . so, I don't know, mixed up about everything. I can hardly remember why I ended it, Tommy."

"Because of Lou." He remembered every goddamn detail of

that final conversation. He remembered how the motel room smelled, of soap and shampoo and sex. He remembered that she was standing in front of the mirror, pulling a comb through her hair, when she said it. *I can't accept the ring, Tommy. I don't want to see you anymore.* And he remembered how something deep inside his chest had broken, come apart. "You ended it because of Lou."

She shook her head, a streak of light caressing the curve of her jaw. "I don't think that's the only reason." And then she covered her face with her hands and started to cry. He had never seen her cry, not once in the course of their affair.

He slipped his arms around her and inhaled the rich scent of her hair and felt the hard reality of her bones against his hands and wondered how he had arrived at this particular point in his life, with this particular woman.

She told him what she knew, he told her what he knew, and when he got out of her car sometime later he felt buoyed, high, stoned out of his fucking mind on what was possible. What might be. The future. And that was something, wasn't it? Wasn't it?

Dear God, he thought, and pressed the heels of his hands against his eyes and saw the fat man in his mind, the fat man begging, the fat man writhing on the ground, the fat man dying. But he also saw a plane lifting from a runway, rising into the vast blue sky, and banking west toward the future, his future and hers if they played their cards right.

If. That was the bottom line.

If.

II

On several occasions, Quin had been on the receiving end of Christine's psychic impressions. But she had never seen her do what she was doing now, swiveling her hips and twisting her bare feet against the sunroom floor. She also kept running her hands together hard and fast, a noise like dry leaves scraping across concrete.

"Should we do anything special, Slick?" McCleary asked.

"Beats me. I never tried to talk to spooks before. All I'm doin now is grounding myself."

They were in Lou's den, where the small wooden chest stood against the wall. "Do you mind if I turn on the recorder?" Quin asked.

"Do whatever you got to, Bones."

The first sentence the recorder caught was McCleary's, who said, "Maybe I should get that trunk out of here." He went over to it, started to shove it out into the hall, but Christine stopped him.

"No, it's okay. Let's see if that there skull's got anything to say."

McCleary hadn't told Christine where he'd gotten the chest; she'd insisted that the less she knew, the more accurate her impressions would be. He flipped back the lid, reached inside for the skull, and handed it to her.

It was wrapped in the black plastic and the stuff crinkled as she moved her hands over it. She walked slowly around the room, a Diogenes seeking a light of truth. Sometimes her eyes were open, fixed on the object she held, and sometimes her eyes were shut.

The sky had clouded over and the muted afternoon light touched Christine's smooth, black arms, a benediction. Somewhere distant there was a squeal of brakes and, closer to the house, the shriek of an owl. Then there was only a thick, pervasive quiet that seemed to seep from the center of the room and bleed into the air until she was breathing it.

The stillness spread through Quin's lungs and her chest and her head. It was a soft, comforting warmth that relaxed her so deeply she could feel herself separating from her skin and her bones. It frightened her and she snapped back, sat up straighter on the couch, and realized Christine was perched at the edge of an old rocker near the window.

She had removed the plastic wrapping from the skull. It was balanced on her legs now and her hands slipped over it, utterly black against that strange, weathered white bone. Her eyes had rolled back in her head, narrow white slits. When she began to talk, her voice was soft and hoarse, punctuated by numerous pauses. Just watching her, Quin felt like the sorcerer's apprentice, armed against mythic forces with nothing more than a mop and a broom.

McCleary moved the recorder closer to Christine; Quin had to strain to hear what she said.

"A young man. Not very tall. Muscular. Skin like dark chocolate. He died from the bite of a mosquito."

The forgotten son, Quin thought. This was his skull.

"He didn't fit in," Christine went on. "He wasn't black, he wasn't white, he wasn't Spanish, he wasn't a slave." She paused. "He was just a bastard, he was nothing. That was how he grew up thinkin about himself." Another pause. "From the time he was just a boy, he knew who his old man was. His mother told him and for a long time he hated her for that." Pause. Her eyes rolled back into place again, chips of glossy obsidian. "Hated her for the truth."

Her hands moved more quickly over the skull now, fingers dipping into the smooth sockets of the eyes, into what had once been the mouth. "He punished her by leaving the island . . ." Christine shook her head. "I don't know how long he left for, but it was a long time. Three or four years.

"During that time, he loved men. He became what he always was, but he couldn't handle it, he was all eaten up with this"—her hands lifted from the skull, fingers fluttering just above it like black moths—"this guilt shit, Catholic guilt." Her hands glided down to the skull again. "He came home. Not too long after that the mosquito bit him."

Quin had told her nothing of what she had discovered in the rectory archives about Luz, the pirate, their son.

Christine stopped, blinked, then set the skull carefully inside the chest and wiped her damp face on the sleeve of her T-shirt. Her head snapped up suddenly, she sniffed at the air like a dog, and whispered, "Jasmine."

Quin didn't smell anything.

Christine pushed to her feet. She moved with the swiftness of a panther, a cougar, some large and graceful cat, and headed out of the den. Quin and McCleary glanced at each other, neither of them quite sure what they were supposed to do. He grabbed the recorder and they hurried after Christine.

She stopped in the kitchen, at the sink, her fingers folded over the edge of it, her face toward the window, eyes focused on something outside. Quin had the sudden, clear impression of Christine as a liquid pillar of energy that would short-circuit everything inside of her unless she did what she was doing now, standing still, rooted. The energy coursed through her and into the floor, the foundation of the house, the very earth itself. Her hair had gone a little wild, sweat glistened on her arms, her face. She looked, Quin thought, like a schizophrenic in the midst of an epiphany.

The afternoon had grown progressively darker. Through the window, Quin saw clouds that sagged over the grove, threatening to brush the treetops. Thunderheads. You didn't see the likes of these suckers anywhere else but Florida, she thought, huge, billowing flowers that climbed thirty and forty thousand feet into the atmosphere while their bellies brushed the treetops in the grove.

Lightning flashed briefly in the window, a stroboscopic explosion whose brilliance struck Christine full in the face. And for seconds Quin didn't recognize her. Her profile seemed prouder, almost regal, like something rendered on the surface of a coin. Her rich, black skin shimmered. Her features seemed fuller, her neck thinner and longer. Quin had the strangest impression that the woman in front of her wasn't Christine.

She reminded Quin of a black swan she had seen once on a family vacation when she was a kid, an elegant creature that had landed on a lake somewhere in upstate New York. She must have been nine or ten at the time and was down at the lake tossing bits of bread to the birds that frequented the place at dusk.

And suddenly, there was the swan, wings fluttering as she landed almost soundlessly on the water. It had to be a she. No male could ever look as lovely as this swan had looked, the very essence of femininity, grace, instinct.

Quin could still remember the texture of the dusky light that had fallen across the swan's ebony feathers. She could see the bird's long, graceful neck bending, twisting slightly as she regarded Quin on shore, a young girl with a bag of stale bread.

She'd felt then as she did now, a connection to something so large, so vast and complex, she could never take it all in, much less comprehend it. The swan had symbolized all that was greater than herself, all that was mysterious and unknowable. It was the ultimate black hole, the ultimate riddle, a Zen koan, unanswerable.

"The mother. She died here." Christine wrenched back as she said it. Her balled hands were pressed now to the center of her chest. "Her heart. She was standing here thinkin of her boy and her grief was so deep her heart clenched up and that was it." Christine's voice was very soft, awed, and the recorder whirred, getting all of it. "She was miserable when she died. She hated her son's father. He built this house for her but he never lived here. I think he married a white woman. Yeah, a Spanish girl. She was young, still in her teens. He married her and kept the black woman as his mistress."

"Do you get a name?" McCleary asked.

"Loose. Does that make sense? Loose."

The phonetic pronunciation of Luz.

"Did you tell her?" McCleary mouthed to Quin.

She shook her head.

"I see kids around her, okay? Mulattos like her son, little bastard kids." She lifted her arm and pointed through the window. "They had school outside. She taught them art." Her arm dropped to her side, she took another step back, then brushed past Quin and McCleary as though they didn't exist, as though *they* were the ghosts.

She was sniffing the air again, pursuing a scent that Quin smelled intermittently, the odor of jasmine. Quin wasn't surprised when Christine entered Lou's den again. She stopped just a few feet inside the door. Minutes ticked by, but Quin lost track of how many minutes it was. Her awareness, it seemed, was no longer measured by the ticks of a clock. She heard the whisper of air through the tiny ceiling vents. She heard a low rumble of thunder, a sudden explosion of rain against the windows.

Christine walked over to the bookcase, reached out, reached, Quin knew, for *One Hundred Years of Solitude.* McCleary glanced at Quin again, his eyes asking if she had told Christine about the stone room. McCleary's reality check, she thought, and shook her head. Hell, she knew the rules. You use a psychic on a case, you offer only the bare minimum.

The bookcase creaked.

Christine walked into the stone room, passed the surface of her palms over the back of the chair at the rolltop desk. She touched the walls, the empty filing cabinets. She sat at the edge of the cot, her body blocking the hole McCleary had made in the wall. She propped her elbows on her thighs and rested her chin in her hands.

Only hours ago, Quin thought, Marion had sat where Christine was sitting now and had told her she and Lou had been lovers. Was this any stranger? Any more unexpected?

"This was her private room. It looked real different back then. Bigger." Christine turned slowly, her arm lifting again, finger pointing at the wall behind the cot. "I think there was a window here. The white man used to come to her in this room. Her son was born here."

For the first time, Christine noticed the pair of paintings on the desk. They weren't signed, they weren't even completed, but Quin knew that McCleary had done them. The pencil on the floor near the wall was one he'd been using earlier today, when she and Christine weren't here. She could see the faint markings on the stone.

"That's it," Christine said softly, pointing at the painting of an arched window. "That's what I keep seeing. That's how the window looked." She paused, breathed deeply several times, then whispered, "A man. There's a man at the desk. Dark hair, jeans. Someone from this time. He's going through papers, looking for something."

"What's he look like?" Quin asked.

"Can't see his face."

McCleary said, "Try to get a closer look at him or the papers."

"Don't know if I can. He's, like, frantic now. Scooping all them papers up, shoving them into the desk, slamming the top down."

She moved past them, pursuing something that was invisible to them. It was as if she treaded a border between worlds, between dimensions, between here and *there,* and it required an enormous effort just to sustain her focus.

As she stepped into the hall and turned left toward the front door, Quin caught a whiff of ozone and the rich scent of earth in the air. The storm, Quin thought. It was just the smell of the storm. But she knew it was more than that. So did McCleary.

He stopped, she did, too. And then she felt it, the charge in the air, as if the room had been infused with an enormously powerful electrical current. It raised the hair on her head and arms, made her mouth pucker as though she had bitten into something horribly sour. Then there was a tremendous boom outside and at the same moment the house sprang to life.

The lights blazed, the radio and TV exploded with music and voices, the garbage disposal in the kitchen clattered, the appliances went berserk, a ceramic vase on a table in the hallway exploded and shards flew in every direction. The doorbell rang, a shrill, endless note. Quin slapped her hands over her ears and ran through the kitchen, where the lights flashed and the appliances were still going nuts, and charged into the utility room.

Just as she jerked open the door of the circuit breaker box, lightning struck so close to the house she smelled it. She heard the sizzling hiss as it raced through cables, wires, electrical connections, heard the sharp *pop pop pop* as switches blew out of the panel. Then she was hurled back and a black, soundless wave swallowed her completely.

Quin Quin Quin. The voice kept poking at her, stabbing at her. She opened her eyes and saw death charging toward her on horseback, a blood-red helmet on his head, his face a gleaming white skull, his mouth a frozen rictus of bone. Behind him, surrounding him, were people she and McCleary had known and loved, all of them dead. McCleary's sister, Sylvia Callahan, the man she had been living with before she had met McCleary, a movie producer, even Lou. But they were moving, they weren't dead, they were all talking to her at once and she couldn't hear them. The only thing she heard was the voice, stabbing at her.

Quin Quin Quin.

The people dissolved, aspirin in water. She opened her eyes again, everything was blurred. She was aware of a weird, thick taste in her mouth, of an unpleasant tingling in her fingertips. There was a strange odor in the air, of burned wires. The room solidified around her. McCleary was clutching her shoulders and his face was completely white.

"Jesus, Quin."

She realized she was lying on a cushion of clothes, that she must have fallen back into the hamper and toppled it. She pushed up on her elbows. "Okay, I'm okay."

"You gave us some scare, Bones."

"I . . . the panel . . ."

"We got hit by lightning," McCleary said. "It blew switches right out of the circuit breaker panel and threw you about twenty feet."

"How long was I out?"

"A few seconds, it couldn't have been more than that. Do you feel okay? Can you stand?"

Yes, she could stand and yes, she felt okay. But she didn't feel *right.* There was a terrible buzzing in her left ear, her organs felt as if they had been rearranged, and the tingling in her fingers hadn't gone away.

"I'm hungry," she said.

McCleary and Christine glanced at each other. "If she's talkin about food, she's fine," Christine said.

"With the power off, I can't cook anything," McCleary said, holding her arm as though she were a cripple, an invalid. "How about a sandwich and a salad?"

"Great. Thanks."

"I'll fix it," Christine said, and hurried off.

McCleary didn't let go of her arm until they were in the sunroom, where there was no sun. Rain ran down the picture windows, blurring the gloom outside.

"Sit here," he said, arranging the throw pillows on the couch so she could stretch out. She sank against them and McCleary removed her shoes, her socks, and rubbed the soles of her feet. "You sure you're okay?"

"I feel kind of weird."

"Weird how?" he asked, his anxiety so blatant, so raw, she felt sorry for him.

"Weird okay." The shorthand of marriage, an oxymoron at best.

She rubbed her eyes with the heels of her hands. In the dark inside her head she saw death on horseback, the faces of the dead. "This is going to sound nuts, Mac. But I saw your sister. And Sylvia Callahan. And Grant Bell. And Lou, even Lou. He was standing at the back of . . ." Of what? A room? The crowd? She didn't know. The vision or whatever it had been was no longer as vivid in her mind. "They were all talking to me at once, I couldn't hear any of them."

McCleary ran his hand over her hair, brushed his mouth against her forehead. "That's all you remember?"

"Yeah."

Another man, she thought, might say it was an hallucination, that she'd imagined it. But not McCleary. "What do you think it meant?"

"I don't have any idea. But it seemed that just about everyone we've lost over the years was there, trying to tell me something."

"If you just let it go, the answer will eventually come to you." He squeezed her hand, released it, stood. "Unless we get an electrician out here this afternoon, we're going to be spending the night elsewhere. It's too hot to stay here without AC. I'll call from the car phone. Be right back."

"Mac, wait. Did the lightning happen before everything in the house went off?"

"I don't know."

"The house went crazy first," Christine said, wheeling a cart into the room. It held a platter of sandwiches, a huge bowl of salad, plates. "I'm sure of that."

"If I can get an electrician and the phone company to come out here this afternoon, would you two mind waiting around? I've got to meet Ferret around seven."

"No problem," Quin replied. "I don't feel like doing much of anything right now."

"Don't worry none 'bout us," Christine said, setting everything on the coffee table. "We'll finish what you started in that room."

As McCleary vanished into the hall, a sliver of ice worked its way up Quin's spine. She was suddenly afraid that once he walked out the door this evening to meet Ferret he would never walk in again.

Ridiculous, she thought, and devoured her sandwich as if to fill some huge inner void.

20

I

At 5:37, the ferry docked at Tango Key and Blade walked right past the cop who had been riding back and forth most of the day. The guy never looked twice at him. It was the weirdest sensation, as though he were passing through a world where he was less dense than a shadow.

He headed for the parking lot. His shoes clicked against the concrete, every step pinched his toes. His gray stockings rubbed together, his dress flapped at his knees. The bra he wore, stuffed with rags, kept threatening to slide off his shoulders. His hands were jammed in the pockets of his raincoat. He was afraid the wet wind would whip off the raincoat's hood, so as soon as he was out of the cop's line of vision, he slipped his hand from the pocket and held on to the hood.

He had shaved off his mustache and beard and had made himself up with powder and lipstick and shit from the box of lost-and-found articles on the ferry. Ross Blade, cross-dresser, transvestite. Even Lou wouldn't recognize him now. But for the first time since the night he'd found Lou, he allowed himself to believe he might actually have a chance.

Charlie's Miata was parked by the Dumpster, exactly where she had said it would be. She was leaning against the door, smoking a cigarette, the collar of her raincoat turned up in back, her dark hair glistening with raindrops. She glanced at him, then looked past him, toward the ferry, obviously not recognizing him.

"Hey," he said softly.

Her eyes snapped toward him and she burst out laughing. "Ross."

"Rose," he said, and opened the passenger door and slid inside, his canvas bag in his lap.

She didn't waste time getting out of the lot. "I was afraid you wouldn't show."

"I almost didn't." He checked the side mirror for cars.

"I wasn't followed, Ross. I drove around for an hour before I got here. I also swung by the bus station first and the Rambler's just where he said it would be, in the back lot. I'll just pull up next to it."

"I have to go inside. I left some things in a locker. You can just drop me off."

"There're cops at either end of the bridge, a cop riding the ferry, there're probably cops at the bus station, too."

"C'mon, you really think some cop who's never seen me before is going to recognize me? I don't think so."

She laughed again. "Well, just in case, I'll wait until you're out of the station and inside the Rambler."

"Bad idea, Charlie."

"Just listen to me, okay? My whole family's fucked up. I've been in boarding schools since I was in seventh grade because my parents never got the hang of being parents. I was a total shock to them from the day I was born. I was an intrusion, an inconvenience. I messed up their dinner parties, their vacations in Aspen and Europe. Even after I went to boarding school, I spent most of my vacations here on Tango. You're the most decent human being I've met in ten years."

The words had rushed out of her with a kind of breathless

urgency and now she looked completely horrified that she had said what she had. "Jesus, I'm sorry. I didn't mean to unload on you."

Blade sat there in a shocked stupor, the car idling at a stoplight, the wipers whispering back and forth across the windshield. No girl like Charlie had ever said anything comparable to him before. It embarrassed him, thrilled him, tied his tongue in knots. Color poured into his cheeks and into hers, as well. They both laughed, quick, nervous laughs, and Blade suddenly did what he had wanted to do since the moment he had seen her. He leaned toward her and kissed her, a soft, shy kiss that he felt all the way to his toes.

Everything else fell away from him—the noise of the rain, the hum of the engine, where they were. There was only the soft shape of her mouth, the sweet scent of her hair and her skin. He wasn't sure who broke apart first, but her eyes were mirrors of his own, bright and happy. "It's not every day I get to kiss a man with fake boobs."

He laughed.

Horns blared behind them, the light had turned. Charlie drove on and a few moments later she turned into the bus station parking lot. Blade grabbed his bag off the floor, kissed her quickly again. "I'll drive around to this side and you follow me."

"Right."

He walked quickly but not too quickly toward the front door. Lou used to say that the Tango depot reflected the state of bus travel in south Florida. It was a small, decaying building that looked hunched over, as if cowering against the threat of destruction. A Greyhound had just pulled in and passengers were standing around in clusters, waiting for their luggage.

Blade threaded his way through the crowd, everyone hungry and thirsty and anxious to get somewhere. It wasn't much better inside, people standing in lines for the phones, the rest rooms, the vending machines, the doors to the rear lot opening and shutting as taxis and car rental vans pulled up. Chaos, it was easy to lose yourself in chaos.

The lockers were in the now crowded hall near the rest rooms. He got a few curious looks, maybe because he was still wearing the hood of his raincoat or one of his boobs had slipped or because his eyebrows were too bushy or something. No time to think about it. The key to locker 15 was in his hand.

A locker at the end, on the left-hand side. He crouched, slipped the key into the lock, turned it. The flight bag was inside, of course it was, what the hell had he expected? Just because Rico had brought him here first and was now dead didn't mean the bag would be gone.

Blade pulled it out, shut the door, stood. And suddenly someone whipped off his hood from the back and he spun around. "It's innovative, Ross. I'll give you that much," said Detective O'Connor. Her face was so close to his he could smell mint on her breath. "I didn't recognize you when you got into Charlotte's car. In fact, I probably wouldn't have figured it out if Doris Lynch hadn't told me how odd her granddaughter had been acting since you dropped in at their place the other night."

She wasn't holding a gun on him. He didn't see any other cops nearby. People jostled them on either side, men and women coming and going from the rest rooms. His spine was up against the lockers, he was still clutching the flight bag to his chest, and his head was racing.

"C'mon, Ross. Say something. 'Fuck you, Detective O'Connor.' Yeah, let's hear that for the old days. I think the first arrest was where you said that. And the second and the third and the . . ."

"I didn't kill Lou," he said hoarsely.

Detective O'Connor smirked. "Of course you didn't, Ross. That's why your knife was in his chest." She rocked back on her heels. "And I don't suppose you killed your pal Rico either. Drop both bags on the floor and kick them over here." She gestured at the flight bag. "That one first."

This time there wouldn't be a juvenile hall, a detention center, a rehab program, none of that. This time there would be a double murder charge and a year or more in the county jail before he went to trial as an adult. This time he would be fucked.

"Drop it!" she snapped, and reached inside her raincoat for her gun.

Blade swung the flight bag up and out, swung it hard and fast, and it slammed into her arm, knocking it away from her raincoat. Then it struck her chin and threw her off-balance. She stumbled back and Blade charged her in a wild, desperate panic, his arms thrust out in front of him like a blind man's. He literally ran her over and kept right on moving, oblivious to the screams and shouts in the crowded bus station as people scrambled to get out of his way.

The door, his eyes were on the door, a double door made of glass. Through it he could see the fading light, taxis, throngs of people with their bags. And behind him Detective O'Connor shouted, her voice as swift and powerful as some raging river that swallowed every other sound. But he had no idea what she shouted. He exploded through the doors, stumbled over suitcases, and people leaped out of his way. He raced toward the row of cars, toward the Rambler, a rusted piece of junk whose engine he knew as intimately as his own skin.

His shoes slapped the asphalt, his bags bounced against his hips. O'Connor's shouts were directly behind him now and he knew he wasn't going to make it, knew some rookie cop would pop out of the car, grinning like Freddy Krueger inside the girls' locker room.

Shit damn fuck curtains.

He made it to the Rambler. He didn't know how, but he did, and he threw open the door, hurled himself inside. He slammed the side of his fist against the button on the glove compartment. The lid fell open, the key was inside. Blade jammed it into the ignition and the rusted piece of junk roared to life.

He slammed the shift on the column into reverse, pressed the accelerator to the floor. The car shrieked back, then shot forward, out of the lot and into the street. Second gear, third, Christ oh Christ, she was right behind him, a blue, swirling bubble on top of her van.

The needle on the Rambler's speedometer leaped toward seventy and kept on rising. One-ten was its top speed, and if he hit it the car would probably fall apart. A fender, a door, a goddamn tire.

Blade hung a right on two wheels, then a left on a prayer and a heartbeat, then he was on the four-laner that cut straight through the heart of the island from north to south, and he opened her up wide. For sixty seconds the road was his. The wind whistled in his ears, the landscape blurred past, water flew off the windshield. Then he reached a wall of red taillights, rush-hour traffic, and he tore up the shoulder of the road and swerved off the exit and swung into a U-turn.

He passed her headed in the opposite direction. She saw him and veered across the meridian, a maneuver he wouldn't try in a million years. Blade shrugged off the straps of the bag that were draped over his shoulders and thrust his hand into the glove compartment for the sacks of goodies Ferret kept inside.

Blade had worked on this car so often he knew the contents of each sack. He had investigated each one. He had snooped. Flares, a sewing kit, a dental bridge, firecrackers, glass marbles, tacks, nails. Nothing was related to anything else. These were Ferret's whims.

He grabbed a bag of nails and emptied it out the window. But O'Connor kept on coming, relentless in her fury. The van loomed in his rearview mirror like some huge, mutant dog hell-bent on revenge. He scattered tacks across the road, but she clung to him, narrowing the distance between them. With the cigarette lighter, he lit one of the firecrackers, a sucker about five inches long with a kick that could blow off your fingers. He swerved to the right and dropped it out the window.

It blew up right in front of her, a Fourth of July shower of colorful sparks and an explosion that probably wiped out two years of her life. She swerved, the van slammed across the grassy meridian, then Blade turned and couldn't see her anymore.

He drove like a lunatic, his head locked inside a great white void. When he finally became aware of his surroundings, he was deep in the preserve but damned if he knew where. The Rambler bounced through potholes, trees towered on either side of him, dark skyscrapers that blocked much of the rainy gray light. He slammed on the brakes and collapsed against the steering wheel, shaking so badly his teeth chattered.

After a while he lifted his head, his arms dropped to his sides, and he strained to hear something other than the woods. He quickly removed the clothes in the flight bag, men's clothes, his own goddamn clothes, and changed into them. He didn't have any idea where in the preserve he was, but Charlie had said something about directions.

He didn't find directions in the glove compartment or tucked into the visor. But when he slid out the ashtray, a scrap of paper was neatly folded inside, against the bottom. It read: *Okay, Ross. Here it is. Directions to Ferret's hideout in the preserve. Burn this when you arrive. The IRS loves secrets.*

Attached to the note was a hand-drawn map. Blade studied it, then burned the note in the ashtray, smoothed the map on his thigh, and set out to find Ferret's hideaway.

II

Quin and McCleary stood outside by the Camaro. The grove was eerily quiet, not so much as the click of an insect. Either the fire had obliterated the bugs and frogs, she thought, or the survivors had decided to live elsewhere. Shoots of evening light pierced the damaged trees and shimmered in the air. The rain had diminished to a warm drizzle; she could tell he was anxious to get going.

"I have a bad feeling about this, Mac."

"Slick's here with you."

"No, I mean about wherever Ferret's taking you."

"I trust Ferret."

"So do I. I just have a weird feeling in the pit of my stomach."

"Look, if I'm not back by one A.M., call Gene Frederick. His home number is on the refrigerator. He knows what's going on. You keep the car phone."

McCleary reached into the car for his pack, where the phone was, but she touched his arm. "You keep it and I'll call you later from a pay phone. Or from here, if the phone company gets it fixed tonight."

McCleary stroked her hair, then cupped her chin and kissed her. His mouth tasted of the dampness that clung to the air, a kind of sweetness. "Relax, okay? The only thing that's going to happen tonight is Blade." Then he slipped behind the wheel, shut the door.

The window framed his face and the camera in her head snapped a picture of it, those smoke-blue eyes, the trim beard, the dark hair paling to gray at the temples.

"What?" McCleary whispered, cocking his head.

She leaned into the window. "I love you."

"You really *are* feeling paranoid."

"Habit."

"Well, think about this. Gene offered us a job. We'd be independent contractors, special liaisons between the Tango sheriff's department and federal law enforcement agencies. It would start sometime after the first of the year. Does that interest you?"

Typical, she thought. Save the best for the very last. "Definitely."

"That's it? You don't want more details?"

"How's the money?"

"We'd be making less than we are now, but if we sold the house and fifty percent of the firm to Tark, we'd do pretty good."

He'd already figured the angles. "What'd you tell Gene?"

"That I'd talk it over with you and get back to him in a few weeks."

"The island would be a better place to raise Michelle."

"The dog would love it, but the cats would go into shock with another move."

She laughed. "They'll adjust."

"Will we?"

"Definitely. Tell him yes."

"You sure?"

"Positive."

He squeezed her hand. "See you later."

She stood there as he headed away from the house. Her unease was tempered considerably by his news. It wasn't just the idea of living on Tango Key but that they would be leaving behind the risks inherent in the kinds of cases they'd been investigating for the last ten years. The six of swords, she thought. There it was. Moving away from one thing and toward another.

She thought about the other cards in the reading Janna had done on her. The Tower, she thought, was the fire; Ferret was definitely the knight of rods, the bearer of news; Christine was the queen of cups, the clairvoyant who would help; the Devil, her own fears, had been her obstacle since the beginning; the five of swords, confusion about professional issues, might be resolved as a result of Frederick's job offer, which would nullify the stalemate of the two of swords. That left the ten of swords and the Death card.

The Camaro's taillights vanished around the curve in the driveway. Moments after she went inside, the electrician arrived. He was an aging Tango fritter, scrupulous in his examination of the air conditioner and all of its complex components. He made the rounds from the AC unit outside the house to the temperature control on the wall in the hallway to the circuit breaker panel in the utility room.

"If that don't beat all," he said finally, shaking his head as

Quin and Christine stood on either side of him. "Five circuits blown right outta the panel."

"You've never seen lightning do that?" Quin asked.

"I've seen lightning do all kinds of things, ma'am. Did it start the fire that damaged them trees outside?"

"No. Where'd the lightning strike, anyway?"

"Right next to the air conditioner. It zipped through the cable, scorched the circuits in the temperature gauge in the hall, and if it hadn't blown out the breaker, it probably woulda started a fire here in the house. I bet every phone and alarm in the house went off, huh?"

"Everything but the phone. It's out of order," Quin replied. "Every appliance in the kitchen went nuts."

"Yeah? I've never heard of that, but when it comes to lightning, nothing surprises me." He popped the blown circuit breakers out of the panel and went to work. "If the AC had been on when it happened, you'd be looking at a new compressor and that runs into plenty of money. I think the problem's in the relay switch and that won't be more than one-sixty. Got to charge you overtime."

"How long will it take?" Quin asked.

"No more than an hour."

Quin and Christine left him to his business and went into the den armed with several powerful hurricane flashlights, a toolbox, and the material from the church archives that she had Xeroxed. "Maybe you oughta be takin it easy, Bones."

"I'm not sick. I feel fine."

Fine and yet still not quite right. "Let's make sure we agree on the basics, Slick. Is the air in here warm or cool?"

"Warm. Sticky. You smell jasmine?"

"Nope."

"Me neither."

Quin set one of the flashlights on the floor in front of the bookshelves, its beam diffused against the ceiling, and pulled *One Hundred Years of Solitude* toward her. The bookcase began to swing open.

"Been a sight longer than a century of solitude for the spook in this house," Christine remarked. "If I'd spent nearly three hundred alone here, I'd be nuttier than she is."

"How's she nutty?"

"Shit, girl. Think about it. I'm pretty sure the man I saw at the desk was Lou and that it was the night he died. I was following him into the hall, he was going to answer the door. If his killer was out there, I would've seen the person's face, I'm sure of it. So what's this nutty spook do? She interferes, that's what. She sets off every goddamn electrical gizmo in the house."

"I thought the lightning was responsible."

"Bones, this spook didn't want me to see who killed Lou, because she was afraid we'd forget about what she's been trying to tell us."

"Which is . . . ?"

"I don't even want to make a guess. Let's go see what, if anything, that room has to tell us."

Quin left one of the flashlights right outside the room, the beam aimed at the ceiling, and she and Christine went in with a flashlight each. The air was slightly cooler, but Quin attributed it to all the coquina stone. Just the same, her pulse quickened, her palms dampened.

It was as if the mere act of entering the room where Lou had spent so much time during the final months of his life brought home how far over the top he had stepped. Normal men, after all, didn't dig up graves, didn't hide skulls in walls, didn't lock themselves up in their homes for days at a time and paint scenes of places they had never been or portraits of women who had lived three centuries ago. They didn't do any of the things Lou had done toward the end of his life.

Quin spread the archive material on the floor and Christine brought over McCleary's unfinished paintings and several felt-tip pens. They crouched in front of the wall with the hole in it. Christine stuck her arm down inside; it vanished to the forearm.

"Empty," she announced. "With any luck, though, the hole weakened the rest of the wall."

Quin ran her hands over the stones inside the arch shape that McCleary had partially marked on the wall. Cool and rough. She could see and feel the tiny fossils embedded in them.

She found the archive sketches of the window and compared them to McCleary's painting. They were startlingly similar, depicting an erratic arch that began a foot or two above the floor and extended almost to the ceiling. And yet McCleary hadn't seen the sketches before he had done the painting. So he evidently had tapped into something. Or Luz had worked through him. Or maybe he'd just gotten lucky. Maybe this, maybe that.

The real question here was the significance of a window that had existed three hundred years ago but didn't exist now. It was entirely possible that the window had been filled in during one of the many renovations of the house. Lou's father might have done it at the same time the room had been sealed off from the rest of the house. Or maybe the Tripps had done it in the forties. But she somehow didn't think so.

Christine handed her a pen and pointed at the wall. "You start sketching in the shape from the right, I'll work from the left. Then we'll knock the fucker down."

"Sure. With hammers."

"Just start sketching, Bones."

She was vaguely aware of the electrician coming and going from the utility room, but after a while she ceased to hear him. Her world shrank until it contained only the wall of stone, the vague outline of an arch that hadn't existed for centuries, and a slow, creeping chill.

III

A little bad weather never stopped the freaks, Roey thought, and tonight they were out in great numbers on the boardwalk. They performed under the glow of lights from the shops—the fire-eater, the sword juggler, the Grecian statue, the guy whose cat jumped through hoops of fire. Ferret's weirdo pals.

Roey didn't get it; he didn't give a shit who could do what. But a lot of other people did. The crowd tonight was packed onto the boardwalk and spilled over onto the beach. Roey made his way from act to act, searching for Ferret or Bino, whom he had followed down here from the garage. It was possible they had come just to see the freaks perform, but Roey doubted it. This smelled like a rendezvous.

He paused at the edge of the crowd around the Grecian statue freak in his spray-painted skin, his white hair, his short white tunic. He was standing on a square pedestal, balanced on one leg, his arms frozen in midair, just his eerie eyes moving.

A man with a little girl riding on his shoulders went up to the faggot and the girl held out a dollar bill; the freak's arm came down ever so slowly, took the bill from the little girl's hand and tucked it inside his tunic. His hand emerged from the folds of spray-painted fabric clutching a lollipop.

The girl refused to take it; the freak held his arms out and her old man handed her to him and she began to cry, then to wail, then to shriek. Roey knew just how she felt, all right, and turned away in disgust.

And that was when he saw McCleary. His back was to Roey, he was talking to the fat cookie lady who rode her bike up and down the boardwalk hawking homemade cookies. Another one of Ferret's freak friends. McCleary bought a bag of cookies from her and walked with her along the edge of the boardwalk. Roey followed them at a distance and continued to scan the crowd for Bino or Ferret.

McCleary and the cookie lady stopped in front of the windsurfing shop. She pointed up the alley on the other side of it, then pedaled on and McCleary strolled past the shop, stopped, and glanced around. Roey quickly bowed his head and tugged his baseball cap lower over his eyes. When he looked again, McCleary was gone.

Roey pushed his way through the crowd and ducked down the first alley he reached, several short of the one McCleary had taken. He ran through it, toward the parking lot of a bank on the other side. Bino's black Blazer was just speeding out of the lot, two heads visible in the rear window.

He charged for his Volvo, which was parked at the curb across the street from the bank, leaped inside, and tore away from it with the fury of a man who knew his last stab at something better was about to disappear.

He lost fifteen minutes circling the immediate vicinity and finally spotted the Blazer headed for the four-lane highway that shot north across the island. He laughed out loud and slipped into the turn lane three cars behind them.

San Miguel de Allende had suddenly gotten a lot closer.

21

I

Blade nosed the Rambler into the trees near the cabin. He scooped the firecrackers out of the glove compartment, half a dozen of the long ones with the wicked booms and a box of fifty smaller ones. He shoved them in a side pocket of the flight bag, reached under the seat for the flashlight, then got out of the car.

He stood for a moment in the absolute darkness, the night sounds rising and falling around him. The rain had stopped, but lightning seared across the sky and thunder echoed through the trees, promising more. He strained to hear the noise of other cars, other people, but the only noises out here belonged to the wild.

Blade turned on the flashlight and hiked up the steep, muddy hill to the cabin. It looked basic from the outside, an old small cabin squatting on very short stilts that lifted it, at most, two feet from the ground. The porch door hung on a single hinge and here and there the screen was torn.

The only pieces of furniture on the porch were a wooden rocker that would probably break if he sat in it and a wooden table with three legs that was propped at one corner on a stack of bricks. The front door, though, was solid pine, a foot thick, and the key to it was taped to the underside of the rotting rocker.

Inside, he found three rooms and a small basement. There was no electricity. Water was hand-pumped at the sink. The kitchen appliances consisted of a one-burner gas stove and a small, gas-fueled fridge. The furniture was old and musty, forget hot water. But the pantry was well stocked; Ferret had prepared for the end of the civilized world.

Blade stuffed a can of tuna fish and several small bottles of water into the flight bag. He drank down a warm Pepsi as he dug out the cellular phone to connect it to the computer. He needed to talk to Charlie, to know she was okay. But the phone was dead. He shoved it into the bag with the notebook and stashed it in the woodpile in the basement.

Upstairs again, he paused long enough to wash the makeup off his face. He wiped the sink dry with a paper towel, started to toss it into the empty trash can, but stuck it in his pocket instead. He didn't want any traces of himself here. He scooped some matches out of a drawer, shoved them into the bag, and slipped out the rear door.

Yeah, he was paranoid. But look what had happened when he had let his guard slip at the bus depot. Better this, he thought, that the inside of a miserable little cell.

The rear porch wasn't screened and he went over to the railing and shone the flashlight around, looking for a place to hide. But the only thing he saw were more trees, huge dripping trees that formed a wall just beyond the cabin.

He swung over the railing, landed softly on the spongy ground, and dropped into a crouch. He shone the flashlight under the cabin, across the piles of firewood, over the floorboards, into the space under the porch stairs. He scurried along the side of the cabin, and when he reached the stairs, he ducked under and pushed back into the space.

And there he waited for Ferret to arrive.

II

The shape of the arch was clearly visible now, drawn in black magic marker. It started eighteen inches above the floor and ended a foot or so from the ceiling. Quin stared at it so long her vision grew fuzzy at the edges. She could sense that distant past around her, swirling in the very molecules of the air she breathed.

Gradually, the shape began to brighten, to assume dimension and scope, and suddenly the stones vanished and there it was, the window as it had existed then, the arch as a portal to another world. The rich, emerald leaves rustled in a warm breeze. She could hear birds. The scent of the warm sea air washed over her. And the light, she had never seen light quite like this, possessed of such preternatural clarity.

Quin wanted to feel it against her face, hold it in her hands. She wanted to lean out into this other world and inhale its air, its density, its reality. Infused with something she couldn't explain, she lurched toward the window.

She would wait for him there, her back against the cool hardness of the stones, her legs drawn up against her chest, the glimmer of the sea visible through the trees. He would ride up on his horse, she would wave, he would sweep her out of the window and they would gallop off into the woods. That was how it would happen, how it always happened, how—

She ran smack into the wall and stumbled back, rubbing her nose and forehead.

"Jesus, Bones, what the hell's wrong with you?" Christine hurried over to her.

Quin ran her hands over the stones. Impossible, she thought. It had seemed so real, all of it, not just the sights and odors and sounds, but the rest of it, that he would ride up on his horse and . . .

"Hey, Bones." Christine grabbed her forearm, snapping her back.

"Hello, Mrs. McCleary?"

The electrician's voice rang out, a lamp flared in the den, she heard the AC click on. The real world. Pay attention to the real world. "Let me take care of him and I'll be right back, Slick."

He was waiting in the hall for her, proud that the power was restored. Quin wrote him a check for $152 and change and walked to the door with him, eager to be rid of him, to return to the room and finish what she'd been doing. Then he was gone and she rushed around the house, shutting the windows they had opened earlier.

When she entered the den, Christine had turned on all the lights, connected the lamp to an extension cord, and moved it into the stone room. "Now we'll at least be able to see what we're doing," she said without looking up. She was going through the toolbox and plucked out a hammer, a chisel, and a heavy-duty electric drill. She picked up a box of drill bits and selected the largest mortar bit.

"This looks like something you'd use on a floor, to take up tile. If it works on rock, it'll be faster than a hammer and chisel."

Quin, sitting back on her heels, said, "We don't know for sure that anything else is hidden in the wall, Slick. Maybe we should just let this whole thing alone. Mac already made a mess here."

Christine snorted. "Jesus, girl. Sometimes you chug along in right-brain mode and I think there's hope for you. Then you say something like that. I mean, what the hell are we doing in here if there's nothing in the wall?"

"Okay, okay."

Christine pulled an extension cord from the toolbox, plugged one end into the drill and went into the den to plug it into an outlet. She turned on the drill, testing it. "Seems to work okay."

"We'll start where the wall sounds hollow."

Quin began tapping the stones about a foot and a half up from the floor. She located a hollow spot three feet up, equidistant between the lines that defined the arch shape of the window. Quin slammed the hammer against it, loosening the mortar. "Try right about here with the drill."

"Right." Christine touched the drill bit to the loosened mortar and turned on the drill.

A high-pitched shriek filled the room, a noise like a thousand fingernails clawing a blackboard. Quin clenched her teeth and pressed her hands to her ears. The drill began to smoke, Christine turned it off, and Quin struck the area with the hammer again.

Chips of mortar fell away and a long fissure raced through the coquina rock. Christine flashed her a thumbs up, grinned, and they fell into a mesmerizing rhythm—the drill, the hammer, the drill, the hammer. And when the block started to crumble, they went after it at the same time until the rest of it surrendered, raining down in dusty bits and chunks.

The opening was just big enough to squeeze her hand through. Quin switched on the flashlight and shone it inside, but she couldn't see much of anything except more wall on the other side of the hole. The exterior wall of the house. "We need to widen it."

Christine plucked a pair of stained gardening gloves from the toolbox and pulled them on. "Let me try." She gripped the broken edges of the opening and pulled. More bits and chunks fell away. "We need the drill again."

Quin picked up the hammer once more and started tapping the stones in the immediate vicinity of the opening. She located another hollow spot and they went to work on it and quickly found the rhythm again. Drill, hammer, drill, hammer.

The loss of the first stone had weakened the others, and the mortar that kept these suckers together was old. She wondered how many they could remove before the entire wall collapsed. Five? Ten? Fifteen? And then what? Suppose there was nothing hidden in the wall?

"Screw it, Slick. This is ridiculous." She dropped the hammer, brushed her hands together, and started to push to her feet when the lamp suddenly blinked and the cold seeped slowly into the room.

She and Christine glanced at each other, but neither of them said a word. They resumed their work. Now and then Quin was aware of a cool breath of air against the back of her neck, but she tried not to acknowledge it, tried instead to focus on the ever-widening circle in the middle of the wall.

Another stone gave way and Quin thrust her hand inside. She could feel the exterior wall of the house, jagged edges of coquina rock and mortar, and then a cleft in the mortar that was barely large enough to accommodate her index finger. "There's something here, Slick."

"Can't see worth a shit. Let me move the lamp closer."

The light helped. Quin was able to approximate the location of the cleft relative to the wall they'd been dismantling bit by painful bit. She made an *X* on the spot, then Christine went at it with the drill and Quin used the hammer to pound the area around it.

The stone collapsed, exposing a small, bowl-shaped depression that was filled with what appeared to be small rocks, pebbles, dirt, shells. A perfect hideout for scorpions, spiders, and other creepy critters. Christine, obviously thinking along the same line, said, "Ain't puttin my hand in there. Uh-uh, no way. We need a shovel."

"The shovel's buried somewhere under the mess in the shed. I'll get some spoons."

Christine pushed to her feet, rubbed her hands over her arms. "I need a sweater."

They exchanged a glance, but neither of them voiced the obvious, that the air in the room had grown progressively cooler until it was now downright chilly. They hurried through the den, which was noticeably warmer, and when they reached the hall, Quin whispered, "She's in there, Slick. Watching us."

"You want to quit?" Christine whispered back.

"No. Do you?"

"No. But I need a sweater or a jacket. You got something that'll fit me?"

"Probably in the laundry room."

The farther they got from the stone room, the easier it was to talk. But they kept whispering, as if they were afraid she was listening to them, eavesdropping on them. Hell, maybe she was. Just when Quin had been ready to quit, the lamp had blinked. Yes, there were other possible explanations—a bad connection, a flawed cord—but she knew it was none of those. The spook had been telling them to stay, to see it through to the end.

III

Everett, the escape artist, drove like a little old man who had never ventured beyond his own neighborhood. He was hunched over the steering wheel and kept rubbing his hand across the glass to clear it.

"I'm supposed to take you to the wharf. That's where Bino will pick you up."

"The wharf is five minutes from where you picked me up. We've been driving around for forty minutes."

"Precautions, Mr. McCleary. Oh, I almost forgot." He fished in the side pocket on the driver's door and brought out a baseball cap. "Put that on."

"For what?"

"I don't know, man. I'm just telling you what Ferret told me."

McCleary put the hat on. "Any other instructions?"

"Nope." He kept glancing in the rearview mirror. "I see a couple of cars back there, but I don't think we were followed."

He exited the highway and headed south on Old Post. He twitched a lot, but it wasn't a nervous affliction. It was as if he were trying to compress his bones, make himself smaller.

"You known Ferret long?" McCleary asked.

"Half my life. I was seventeen, doing escape gigs in local theaters. Ferret saw my act, told me about the boardwalk, rented me an apartment, and here I've been ever since."

"And Bino?"

"Shit," he laughed. "They've known each other forever. They're half-brothers, same old man." He pulled into a lot behind one of the warehouses on the docks, nosed into a space between a pickup truck and a high-top van. "End of the road, Mr. McCleary. Bino's in the truck."

"Thanks."

"Good luck."

As he got out, a man emerged from the van, trotted over to the Blazer. He wore a baseball cap and was about McCleary's height and weight. He grinned, tipped his cap in greeting, and slid into the seat McCleary had just vacated.

The pickup's passenger door swung open, McCleary climbed inside. "Sorry about the detour," Bino said, backing out of the space. "Blade nearly got nabbed earlier, so Ferret thought we'd better take precautions."

"Nabbed where?"

"Bus depot. Detective O'Connor was there. He created a ruckus and got away, but Charlie Lynch was taken in for questioning. Ferret doesn't think she'll mention his name, but in case she does, we just want to be prepared."

"Where's Blade now?"

"That's where we're going." He headed for the exit at the other end of the lot. "Better take off the cap and slide down in the seat."

McCleary did. The pickup bounced over a speed bump and whatever it had in the back clattered and slid around. Then the truck turned and McCleary felt road beneath the wheels. "We're in traffic now," Bino said. "It's okay to sit up."

"Where're we headed?"

"The preserve. What do you know about Tom Roey?"

"Just that he's some guy Lou's ex dated." And that he didn't show up anywhere on the computer check Marion had run on him that night at the lighthouse.

"I'm afraid he's a little more than that. I happened to be in the Cove the other morning and saw Roey drop Janna Hilliard at her office. It was obvious they'd spent the night together. For some reason, that kept bugging me, so I made some inquiries and found out that Janna and Rico, Blade's astrologer buddy, used to trade readings.

"So then I had to ask myself if Janna knew that Blade and Rico were friends and if she told Roey. The bartender at the Pink Moose had seen them leave together. I figure Roey split from Janna's sometime before dawn, called Rico with some story about information on Blade, and Rico met him somewhere or picked him up, something like that. And then he pulled a gun on him when they were up in the preserve and shot off his fucking kneecap to get Rico to tell him where Blade was hiding out. He killed him, drove the car into the woods on Old Post, and beat feet back to Janna's. She was his alibi just in case."

"But he never found Blade."

"I think the kid had moved by the time Roey tracked down the houseboat. The guy who runs the boat rental place up at the marina said he rented a skiff to Roey, that he took off into the mangroves on the Tango River. So I decided to take a look earlier today. I found Lou's houseboat, all right. What was left of it, a hulk that reeked of gasoline. If we hadn't been having so much rain and the heat was as bad as it usually is in September, the gas probably would have ignited."

"You're making some huge assumptions about Roey having killed Rico."

"Not so huge. Miami, 1975. A poker game in a warehouse owned by a guy named Sean Korelli, a minor-league loan shark. During a poker game, Korelli ripped off a fifteen-year-old kid named Tom Roey, who made a stink and got tossed out. Eight months later Korelli's body was fished out of Biscayne Bay. He'd been shot in the knees and point-blank in the neck, just like Rico. No leads, no clues, the case is still open.

"Roey moved around south Florida afterward, hiring out with fishing charters, shit like that. He played the track, made some money, some connections, and moved to the islands, where he ran a casino for the cartel. There was trouble, he split, moved around again for a while, did some bounty hunting for bail bondsmen in different parts of the state.

"He ended up on Tango, connected with David Vicente, started managing some of his rental apartments. He was still doing some bounty hunting on the side. Three years ago, Gracie hired him to track down one of her skips. Petty shit, a three-thousand-dollar bond. He found the guy, brought him in. Then last winter she hired him again to track the expensive skips and he fucked up. The bonds were forfeited, Lou had to pay big time."

Gracie claimed that Lou had hired a bounty hunter. One more little lie. "And you think Vicente paid him to get rid of Blade so that he'd have an easier time getting his hands on the grove?"

"Very likely. It's also likely that he hired Roey to waste Lou and to scare you and your wife off the island."

The threatening calls, the fire, yeah, it made sense. Now all he had to do was prove it. "Have you told Detective O'Connor any of this?"

"No way. There's only one cop me and Ferret deal with and she's out of the country." He glanced at McCleary, his red eyes like hot coals. "That's why you're sitting where you are, Mike. You're our connection."

"You ever had any dealings with Gene Frederick?"

"A few. Our buddy Kincaid works with him from time to time."

"Kincaid is the guy who owns the lighthouse where Detective O'Connor is staying, right?"

"He and Aline own it. She's the cop we deal with."

Their world sounded more complicated than his own.

Bino pulled into the last gas station before the preserve. "Got to fill up. We'll be leaving this truck for the kid."

Bino and McCleary went inside. While Bino prepaid for the gas, McCleary headed down a dingy hall at the back of the store. He called the station, but Frederick wasn't in. When he called his home number, McCleary reached the answering machine. He didn't want to call later on the car phone, it wasn't private, so he left a message.

"Gene, it's Mike. I'm on my way to meet Blade. Check out a guy named Tom Roey. He manages some of Vicente's rental complexes. No record, Marion ran his name a couple of nights ago. But he may have killed Rico and his alibi's going to be Janna Hilliard, the tarot card reader whose office is across the courtyard from Lou's. I'll be in touch."

He tried the house, but reached a recording that the number wasn't in service at this time.

Half a mile up the road from the station, Bino pulled alongside a dark sedan that was parked on the shoulder. Ferret hopped out, McCleary opened the door, and he climbed inside.

"We clear, Bino?"

"As clear as it gets."

"Good." He grinned at McCleary. "It's not far now."

"How do you know Blade is there?" McCleary asked.

"I don't. But we know he was driving the Rambler when he fled the bus depot and he had directions. I'm hopeful."

McCleary wished he could say the same. But ever since he'd made his calls, an inexplicable dread had been bumping around inside of him, a feeling that he shouldn't have left the grove, that something, somewhere, was about to go very wrong.

22

I

The room had grown progressively colder. Quin's fingers were now so stiff it was difficult to dig. The floor around her and Christine was already strewn with stuff that had been inside the wall since the window had been sealed up. Rocks, pebbles, bits of mortar, shells. The shells that were still intact were embedded with fossils and streaked with intricate swirls of color. They weren't typical of what you found on Tango's beaches today.

When the hole was clear of debris, Quin dropped the spoon and worked her fingers through the floor of sand and grit inside. She felt something hard and cold at the bottom. "What is it?" Christine asked, holding a flashlight over the depression, straining to see.

"Metal, a small metal container." One end of it seemed to be caught under a protrusion of rock inside the hole and she had to work the container from side to side to free it. When she finally lifted it, she was disappointed that it was so light. Nothing this light could possibly contain gold or gems, the remains of Domingo's treasure.

Quin pulled it out of the hole and set it on the floor. It was a black iron box about six inches long on either side and a foot high. "Looks old," she said softly and ran her hands over it. It felt old, too. She couldn't say exactly how an object could feel old, but this did. There was something radically different between this iron, for instance, and an iron frying pan from Kmart.

"The lid's been welded to it," Christine remarked, and placed her own hands against it.

She shut her eyes and began a deep, rhythmic breathing. Quin closed her own eyes as well and began to breathe as Christine was breathing. Her fingers tingled, a pins and needles sensation that rose up into her hands, her wrists, her arms. It was the same odd tingling she'd experienced when she had come to on the laundry-room floor, but it was more pronounced this time, ran deeper into her tissues, her blood, her very bones. It was as if the metal had retained a residue of the individual who had last touched the box and she could sense it. Sense him.

"A man," Christine said. "I'm picking up a man."

Quin didn't say anything, but it seemed she sensed the man's hands against the iron—small, powerful hands. Now he took shape in her mind, just his face at first, a vague, undefined face, like a sketch a kid might make. Then certain details leaped into clarity—an eye patch, a hooked nose, long, graying hair. Disney World bullshit, she thought, that's all this was. Captain Hook without the hook.

"What're you getting?" Christine asked.

"It's stupid."

"It's never stupid, Bones. Trust your first impression. Just say it."

"He wore an eye patch," Quin said.

"He smelled bad."

She hesitated, uncertain again.

"Anything else?" Christine prodded.

"I don't know."

"You know. Say it."

"Gray hair, shoulder-length."

"Yeah, I get that, too. And he had a gorilla body, short, solid, hairy. It's him. The pirate. Gotta be."

They opened their eyes at the same moment, removed their hands from the chest simultaneously. Christine grinned and wiped her face with the sleeve of her shirt. "Whatever happened to you earlier seems to have opened you right up, girl. C'mon, let's break into this fucker and see what Domingo left behind. I don't think it's a treasure, but this ol' box is why the spook lady hung around all these centuries."

"We need a blowtorch to get into this," Quin said.

"Shovel might do it. C'mon, let's carry it into the other room where it's warmer."

They set it on the floor in the den, then Christine went back for the lamp and tilted the shade up so the light spilled more directly on the metal box. She stood over it, pushing up the sleeves of the sweater Quin had lent her. "Better be a big shovel."

"I think I saw one in the basement. I'll get it."

"You stay put. I need to get my blood moving."

"The cellar door is off the kitchen."

When she had left, Quin put her hands on the box again, shut her eyes, breathed as she had done before. Her fingers started to tingle and she felt something shift inside of her, as if to accommodate this invisible conduit. And then images flashed across the inner screen of her eyes, impressions that rushed at her too quickly to process, to understand. She jerked her hands away, the images stopped. A short-circuit, she thought.

"This should do it." Christine brought the shovel over to where Quin was. "Scoot outta the way, Bones."

Quin moved back and Christine heaved the shovel over her head and slammed it down against the chest. She did it again and again and again; the clatter of metal against metal rang out with the clarity of a church bell.

When Christine got tired, Quin took over. She tilted it onto the side and struck the place where the lid had been soldered to the box. They switched back and forth twice more before the metal suddenly split open.

Inside was a rolled-up parchment, that was all. The edges of the paper had crumbled away over the centuries and the wax seal had long since broken. But it looked remarkably well preserved. Quin unrolled it and Christine held the bottom edge to keep it from furling up again.

The script was small and florid, with many elaborate swirls that would make it difficult to read in English, much less in Spanish. "At least it's not in Latin."

"You can read it, can't you?" Christine asked.

"I need a pencil and some paper. It'll be easier to do it that way."

It took her a while, but Christine took it down word by word. It read:

19 July 1734
I, Juan Sebastian Domingo, son of Don Esteban Domingo of Barcelona, Spain, do hereby acknowledge that Luz Jacinto is my lawful wife, wedded to me at sea in the summer of 1701. I am the father of Tomás Xavier Jacinto, born to Luz Jacinto on 3 April 1704. This shall be entered into the official church records and shall entitle my son to all the rights to which he is permitted under the laws of Spain and the laws of God.
Juan Sebastian Domingo

"Goddamn," Christine breathed. "That's why she hung around all these years. Not the loot, but a letter from this prick saying he was the father of her boy."

The forgotten son, Quin thought. "Domingo was married to a Spanish woman then, so he was a bigamist to boot. No wonder the document never made it into the church records. If I remember correctly, Luz's son died on July twentieth, one day after this document is dated. So it took Domingo thirty years to admit paternity and he didn't do it until his son was on his deathbed."

"Shit, then she has to hang around for another three centuries." Christine made a disgusted noise. "That's the problem with heroes. They usually fuck up." She released the bottom of the parchment and it rolled up again. "You got to make sure that two-faced priest fixes the records."

"C'mon, let's clean up in there and drive over to the church."

While Quin fetched the broom from the kitchen and began sweeping up the mess in the room, Christine gathered up the drill bits, drill, and the shovel and headed toward the cellar. Quin paused once to reread the document and found that each swirl of ink, each beautifully written word, even the texture of the paper itself yielded some small intuition about the man who had written it.

The lamp flickered once and she raised her eyes, noticing that the cold from the stone room had oozed into the den. "I'll go to the church," she whispered. "Just don't do any more weird shit. We have a deal?"

The lamp stayed on. She set the document on the rolltop desk and was about to resume her cleanup when the doorbell rang. The phone company. Finally. Quin shut the door to the den as she left and walked quickly down the hall.

It took her a moment to recognize the man who stood there in jeans, a guayabera shirt, sandals, and rain jacket. In his photos he usually looked like a businessman; now he looked like a Latin tourist.

David Vicente said, "You must be Mrs. McCleary."

She managed a tight, barely polite smile. "What can I do for you, Mr. Vicente?"

"I'd like to speak to your husband. I phoned, but the number seems to be out of order."

"He'll have to call you in the morning. He's working and doesn't want to be disturbed."

Why did I say that?

Because she was suddenly afraid of this man. Because this was exactly what Lou had done, opened the door to his killer.

The thought apparently showed in her eyes because his arm shot out to hold the door open and he was suddenly holding a gun on her. A thirty-eight. "Put your hands on top of your head and step back into the house, Mrs. McCleary."

She never argued with a gun. She laced her fingers together on top of her head and stepped back; he stepped in and shut the door. *Stay put, Slick. Listen up. Let's get this right, please let's get this right.* "Just what is it that you want, Mr. Vicente?"

"To look around, if I may."

"You've got the gun. You don't have to ask permission."

He smiled at that, a courteous gentlemanly smile, a Cuban smile filled with hospitality. "Quite true. Into the den, Mrs. McCleary. What I'm looking for is in that part of the house."

She didn't want to turn her back on him, so she moved down the hall facing him. A McCleary axiom. *Always look them in the eyes when they've got a gun on you, and keep talking—it makes it harder for them to shoot.*

"And what would that be?"

"A legal document."

"Ask Craig Peck. He's been rather liberal with information about Lou's will."

Vicente cocked his head and flashed another one of those irritating gentlemanly smiles. This guy, she thought, would be smiling like that when he pulled the trigger. "Very good, Mrs. McCleary."

"And I suppose you're also looking for Domingo's treasure."

"That would be a pleasant surprise."

"Christ, don't you have enough money?"

He seemed to get a kick out of that. "You're quite right. I have more money than I'll be able to spend before I die. For me, it's actually a matter of principle. This land was supposed to be mine. The last family to own it before the Hernandos went bankrupt and the land was repossessed, then sold at auction. Manuel, Lou's father, was supposed to bid on it for me. Instead, he bid on it for himself and kept it." Vicente laughed, a small, bitter sound. "It's one thing to lose fairly. It's quite another to lose because you're betrayed by a man as close to you as blood."

"So you *did* kill him," she said quietly, taking small steps as she moved backward down the hall.

"I'm afraid I can't claim credit for that."

"Maybe I should rephrase it. You hired someone to kill him."

"I had nothing to do with Lou's death. Unfortunately, someone else beat me to it. Into the den, please."

C'mon, Slick, help me out on this one. She groped behind her for the knob, turned it, backed into the den. "If you're acting on principle, then I guess that means Doris Lynch is acting out of greed."

"Doris? Greedy?" He laughed again. "Please. It's hardly that complicated. Doris simply likes control, Mrs. McCleary. And it doesn't matter whether it's people or birds or land she has coveted since the day she saw it. She doesn't care what's done with it as long as *she* owns it, controls it, calls the shots." He paused, his eyes darting from her to the stone room and back to her again. "My, you have been busy. And what did you find in the wall?"

"A skull. Probably what was left of Domingo's son."

He laughed again, a soft, ugly sound, then stepped toward her and struck her across the face so hard stars exploded inside her eyes. She stumbled back and stood with her spine against the wall, wiping at the blood that oozed from a corner of her mouth. "I guess that means you don't believe me."

"What I believe, Mrs. McCleary, is that you and your husband are a complication I don't need. What did you find in the wall?"

"Like I said, a skull. And that." She pointed at the document on top of the desk.

Vicente sidestepped toward it, never taking his eyes from her, the position of his gun never faltering. He unrolled the parchment with one hand, weighted it at the top with a book, glanced at it briefly, then looked back at her.

"This was in that black box?"

"Yes."

"And that's it."

"Yes."

He fired the gun then and the bullet struck the floor only inches from her feet. She wrenched back, the explosion echoing in her skull, and Vicente smiled politely. "I don't believe you, Mrs. McCleary. So let's go through it again."

Quin saw the shadow that fell across the floor behind him. *Keep him occupied,* she thought, and started telling him how McCleary had found the skull, what she had learned from the church archives, anything to distract him. Christine crept into the room with the shovel raised over her head and suddenly Vicente spun around and fired. The bullet glanced off the shovel, slammed into the wall on the other side of the room, then the shovel crashed into his arm and the gun went flying.

Quin dived for it and Vicente, squealing like a stuck pig, stumbled back and tripped over the desk chair. And there he remained, clutching his bleeding arm against his body, moaning, "You broke it, Jesus, you broke my fucking arm."

"Shut up," Quin snapped, cocking the gun, aiming it at him. "Slick, there're handcuffs in the kitchen drawer closest to the fridge. Can you get them?"

"Sure thing."

She tore out of the room and Quin stepped back to a safe distance, the gun never wavering from her target. Vicente watched her with his small, dark eyes, glazed now with pain. He didn't try to get up, didn't make any sudden moves. But there was something deeply disturbing about the silence and the way he watched her. She had the distinct impression that he was gloating.

Christine returned to the room with the handcuffs, told

Vicente to roll onto his stomach, then straddled him like a rider on a horse, grabbed his arms, and jerked them behind him to snap on the cuff. He shrieked from the pain, his arm bled all over the floor.

"Quit your yellin, asshole," Christine muttered, and proceeded to gag him with a table napkin. Then she bound his ankles with an extension cord, stood up, and brushed her hands together, surveying her work with the pride of a cowgirl who has just roped a calf at the local rodeo.

Vicente writhed and screamed into the gag.

"Let's get him down into the cellar," Quin said.

"I'll get the afghan from the sunroom. We can wrap him in that."

When he was bound like a mummy, just his head showing, they carried him down into the cellar and propped him in a corner. His eyes bulged in his cheeks, he screamed into the gag. Christine held the gun on him while Quin peeled open the afghan at the front and searched his pockets.

She found an unaddressed envelope that hadn't been sealed. Inside was a Xerox copy of a document from the county tax appraiser's office, describing a five-acre plot of land in the preserve that had sneaked in under the grandfather clause. It cost two hundred a year in taxes and was registered to J. Ferret and R. Bino. She knew, she suddenly *knew,* where Blade was hiding out and where McCleary had gone.

"What're you doing with this, Mr. Vicente?" Quin held up the sheet with one hand and jerked the gag from his mouth with the other.

He swore at her in Spanish, spittle flying from his mouth.

"Oh, let me ask him," Christine said impatiently, and knelt at his right side. "It's this little ol' arm that's hurt, isn't it, Mr. V. How much does it hurt, hmm?"

And she closed her fingers around it, his eyes bulged in his cheeks, and he gasped, "Okay, okay, I'll tell you."

Christine eased back on the pressure. "I'm waitin, Mr. V. And I'm not a patient woman, you hear what I'm sayin?"

"Ross worked for Mr. Ferret. I . . . I think that's where he is."

"Ah." Christine's head bobbed up, down. "And you want the kid outta the way. So he doesn't inherit."

"Yes." He whispered it.

"Then what the hell are you doing here?" Quin snapped.

His lips rolled together. "I . . . that is . . ."

Christine clicked her tongue against her teeth. "Shame, shame, Mr. V. The lady done asked you a question. You got ten seconds."

He was in so much pain the words rushed out of his mouth. It took her a moment to absorb the full impact of what he had said. Tom Roey. McCleary and Blade. Two hundred grand.

But when it all sank in, a thick and terrible loathing swept over her and she kicked him in his arm, his broken arm, and he passed out.

"You got any idea how to get to this place in the preserve?" Christine asked.

"No." And there weren't any directions in the document. "The nearest phone's on Mango Road. I'll call Mac on the cellular phone."

Less than sixty seconds later, they sped out of the grove in the Camaro, the three-hundred-year-old paternity document locked in the glove compartment.

II

Blade heard the car a long time before he glimpsed the headlights. The sound rode the damp night air like some sort of animal's call. *Hellooo, are you there? Is anyone there?* That kind of call.

He pushed back as far as he could into the dark space beneath the stairs. He felt alternately cold and hot, terrified and calm. He could see through the slats, lights that winked through the trees, but he couldn't hear voices yet. He clutched the flight bag closer to his chest and pressed his face into it.

A soft whistle drifted through the air and Blade raised his head and peered through the slats again. Flashlights. Three people at the top of the slope. One short, one tall, one in between. Ferret, Bino, and a third man, maybe McCleary. But he stayed where he was, listening for their voices. He wanted to be sure. He had come too far not to be sure.

". . . doesn't look like anyone's here."

Blade didn't recognize the voice.

"He's been here, Mike," Ferret replied. "I can smell him."

Mike: that was McCleary, Blade thought.

"Smell him?" McCleary again.

"Ferret's got an acute sense of smell," Bino explained.

They climbed the stairs to the porch. "Key's gone," Blade said. "Door's unlocked."

They went inside the house. Through the floorboards, he could see the flicker of a lantern. Their voices now were muted, he couldn't make out what they were saying. Someone walked from one end of the cabin to the other. He heard the rear door creak open, heard someone come out, heard the familiar soft whistle. It was Ferret.

"Hey, Ross," he said. "I know you're nearby. It's okay to come out. It's just me, Bino, and McCleary."

Blade crawled out from under the house and reached the porch just as Ferret was coming down the steps. They both stopped. "Goddamn, kid, it's good to see you."

A lump swelled in Blade's throat and he threw his arms around the little man, hugging him hello. "Thanks for everything, Ferret." He could barely get the words out.

"Don't thank me yet. Let's get things squared away and see where we stand."

"What do I smell like anyway?"

Ferret laughed and slapped him on the back. "Scared shitless, Ross. Scared shitless. Let's go inside."

III

Roey couldn't stand it anymore. He threw off the tarp, sat up, and pulled the sweet, wet air into his lungs. He didn't know how long it had been since he'd climbed into the back of the truck at the gas station, while Bino and McCleary were inside. Half an hour, an hour, what the hell difference did it make at this point? By now the three musketeers were settled in the cabin.

He eased between the boxes and swung over the side of the truck. He landed soundlessly on the soft, spongy ground, slipped out his nine millimeter, flicked off the safety. Two at once, what could be easier? He walked around the truck, puncturing the tires with his knife.

Just as he finished, a phone inside the truck began to ring. The sound was muffled because the door was shut and the windows were up, but there was no telling how far a noise traveled out here. He threw open the door, grabbed the phone off the seat, and pressed the button before it could ring again.

The woman's voice reached him as if from a great distance. "Mac? Mac, you there?"

The Mrs. The Mrs. with the long legs. Too bad, he thought, and disconnected. Before she could call back, he popped the batteries out and hurled them and the phone into the trees.

Then he started up the muddy hill toward the cabin, juggling two plans in his mind, both equally clear. He could wait for them to leave the cabin and pick them off one by one. Or he could lure them out somehow and do the same. Either way, he had the element of surprise in his favor.

IV

Quin hung up, alarmed that she hadn't been able to get through to McCleary. And yet she was sure someone had answered it. She had heard the click, the open line, and then the void as the connection was severed. An electronic glitch, something misfiring in a satellite two hundred thousand miles from Earth, that had to be it.

But she sensed that wasn't it at all.

She punched out the number for the Tango Key sheriff's department. The dispatcher who answered said Gene Frederick wasn't in, could anyone else help her?

"Is there another number where I can reach him? It's very important," Quin said.

"Your name, ma'am?"

"Quin McCleary."

"Just a minute. I'll have to put you on hold."

She waited through an excruciating silence punctuated by soft, even beeps that indicated the call was being recorded.

"Mrs. McCleary? You still there?"

"Still here."

"I'm going to patch you through to the captain."

Moments later, Gene Frederick came on the line, his voice gruff and urgent. "Mrs. McCleary, I got a message from Mike on my machine at home. Do you know where he is?"

"Yes, but I don't know how to get there." She quickly told him about Vicente, Roey, Ferret's land in the preserve.

"Christ. Are you at the house now?"

"No."

"Can you meet me at the airport?"

"You bet. I'll even bring a pilot."

"Can he fly choppers?"

"She can fly just about anything."

"Good, that'll save us time. I'll meet you at the flight service office."

"What do you look like?"

"Short and squat, like a troll," he said, and hung up.

Quin ran over to the car and leaped in. "You've got to fly a chopper."

"A chopper? I'm not rated for a chopper."

"So you can't do it?"

"I don't know. I never tried."

"You'll do it. I know you will."

What she didn't know was if they would reach Ferret's cabin in time.

23

I

McCleary listened to Blade's story from beginning to end and the tape recorder whirred, getting every word. When the kid was finished, he slumped against the couch, as if the telling had exhausted him.

"Can you describe the car you saw speeding out of the firebreak the night of the murder?" McCleary asked.

"I didn't see it very well. It was too dark."

"C'mon," Bino said. "You've worked on just about every car that's made. What'd it sound like?"

Blade pressed the heels of his hands against his eyes and cocked his head, as if listening to the car he'd seen that night. "Big."

"Big," Ferret repeated. "Okay, that's something. Big how? Six cylinders? Eight? What?"

"Six."

"You're sure," Ferret said.

"Yeah."

"Six. Okay, let's see. Gracie drives a six-cylinder. So does

Felicity. Doris Lynch's Benz is a six. You'll have to give us more than that, Ross."

"There isn't any more." His hands dropped to his lap.

"Was the car white?" McCleary asked.

Blade blinked, thinking, then slowly shook his head. "No, it was so black that night I would've noticed if it was white."

"Let's rule out pastels," Bino said. "Let's say it was dark. A dark-colored six cylinder. Did you check the tire marks?"

"No."

McCleary interrupted. "Let's forget the car for now. I'm interested in the evidence you've got, Ross."

"In here." He dug into the canvas bag that rested next to him and brought out one item after another. He named each object as he passed it to McCleary: Lou's journal, sketches and blueprints of the house at various stages in its long history, a more recent version of Lou's will with quite different provisions than the one Peck had shown McCleary and Quin, a revealing letter to Lou from Doris Lynch about the sale of part of the grove.

There were also files on Lou's business which made it clear that Gracie had forged his signature on the bonds that were forfeited, and that Lou had intended to buy her out.

McCleary paged through the journal as he questioned Blade about Lou's women. Many of the entries detailed Lou's obsession with Luz, the spook. These interested McCleary less than the references to the flesh-and-blood women. He rarely used their names, but they obviously weren't the same woman.

One warranted disparagement and he usually referred to her as the bitch; McCleary pegged her as Gracie or Felicity. Another was described with a certain nostalgic fondness, Felicity or maybe Janna Hilliard, it was difficult to tell. There was another woman for whom he had felt enormous pity, an older women, probably Amelia Vicente. The fifth woman was described in the same passionate tone he used when writing about his encounters with Luz. In several entries it was impossible to determine who Lou was writing about, the real woman or the spook.

Marion O'Connor was mentioned several times in connection with work, but there was no reference to a personal relationship. McCleary considered the omission a telling detail about the restraints their jobs imposed on their personal lives.

"Did Lou ever say anything to you about Marion O'Connor, Ross?"

The kid shrugged and rubbed his palms over his jeans, obviously uncomfortable with the question. "We didn't talk much about her. He knew I didn't like her. Don't like her. Will never like her."

"Because she busted you."

"Maybe that's part of it, but I really don't think I'd feel any different even if she hadn't busted me."

"So you didn't know they were sleeping together?"

Blade made a face. "Fuck, no. O'Connor and Lou?" The lantern on the coffee table hissed and flickered, as if in response to the kid's astonishment.

"Bad combo," Ferret remarked.

"But not off the wall," said Bino. "He bonded her busts, they saw a lot of each other professionally."

"And she was lonely," McCleary said, thinking aloud.

"And Lou was losing it bad," Bino said, nodding. His bright red eyes bored into McCleary, understanding what he hadn't said. "Yeah, it might fit."

Blade looked from one man to the other, not getting it. "What could fit?"

"That O'Connor killed Lou," Ferret said, his voice flat.

The enormity of Ferret's statement seemed to sink into him bit by bit. First his hands curled into fists against his thighs. Then his body tightened and the dark of his eyes deepened until they were black pools in his cheeks. His mouth moved but nothing came out.

"You were her perfect fall guy, Ross," said McCleary, his voice quiet. "She knew your history. She probably had access to the houseboat and found your knife there. Maybe she wasn't consciously thinking of killing Lou, maybe the intent was barely formed in her own mind. But she took the knife and she was carrying it the night she drove out to the house."

The incompleteness of the thought hung in the silence, a picture that screamed for definition, details, a story that begged for an ending. Blade's face sagged beneath the weight of the truth. "But why?" Blade whispered. "Why would she kill him?"

"Jealousy," said Ferret. "She knew about the other women and couldn't handle it. Or maybe she just couldn't deal with the fact that he dumped her. That it was over."

Bino said, "That van she drives has six cylinders."

"It's not enough to get a warrant," McCleary said. "But it's a beginning."

The window behind the couch suddenly exploded inward, the lantern shattered, and the spilled kerosene burst into flame. Blade shot to his feet and McCleary tackled him, bringing him down hard and fast to the floor, then he scooped up Blade's evidence from the couch and shoved it into the kid's pack. Bino rolled across the floor and fired through the shattered window. Ferret was trying to smother the flames with a couch cushion, but the fire was spreading too fast.

"Mike, get him outta here fast," Ferret hissed. "Through the cellar. Behind the washer there's a metal plate that opens into a tunnel. It leads to the road. We'll follow."

Another window exploded. Silencer, McCleary thought, and slung the pack over his shoulder and scrambled after the kid toward the cellar door.

II

Marion was pacing outside the flight service office when Quin and Christine arrived at the airport. "Gene's out on the tarmac," she said without prelude and hurried up the breezeway, Quin and

Christine falling in on either side of her. She introduced herself to Christine. "Have you flown police choppers before?"

"Nope."

"Shit." Marion looked accusingly at Quin. "I thought you told Gene that . . ."

"She'll do fine," Quin said quickly.

Christine gave her a dirty look, but kept her mouth shut.

"Personally, I think it's a mistake to go in like this," Marion went on. "You don't tip off men like Roey."

"It's not your husband up there," Quin said crisply.

Marion had the good sense not to say anything more about it.

The police chopper stood alone at the end of the tarmac, a giant, overfed bumblebee. A short man whom she presumed was Gene Frederick was already in the passenger seat, studying a county map and talking with someone on the radio. As soon as he was finished, he swung down to the ground and thrust his hand at Quin.

"I was hoping we could meet under better circumstances, Mrs. McCleary. Hop into the back with Marion." Without skipping a beat, he handed Christine the aviation map. "From what I've been able to find out, the cabin is about a mile due north of the fire tower." He tapped the red circle he'd made on the map. "Right about here."

Christine studied the map, nodding slowly. "Let's get moving."

Quin and Marion climbed into the back and snapped on shoulder harnesses, Frederick and Christine shut their doors, and the engine leaped to life with a high-pitched whine. The rotors began to turn, the chopper lurched upward. Quin suddenly wished she were elsewhere. She felt as if she were inside a transparent plastic bubble that had been hermetically sealed. With Marion crowded in beside her, she barely had enough room to move, to breathe.

A strong eastern wind buffeted the chopper as it rose. The

lights of the airport fell away and the preserve stretched in front of them, a black sea. Christine turned on the search light and its brilliance burned across the treetops five hundred feet below. Marion leaned toward Quin. "We'll never find it like this."

"Then what the hell do you suggest, Marion? Parachuting? A nosedive? Doing it on foot?"

She bit at her thumbnail. "I don't know. But this is a mistake. Roey will see this chopper coming and try to shoot it down."

As if she knew all about Roey, Quin thought, and willed the chopper to move faster. Faster.

III

Roey snapped another clip into his gun, leaned back against a thick, sturdy branch in the ficus tree he had climbed, and sighted through a nightscope. It reduced everything to bare essentials—the front porch, the shape of the cabin, the flickering glow inside of it.

He hadn't intended to hit the lantern, to start a fire. But now that he had, he would take advantage of it, he would flush them out. He squeezed the trigger, spraying the front of the cabin, then scrambled higher into the tree. Shots exploded several feet below him and he smiled and thought, *Come out, come out, wherever you are.*

They might flee into the surrounding woods, but he was betting they would head for the pickup, the fastest way out of here. He scanned the road and the pickup through the nightscope, certain that San Miguel de Allende was just that much closer. White beaches, a snug little hideaway, breathtaking sunsets, the two of them baking in the sun until they were as brown as the coconuts. Better than the old days because this time it would just be the two of them. Lou wasn't around to fuck things up.

He could taste the dream now.

IV

Blade climbed into the tunnel first. His flashlight was still upstairs, but he had the wooden matches in his pocket that he'd taken from Ferret's kitchen. He struck one against the wall of the pipe and held it up so McCleary could see well enough to pull the metal plate back over the opening.

The tunnel was concrete, with curved sides like a water pipe, and appeared to be large enough to move through at a crouch. The glow of the match didn't reach far, but it looked as if the tunnel sloped steeply downward just ahead.

The match went out, the blackness bit down. A moment later the lid clattered shut and McCleary whispered, "How many of those matches do you have?"

Blade fingered them in his pocket. "A handful."

"Shit. Let me have a couple."

Blade dug some out of his pocket. "Give me your hand."

"Here."

He put four matches in McCleary's palm. "I've also got some firecrackers."

"Yeah? Big ones?"

"Big and small."

"Good. Hold on to them. Maybe they'll come in handy. Move, I'm right behind you, Blade."

Blade crept forward, feeling his way, hands against either side of the pipe. The concrete was cool and damp and got progressively damper. He kept wanting to raise up. He kept waiting for the moment when his eyes would seize on some small bit of light, but there wasn't any light.

The blackness swam around him. He could barely breathe. His heart hammered. Sweat sprang from his pores. Match, he thought, just one more match. But his hand touched something wet and slimy, something that moved, that fucking *moved.* He wrenched back and lost what little equilibrium he had and suddenly he was tumbling down the steep, slippery incline. His arms flew up around his head to protect it, but it thudded against the concrete. Thump thump thump, hard and rhythmic.

A single, desperate note issued from his mouth and slammed back and forth against the walls of the pipe like a tennis ball. Then he stopped, facedown in a pool of stale water, sucking the shit into his mouth. He flew upward, coughing, spitting, and his head slammed against the roof of the tunnel.

"Take it easy, Jesus, don't move," McCleary said, and scraped one of the matches against the concrete.

The first thing Blade saw was something he would see for months afterward every time he shut his eyes. A nest of snakes. They swarmed over the floor of the pipe about fifteen feet beyond him, dozens of them, skinny little fuckers that were red, black, and yellow. They slid over and around each other, a quivering mass, rainbow Jell-O.

"Fuck," he whispered.

"Fuck doesn't begin to describe it."

"Are they poisonous?"

McCleary emitted a soft, choked laugh. "They're coral snakes."

"We've got to go back up the tunnel."

"We can't go back. Take a good whiff, Blade."

Smoke, seeping into the tunnel.

"Shoot them," Blade said, scooting slowly back on his buttocks, out of the water, closer to McCleary. "Shoot the fuckers."

"Too many of them. Give me those firecrackers, the biggest ones you have."

He unzipped the pocket of his windbreaker, scooped out what was left of the firecrackers he'd gotten from Ferret's glove compartment. "That's it." He poured them into McCleary's outstretched hand. "That's all there are."

The match went out. In the utter silence, he could hear the soft, scraping sounds the snakes made as they slithered over each other, over the concrete, a sound like palm fronds rubbing together in the wind.

McCleary struck another match and held it above the firecrackers. "We need three dry ones."

He picked through them. His fingers felt stiff, huge, awkward. "Christ, they're all damp."

"Pick three, hurry up. They don't like the light."

He chose two boomers and one of the firecrackers that would sizzle like bacon on a hot griddle before it exploded. They were moist, but not hopeless. As McCleary stuck the rest of the firecrackers in his pocket, the flame sputtered and went out.

He hated the way the dark clamped down over them, relentless, absolute, a kind of death. "Let's move back a little before we do another match," McCleary said softly. "We'll light these suckers at the same time and toss them about four inches this side of the snakes. That should scare them away from us."

In the dark, Blade simply nodded. He was too frightened to speak.

They moved back through the pipe, their jeans scraping against the concrete. McCleary struck a match and their eyes met briefly over the flame. "We light them and on the count of three we toss."

"Right."

Blade stuck the fuse of his boomer into the flame, McCleary lit the other two. The fuses sputtered, then caught, and Blade stifled the urge to hurl his immediately. McCleary's voice seemed to echo inside his aching skull. *One . . . two . . . three . . .*

Two of the firecrackers arched through the air side by side, as if joined by an invisible cord. The third trailed behind them and hit the floor of the tunnel seconds later. One of them promptly fizzled, the other two went off. They were boomers.

The explosion in such a small, closed space sounded like a bomb and the tunnel lit up, brighter than the Fourth of July. Those snakes that survived whipped away in a wild panic. Two came straight toward them and McCleary shot them with the Magnum, a noise like the end of the world.

Then silence, the stink of the smoke, the horrible blackness again.

McCleary lit another match. "Tuck your jeans into your socks and keep your arms above your head just in case any of them are still alive."

Jeans into socks, arms above his head, yeah, he got it.

Right foot, left, right foot again. Christ oh Christ, he could see them in the pale glow of the match, the dead snakes, the injured snakes, and the writhing, frantic mass that worked its way toward the end of the tunnel.

And just when he thought he could make it without puking, without losing it, an explosion above them rocked through the tunnel. Blade fell into McCleary, the match went out, and McCleary shouted, "The gas tank in the kitchen just blew! Get out of here fast!"

Blade scrambled blindly forward, a wild, white panic burning through his head.

V

"Down there," Frederick shouted, pointing below.

Quin pressed her face to the window. A ball of fire and black, greasy smoke leaped upward through the trees two hundred feet down. Explosion, she thought, and suddenly an updraft of furious wind seized the chopper. Marion screamed. The engine shrieked as Christine struggled to keep the chopper airborne. It lurched into a wide, erratic circle and Christine shouted, "I'm putting it down over there!"

Then the ground rushed upward, as if to embrace them.

VI

Roey charged away from the fire, the heat and flames at his back, the air like molten glass. Despite the recent rain, the trees around him were now catching fire, branches crackling, snapping like toothpicks, crashing to the ground.

In his haste to get away from the fire, he tripped as he was descending the steep, slippery incline to the road, and pitched forward. Suddenly he was tumbling downhill, his head slamming against rocks, branches, forest debris. His pack was torn off his shoulder, but he somehow managed to hold on to his gun.

He slammed into a ditch at the bottom of the hill, too stunned to move. The world spun around him, a carousel out of control. The air lit up, a sunlike brilliance that snapped his vision into utter clarity and exposed everything like an X-ray—the mouth of a pipe that protruded from the hill, the road, the pickup, and McCleary and the kid racing toward it.

It wasn't going to get any better than this.

He bolted forward, aimed, fired off four quick shots, and saw both figures fall before the light vanished behind the trees and the chatter of a helicopter reached him. Cops, he thought, and leaped up, adrenaline pumping through him as he stumbled through the ditch, heading for the deeper woods. In his haste to escape before the cops landed, he wasn't watching where he stepped. His shoes came down over something soft and mushy, muddy leaves or damp, rotting sticks, and he felt a sharp, excruciating pain near his ankle. He looked down, down at the snake that clung to the top of his sneaker, its fangs embedded in his foot.

Roey shrieked and danced around, hitting it with the gun until it fell off. But there were more, snakes everywhere, surrounding him as they whipped through the ditch to escape the fire. Firelight washed over their slithering shapes, their luminous skins, the red, the black, the yellow stripes.

Coral snakes.

Panic crashed over him and he spun in place, squeezing the trigger again and again and again.

VII

The first thing Quin saw as the chopper hit the ground was Bino, standing at the edge of the clearing, holding Ferret in his arms. In the glare of the searchlight, his pale skin looked even whiter than usual. His face and clothes were streaked with smoke and dirt.

Marion leaped off first, Quin and Frederick right behind her. "His leg's busted bad," Bino said when they reached him. "He got caught under a beam when the porch caved in. I had to knock him out. Mike and Blade got out through a tunnel that empties into the road down there."

"Where's Roey?" Frederick asked.

Quin didn't stick around for his answer. She pulled out Vicente's .38, knocked off the safety, and ran into the pines where the fire hadn't reached yet. The smoke drifted through the branches like ectoplasmic tendrils, the din of panicked wildlife echoed eerily.

Marion caught up with her and grabbed her arm. "Hold on, just hold on," she hissed. "You're not a cop. Go back to the chopper."

"Fuck off."

Quin wrenched her arm free, but Marion shoved her hard, knocking her to the ground, and sprinted away. Quin clambered to her feet and raced after her, certain that she had plans for Blade that she didn't want anyone else to witness.

The firelight was sufficiently bright to make out the spaces between the tightly packed pines. She ran faster, arms pumping at her sides, and skidded down a steep incline. The pines thinned, the brush thinned, she could finally see the dirt road where Marion stood over a figure sprawled on the ground, her gun aimed at him.

Blade, Quin thought, and ran toward her, shouting, *"Don't do it, Marion!"*

But she fired and Quin dropped to the ground, aimed, squeezed the trigger. Marion's legs buckled and she crumpled to the road. When Quin reached her, she was clutching her thigh and sobbing, "I'm bleeding, Christ, I'm bleeding."

The man on the ground was Tom Roey, not Blade. He was crawling toward Marion, blood spreading across the back of his shirt, his broken voice a litany. "Oh God, babe, oh God, I thought . . ."

"Babe?" Quin didn't realize she had spoken aloud until Marion raised her head. Quin saw the truth in her eyes, that Marion had been Roey's lover and perhaps still was, that she had killed Lou in a jealous rage and carefully framed Blade for the murder.

"It was a mistake," she said hoarsely.

"You murdered Lou and it was a fucking *mistake*? And what about this schmuck, Marion? Is Roey a mistake, too?"

"Snakes," Roey moaned. "Help me."

"I didn't have any idea he was up here," she said quickly.

Roey managed to lift his head and hissed through teeth clenched against pain: "Lying bitch. San Miguel. We were . . . going . . . San Miguel."

A primal rage rushed into Marion's eyes and she lunged for her fallen weapon. Quin fired at the ground and Marion wrenched back. "Don't give me a reason, Marion."

Frederick ran up to her, breathless, his sweaty face bright red. "I'll cover them. Find Mike and the kid. More choppers are on the way."

Quin turned in place, shouting their names, and trotted along the road until she heard a voice that was not McCleary's. It was coming from a pocket of shadows in the trees just beyond the pickup. Blade's legs were stretched out in front of him, one of them bleeding and obviously broken. McCleary's head rested against his thigh and Blade was leaning over him, holding his bunched shirt against McCleary's chest.

"Oh God," she whispered, and dropped to her knees beside McCleary.

"He took it in the chest," Blade said softly. "One of the shots meant for the snakes. He's bleeding real bad."

Quin could hear the wheeze of his breath, the rattle in his chest. She was afraid to touch him, afraid not to touch him, and finally pressed her hands over Blade's and felt the warm stickiness of McCleary's blood. "Hold on, Mac," she whispered. "Just hold on."

VIII

Hold on, hold on, hold on. Her voice sounded distant, unreal, a voice in a dream. But McCleary could see her face now and despite her best efforts to conceal her horror, he knew it was bad. There wasn't much pain, just an unfocused ache somewhere deep inside him. Some of his senses seemed preternaturally acute, like the smell of the smoke, a scent of autumn nights straight out of his childhood.

He struggled to raise up, but his body refused to cooperate. It was harder to breathe now, his awareness blinked off and on, time pulsed and echoed. Then hands were lifting him, the firelight shimmered against Quin's wet cheeks.

Every step they took jarred him to the bone. The sky listed to the right, the left, then turned inside out and he turned his head to the side and saw his sister, his youngest sister, his dead sister, Catherine.

You've been here before, Mike, she said.

No. He turned his head to the other side, his eyes on Quin. No, he wasn't ready.

But every breath was an effort that exhausted him. He shut his eyes, opened them. He was in the chopper now and she was squeezing his hand, leaning over him, her hair brushing his cheeks. Her voice was a choked whisper. "Don't leave me, don't you dare do this, don't don't don't . . ."

McCleary clenched her hands and released everything inside of him, forty-five years of choices, of triumphs and losses and love, and it flowed from him into her, sealing something between them. Then he turned his head and saw Catherine again, smiling, and he reached out and took her hand. He lifted up, up, out of his tired bones, his ruined body, until he was floating just above Quin.

She'll be okay, his sister assured him, and he believed her.

Then he let go.

Wednesday, September 20

Quin steered the skiff out into the Tango River. It was deserted at this hour of the day, minutes from sunrise. The horizon was violet fringed in a furious orange and both colors sprayed across the water, where they melted together like wax.

She was alone with the gulls that swooped over the river, alone with the silence of sunrise, alone, the only way she could do this. She steered into the widest part of the river and throttled back on the engine, then killed it. The skiff, which she had borrowed from Ferret, bobbed in the river's current.

From her pack on the floor, she removed a glass bottle, blue glass, an antique that had been in McCleary's family for years. She popped out the cork and tilted the bottle to her palm until some of the ashes spilled out. She stared at this tiny pile of dust, a dark stain against her skin.

These ashes, she thought, should have been Roey's. Or Marion's. Or Vicente's. But Marion was in the county jail awaiting trial for Lou's murder and Vicente was being held without bond for conspiracy to commit murder. Roey had died of the snakebite before he reached the hospital and was buried with the other indigents on the old Pauper's Hill.

Quin blew the little pile of ashes into the air, where they scattered like fireflies.

From her pocket, she removed a gold locket that her daughter often wore. She opened it and looked at the miniature photo of her, McCleary, and Michelle. It had been taken when Michelle was six weeks old by a roaming photographer in a Mexican restaurant. She snapped it shut and dropped it, chain and all, into the bottle. From another pocket she brought out a narrow smooth stone, one that Michelle had picked up yesterday at the beach. She pushed it through the opening to weight the bottle, then corked it.

The sun shoved its way upward, peeking above the horizon, a yellow crescent. She clutched the bottle against her, suddenly reluctant to let it go, and squeezed her eyes shut against the rush of memories. More than thirteen years, the best and most perplexing years of her life: nothing could take that away from her. Not even death.

Light streamed across the trees, the surface of the river, and she hurled the bottle away from her. It struck the water with a soft, innocuous splash and bobbed in the current, as if keeping rhythm with the boat, the river, the very pulse of Tango Key.

Then it sank.

She stared at the water for a very long time, hoping the bottle would reappear. Or that she would feel McCleary's presence. But nothing changed. There was only the whispering current, the violet light, and the soft, choked sounds of her grief.

Quin finally cranked up the engine and steered the skiff through the exquisite light, back toward shore and whatever awaited her there.